YEAR'S BEST

YA SPECULATIVE FICTION 2013

EDITED BY
JULIA RIOS &
ALISA KRASNOSTEIN

First published in Australia in December 2014
by Kaleidoscope

www.twelfthplanetpress.com

Design and layout by Amanda Rainey
Typeset in Sabon MT Pro

National Library of Australia Cataloguing-in-Publication entry

Title: Year's best Y A speculative fiction 2013 / editors, Julia Rios, Alisa Krasnostein.

ISBN: 9781922101273 (paperback)

Target Audience: For secondary school age.

Subjects: Short stories, Australian--21st century.

Other Creators/Contributors:

        Rios, Julia, editor.

        Krasnostein, Alisa, editor.

Dewey Number: A823.408

Table of Contents

Summation: YA in 2013

t's a relatively new category in publishing terms, but YA (Young Adult) fiction has been growing at a brisk pace for several years, and by 2013 its foothold was well established. With large sections in bookstores, multiple movies and television series based on YA novels, and a robust YA book blogging community, YA in 2013 was not an emerging category. It was a strong presence.

On the big screen, 2013 saw adaptations of *The Hunger Games: Catching Fire*, *The Mortal Instruments*, *The Book Thief*, and *Beautiful Creatures*, among others. On television, *The Vampire Diaries* went into its fifth season and launched a spinoff series called *The Originals*, and *Pretty Little Liars* went into its fourth season and also announced a plan for a spinoff.

In terms of novels, dystopian YA was still hot in 2013. *Allegiant* by Veronica Roth (#3 in the Divergent series) won the

Goodreads Choice Award for YA science fiction and fantasy (a popular vote award by members of the Goodreads community), with other dystopian contenders such as *Requiem* by Lauren Oliver (#3 in the Delirium series), *Unravel Me* by Tahareh Mafi (#2 in the Shatter Me series), and *Prodigy* by Marie Lu (#2 in the Legend series) among the finalists. The Goodreads list was not limited to dystopian fiction by any means, though. Other popular titles included steampunk books like *Clockwork Princess* by Cassandra Clare (#3 in The Infernal Devices series) and *Etiquette and Espionage* by Gail Carriger (#1 in the Finishing School series), science fiction like *Scarlet* by Marissa Meyer (#2 in the Lunar Chronicles series of science fiction fairy tale retellings), and epic fantasy like *Steelheart* by Brandon Sanderson (#1 in the Reckoners series).

One of the clearest patterns was that series remained popular among readers. In addition to all the series books mentioned above, Sean Williams and Garth Nix released *The Mystery* (aka *The Mystery of the Golden Card*, #3 in the Trouble Twisters series), Malinda Lo released *Inheritence* (#2 in the Adaptation series), Sarah Rees Brennan released *Untold* (#2 in the Lynburn Legacy), and Beth Revis released *Shades of Earth* (#3 in the Across the Universe series). Of course, series aren't everything. 2013's standalones included *Sister Mine* by Nalo Hopkinson, *The Coldest Girl in Coldtown* by Holly Black, and the runaway bestseller of the year, *The Fault in Our Stars* by John Green (which was not a fantasy or science fiction book, but which contributes to the overall trend of booksellers and publishers paying attention to books aimed at teens).

The Andre Norton Award (a juried award for best YA speculative fiction book) went to Hopkinson's *Sister Mine*. On the Norton shortlist were Black's *The Coldest Girl in Coldtown*, *September Girls* by Bennett Madison, *The Summer Prince* by Alaya Dawn Johnson, *When We Wake* by Karen Healey, *Hero* by Alethea Kontis, and *A Corner of White* by Jaclyn Moriarty. Other YA specific awards and honour lists included the American Library Association's Alex Awards honouring ten adult books with teen appeal. Wesley Chu's *The Lives of Tao* stood out as the lone speculative fiction work on that list, but speculative fiction fared better on the Rainbow Book List (another ALA list honouring books with QUILTBAG content) with more dystopians including *Love in the Time of Global Warming* by Francesca Lia Block, *The Culling* by Steven Dos Santos, and *Proxy* by Alex London. Johnson's *The Summer Prince* and *Pantomime* by Laura Lam also made the list.

YA book blogs in 2013 included several devoted to celebrating diversity. *Diversity in YA* (started in 2011 by Malinda Lo and Cindy Pon) was still going strong with lots of news about diverse YA releases and statistical breakdowns of diverse content in books released by major publishing houses. *Rich in Color*, a blog devoted to reviewing books featuring characters of colour, listed Mafi's *Unravel Me*, Lu's *Prodigy*, and London's *Proxy* among its 2013 diverse YA favorites. *The BookSmugglers*, Ana Grilo and Thea James, also paid attention to diversity in their reading, noting their personal statistics over the course of the year. Ana's best books of the year included Madison's *September Girls*, *Sorrow's Knot* by Erin Bow, and *Into the Grey* by Celine Kiernan, while Thea's included *Quicksilver* by R.J. Anderson (which she noted featured an asexual heroine and a love interest who was a character of colour), *Light* by Michael Grant (#7 in the FAYZ series—this one was also on the Goodreads shortlist), and three more dystopians: *In the After* by Demetria Lunetta, *The Different Girl* by Gordon Dahlquist and *Orleans* by Sherri L. Smith. Moriarty's *A Corner of White*, Lo's *Inheritance*, and Black's *The Coldest Girl in Coldtown* made *The BookSmugglers*' honourable mention list along with several other titles including *Raven Flight* by Juliet Marillier (#2 in the Shadowfell series).

Australia had a healthy crop of YA titles in 2013. In addition to the third Trouble Twisters book, Sean Williams released the first of his Twinmaker series, *Jump (Twinmaker* in Australia*)*. Juliet Marillier was also quite active. Apart from her Shadowfell release, she also won the Aurealis Award for Best Young Adult Short Fiction with "By Bone-Light" from her collection *Prickle Moon*. The Aurealis Award for Best Young Adult Novel ended up in a tie between *These Broken Stars* by Amie Kaufman and Megan Spooner (also on *The BookSmugglers*' honourable mention list) and *Fairy Tales for Wilde Girls* by Allyse Near, with *Fairy Tales for Wilde Girls* also picking up the Best Horror Novel award. Finally, the Best Collection went to Joanne Anderton's *The Bone Chime Song and Other stories*, of which "Mah Song" was shortlisted in the Best Young Adult Short Fiction category. Also popular from Australia were paranormal romances featuring angels with titles such as *Haze* (#2 of the Rephaim series) by Paula Weston, *The Chronicles of Blood and Stone* (#2 in the Legend of the Archangel series) by L. L. Johnson, and *Ominous Love* and *Ominous Angel* (#2 and #3 of the Ominous series) by Patricia Puddle. Other popular non-angelic fantasy titles from Australia included *Chasing the Valley* (#1 in the Chasing the Valley series) by Skye Mleki-Wegner, *Lucien* (#3 in the Silvermay series) by James Moloney, *Hunting* by Andrea K. Höst, and *Alpha Girl* (#1 in the Wolfing series) by Kate Bloomfield.

The Canadian Library Association Young Adult Book Award went to a non-speculative book (*Graffiti Knight* by Karen Bass), but three of the ten finalists were fantasy. Two (*The Gypsy King* by Maureen Fergus and *The Oathbreaker's Shadow* by Amy McCullough) were high fantasy while the third (*Not Your Ordinary Wolf Girl* by Emily Pohl-Weary) was contemporary fantasy. Other popular Canadian releases from 2013 included Bow's *Sorrow's Knot*, *Undercurrent* by Paul Blackwell, *Dualed* (#1 of the Dualed series) by Elsie Chapman, *Rush* (#1 of The Game series) by Evie Silver, and *Apparition* by Gail Gallant.

British YA held up the dystopian trend with titles like *Fractured* (#2 in the Slated series) by Teri Terry, *The Lost Girl* by Sangu Mandanna, *Linked* by Imogen Howson (#1 in the Linked series), and *Acid* by Emma Pass. Other popular speculative titles from the UK included *Earth Star* (#2 in the Earth Girl series) by Janet Edwards, *Legacy* and *Fracture* (#2 and #3 in the Night School vampire series) by C.J. Daugherty, and *The Night Itself* (#1 in The Name of the Blade series) by Zoë Marriott. Another UK trend was witches with titles including *Witchfall* (#2 in the Tudor Witch Trilogy) by Victoria Lamb, *A Witch Alone* (#3 in the Winter Trilogy) by Ruth Warburton, and *Witch Fire* (#2 in the Burn Mark series) by Laura Powell.

In short fiction, there were a few dedicated YA anthologies, the two most notable being *Futuredaze: An Anthology of YA Science Fiction* edited by Erin Underwood and Hannah Strom-Martin, and *Defy the Dark* edited by Saundra Mitchell. Both anthologies were particularly strong with several outstanding stories. *Rags and Bones: New Twists on Timeless Tales* edited by Melissa Marr and Tim Pratt was another strong anthology marketed as YA, but we found that many of the stories didn't meet our definition of the category. Standouts from this anthology included "The Sleeper and the Spindle" by Neil Gaiman, and "Without Faith, Without Law, Without Joy" by Saladin Ahmed, the latter of which examined the events of Edmund Spenser's *The Faerie Queen* from the point of view of one of the Muslim villains.

Apart from anthologies, we found several excellent YA stories in speculative fiction magazines not aimed at teens, two of which gained significant awards recognition. Sofia Samatar's "Selkie Stories Are For Losers" originally appeared in *Strange Horizons*, and went on to receive nominations for the Nebula, Hugo, and World Fantasy Awards. Sam J. Miller's "57 Reasons for the Slate Quarry Suicides" originally appeared in *Nightmare*, and won the Shirley Jackson Award.

This brings us to the question of what exactly makes something YA? To some it seems anything that is marketed to teens, but we find that troubling as some of the stories we love and feel would speak to teens are marketed to adults, and some of the stories marketed to teens don't relate to teen issues (certainly most of the things we had as required reading in school were more about the lives of adults). We needed a boundary for the label that would by default include teens and teen experiences, so we settled on defining YA as having teen protagonists and relating to teen lives. In the research for this book, we read far and wide, scouring magazines, anthologies, awards lists and single author collections aimed at all markets. What we have assembled showcases the breadth and depth of excellence in YA speculative fiction in 2013.

Our selections come from multiple countries and diverse viewpoints, and the original sources range from large publishing house anthologies to self-published authors, with all sorts of publication types in between. We have done our best to include dark and light themes, a mix of science fiction and fantasy, and a variety of story lengths, with the shortest pieces counting as flash fiction and the longest ones edging over the line into novelette territory. It is our hope that every reader will find something to love within these pages.

Selkie Stories Are for Losers

By Sofia Samatar

I hate selkie stories. They're always about how you went up to the attic to look for a book, and you found a disgusting old coat and brought it downstairs between finger and thumb and said "What's this?", and you never saw your mom again.

I work at a restaurant called Le Pacha. I got the job after my mom left, to help with the bills. On my first night at work I got yelled at twice by the head server, burnt my fingers on a hot dish, spilled lentil-parsley soup all over my apron, and left my keys in the kitchen.

I didn't realize at first I'd forgotten my keys. I stood in the parking lot, breathing slowly and letting the oil-smell lift away from my hair, and when all the other cars had started up and driven away I put my hand in my jacket pocket. Then I knew.

I ran back to the restaurant and banged on the door. Of course no one came. I smelled cigarette smoke an instant before I heard the voice.

"Hey."

I turned, and Mona was standing there, smoke rising white from between her fingers.

"I left my keys inside," I said.

Mona is the only other server at Le Pacha who's a girl. She's related to everybody at the restaurant except me. The owner, who goes by "Uncle Tad," is really her uncle, her mom's brother. "Don't talk to him unless you have to," Mona advised me. "He's a creeper." That was after she'd sighed and dropped her cigarette and crushed it out with her shoe and stepped into my clasped hands so I could boost her up to the window, after she'd wriggled through into the kitchen and opened the door for me. She said, "Madame," in a dry voice, and bowed. At least, I think she said "Madame." She might have said "My lady." I don't remember that night too well, because we drank a lot of wine. Mona said that as long as we were breaking and entering we might as well steal something, and she lined up all the bottles of red wine that had already been opened. I shone the light from my phone on her while she took out the special rubber corks and poured some of each bottle into a plastic pitcher. She called it "The House Wine." I was surprised she was being so nice to me, since she'd hardly spoken to me while we were working. Later she told me she hates everybody the first time she meets them. I called home, but Dad didn't pick up; he was probably in the basement. I left him a message and turned off my phone. "Do you know what this guy said to me tonight?" Mona asked. "He wanted beef couscous and he said, 'I'll have the beef conscious.'"

Mona's mom doesn't work at Le Pacha, but sometimes she comes in around three o'clock and sits in Mona's section and cries. Then Mona jams on her orange baseball cap and goes out through the back and smokes a cigarette, and I take over her section. Mona's mom won't order anything from me. She's got Mona's eyes, or Mona's got hers: huge, angry eyes with lashes that curl up at the ends. She shakes her head and says: "Nothing! Nothing!" Finally Uncle Tad comes over, and Mona's mom hugs and kisses him, sobbing in Arabic.

After work Mona says, "Got the keys?"

We get in my car and I drive us through town to the Bone Zone, a giant cemetery on a hill. I pull into the empty parking lot and Mona rolls a joint. There's only one lamp, burning high and cold in the middle of the lot. Mona pushes her shoes off and puts her feet up on the dashboard and cries. She warned me about that the night we met: I said something stupid to her like "You're so funny" and she said, "Actually I cry a lot. That's something you should know." I was so happy she thought I should know things about her, I didn't care. I still don't care, but it's true that Mona cries a lot. She cries because she's scared her mom will take her away to Egypt, where the family used to live, and where Mona has never been. "What would I do there? I don't even speak Arabic." She wipes her mascara on her sleeve, and I tell her to look at the lamp outside and pretend that its glassy brightness is a bonfire, and that she and I are personally throwing every selkie story ever written onto it and watching them burn up.

"You and your selkie stories," she says. I tell her they're not my selkie stories, not ever, and I'll never tell one, which is true, I never will, and I don't tell her how I went up to the attic that day or that what I was looking for was a book I used to read when I was little, *Beauty and the Beast*, which is a really decent story about an animal who gets turned into a human and stays that way, the way it's supposed to be. I don't tell Mona that Beauty's black hair coiled to the edge of the page, or that the Beast had yellow horns and a smoking jacket, or that instead of finding the book I found the coat, and my mom put it on and went out the kitchen door and started up her car.

One selkie story tells about a man from Mýrdalur. He was on the cliffs one day and heard people singing and dancing inside a cave, and he noticed a bunch of skins piled on the rocks. He took one of the skins home and locked it in a chest, and when he went back a girl was sitting there alone, crying. She was naked, and he gave her some clothes and took her home. They got married and had kids. You know how this goes. One day the man changed his clothes and forgot to take the key to the chest out of his pocket, and when his wife washed the clothes, she found it.

"You're not going to Egypt," I tell Mona. "We're going to Colorado. Remember?"

That's our big dream, to go to Colorado. It's where Mona was born. She lived there until she was four. She still remembers the rocks and the pines and the cold, cold air. She says the clouds of Colorado are bright, like pieces of mirror. In Colorado, Mona's parents got divorced, and Mona's mom tried to kill herself for the first time. She tried it once here, too. She put her head in the oven, resting on a pillow. Mona was in seventh grade.

Selkies go back to the sea in a flash, like they've never been away. That's one of the ways they're different from human beings. Once, my dad tried to go back somewhere: he was in the army, stationed in Germany, and he went to Norway to look up the town my great-grandmother came from. He actually found the place, and even an old farm with the same name as us. In the town, he went into a restaurant and ordered lutefisk, a disgusting fish thing my grandmother makes. The cook came out of the kitchen and looked at him like he was nuts. She said they only eat lutefisk at Christmas.

There went Dad's plan of bringing back the original flavor of lutefisk. Now all he's got from Norway is my great-grandmother's Bible. There's also the diary she wrote on the farm up north, but we can't read it. There's only four English words in the whole book: *My God awful day.*

You might suspect my dad picked my mom up in Norway, where they have seals. He didn't, though. He met her at the pool.

As for Mom, she never talked about her relatives. I asked her once if she had any, and she said they were "no kind of people." At the time I thought she meant they were druggies or murderers, maybe in prison somewhere. Now I wish that was true.

One of the stories I don't tell Mona comes from *A Dictionary of British Folklore in the English Language.* In that story, it's the selkie's little girl who points out where the skin is hidden. She doesn't know what's going to happen, of course, she just knows her mother is looking for a skin, and she remembers her dad taking one out from under the bed and stroking it. The little girl's mother drags out the skin and says: "Fareweel, peerie buddo!" She doesn't think about how the little girl is going to miss her, or how if she's been breathing air all this time she can surely keep it up a little longer. She just throws on the skin and jumps into the sea.

After Mom left, I waited for my dad to get home from work. He didn't say anything when I told him about the coat. He stood in the light of the clock on the stove and rubbed his fingers together softly, almost like he was snapping but with no sound. Then he sat down at the kitchen table and lit a cigarette. I'd never seen him smoke in the house before. *Mom's gonna lose it,* I thought, and then I realized that no, my mom wasn't going to lose anything. We were the losers. Me and Dad.

He still waits up for me, so just before midnight I pull out of the parking lot. I'm hoping to get home early enough that he doesn't grumble, but late enough that he doesn't want to come up from the basement, where he takes apart old TVs, and talk to me about college. I've told him I'm not going to college. I'm going to Colorado, a landlocked state. Only twenty out of fifty states are completely landlocked, which means they don't touch the Great Lakes or the sea. Mona turns on the light and tries to put on eyeliner in the mirror, and I swerve to make her mess up. She turns out the light and hits me. All the windows are down to air out the car, and Mona's hair blows wild around her face. *Peerie buddo*, the book says, is "a term of endearment." "Peerie buddo," I say to Mona. She's got the hiccups. She can't stop laughing.

I've never kissed Mona. I've thought about it a lot, but I keep deciding it's not time. It's not that I think she'd freak out or anything. It's not even that I'm afraid she wouldn't kiss me back. It's worse: I'm afraid she'd kiss me back, but not mean it.

Probably one of the biggest losers to fall in love with a selkie was the man who carried her skin around in his knapsack. He was so scared she'd find it that he took the skin with him everywhere, when he went fishing, when he went drinking in the town. Then one day he had a wonderful catch of fish. There were so many that he couldn't drag them all home in his net. He emptied his knapsack and filled it with fish, and he put the skin over his shoulder, and on his way up the road to his house, he dropped it.

"Gray in front and gray in back, 'tis the very thing I lack." That's what the man's wife said, when she found the skin. The man ran to catch her, he even kissed her even though she was already a seal, but she squirmed off down the road and flopped into the water. The man stood knee-deep in the chilly waves, stinking of fish, and cried. In selkie stories, kissing never solves anything. No transformation happens because of a kiss. No one loves you just because you love them. What kind of fairy tale is that?

"She wouldn't wake up," Mona says. "I pulled her out of the oven onto the floor, and I turned off the gas and opened the windows. It's not that I was smart, I wasn't thinking at all. I called Uncle Tad and the police and I still wasn't thinking."

I don't believe she wasn't smart. She even tried to give her mom CPR, but her mom didn't wake up until later, in the hospital. They had to reach in and drag her out of death, she was so closed up in it. Death is skin-tight, Mona says. Gray in front and gray in back.

Dear Mona: When I look at you, my skin hurts.

I pull into her driveway to drop her off. The house is dark, the darkest house on her street, because Mona's mom doesn't like the porch light on. She says it shines in around the blinds and keeps her awake. Mona's mom has a beautiful bedroom upstairs, with lots of old photographs in gilt frames, but she sleeps on the living room couch beside the aquarium. Looking at the fish helps her to sleep, although she also says this country has no real fish. That's what Mona calls one of her mom's "refrains."

Mona gets out, yanking the little piece of my heart that stays with her wherever she goes. She stands outside the car and leans in through the open door. I can hardly see her, but I can smell the lemon-scented stuff she puts on her hair, mixed up with the smells of sweat and weed. Mona smells like a forest, not the sea. "Oh my God," she says, "I forgot to tell you, tonight, you know table six? That big horde of Uncle Tad's friends?"

"Yeah."

"So they wanted the soup with the food, and I forgot, and you know what the old guy says to me? The little guy at the head of the table?"

"What?"

"He goes, *Vous êtes bête, mademoiselle!*"

She says it in a rough, growly voice, and laughs. I can tell it's French, but that's all.

"What does it mean?"

"*You're an idiot, miss!*"

She ducks her head, stifling giggles.

"He called you an idiot?"

"Yeah, *bête*, it's like *beast*."

She lifts her head, then shakes it. A light from someone else's porch bounces off her nose. She puts on a fake Norwegian accent and says: "*My God awful day.*"

I nod. "Awful day." And because we say it all the time, because it's the kind of silly, ordinary thing you could call one of our "refrains," or maybe because of the weed I've smoked, a whole bunch of days seem pressed together inside this moment, more than you could count. There's the time we all went out for New Year's Eve, and Uncle Tad drove me, and when he stopped and I opened the door he told me to close it, and I said "I will when I'm on the other side," and when I told Mona we laughed so hard we had to run away and hide in the bathroom. There's the day some people we know from school came in and we served them wine even though they were underage and Mona got nervous and spilled it all over the tablecloth, and the day her nice cousin came to visit and made us cheese-and-mint sandwiches in the microwave and got yelled at for wasting food. And the day of the party for Mona's mom's birthday, when Uncle Tad played music and made us all dance, and Mona's mom's eyes went jewelly with tears, and afterward Mona told me: "I should just run away. I'm the only thing keeping her here." My God, awful days. All the best days of my life.

"Bye," Mona whispers. I watch her until she disappears into the house.

My mom used to swim every morning at the YWCA. When I was little she took me along. I didn't like swimming. I'd sit in a chair with a book while she went up and down, up and down, a dim streak in the water. When I read *Mrs. Frisby and the Rats of NIMH*, it seemed like Mom was a lab rat doing tasks, the way she kept touching one side of the pool and then the other. At last she climbed out and pulled off her bathing cap. In the locker room she hung up her suit, a thin gray rag dripping on the floor. Most people put the hook of their padlock through the straps of their suit, so the suits could hang outside the lockers without getting stolen, but my mom never did that. She just tied her suit loosely onto the lock. "No one's going to steal that stretchy old thing," she said. And no one did.

Selkie Stories Are for Losers | Sofia Samatar

That should have been the end of the story, but it wasn't. My dad says Mom was an elemental, a sort of stranger, not of our kind. It wasn't my fault she left, it was because she couldn't learn to breathe on land. That's the worst story I've ever heard. I'll never tell Mona, not ever, not even when we're leaving for Colorado with everything we need in the back of my car, and I meet her at the grocery store the way we've already planned, and she runs out smiling under her orange baseball cap. I won't tell her how dangerous attics are, or how some people can't start over, or how I still see my mom in shop windows with her long hair the same silver-gray as her coat, or how once when my little cousins came to visit we went to the zoo and the seals recognized me, they both stood up in the water and talked in a foreign language. I won't tell her. I'm too scared. I won't even tell her what she needs to know: that we've got to be tougher than our moms, that we've got to have different stories, that she'd better not change her mind and drop me in Colorado because I won't understand, I'll hate her forever and burn her stuff and stay up all night screaming at the woods, because it's stupid not to be able to breathe, who ever heard of somebody breathing in one place but not another, and we're not like that, Mona and me, and selkie stories are only for losers stuck on the wrong side of magic—people who drop things, who tell all, who leave keys around, who let go.

By Bone-Light

By Juliet Marillier

Author's note: The Russian story Vasilissa the Fair, with its nearly all-female cast, is one of my favourite fairy tales. I'm especially fond of the crone Baba Yaga, who, like the fire she guards, can be both destructive and life-giving, and who must be approached in the right way if one wants a favour. 'By Bone-Light' is my first re-imagining of the story, but it probably won't be my last.

'We need light,' says Susie.

The power's gone off again; that happens a lot at Woodland Gardens. This place must have been named by a clown—instead of numbers, the floors have names, Chestnut Level, Willow Level and so on, a whole tower of trees. Woodland Gardens itself is a concrete high-rise with no redeeming features. Along with dodgy power it has blocked drains, creeping mould and lifts that make everyone use the stairs, even people who live on the top floor—Oak Level—like us. If something can break, you can be sure it'll be broken at Woodland Gardens. Down the bottom, outside, there's a sad playground with a metal swing and a climbing frame on dirty sand. In the daytime it's usually empty because mothers don't want their kids stepping on dog poo or used syringes. At night it's a meeting place for dealers.

We're sitting in our flat in the almost-dark, my stepmother, my stepsisters and me. Our torch batteries are flat, Susie's lighter is used up and we've managed to run out of both matches and candles. It's nearly dusk outside and the heater's gone off along with everything else electrical, so it'll soon be icy in here. But I know better than to suggest early bed. Susie wants our projects finished tonight, so she can get them in the mail first thing. Since it's already too dim in here for us to see our work, one of us will have to fetch light. It's not going to be Sophie or Miranda, because they're Susie's own daughters, her flesh and blood, and she never makes them go downstairs in the dark. I am my mother's daughter, and my mother is dead.

'Won't the shop be shut by now?' I say, hating the way my voice shakes. 'I think they close at five on a Thurs—'

Before I can finish I'm hauled up onto my feet with Susie's fingernails pressing into the soft flesh of my arm. I sink my teeth into my lip; I won't give her the satisfaction of hearing me cry out. My heart's thumping hard.

'You think I'm stupid or something?' Her hand tightens.

'You'll have to go to the basement,' Sophie says.

'Better hurry, Lissa,' puts in Miranda. 'It'll be dark soon.'

There's a silence. I feel the weight of their gaze, the three of them, and I hear them thinking: *Go. Now. Before we make you.*

'That concierge woman's supposed to have everything,' Susie says, and the hold on my arm slackens slightly. 'You know, what's-her-name, the one they all talk about. Go down and ask her for candles and a lighter.'

We haven't been at Woodland Gardens long. Susie got word that Dad's deployment was extended another six months, and almost straight away she sold the house that had been my home for all of my fifteen years. Home and haven. The house where my mother gave birth to me, her only child. The house where, only a year and a half ago, she gave me a gift, then died. Susie moved us so fast there was no time to ask questions. There wasn't even time to cry. It felt as if I blinked, then opened my eyes to find everything gone.

This flat is small. Two bedrooms: one for her, the other one for the three of us, with me on a trundle bed. Apart from my clothes, I got to bring one book—*Grimm's Fairy Tales*, which she had to let me keep because it was a Christmas present from Dad—and Mimi, who didn't get given to the Salvos because she was hidden in my pocket.

Susie had Wilmot put down. For that, I can never forgive her. She didn't have to choose a place with a no pets policy. She didn't have to move us at all. I thought I was going back to school at the end of the holidays and instead here we are in a completely different neighbourhood. When I asked about school—the kids at Woodland Gardens go to Westmoreland High—she said some stuff that frightened me so much I never asked again. Stuff about how screwed up in the head I was, and how much worse it would get if I was around people. Stuff about what she'd do to me if I told anyone what she'd said, ever. Miranda and Sophie never finished high school and now I have an idea why.

'Her name's Barbara,' says Sophie, reminding me sharply of what's ahead.

None of us has ever been down to the basement. None of us has ever met Barbara the concierge in the flesh. But we've heard about her. Everyone at Woodland Gardens talks about her in the same way, hushed and scared like an olden-days person speaking of a witch. She's supposed to have lots of stuff down there, not only candles but old-fashioned oil lamps, fuses, all kinds of tools, probably matches and firelighters too. And weird stuff, so Kye told me. Kye is the only kid I've spoken to since we moved in here. Susie doesn't like letting us out, and we're not supposed to talk to anyone. Her reason is, the building's full of druggies and perverts. But doing the washing is one of my jobs, and that gets me as far as the communal laundry along the end of Oak Level. When I'm there I hear people talking. And I see Kye sometimes, not washing, just hanging around. He told me people go into Barbara's basement and never come out again. He told me she has a human bone for a door knocker. He said his uncle told him

Barbara came from some country where they do voodoo, black magic, and that weird people are always visiting her to get spells. If that was true, if magic was real, I'd ask her for a spell myself. I'd get one to bring my father home right now. He probably thought he was doing the right thing when he married Susie so soon after Mum died. He must have thought I needed a mother, since we have no other family and he's away so much. And Susie wasn't so bad back then. Dad couldn't have known she'd turn into a monster the moment he was gone.

I've thought of asking Kye if I can make a phone call from his place, to … I don't know who, but there are welfare people who are supposed to help the families during a deployment, and I could look up their number. Or I could call my old school, speak to Mr Turner or Mrs Moss. I've thought of giving Kye a letter to post to Dad, because I suspect Susie rips them up, or Dad would have sent some back the way he always used to. Only Susie's so good at lying, and she's his wife now. She'd tell the welfare people I'm emotional and confused, and say she's getting professional help for me. And then she'd punish me. She's good at punishments. I have lots of bruises, the kind that show on my body and the kind that are deep inside where nobody can see.

'Off you go, Lissa,' she says now. 'Don't take too long about it. You're way behind with the orders; at this rate you'll be up all night getting that one finished.' What we make, Susie sells online. Sophie's fine shawls; Miranda's Aran sweaters; my one-of-a-kind dolls. I make a lot of dolls, so I guess they're popular. Susie won't let us use the internet, so I don't see the customer feedback. No internet means no email either. Dad could be on another planet. He's been gone eight months, and in those eight months my whole world has changed.

'What are you waiting for?' Susie snaps. 'Pitch darkness? Go! Now!'

There's no refusing. And with Susie standing over me, there's no getting a coat or gloves even though it'll be freezing in the stairwell. At least I have Mimi. She's about all I do have these days.

Susie locks the flat door behind me. Locks me out. When I get back with the candles I'm supposed to knock on the door three times, count to five, then knock three times again and wait for her to let me in. The two times three knocks are so she won't open up to some kind of crazy person. Though that's what she told me I was: crazy. A crazy girl can't go to school, but it's okay for her to sit at home making dolls for her stepmother to sell. I hope my dolls go to better homes than mine, homes where people love them and look after them and whisper secrets in their woollen ears.

The hallways in Woodside Gardens are long and grey. At this time of day all the doors are shut. There's still enough light from the tall windows down the end for me to see my way to the lift, and beside it the stair door. This door's broken, falling off its hinges. I step through and start down the twelve flights.

The stairwell stinks of wee. I'm hoping not to meet the perverts and junkies Susie talks about, though the shadowy landings seem like places where bad stuff might happen. I reach Willow Level,

Aspen Level, Juniper Level, and the light's almost gone. I have to slow down or I might fall. There'll be no sympathy from Susie if I break my ankle, only a reprimand for being clumsy and costing her money for a trip to the doctor. I wonder if the doctor would believe me if I told the truth about my stepmother? For a moment it seems almost worth breaking my ankle to find out. I sit down on the top step of Juniper Level to stop myself from jumping. I take Mimi from my pocket and put her on my knee. There's just enough light left to make out her little face, her dark beady eyes, her snub nose, her mouth that's not smiling and not frowning but something in between. Her black embroidery-silk hair; her moss stitch gown in my favourite purple.

'I'm scared, Mimi. Scared of Susie and scared of myself. Scared of going down to the basement.'

Give me a kiss, says Mimi.

I oblige with a peck on her knitted lips.

Give me a hug.

I press her against my cheek. My mother's last gift was teaching me how to knit. How to put love and hope and courage into every doll I make, so the person who gets that doll will have a true friend in good times and in bad. Mimi was the first doll I ever made, and knitted into her body is a strand of hair my mother cut from her own head as she lay dying. 'When you are sad, Lissa, when you are lonely, when you are at your wits' end, she will help you,' she told me. And it was true. I don't think Mimi is truly magic—how can she be, when I made her myself with wool and needles?—but when

27

I speak to her in the right way, I can hear her speaking back to me.

Now let me fly!

I toss Mimi up in the air. She performs a triple somersault and I catch her on the way down, setting her upright on my knee again. She's only a little doll, ten centimetres from the top of her head to the soles of her knitted shoes. In the dim light it seems to me she's looking quite pleased with herself.

Why are we going downstairs in the dark?

'To visit Barbara in the basement. To ask her for light.'

Mm-hm. Mimi seems to be considering this. *We'll need that if we're to find our way back up. Did you say you were scared?*

'I'm scared of Susie because she hurts me and I never know when she's going to be angry. And I'm scared of Barbara the concierge because everyone else is.'

Mimi appears to be waiting for more.

'And I'm scared of myself. A moment ago I was going to throw myself down these stairs and hurt myself on purpose, and that would make what Susie says about me true. I wasn't crazy before she came, Mimi. I'm sure I wasn't.'

Was your mother ever afraid of anything? Even at the end?

I remember Mum lying on the bed, hooked up to a drip, a skeleton with a fine layer of white silk for skin. Her eyes huge; her mouth stretched in a terrifying smile. Speaking words of hope. I shake my head.

You are your mother's daughter, Mimi says. *Get up, walk down, fetch light. I will help you.*

We go on down. Poplar Level, Cypress Level, Eucalyptus Level. I can hardly see the steps now. Ash Level, Elm Level. Somewhere below me a door clangs open, and I hear someone charging up the stairs toward me. I shrink back against the wall, stuffing Mimi into my pocket for safety. My heart's in my throat. A drug deal gone wrong, someone being chased with a knife, someone desperate… The person reaches the landing below me and comes straight on up. *Don't see me,* I beg. *Just go on past, please, please…*

It's a man dressed all in black, leather pants, hoodie, chunky Doc Marten-style boots. He hurtles past me. Either he's a top athlete or he's terrified of what's coming after him. His face is as dark as his clothes; there's a hint of gleaming eyes, and he's gone. I wait, making myself remember to breathe. Wait for whatever is coming next. I count up to fifty but nobody comes. Mimi says nothing, but I imagine her thinking, *What are we waiting for?* As well she might, because since the man ran past me, it's gone so dark I can't see my hand in front of my face. I pray that Barbara the concierge is home, and that she does give me light.

The lower levels, I navigate by touch. One hand on the iron railing, the other stretched out toward the concrete wall of the stairwell, I go down foot by cautious foot, hoping there are no broken steps, no missing stretches of rail. The dark's like a presence pushing at me, weighing me down. I feel as if I'm deep underground, though I think this is only Yew Level, third from the bottom. There's no reading the signs anymore, so I start counting the steps, counting the turns in the stairs. This stairwell comes out on the ground floor; I've been down here in the daytime, when Susie took a risk and sent me to the shop on my own. Back then, I thought of running away, asking the shopkeeper if I could use the phone, asking someone, anyone, for help. I didn't. Susie's got a long reach. As I go down the last flight of steps to ground level, I start wondering if she actually doesn't want me to come back tonight. She might be hoping I run into a murderer so she can get rid of me with a neat explanation for Dad. It's not as if my dolls are making Susie a fortune, or we wouldn't be living here in Woodside Gardens. I wonder what's happened to Dad's Navy pay. What if he's sick or even dead and she hasn't told me? But that couldn't happen. Could it?

The stairs come to an end. I stand still, trying to get a sense of direction. Somewhere in front of me I know there's a door that leads out to the so-called plaza, where kids ride skateboards and do graffiti during the day and adults shout and smash bottles at night. Between me and that door there's utter darkness. I can't even see a line of light around the doorway, though surely there's at least one street light working out there. I creep forward with my hands outstretched, hoping I'm not about to fall down a flight of steps I've forgotten about. My heart's jumping around like crazy.

My hands touch the concrete wall. I work my way around till I find the door and pull on the handle. It's locked.

For a bit I just stand there, thinking of the long way back in the dark, imagining myself telling Susie I failed, guessing what might happen then. Susie making me stand in a cold shower till

I'm blue and shivering. Susie making me stand out on the balcony in my underwear. Susie shoving my head into the wall. Susie has a great imagination.

I sink down onto the floor and get Mimi out of my pocket. I sit her on my knee. 'I don't think I can go on,' I mutter.

I can't see her face in the dark, but I hear her familiar voice.

Give me a kiss.

I touch my lips to her face.

Give me a hug.

I hold her to my cheek and find that I am actually crying a bit.

Now let me fly!

I flip Mimi up into the air and manage to catch her, blind.

So, we're down here in the dark. And you're curled up in a ball crying.

'I do try to be brave.' I scrub a hand across my cheek. 'But sometimes it's too hard.'

There is a light to be found in every darkness. You are your mother's daughter. Find it.

'But—' I fall silent, because it seems Mimi's right. The blanketing dark has lightened just enough for me to see that there *is* another set of steps, leading not up but down, and from somewhere below a faint glow is coming. I thought you could only reach the basement by the lift or a flight of outside steps. But maybe there's a third way.

With Mimi in my hand I creep across to the steps, which don't have any kind of guard rail. We go down. The dim light gets a bit brighter. There are only seven steps, and here we are at another level, with a short landing and one door at the end. The door is painted in blood-red gloss, and on a shelf beside it is the source of the glow: a lamp made from what looks like a real human skull, with a tea-light candle inside. It makes weird flickering shadows all over the stairwell walls. And there, dangling beside the door, is that knocker Kye told me about. If it's not a human shin-bone I don't know what it is. Now I'm really cold.

There's a little brass plate on the red door, and on it is some lettering, only it's not the letters I know, but a foreign alphabet of some kind. It might say anything from 'Concierge' to 'Visitors will be eaten alive.' I gather my courage, put my hand around the leg bone and rap on the door.

I wait. It feels as if getting downstairs took a long time, far longer than it should have done, and I wonder if Barbara has gone to bed already, in which case she won't be well pleased if I go on knocking. Maybe she's out. Maybe Mimi's instincts are wrong for the first time ever.

After a while I knock again, not too hard. I call out, 'Is anyone home?'

The door opens so suddenly I yelp with fright. There's a woman in the doorway, long straggledy white hair falling out of a bun, little bright eyes, skin with a million wrinkles. She's wearing a knitted garment in exactly the same purple I used for Mimi's dress, and in her arms she's holding this humungous ginger cat. It is the biggest cat I've ever seen in my life and it has a mean look in its eye. I know cats, though. I see right through this one.

Barbara—who else could this be?—hasn't said a word, so I speak up before things get embarrassing.

'Sorry to disturb you. I'm—'

'Lissa from 1205. You'll be wanting light, yes?'

I gape, but only for a moment. Behind her the room looks dark and bright at the same time, full of changing light that shows me rich colours and elaborate patterns. Unlike ours, Barbara's place is full of interesting stuff.

'Come in,' she says as if reading my mind, and steps back to let me go past her.

There are bones everywhere. Skulls with lights in them, their glowing eyes following me as I move cautiously across the room. Leg bones and arm bones and goodness-knows-what bones hanging from the ceiling like mobiles. Colourful pottery bowls full of tiny bones that must be from shrews or voles or something. There's a smell like incense, a lot better than the stink in the stairwell. I start to feel a bit dizzy and have to remind myself why I'm here.

'Our power's off,' I say as Barbara puts the huge cat down on an overstuffed sofa. It settles on an embroidered cushion, looking at me through narrowed eyes. 'My stepmother sent me to ask you for candles and a lighter. Please.'

She just stands there examining me, her arms folded. I can't think of anything else to say, so I crouch down beside the cat and put my hand carefully out where he or she can smell it and decide to be friends or not. 'Beautiful one,' I whisper, remembering Winslow with his silky hair and lovely blue eyes. 'Aren't you a fine cat, then?'

The giant feline deigns to sniff my hand, then gives itself a cursory lick. It raises no objection when I stroke it gently.

'She bites,' says Barbara.

I don't think this cat's going to bite me. She's purring now. 'What's her name?' I ask.

'Rory. Aurora.'

I go on petting her for a while, and Barbara goes on standing there watching me.

'Sorry,' I say eventually, remembering that it's late. 'I miss my own cat. Is it okay for me to have some candles, please?'

'Ah,' says Barbara, and I realise the door is shut and I'm alone with her and her house is seriously weird. I get to my feet and think about the twelve flights of stairs and the dark. 'I have candles,' she says. 'I have lighters. I have all manner of things down here, as no doubt you've heard. They tell all kinds of stories about me.'

'I don't get out much,' I squeak. 'But I did hear you have candles, yes.'

'Can you pay?'

'Oh.' My heart sinks. 'My stepmother didn't give me any money.' Stupid! I should have thought of this.

'Nothing's free, young lady. But there are other ways of paying.'

I back away toward the door. If I can get out, if she hasn't locked it, I should be able to outrun her. She's a big heavy woman and she looks sixty at least, maybe even older.

'Can you cook?' Barbara asks.

I stop backing. 'Yes,' I say. I've been cooking since I was a little kid. Since Dad went away I've been doing pretty much all the housework, including preparing meals for four. If that's all she wants me to do, fine. Even if it takes until midnight.

Barbara flings open an inside door to show a dark old kitchen lit by more skull lamps. The stove is one of those ancient iron ones with a wood fire in a little compartment; there's a basket of logs sitting next to it. Bunches of herbs and onions and garlic dangle from the ceiling. In the middle of the room there's a wooden table and on it are a big bowl of fruit and veg, a basket of eggs and some little sacks that look as if they might hold rice or beans. In the corner stands a big red cupboard with a design of fruit and flowers painted on it, like something out of an old fairytale book. *Then she shut her little brother in the red cupboard, and when she opened the doors again he was quite, quite gone.*

'I'm going out,' Barbara says. 'Work to be done. You'll make my dinner, three courses, each finer than the last. Lay it out on this table before I return home, and be sure it's a meal fit for a queen. If I'm satisfied I'll give you what you came for. But take care you leave my kitchen tidy. If I find the smallest thing out of place, I'll consider eating you for my dinner instead.'

Seems as if she's heard most of the things the tenants of Woodland Gardens say about her and finds them amusing, not upsetting. I'm beyond being surprised by anything at this point, so I put on an apron, wash my hands and get to work. My gran had a wood stove like this so it's not too much of a challenge.

Making a three course dinner takes me a while. I put Mimi on the table, propped up against the fruit bowl. Rory the cat comes in at a certain point and hunkers down in a corner to supervise. As for Barbara, she's flung on a cape and gone off, slamming the front door behind her. It's pretty trusting of her, seeing as she's never met me before tonight. I wonder what work she could be doing at this hour.

I think about Susie, upstairs getting angrier and angrier in the dark. The doll I was working on will be lying on the table up there, all lonely, waiting for me to finish embroidering her face. Like all the dolls I make, she has in her a hair I plucked from my own head and knitted in with the wool. Someone's out there waiting for that doll, and unless I get this job finished and take the candles upstairs they'll have to wait a day longer, and Susie ... I can't let myself think too hard about that; I have to concentrate. I dare to open the red cupboard and find it's a pantry full of useful ingredients. It's a long time since I've had so much good stuff to work with.

For starters, I make a tomato and basil soup, with shaved Parmesan and a herb scone on the side. I put together a spiced fruit compote and vanilla custard—there's no fridge in Barbara's kitchen, but the bottle of milk in the pantry is still okay, and so is the chicken waiting to be jointed and cooked. The main course will be breaded chicken pieces on herbed couscous, with vegies baked in olive oil and rosemary. In herb lore, rosemary means a strong woman, so it seems a good choice. I hope the meal's substantial enough for Barbara. She looks like she might be a big eater. I wonder who would have cooked her dinner if I hadn't been here.

It's starting to feel as if midnight might have been and gone, and my eyes are gritty with tiredness. The meal is pretty much ready, with only the couscous to steam. I make myself coffee, give Rory some chicken scraps in a bowl that looks like it might be hers, and sit down at the table for a bit. The kitchen's full of good smells; even with those skulls staring down at me, it feels safe in here. The coffee should give me enough energy to clean up, then I only need to set the table and I'm done. If Barbara likes the meal, I can grab the lighter and candles and head on upstairs, and I'll still have time to finish the doll before morning.

I find crockery, a glass, knives and forks. I check the kitchen: bench wiped clean, dishes washed, dried and put away, floor swept, fire made up, kettle steaming on the wood stove. Everything's ready. And I hear noises from outside the front door—Barbara's back.

Whoosh! Rory leaps onto the table, sending the open bag of couscous flying. Around two kilos of the stuff spill out all over the floor, the tiny granules rolling and scattering into every corner. I jump up and they crunch under my shoes. Rory has terrified herself; now she's standing on the table with one paw planted on the clean plate, fur on end, yowling. There's a rattle at the front door as Barbara sticks her key in the lock. What was that she said about eating me for dinner?

I scramble for the red cupboard where there's a dustpan and brush, and I slip over on the carpet of little grains. I land on my hip, putting new bruises on the old ones. I want to curl up on the floor and cry. Instead I look at Mimi, who's still standing beside the fruit bowl.

Give me a kiss, says Mimi.

The front door squeaks open. I struggle to my feet, reach out for the doll, kiss her embroidered mouth.

Give me a hug.

Quick, quick, I will her as I lay my cheek on hers.

Now let me fly!

I throw her high; in the few seconds we have left before fate catches up with us, she may as well enjoy herself. She twirls, tumbles, falls back into my waiting hands. Dear Mimi, my true friend in good times and bad.

Sit on the chair, close your eyes, lift your feet and keep that cat out of my way.

I manage to gather up Rory, who weighs half a ton, and sit down at the table again. I can hear Barbara walking about in the other room, muttering to herself. There's no way this can be cleaned up before she comes in, no way.

Somewhere near my feet there's a little sound like rats scuttling about. In my arms Rory tenses, making a deep-down whining noise. My body feels like it's strung on a wire, every bit of it jangly and terrified.

Hold on to that cat and keep your eyes shut.

Something small and woollen brushes against my ankle and is gone. The scuttling moves around the room, from cupboard to table, from table to bench, from bench to stove.

How much couscous does your recipe require? asks Mimi.

'A cup.' This is crazy.

The scuttling moves up onto the table; becomes more of a pouring sound.

Done.

I open my eyes. The floor looks completely clean. Mimi is exactly where she was before, regarding me with her woollen gaze, and the couscous is back in the bag, most of it anyway. The enamel cup I had ready for measuring is filled precisely to the top.

The door opens and there's Barbara, tall and imposing, her dark eyes taking in the tidy kitchen, the neatly laid table, the various serving dishes waiting. I put the cat down, then move the couscous over to the bench and measure a cupful of water into a small iron pot.

'Please, do sit down,' I say a bit shakily. 'Are you ready for the first course now?'

She sinks weightily onto the chair. 'I could eat a horse,' she says, sounding as if she actually means it.

Barbara eats the tomato and basil soup, the parmesan and the herb scone without saying a word. While she's getting through that, I steam the couscous, which seems none the worse for its stint on the floor.

'Good.' Barbara wipes her mouth with a large hand. 'What's next?'

I serve the couscous, the chicken pieces and the baked vegetables: creamy potatoes, golden pumpkin, ruby-red beets, glistening onions. My mouth is watering, but she doesn't suggest I sit down and share her feast, and I don't either.

When she's eaten about half the main course, she sets down her knife and fork and stares at me. 'I need entertainment,' she says. 'A story. Think you can manage that?'

I'm okay at cooking and I guess I'm okay at stories too, thanks to *Grimm's Fairy Tales*. I start to tell her a story about a girl who goes into the woods to find an old witch who lives in a hut on hen's legs, only Barbara keeps interrupting and asking questions, and it turns into a story about a girl whose stepmother takes her away from everything familiar, until the only friend she has in the world is the little doll her mother taught her how to make. A girl who only gets let out when her stepmother wants something; a girl who's lost touch with the good things of her past, and only sees the cruelty and loneliness of her future.

'Is this the doll?' Barbara asks, looking at Mimi, who stares back boldly from her spot by the fruit bowl.

I tell her. I explain about the other dolls I make and how Susie sells them as fast as I can get them finished. I don't tell her about the strands of hair; that feels too secret, even though Barbara's listening with interest and her expression's quite kindly. She's finished the main course, a meal big enough to go around all four of us at 1205 with leftovers to spare.

'Ready for dessert?' I ask politely, wondering what the time is and whether Susie will have given up on me and gone to bed by now. Maybe I can sneak in without waking her up.

'Mmm.' Barbara stretches, moves her chair back a bit from the table. 'Who taught you to cook, Lissa?'

'My mother.'

'She did a good job. You could be a chef someday.'

I say nothing. You don't get to be much at all if you haven't finished high school. I bring out the fruit compote and the custard, and I make a pot of tea.

'Sit down,' Barbara says at last. 'Fetch yourself a cup, a bowl and a spoon.'

We eat the dessert course together. It tastes wonderful; each mouthful reminds me of summer and sunshine and being safe. It reminds me of Mum and Dad and the way things used to be.

'Well, then,' says Barbara when the compote and custard are all gone and we're sitting over our cups of tea. 'You've told me your story, and a fine one it was, full of joy and sorrow, good times and bad. Now it's your turn. I'm sure you have plenty of questions for the old woman in the basement with her voodoo spells and her cantankerous familiar. Go ahead, ask them.'

My mind fills with questions. I'd love to know about her past, and what brought her to live at Woodland Gardens, where she doesn't belong at all. I'd like to know what the brass plate on the door says, and what language it's in. I'd love her to tell me what work she does out there at midnight. And I want to know about spells: whether there's one that will rescue me from Susie.

Suddenly it seems dangerous to ask much at all. It feels like prying into something best left alone.

'I only have one question,' I say.

Her eyebrows go up.

'Is magic real?' I ask, hoping she won't laugh her head off.

She doesn't say anything, just looks at me, and I remember the thing with the couscous. I think of the hair I put into my dolls, as if that might somehow make them as real to their owners as Mimi is to me. Of course magic is real. But then I remember Susie and my bruises and how I've never been brave enough to ask Kye if I can use his phone, and I think no, it can't be.

Barbara goes on looking at me and sipping her tea, and I think she isn't going to answer at all until she gets up, goes to the red cupboard, opens a little drawer at the bottom and brings out something that looks a bit like a melted candle. When she shows it to me I see it's like a doll, with arms and legs and a head, but blobby and crude as if someone got tired of making it halfway through.

'What if I told you this was a voodoo doll?' she asks, and a shiver runs through me. It doesn't take much to imagine this little thing with pins stuck all over it, or being held over a lighter flame until it drips away to nothing. 'What if I taught you how to work a curse?'

Now the room is bristling with magic, the Grimm's fairy tale kind where girls try to hide terrible secrets and wicked stepmothers dance in red-hot iron shoes. I take a deep breath, then reach out and pick up Mimi. 'No,' I say. 'Not even if it gets me out of trouble. Not even if it fixes up the future the way I want. It'll cost too much. That kind of thing always does.'

Barbara smiles. She reaches over toward the stove, opens the iron door with her bare hand and throws the wax thing inside, where it sizzles, making a vile smell. She clangs the door shut. 'You'll be wanting that light, then.' She stands, takes one of the skull lamps from the shelf and hands it to me. There's a wire running through a couple of holes on the top, so I can carry the skull. The tea-light candle inside has been burning a while; this lamp may be out before I even get to Oak Level. Perhaps the power will be back on by then. Perhaps Susie won't hurt me. After the voodoo thing, I can't seem to make myself ask for more.

'I'll see you out,' Barbara says, leading me through the room with the embroidered cushions to the red front door. When she opens it, Rory streaks out, quicker than her bulk suggests is possible, and darts up the steps to the ground floor.

'Thank you,' I say. 'It's been interesting talking to you.'

Now she does laugh, but in a good way. 'And you,' she says. 'Hasten upstairs, Lissa. Dawn is breaking, and a new day comes.'

A new day? Already? I see that she's right, because up the top of the seven steps the door to the plaza is open, and as Rory sprints out, the darkness starts to lift. Out there, it's nearly dawn, and upstairs in 1205 Susie's going to wake up and find I've been away all night. Can I really have been talking for as long as that? Did I somehow fall asleep and not even notice? Either way, this is a disaster.

'Farewell, Lissa,' says Barbara softly, and the door closes behind me.

Grimly, I start the long climb. Pine, Cedar, Yew. Beside each painted name there's a little silhouette of the tree; nice idea, wrong place. Beyond the stairwell windows the sky turns violet, pink, gold. Elm, Ash, Eucalyptus. Let her be still asleep. Let me get inside and be sewing before she wakes up. But that isn't going to happen, because I have to do the twice three knocks on the door. She's going to kill me. Cypress. Poplar. My legs are on fire; I have to stop and catch my breath. I sit down on the steps with Mimi on my knee, and look out the window as somewhere beyond the concrete towers the sun edges over the horizon.

Down below, the stairwell door opens. The guy who walks through is not much older than me. His hair's the colour fairy tales call golden, and he's wearing snowy white overalls with a logo on the pocket, a smiling sun with Day and Son, Fresh Food Deliveries underneath. The guy's carrying a little crate, and in it are loaves of bread and bottles —old-fashioned glass bottles—of milk. Like the one in Barbara's pantry. 'After you,' he says politely.

We go on up, me first, the milk guy—Day Junior—second. I wait for him to ask me what I was doing sitting on the stairs at what must be about five in the morning, or to comment on the skull lamp, but all he says is, 'Going to be a lovely day.'

'Mm,' I say, my mind full of Susie. Why am I so stupid? Why didn't I ask Barbara if she'd let me use her phone to call the welfare people, instead of cooking her a giant dinner and asking her about magic? No wonder I'm in so much trouble.

Day Junior and I climb through Juniper, Aspen and Willow. Outside, the sun comes up and proves him right; weather-wise, at least, it's shaping up to be a beautiful day. Seems as if he plans to start his deliveries at the top. When we get to Oak Floor, he balances his crate on one arm and uses the other to hold the broken door back so it can't fall on me as I go through.

'Thanks,' I say, and head off toward 1205, not looking back to see who on Oak Floor can possibly afford a fresh food delivery.

The hallway is full of light; outside, the sun's climbing. I reach our door, knock three times, wait, knock three times again. The door flies open. She's been waiting. Her face is all squeezed up with rage. Her arms stretch out to drag me inside.

'Here,' I say, holding out the skull with its pitiful, flickering candle inside. Too little, too late. Susie takes it, and the look on her face makes my flesh crawl. My fingers move to touch the comforting shape of Mimi in my pocket. She's not there. Somewhere on the long climb up, I've dropped her.

No time to think. I turn my back on Susie and bolt for the stairwell. Day Junior hasn't got past the first doorway, and when he sees me rushing down the steps he comes after me.

'Hey! Slow down or you'll hurt yourself. What's wrong?'

I gasp out an explanation, and instead of laughing at me he helps me search. As we go down, Willow, Aspen, Juniper, checking every step, I do wonder why Susie hasn't come after me, but nothing's as important as finding Mimi. Without her, a bit of me's missing, and I don't have a lot to spare.

It's Day Junior who locates Mimi, wedged between concrete step and iron railing on Poplar Level. He gets her out carefully, dusts her off, hands her back to me. 'Safe and sound,' he says.

'Must have jumped out of your pocket.'

I'm just starting to say thanks when there's a massive *Boom!* from somewhere up above. The two of us shrink back against the wall, Day Junior acting like a fairytale hero as he spreads out his arms and shields me. The noise is over quickly, but now there's a strange light from up there, not the rising sun or a little skull lamp but a big, hot, hungry light. And people shouting. *Fire!*

Day Junior takes my hand. 'Downstairs, quick!'

I hesitate for about two seconds, then people start streaming down the stairs from the floors above us, and the only thing we can do is go down with them. There's an alarm woop-wooping, and smoke starting to fill the top of the stairwell. People are in their nighties and pyjamas, with kids wrapped in blankets and old folk clinging onto the dodgy hand-rail, but nobody's panicking, and we all make it down to the ground floor and out onto the plaza where the Day and Son delivery van's parked, gleaming white in the sunlight.

The fire fighters arrive and we get moved away from the building. The fire's on Oak Level. I can see smoke billowing out of the windows. I look around for Barbara, but I can't spot her or Rory in the crowd. Still, the fire's a long way up; in the basement they should be safe. Firies head up the stairs; down here on the plaza there's a truck with a massive extension ladder and hoses being screwed onto water mains and lots of activity. Someone asks Day Junior to move the van. He asks me if I'm okay and I say yes, so he hops in and drives it away.

I haven't seen Susie. I haven't seen Sophie or Miranda. But Kye's here with his mum and his little brother, and they live on Oak Level. I can't make myself go over and talk to them. My head's gone muzzy and my legs feel weak. I collapse onto a bench with Mimi on my knee, staring up at the thickening smoke and thinking about that lump of wax Barbara threw into the stove. How it sizzled and burned. How it filled my nostrils with a smell like death. I want to say a prayer, but I can't think what should be in it, so I put my head down on the bench and press Mimi against my cheek and close my eyes. Magic *is* real, just like in Grimm's fairy tales.

The day after the fire, I'm leaving Westmoreland Hospital, where they've kept me in overnight for observation. A social worker from Defence Welfare is letting me stay at her place until Dad gets home on compassionate leave. Her name's Siobhan, she lives near my old house and she's told me she has three cats called Winken, Blinken and Nod. Siobhan seems to know a lot about what's been happening to me, even though I've hardly said anything. She tells me a Mrs Barbara Jaeger rang the office and told her where I was and that I needed help. And Mrs Moss from school rang too, a while ago, asking why I hadn't come back this term and if I was okay. I ask Siobhan if Mrs Jaeger is the concierge at Woodside Gardens and she says yes, and that Barbara said to pass on her best wishes for the future.

Before I go home with Siobhan, I visit my stepsister Sophie, who's in a different ward getting treated for smoke inhalation. Miranda's in surgery this morning—her hands got burned—so I can't see her. Sophie looks terrible, hospital-sheet-white with big bruises under her eyes, but she scrapes together a smile.

'Lissa. You're okay,' she whispers.

'I'm okay. And you will be, too.' I know the next thing I should say is that I'm sorry about Susie, but the words won't come out. I'm sorry it happened the way it did. But I can't be sorry she's gone.

'Look in the drawer,' Sophie says on a rasping breath. 'Got something for you.'

I open the drawer in the bedside table, and there's the little doll I was making before Susie sent me down to get light. She's unharmed, just waiting there quietly for me to fetch her so I can finish embroidering her face. She's lying on the lacy shawl Sophie was knitting, and under that I see Miranda's Aran sweater with the fancy cables. I want to laugh and cry at the same time.

'Our Dad's coming,' Sophie says. 'They let me call him. He cried when he heard my voice. All this time, he didn't know where we were.'

I start to understand why my stepsisters were sometimes unkind to me. I guess they were every bit as lost and afraid as I was. I feel strange, sort of sad, sort of relieved, but mostly just very tired.

'Miranda stopped to grab our work as we were running out.' Sophie's looking at the doll, which is on my knee now. 'That's how her hands got burned. I'm sorry we couldn't save your book, Lissa. I know you loved it.'

A book is only a book. It's the stories in it that matter. 'Thank you,' I say, putting my hand on hers.

'Mum,' Sophie whispers. 'She threw that skull thing across the room, and suddenly there was fire everywhere. I don't know how it could … I don't understand…' Her voice fades to nothing.

'They think it may have been an electrical fault,' puts in Siobhan from the doorway.

There's a silence, then I say to Sophie, 'Let me know how you're getting on, okay?' When it's finished, this doll will be for her, and I'll make another for Miranda. Companions for a new life.

Siobhan comes in to put a little card on the bedside table, with contact phone numbers and addresses so Sophie and Miranda can find me if they want to.

'I have to go now,' I say. I look at Sophie, and she stares up at me with her shadowy eyes, and the thing unspoken between us looms as huge and dark as the monster in every child's worst nightmare. 'It'll be all right,' I say, which is the best I can do at the moment.

Before she closes her eyes, Sophie whispers something. Maybe, *sorry*.

On the way to Siobhan's house, we drive past Woodland Gardens, where the clean-up is still happening. I don't look up at Oak Floor. An old woman in a purple dress is walking across the plaza, with an enormous ginger cat dawdling along behind her. I fish Mimi out of my pocket, hoping Siobhan's too busy driving to notice. I have a big question for my doll, a question about right and wrong and magic and responsibility. It's a question that's too big to be put in words.

Give me a kiss! demands Mimi.

I touch my lips to her woollen mouth.

Give me a hug!

I hold her against my heart, hoping the faceless doll in my other pocket won't get jealous. Her time will come.

Now let me fly!

One flip is all she gets, and not a very high one. I stand her on my knee, gaze into her knitted eyes and ask my question.

'All right?' asks Siobhan, giving me a sideways glance but keeping her hands firmly on the wheel.

'Fine,' I tell her. 'Could you drive around the block before we go home, please?'

Being a social worker, Siobhan is probably used to people acting weird. At the next corner she turns left and we begin a circuit of Woodland Gardens.

Start working on it now, Mimi says, *and by the time you're an old woman with white hair, you might know the answer to that question. Now can we go home, please?*

As we come around the plaza again, Barbara's still there, waiting while Rory does her business in a patch of dirt. I don't open the window and shout. I don't ask Siobhan to stop. I just look across at the two of them and mouth the words, 'Thank you.' Barbara turns and looks straight back at me. She lifts her hand in a sort of wave. Her mouth is not smiling and not frowning, but something in between. We drive on past, leaving Woodland Gardens behind us.

The Myriad Dangers

By Lavie Tidhar

1.

The aliens invaded at two fifty-seven in the afternoon, three minutes exactly to three. Which was a good tactical choice—most adults were asleep, taking a well-deserved afternoon nap in dark rooms where the only sound was the soft burr of the air-conditioner or the gentle hum of a fan as it turned this way and that.

It was hot.

The heat felt like the aliens' laser beams. It lay over the sea and blasted the sand and made the grass sweat. When you blinked the sweat got in your eyes and everything looked hazy and distant and impossible.

The aliens were small and green and wore purple. Their blasters looked like toys and the aliens looked like wizened children dressed for a Purim party. Hardly anyone saw them. Their flying saucers hovered silently above the white buildings of Tel Aviv. There were hundreds of them. Thousands. The saucers came from the sky and some hovered over the city and some hovered over the sea and some blasted cars as they came along the Ayalon Highway, but not like they were being mean. Like they were just a little bored, and maybe wanting to break things.

Danny was alone when the aliens came. His parents were asleep in the room upstairs and he was outside, despite the heat, standing by himself next to the swings, waiting for someone, anyone, to come along so he could play with them.

It was Rosh Hashana, or would be in the evening. They'd welcome the new year as they always did, by going to see his grandparents. They'd go in the car, and his father would hum along with the radio and make up his own words to songs, and when they'd get there Danny's uncles and aunts and cousins and everyone would be there, and there'd be some singing, and not-so-good food, and the television would be on for the news, and it would be one of those long summer evenings that seem never to end without quite leading anywhere, and suddenly he wanted very badly not to go, which was at exactly two fifty-seven in the afternoon, when the aliens came.

The aliens came marching down the street, like ants, or Israeli Defence Force soldiers. They marched in lines and their hands moved in rhythm but they didn't make a sound. The whole city seemed to be asleep, its defence systems down, its awareness diminished, a whole city dreaming, restlessly, of other white cities, and coolness, and matzo ball soup.

Danny watched the aliens go past. They ignored him, but one of the saucers, hovering overhead, shot out a laser beam that made the swing melt and hiss on the ground.

'Cool…' said Danny.

The word, small and alone, hung in the hot, humid air of the invasion before fading softly. Danny watched the melted metal on the dry ground.

After a while he saw that there were now alien soldiers in front of every door that he could see. There must have been millions of small alien soldiers all throughout the city, standing before every doorway and in apartment block hallways throughout the city. They still hadn't made a sound.

'What are they going to do now?' said Danny, but there was no one there to answer him, so he just watched instead.

At three sixteen, in the hot afternoon, the aliens approached each of the doors they were watching and opened them. If they couldn't open them they used their blasters to melt the locks and then they went in. Every house and every apartment, even my one, and you have to get in through a locked courtyard first.

Then they started carrying people out.

Danny watched. He was the only one awake, in the whole wide city. In the whole world, maybe. He watched the strange little aliens carry his mum out. It took four of them to hold her up. She was asleep, and her eyes were closed, and there was a little bit of drool at the corner of her mouth. Two more aliens carried out his dad and three were bringing out the neighbour, Shula, who wore a flower patterned dress and dyed her hair blue and had false teeth that she kept in a tea glass on her bedside table. The teeth floated there in the murky liquid and grinned at nothing. He had seen them once, when he had to go and borrow a cup of sugar for his mum.

The aliens carried people out of their homes. There were old people and little babies and plumbers and school teachers on the summer holidays. There were computer programmers and belly dancers and bakers and cinema ushers and homeless people (but the aliens picked them up in the street, gently, the way you would a baby). There were fat hairy men in big white underpants and women with curlers in their hair and men in blue overalls spattered with paint and old people with catheters and a kid in a wheelchair and a couple still entwined, in sleep, in each other's arms.

'I wonder where they're taking them,' said Danny, but there was no one there to answer him, by the silent swings. He watched the aliens take all the people out of their houses and apartments and then they stopped, and stood motionless in the silent street.

'Mum isn't going to be happy when she wakes up, you know,' said Danny, but the aliens didn't hear him or, if they did, they chose to ignore him. Or perhaps they just didn't understand. No one expects aliens to speak Hebrew. So Danny just watched and then all the flying saucers, at once, shot out a sort of blue light and the alien soldiers and their cargo were lifted slowly up in the air, floating there in the blue with the sun beating down, untold thousands of sleeping people held in alien arms.

Then they all disappeared inside the flying saucers and the blue light vanished and, at three forty-six in the afternoon they, too, disappeared, just like that.

The city was silent and empty and the only sound he could hear, if he tried really hard, was that of the sea, the sound of small waves lapping against the shore. It was a sound both like and unlike the one of small feet padding along, clad in worn-out trainers. The city lay there, in the hot sun of a summer afternoon, on Rosh Hashana: entombed, empty, free.

'I wonder where they all went,' said Danny. But of course, there was no one there to answer him: not even aliens.

2.

'That was strange,' said Danny's dad the next day.

'What was?' said Danny's mum.

'I had the strangest dream,' said Danny's dad. 'That funny little aliens came and took us all away in their ships.'

'That *is* weird,' said Danny's mum.

Danny wanted to tell them it hadn't been a dream, but didn't. It really happened! He saw it!

The problem was, these weren't his real mum and dad. His real mum and dad were stored on board a spaceship, with thousands and thousands of other human bodies, all floating side by side and in stacks, going somewhere.

When the aliens left, Danny had been left alone by the ruined swing. After a while he went back home, but when he turned on the television there was nothing on, so he turned it off again and went out. He didn't lock the door. There didn't seem to be much point.

It was still Rosh Hashana, though maybe for his parents it wasn't. Did you have Rosh Hashana in space?

He wandered the streets. The sun was getting lower in the sky, sinking towards the sea, and it was very slightly cooler. There was no one around.

There were cats, though. But the cats ignored him. And there were dogs, and some of them barked at him, but mostly they just looked confused. There were a lot of pets in Tel Aviv and, like Danny, they expected to be fed.

He felt hungry so he went into an empty mini-market and took a packet of *Bisli*, grill flavour, and ate it. Then he wandered back outside.

'What do you think you're doing, kid?'

He turned when he heard the voice. Inside the mini-market the air shimmered, and for a moment he saw, through a membrane of air, a shifting blue light and an amorphous shape and then, like something hatching out of an egg, the amorphous blob became a person and stepped out onto the mini-market floor.

It looked—it looked exactly like Shufra, the checkout woman who was always there when he went to the store with his mum. She was in her mid-fifties, with a blue blouse and a name-tag that said SHUFRA on it in big black letters, and she had long nails painted red that she used to punch the numbers on the till with. In fact, it looked exactly like Shufra but for the eyes. The eyes were empty, and behind them was the same blue emptiness, like the sky.

'I was—' said Danny, and then stopped, because he didn't know what to say.

'You need to pay for that!'

'But—'

But there was no one there, he wanted to say, but instead he went over to the creature that looked just like Shufra, and gave it five shekels, and then shuffled his feet when she—it—ruffled his hair briefly and then told him to get back home, his mum would be waiting.

So he went home. As he walked along the empty streets, with the sun slowly setting beyond the sea, more and more human simulacra materialised all around him. They looked like everyday people— builders and policewomen, bus drivers and cable technicians, a homeless guy and the two weird old ladies with the runny makeup who always pushed a shopping trolley between them down the road, ignoring the outraged drivers—but their eyes were windows, and beyond them was a clear and empty blue sky, with no clouds or life.

The dogs, he noticed, were growling at the simulacra. But the cats rubbed themselves against them, and their fur stood on end, as if they had come in touch with too much static electricity.

'Where have you been?'

A simulacra stood in the kitchen. It looked just like his mum.

'I was playing on the swings.'

The simulacra mum looked out of the window. 'Someone ruined one of the swings,' she said.

'It was the aliens,' said Danny.

'Go to your room,' his simulacra-mum said.

3.

Luckily they didn't have to go to the Rosh Hashana dinner after all, because of the zombie invasion.

The zombies came from the north, from the direction of the old cities, of Haifa and Acre and Safed, and they came from the south, from the mountains of Jerusalem, and there were lots and lots of them.

The zombies appeared by lunchtime. Danny was playing by the swings again, because it was still a holiday and there was no school until Monday. The zombies looked just like normal people but they had green skin and bits were falling off them and they smelled bad. The zombies shambled down the street and whenever they saw a person they moaned and groaned and reached for them with green flaking fingers, and when they caught them they bit them, bit them everywhere, on the neck and the head and the ears, on the arms and the fingers, on the belly and on the legs.

And then the people who got bitten, or what was left of them by then, also became zombies.

The Myriad Dangers | Lavie Tidhar

Danny hid. He'd abandoned the swings for a makeshift castle, climbing high on the playhouse's network of ladders, swings and rope bridges until he made it to the very top. He felt safe there.

He watched his mum and dad. His dad was standing in the street outside, sneaking a cigarette. 'What the—?' Danny's dad said. He dropped the cigarette on the ground and by the time it hit the zombies were on him. There were more than ten of them—old ladies with false teeth, a baby that made no sound, a fat man with a hairy back, two school girls, the butcher from down the street and a couple of people who had wandered off the bus at the nearby bus stop. They tore at Danny's dad's arms and bit him, like a pack of dogs fighting over a meal. Danny's dad screamed, once, and then he gurgled.

When Danny's dad stood up again he was no longer Danny's dad. He had bits missing everywhere—big chunks on the arms, both ears, an eye, most of a thigh. His clothes were torn and his short hair was matted with green-grey goo.

'Grrrrrr,' said Danny's dad.

'Arrrrrgh,' said the people who came off the bus.

Danny saw his mum step out of the door, pause, take in the scene, and scream. The scream was long and high and piercing and was the only other sound in the quiet street.

Then she ran back inside and, when she came back out, she was carrying an Uzi that Danny's dad kept in the house in readiness for his reserve military service, which took place at least once a year.

'Take that, zombie scum!' Danny's mum screamed, and pulled the trigger.

Bullets flew, cutting through brains and throats and chests and arms. Danny's dad fell back, his arms rising in the air as he sank to his knees, hit by multiple bullets. 'I always knew this day would come,' Danny's mum said, still shooting. Danny could hear gunfire everywhere now. The city of Tel Aviv had erupted in a desperate war, residents and zombies, guns against teeth. 'But where is the government when you need it?'

She emptied the entire magazine and there was a momentary lull. Zombie corpses lay everywhere, broken, twitching, leaking green puss and blood.

From the neighbouring apartment their neighbour, Shula, stepped out in her flowery dress and an AK-47 in her arms. 'It's started,' she said.

And now, from across the street, stay-at-home mums and elderly ladies and young school girls all came marching up towards them. They were all carrying guns. A couple of them, Danny noticed, were smoking cigars. When they came to the apartment—one elderly lady stepping over Danny's dad's corpse—they all stopped, and saluted as one.

'At ease,' said Danny's mum.

'Supreme Commander,' said one of the women, who was holding a Desert Eagle point five oh in one hand and a butcher's knife in the other, 'we are ready at your command.'

'Troops!' said Danny's mum. 'The zombie invasion has started. The moment we have been waiting for has come. We must make for the mountains! Leave no corpse unturned! Kill everything in your path! Who is with me?'

'We are!' cried her troops.

'Who is with me?'

'*We are!*'

'Then let's go!'

And, firing in the air, she led them back up the street, only looking behind once, to shout, 'I'll be back when I can, Danny! Keep out of sight and remember to wash behind your ears! Love you!'

Danny, perched on his eyrie, watched her go. After a while what was left of his dad got up from the pavement. It looked pretty bad. 'Grrrr?' it said, plaintively.

Danny wondered if there was any food left in the fridge.

4.

'Vampires? Really?' said Danny.

5.

It was two fifty-seven in the afternoon, and it was hot. It was Rosh Hashana, or would be in the evening. They'd welcome the new year as they always did, by going to see his grandparents. They'd go in the car, and his father would hum along with the radio and make up his own words to songs, and when they'd get there Danny's uncles and aunts and cousins and everyone would be there, and there'd be some singing, and not-so-good food, and the television would be on for the news, and it would be one of those long summer evenings that seem never to end without quite leading anywhere, and then they'd go home.

But right now, the Rosh Hashana dinner was far away, light years away in the distant future, and the city of Tel Aviv, *his* city, lay all about Danny as he played by the swings. The city lay quiet and peaceful and empty, in silence, its residents asleep in darkened rooms, like the dormant pupae of an alien species, patiently waiting to hatch.

For now, for just this afternoon, this hot summer day, this holiday, the city was his, Danny's, to do with as he pleased. Anything could happen, a multitude of threats posed for invasion, set and ready to stop the new year from coming, the tedious Rosh Hashana dinner, his aunt's cheek-pinching, his uncle's school-Latin phrases aimed like missiles at Danny and the other children, the too-sweet food and the boring television news turned on too loud.

There were aliens and zombies and weird trans-dimensional simulacra people. Even as he was watching the city was being transformed, giant, hungry, carnivorous plants spreading through rooftops and yards, twining themselves into chained bicycles and parked cars, giant hungry mouths opening, dripping saliva, grinning in the hot Mediterranean sun as they waited to devour the sleeping city.

'Cool...' said Danny.

Danny climbed on top of the swings, and smiled. He surveyed his domain. For just this afternoon, in that twilight moment between the old year and the new, while the city, unaware of the myriad dangers it faced, slept, he, Danny, was free.

The Carpet

By Nnedi Okorafor

My sister and I didn't go to the market with the intention of buying a carpet for the new house. All we really wanted were some souvenirs to bring back to Chicago. We bought a few ebony masks, some bead necklaces, a bronze statuette of the mermaid goddess Mami Wata, stuff like that. We didn't even *need* that carpet. How differently our time in the new house would have gone had we not bought that ... thing.

We were in Nigeria to visit our relatives. Our dad was sick so our mom stayed behind to care for him. I was fifteen, Zuma sixteen, and it was our first time visiting Nigeria without our parents. So though we'd been there many times, it felt new, different, darker. No those are the wrong words ... more mysterious.

We spent two weeks of our trip with our mother's sister in Abuja, which is a city in the central, drier, Muslim dominated part of the country. After we'd fully recovered from our jetlag, we went with our cousin Chinyere to the market. By the time we got back to the house, someone had picked my pocket of the few naira I carried, a group of Muslim men had shouted obscenities at my sister for wearing shorts, and two men threatened to smash my video camera because I had the nerve to record people at the market. I laugh. This was a normal day.

On day fourteen, we were getting ready to travel to my father's village. It would be an eight-hour drive south. My parents had a house built in my father's village and my sister and I were to spend three days there. We went with our cousin Chinyere to the market one last time in search of a few more souvenirs.

"Just *ignore* this man," Chinyere said as we walked through the market and approached a really extravagant-looking booth. The man sitting at it was short and old, his potbelly pushing his long white caftan forward.

"Why?" I asked. My hands were shoved in my pockets to protect my money.

"The Junk Man lost his mind a long time ago," she said. "Everyone knows it."

If he's crazy, then why is his booth packed with people checking his stuff out? I wondered. But I kept my mouth shut; I knew it would annoy Chinyere.

My sister Zuma was a few steps ahead and she hadn't heard Chinyere. Within moments, she had spotted something interesting and she too was drawn to the Junk Man's stuff. Chinyere groaned and rolled her eyes.

"One man's junk is another man's treasure!" the Junk Man announced, looking Chinyere right in the eye, challenging her. He turned to my sister Zuma. "Have a look see, but none of it's free."

"Look at all his ... things," I whispered to Zuma.

"I know, man," Zuma said grinning.

"Just junk," Chinyere snapped, thoroughly annoyed.

The Junk Man's booth was the same size as everyone else's, about twenty feet across, separated from the utensil shop to his right and the basket shop to his left by wooden dividers. But all that was exposed of his twenty feet was a narrow path that led in a semi-circle through his "junk."

Everything was arranged. Some items were on tables, most on the ground or hanging from nails on the wooden dividers. Knives, ebony statues, bronze statues, rings, necklaces and anklets of various metals, piles of colorful stones and pink and clear crystals, ancient looking coins, brown, white and black cowry shells of all sizes, some the size of my pinky fingernail, others larger than my head, scary and smiling ceremonial masks, an eight foot tall ebony statue of a large breasted stern looking goddess, a jar of gold powder, a pile of bejeweled and rusted daggers, baskets and bags of colored feathers.

"What you look for, ladies?" Junk Man asked us in his gruff voice, after helping a customer. The stool he sat on creaked as he shifted. He motioned to all his wares like a proud generous dragon. "Junk or jewels, I sell it to you at a good price."

"Do you mind if I look at..." Zuma pointed to the rolled up

carpet on one of his tables. It had golden tassels on its sides. That must have been what caught her eye. Zuma always loved anything that looked like something Scheherazade would own.

"Go ahead. Don't be shy," Junk Man said. "That's what all this is here for. But *don't touch* the things you don't think you should. And especially, don't touch those parrot feathers over there." He pointed to a bowl full of gorgeous green fluffy feathers. The things were practically begging to be handled. I frowned.

"For some reason, people don't know better," Junk Man said with a smirk. "Then they get home and wonder why all they want to do is chatter about nonsense."

Behind us, Chinyere sucked her teeth loudly and muttered, "See? Told you." Zuma and I looked at each other, uncomfortable. The man was either crazy or, seeing that we were American-born, trying to lay the mystery on thick. He thought we were like those stupid tourists who bought stuff because they thought it was "magical", like those people I saw buying stupid fake Voodoo dolls in New Orleans. Little did he know we'd been coming to Nigeria since we were five and six years old. The country was more like a second home than the "dark continent" to us.

"Ooookay," Zuma said. "I'm just gonna look over here." As she moved through all his junk, she kept her hands close to her sides. The Junk Man chuckled and turned back to me.

"American?"

I nodded.

"Sisters?"

"Yeah," Zuma said as she looked at an ebony mask.

"Who's older? You?" he asked pointing at me.

"No," I said. "She's a year older."

"No, that not older, you're practically twins," he said. "And you de older one. Your sister hasn't been around as many times."

"Uh, sure," I said, trying not to look him in his wrinkly nearly black face.

"Parents born here?" he asked.

"Yeah," we both said.

"Then you from here."

I laughed hard. "If you say so."

I heard Chinyere loudly suck her teeth with irritation.

"You interested in that carpet?" he asked my sister.

"Sort of," Zuma said, putting down a large cowry shell and returning to the carpet.

He nodded. "Go ahead and unroll it." He snickered again. "It won't hurt you."

Zuma dragged the rolled carpet to Chinyere and me.

"This will be a good finishing touch to the house," she said to Chinyere and me. "A good house-warming gift."

"I dunno," I said.

From what we'd been told, the house was already fully furnished. I wasn't sure if there would be room for it.

"It'll make the perfect gift, yes," the Junk Man said. Then he laughed again. The three of us ignored him and unrolled the carpet. People passing behind us kept getting annoyed, sucking their teeth and grumbling with impatience because the carpet took up part of the market path.

"Oh," I said, blinking with surprise. "It's really pretty."

"Yeah," Chinyere whispered, all grins.

The carpet was a bright periwinkle color stitched with intricate symmetric geometrical winding designs of thick black threads. I could stare at it for hours. It was a nice piece of artwork, and the gold tassels were beautiful, too. Zuma quickly rolled it back up and said, "I want to buy this, sir. For … two thousand naira." That was about twenty dollars.

He paused looking intently at Zuma. Then he smiled. "Ok, make I pack it for you. Come on, bring it here."

Zuma grinned, surprised. But I felt a little annoyed. If a seller agreed on a price that quickly, then you'd proposed too high a price. But I know I would have also made the same mistake with such a beautiful carpet. Even Chinyere was surprised.

"It's worth over five thousand naira, I'd think. Even after bargaining down," Chinyere quietly told me. "He really *is* crazy."

Uncle Ralph drove us in his blue Mercedes. The eight-hour drive was long, grueling and hot. The last two hours were spent on red dirt roads pock marked with deep holes from the rainy season. Dusty and tired, we arrived in my father's village, our relatives running out and hugging, kissing, and inspecting us. The house was enormous and lovely, a white adobe mansion in rural Nigeria. When we went inside, we learned that the house was also completely and utterly unfurnished! Empty as hell! Apparently, over the last year, since buying the furniture and placing it in the house, our relatives had gone in and stolen everything. Piece by piece. Nice.

Beds, couches, dressers, lights, tables, chairs, rugs, a refrigerator, all gone. The house also had no electricity or running water. To make matters worse, it was ridiculously dusty from being locked for months. It seemed massive house spiders dwelled in every corner, proud and fat as Shelob from *Lord of the Rings*. Then there were the pink wall geckos that scurried across the ceilings. These were okay because they were cute and ate the mosquitoes and small spiders; I doubted that they could eat the Shelobs. I also saw a pile of larger droppings upstairs in one of the rooms. Not a good sign.

After a tour of the house, we both stood there in what was called the Yoruba Room. Our Aunt Mary and Uncle Daniel stood behind us, quiet. Everyone else who had run out to greet us when we arrived had mysteriously disappeared as we walked into the house. The Yoruba Room was the largest in the house, with high ceilings and a lovely, though dusty, tiled mosaic of frolicking fish on the floor.

"But I thought ... didn't you say that everything was here?" was all I could ask.

"Auntie, Uncle," Zuma said, angry. "What happened?"

Uncle Daniel sighed and shook his head. "No one could stop them," he said. "No shame."

Zuma could barely contain herself. "Why didn't you tell…"

"We thought your parents would come with you," their aunt said. "We didn't think they'd come if they knew."

When people travel to Nigeria, they don't usually disclose who is traveling or when. You give as little detail as possible, or risk armed robbers waiting for your arrival or unscrupulous relatives from heaven and earth coming by to ask for this and that. Best to catch people off guard. People knew my father was sick, but they did not know the extent, that he would be having heart surgery soon. I pushed thoughts of my father's illness out of my mind.

"Well…" Zuma said. She turned and looked out the window at the sky. Then she said, "We're going to stay here tonight."

I gasped and said, "Zuma, I don't think…"

She gave me one of her icy big sister looks and I immediately shut up.

"This is our parents' house and we are their daughters. And we're in Dad's village. We stay here," she said, her voice shaky with emotion and her fists clenched. I understood. Our relatives knew our father was sick, yet they took his furniture. This was his house and they robbed it. His home in his homeland. We would honor our father before all of them by staying in the house he and my mother built.

"You don't have to," my aunt said, looking worried. She motioned to the house next door. "Please, you will stay with us…"

"No," Zuma firmly said. "We stay here."

And that is how we found ourselves in a dusty creepy empty but lovely house in the middle of rural southeastern Nigeria with no running water or electricity, the only furniture being a bed my aunt had had carried in and the carpet Zuma bought. We were to stay there for three days.

The village was made up of the gigantic and not so gigantic houses of our relatives, but it was also surrounded by lush forest that used to be farmed for yams and other crops back in the day. This meant, there were probably all sorts of creatures living in that house.

In the evening, after pleading with us one more time, my aunt had a group of girls bring us a tray of red stew, rice, fried plantain and two bottles of orange Fanta for dinner. We were so hungry and exhausted that it was the most delicious food we'd ever tasted. The girls also brought a barrel of well water for bathing. Even after washing in the dirty bathtub with cups of freezing well water, it was still sweltering hot in the room we'd locked ourselves in.

"Geez!" I said, scratching at my itchy sweaty skin. I planned to dunk my head in a bucket of water to wash my braids tomorrow. "How are we going to sleep in this heat?"

Zuma shrugged, sitting on the bed, looking miserably at the lit candles.

"I almost want to dump water on myself, soak my clothes and the bed!" I whined. I held my little battery-powered hand fan to my face. I sat beside her. We crossed our legs on the bed, afraid to touch the floor with our bare feet.

"And we're probably gonna get bitten up by Malaria-infected mosquitoes with that open window…"

"Will you just shut up!?" Zuma snapped. "If you want to run to Uncle and Auntie's house, go! I'm staying here. What are we supposed to tell Mom and Dad when we get back? You think this is gonna make Dad *feel* better? That a bunch of his relatives are greedy jerks even when he's sick?! Who cares about mosquitoes and Malaria, man. This is…"

Then we heard it and we both shut up.

Softly, *scrape, scrape*. Then *clunk*, like something falling. Then a more continuous *scraaaaape*.

"What's that?" I whispered. It was coming from downstairs.

"Shhh!" she hissed.

Scrape, scrape. Quiet. Minutes passed. Then more *scrape, scrape*. It seemed to be moving away from us, toward the front of the house downstairs. We stayed frozen like that all night. Listening. Come morning, we were still in the same position. In the village, there were night-sounds that were normal, like the hoot of an owl, the clicks and chirps of insects, the screech of some animal we couldn't name. But what we'd heard was in the house and it only stopped at about the same time that the sun rose.

Someone knocking on the door forced us to leave our room.

"Hey," I said smiling tiredly, as we slowly walked down the stairs. I pointed at one of the ceiling corners. "Looks like those nasty spiders are taking off because of us. The webs aren't just empty, it looks like the spiders actually cut them down."

"Cool," Zuma said. "I guess they aren't so stupid. I was gonna ask Tochi to come and crush them all today."

"Good morning," our aunt said when we opened the door. She carried a tray of breakfast; bottles of water, thick pieces of buttered bread, scrambled oniony eggs and a tin of sardines. She looked extremely relieved to see that we were okay.

"Good morning," we both said.

"How was your night?"

"Not so great, but we made it," I said.

"It was fine," Zuma said taking the tray. "Thanks for breakfast."

We quickly ran back upstairs, anxious to eat. Zuma would be the only one eating the sardines, though. Those are nasty. As we walked past the Yoruba Room, I glanced in. Then I stopped.

"What the heck?!" I shouted. "I knew something was missing downstairs!"

"What?" Zuma asked anxiously. She obviously wanted to eat before doing anything else.

I ran into the room without answering. "But how?!" I said. "How did it get here??"

"No way," Zuma said running up next to me, when she saw the carpet. "Did we lock all the doors?"

We spent the next several minutes relocking every door in the house and then locking all the rooms that had windows. "Someone snuck in here last night and is trying to mess with our heads by moving our carpet around," Zuma angrily said as she locked a door. "Not gonna happen again, man."

That night, night number two, we slept a little better. We were exhausted and went to bed at seven PM. Plus, knowing that the noises were probably made by human beings related to us and that all the doors were locked set our minds at ease. At least until about four AM when we heard that scraping sound again. I was terrified, thinking maybe this time the noise was armed robbers or … zombies. My sister, she took it all a different way.

"Dammit," Zuma hissed angrily. "They're not gonna drive us out. This is *so* mean." She got off the bed, this time not caring that her feet were bare.

"What are you doing?" I whispered loudly.

"Gonna see who the hell that is!"

Next thing I knew, she was opening the door and going into the hallway with the flashlight.

"Wait!" I said creeping behind her.

Quietly, we moved down the stairs, toward the scraping sound. My sister peeked around the corner, staying on the last stair. She flashed her flashlight. She gasped, "Shit!"

"What is it? What do you…"

She grabbed my hand and we ran up the stairs.

"What? What??" I shouted. "WHAT?!"

She pushed me into the room, slammed the door and locked it. Then she shut the window.

"Okay," Zuma said, calming down, sinking to the floor. "Okay, okay, okay, okay, okay. Oh my God, I wish we'd have … no not really. Just … man. Alright."

"WHAT?" I sobbed, sitting next to her with my heart pounding. She didn't answer. For minutes, we both just sat there, quiet and listening and sweating. The scraping had stopped.

"What was it?" I finally asked again.

My sister turned to look at me with red-rimmed eyes.

"A snake, a huge black snake."

We spent most of the next day outside with our cousins. We didn't tell anyone about the snake. After sitting there feeling tired and scared and confused, we had both silently thought about Dad and decided to spend the last night in the house. One more night. And then the wildlife in the house could do whatever it wanted ... until people were hired to clean the place up.

Zuma said that the snake was over four feet in length and thick in body. That it was a dusty black and had yellow eyes. We assumed it was poisonous and that it had probably been prowling the house at night searching for rats or mice or whatever else lived in the there.

Our cousins took us for a walk down to a nearby pond and for hours after that we sat and played cards and forgot about our troubles. But eventually we had to return to the house. And that night was the most disturbing of them all. We'd locked the door as always and then we listened for the snake to start its foraging. Around three AM, it did.

"Let's go see," I said. It was our last night in the house and, of course, I was scared, but something in me wanted to see that snake. If only to be able to talk about it when we got back to Chicago.

At first Zuma looked at me like I was crazy. It was a similar look to the one I had given the crazy Junk Man back in that Abuja market. Then she smiled. "Alright. Let's go."

We crept out the room with our flashlight and tiptoed to the staircase, but we didn't go down. We didn't get to see the snake either. Why? Because the carpet was on the stairs. No, it wasn't just on the stairs, it was creeping *up* the stairs. It moved like some giant stingray. We stumbled back as it glided by, hovering about an inch or two off the floor as it swam through the air. Zuma followed it with the flashlight.

Once it disappeared around the corner with a flick of a golden tassel, we both made a run for it to our room and shut the door. Then we just sat on the bed, speechless. I thought about the Junk Man. He would have laughed hard at the two of us trembling in our room like that. Shocked and shivering and mentally shifted. Shit.

"Did you see…"

"Shhh," my sister said as we sat there.

"It was a flying carpet!"

"Shhh," my sister snapped. "Don't talk or something. What if it hears us?"

"Well, we've been here how many days. I think it's probably safe to say…"

"Mukoso, shut up!" she said. "And it wasn't a flying carpet, it kinda just crept over the floor and stuff."

"Whatever, man. A carpet isn't supposed to move!"

"No, really?"

What we both agreed on was that neither of us was leaving the room again that night. Not with snakes, carpets and shit creeping and fluttering around the house. Danger abounded. So we stayed there and went to sleep. For the first time, we slept through what remained of the night. Be it from shock, mental fatigue or just common sense, it didn't matter.

We woke up hours after sunrise, around eight in the morning. We dressed and washed in silence. And when our aunt came with breakfast, we didn't say a word. Instead, we went and sat on the floor in the Yoruba Room and ate.

As we sat there with the empty plates, my sister nibbling on a sardine, I said, "Let's go find it."

"Why?"

"Why not?" I said. "We're leaving today … plus, it doesn't move during the day, at least thus far. I … don't … think, at least." I shook my head. "Come on, let's just *see* it."

"I … I dunno," she said. "Let's just get outta here and act like…"

"But it did!" I said with wide eyes. "We saw it, man."

We found it in the kitchen.

"Hello?" I said loudly.

Zuma frowned.

I shrugged. "Just making sure," I said.

Even as we looked at it, neither of us was dumb enough to start doubting what we'd seen last night. Sure, it was dark, yes, we were tired, and we were scared. But we'd seen what we saw; this periwinkle carpet with black thread designs and golden tassels was alive. And maybe now it was asleep. Who knew?

We stepped into the room, staying close together. Then slowly, we walked up to it. It was spread out flat, taking up about a third of the kitchen's floor. There were a few lumps under it.

I squatted down and touch one of the rug's golden tassels. Then quickly before I changed my mind I lifted and threw the rug back over itself. We both jumped back. What we saw underneath still haunts me to this day. There was a big pile of those huge spiders, black, crushed and dead. There were also several large dead rats and the brown black body of a smashed scorpion, too! To top it off, there was the black snake. I got to see it for myself after all. Coiled up, scaly black-skinned and dead as all the other creatures under the carpet.

As we stood there, the carpet rippled and began to turn itself over and flatten out. Then it floated away from us a bit; later I would think it did this almost shyly. We didn't wait to see anymore. That was enough. We ran upstairs, packed our things, and dragged them down the stairs, trying not to look toward the kitchen. We spent the remaining hours in our aunt and uncle's house. I could almost hear the Junk Man laughing his giggly laugh.

As the airplane took off, flying us back to the United States, I couldn't help but think about the next time we'd visit. I had a feeling that the flying carpet that lived in our house was one piece of furniture our relatives would not steal.

"You think it'll be there when we go back?" I asked Zuma.

The Carpet | Nnedi Okorafor

Zuma looked at me, then we both started laughing. We laughed and laughed until we looked out the window. Then I nearly screamed and Zuma just stared. Do I need to say what we saw?

I Gave You My Love by the Light of the Moon

By Sarah Rees Brennan

There was a creepy guy staring at her in the coffee shop.

Berthe, sitting up at the high table by the window with her two best friends, became aware of it in a gradual, nasty way, like when you were camping for the first time and only realized the ground was damp when the wet had already seeped into your clothes. As soon as she was aware of his stare, she knew it had been going on too long.

She even got up from the table to fetch herself a tiny packet of sugar that she didn't want. She was hoping that he would look at Natalie or Leela, that the stare was just the unpleasant one some guys would give any girl, not personal but something they apparently felt you had brought on yourself by having boobs.

It wasn't. His eyes followed her path to the unwanted sugar, and then back. Berthe perched on the edge of her stool, self-conscious and furious, too, that some idiot just looking at her was enough to spoil her fun with her friends.

Being almost six foot tall and a sixteen-year-old girl made you self-conscious enough most days, and today Berthe had the worst cramps she'd ever had in her life.

So someone giving her the stalker eyeballs was the outside of enough. He looked like a college guy, or maybe he was a bit too young, maybe he was one of those high school boys who couldn't wait to get into college where everyone could appreciate his tortured soul. He was wearing a tweedy hipster scarf and black rectangular-framed hipster boy glasses. His eyes gleamed behind them, pale and intent. In fact, he was pretty pale all over, that particular shade of pale that suggested he was waiting for someone to invent technology that would allow him to get a tan from the light of his laptop screen alone.

Not at all the sort of boy Berthe would have anything in common with, even if he hadn't decided to stare at her like a creeper when she already felt like crap.

Another cramp made Berthe hunch forward, almost tilting off the stool. Her face must have shown some, of what she was feeling because Leela reached over the table and touched her arm.

"Are you all right? You feel hot."

Natalie, the vivacious creature of the group, all laughs and curls and the one who usually drew boys' eyes, raised her eyebrows at that and said: "I bet she does. Rawr."

Leela was too concerned and Berthe was frankly too freaked out to laugh. Berthe didn't feel hot. In fact, the skin at the back of her neck was prickling with cold sweat. She touched her fingertips to her cheek and felt them slide on the clammy surface.

"I just have, you know." Berthe waved her hand at her midsection even as she lied, "A headache."

As if as punishment for her lie, Berthe actually felt a twinge start in her head, a jagged line of pain that went from skull to spine. She put her elbow on the table and put her head down, brow pressed against her palm, until the sharp pain and the slow grind of agony in her stomach eased.

She looked up. Natalie looked serious now, and almost as concerned as Leela. Berthe really didn't like being the center of attention: eyes on her made her feel as if she should be doing something, and was too inadequate to know what. Unless she was playing lacrosse.

"I'm just going to go home," she said abruptly—she didn't want any more *fussing*, she didn't want to spoil their day—and she got up, holding onto the edge of the table as she did, so that she would look steady. "I just need an Advil and a nap. Call you guys later."

She left precipitately, because that was the only way to get away clean without one of them coming with her. They would be held up paying for their coffees and discussing whether to go after her, and she'd be long gone.

When Berthe found herself staggering down the steps of the exit and almost reeling into the alleyway beside it, pressing the clammy-cold prickling-hot skin of her face against the brick wall, she began to rethink her amazing strategy. No matter how awkward she felt about being fussed over, it beat not getting home at all. It was pitch black outside, the night sky pressing down on her dense and dark, and she did not think she could walk.

Pain crumpled her insides like tissue and she made a sound horrifyingly like a whine, like the sound of that animal at the campsite weeks ago. Berthe wanted to touch the bandage on her arm, but she gritted her teeth and kept her hands flat against the wall, braced. She wasn't going to fall down.

"You can't stay here," said a voice behind her.

Berthe wanted to spin around, but the voice barely cut through the waves of pain. The most she could do was force her eyes slightly open.

The boy from the coffee shop swam in her vision, his pale face blurring into moonlight and then coalescing into features behind spectacles again. Sweat stung Berthe's eyes. A stalker had her cornered in an alleyway at night, and she could hardly bring herself to mind.

"Oh, give it *up*," she said, always bad at being tactful and now not even able to be polite. "Do you have some sort of fetish for girls getting sick on your feet?"

"I implore you not to give me the chance to develop one," he said. "But you need help."

His face kept disintegrating with each new wave of pain, nothing but glittering shards of moonlight in her vision for too long. Berthe put her hands to her stomach, clutching at it, and realized her mistake when she almost toppled over sideways.

The boy had hold of her arm suddenly, grip cold and firm and inexorable, like being held up by a piece of machinery. Berthe was vaguely startled that he could hold her up at all, since they were the same height, and he was so skinny.

Berthe was starting to think she did need help. But that didn't mean she had to accept it from him.

"So g-get my friends," she said, her teeth chattering so hard that she was afraid they would smash like porcelain. "They're in the—you know who I mean, you were staring like a—you're creepy."

He seemed entirely unaffected by this assessment. Possibly it was not news to him.

He said, as if she had not spoken at all and in relation to nothing, as if he was just plucking random words out of the air: "You don't want to hurt anyone, do you?"

It was strange enough that Berthe opened her eyes all the way, even as another snake of pain uncoiled and struck in her belly. He looked at her, eyes unblinking behind his silly glasses, everything she saw about him at odds with his stone-fast grip. She saw he was perfectly serious.

"Of c-course I don't want to hurt anyone," she gasped out.

"Come with me," the creepy boy said. "Or you'll kill someone."

Come with me, if you want someone else to live, Berthe thought, her mind so muddled she could not even remember what movie she was mangling a quote from.

She wouldn't have responded to a threat to herself: she would have screamed and hit out at him, not because she was brave but because that was something life prepared you for, creepy guys threatening you in darkened alleyways. She was not prepared for someone to say that she could be dangerous. It was not a warning she could ignore.

Berthe staggered, a violent enough lurch so she was almost jarred out of even this boy's grasp. "All right," she got out, between stiff lips and chattering teeth.

The creep from the coffee shop wasn't just strong, he was fast. Berthe stumbled in the boy's speeding wake, and after a few streets, tilting into swathes of moonlight and then back to shadowy road, he stopped at a door. Berthe leaned her face against it, forehead pressed to peeling gray paint, and the boy fished out a key from the pocket of his skinny jeans and opened the door.

She went sprawling into a tiny coffin of a hall.

"Come on, come on," the boy muttered, his keys falling to the floor with a clatter and a thud. He hauled her up again, arm an iron bar across her midsection, and pushed her up stairs covered in brown carpeting, worn white with the constant passage of feet.

Even the white traces of age on the carpet shimmered in Berthe's eyes like moonlight.

They got up the narrow little stairs and into another tiny hall, then through a door that looked out of place, heavy and dark in the midst of all this cheap flimsiness. The boy towed Berthe inside the door.

There were shutters on the windows, heavy and dark like the doors. There was a single bed in the corner, neatly made.

Sick and staggering, Berthe still felt a panicked fist clutch at the inside of her throat. She remembered what she had allowed herself to forget amid all the pain—that what she was doing was crazy.

"Oh no," she said weakly, and backed right into the boy. She spun to face him, even though the sudden movement made her stagger and sway. "No—" she repeated, raining down blows on his narrow chest. They landed like kittens on lilypads.

He caught her wrists in that stone grip of his, pushing her firmly into the room and stepping backward over the threshold as he did so.

"Trust me," he said. "You couldn't pay me to stay in this room with you."

He slammed the door shut. Berthe did not even feel afraid that she was now trapped in a stranger's bedroom. She was just relieved to be alone with her miserable sickness, not to have to split her focus between current agony and present danger.

She sank down onto the carpet on her hands and knees, and arched her back; she felt as if her spine was made of metal and somehow turning molten inside her skin, dissolving and burning at once. She gagged, wrenching pain all the way through her, as if her insides were being torn out. The bite on her arm where the creature from the campsite had sunk in its teeth throbbed as if it might start bleeding again.

Berthe sobbed. She was scared that she would choke up her internal organs, have them laid out ruby red on the carpet before her, her heart bitter in her mouth.

Her fingers clawed on the carpet before her, tearing it into ragged shreds. Berthe howled her agony and her vision whited out, all moonlight, moonlight, moonlight in the dark.

Berthe woke up aching in a nest of chaos. She lifted her head, her hair a snarled blond veil between her and the world. When she lifted her hand to brush it back, her whole body shuddered in protest.

The room she had seen last night was destroyed. The bed was a metal skeleton, scraps of cloth that had been sheets and a mattress hanging on it like mournful ghosts. There was a cupboard at the other end of the room that she had not even noticed: its door was torn off its hinges. The walls had been beige: now they were carved with deep gray lines. The boards beneath the ripped carpet were savagely scored as well, the floor a mess of splinters and nails.

Berthe was naked. She very urgently did not want to stay naked, curled up and whimpering like an animal.

She climbed gingerly to her feet and went over to the cupboard with its door ripped off. There were clothes inside, boys' clothes, and weird boys' clothes at that, but beggars couldn't be choosers and naked people couldn't be fussy about fashion.

There were a lot of button-down shirts that did not fit across her boobs, but she got into a T-shirt that said ORGAN DONOR, INQUIRE WITHIN. The fit made it embarrassingly obvious she wasn't wearing a bra.

She went down the stairs barefoot.

It was silent in the house, so silent she thought that perhaps she was alone here, that she could just open the door and go home now without having to face anything.

She pushed open the other door in the little hall, just the same.

Inside was a kitchen-cum-living-room, all the blinds drawn down. In the dimness she could see clean countertops, a battered sofa, and on a low table a cup of tea with a biscuit lying beside it.

In the darkest corner of the room stood the creep from the coffee shop.

He was still wearing his jacket and his dumb scarf, and he had his hands in his pockets. He looked up as she came in.

"I suppose you have a lot of questions."

"No," said Berthe. She was grateful, suddenly, that he put her back up. It pulled her away from the edge of screaming senseless terror. "I went out camping in the woods, and I was bitten by something that I thought was a wild dog. Last night was the full moon. And I've seen horror movies before. I think I know what's going on."

She did not know until he just kept looking at her, gaze level and undisturbed, that she had wanted him to come up with another explanation. She'd wanted him to tell her he was crazy.

"What I don't know," she said, hearing her voice go high and unpleasant, "is how you knew."

He didn't say a word.

She plunged on. "I mean, do you make a habit of staring like a freak at girls and then if they seem ill, dragging them into your bedroom on the off chance they're…"

"I can tell," he said. "I could smell you."

She felt a flash of shame stronger than terror, so ferocious and so unreasonable—that she could care how she *smelled*, with all this—it made her furious with herself and him.

"And how could you—what were you—" Embarrassment as well as rage throttled her. She could not believe she could not even ask him something important about her own body.

"You'll be able to do it as well," he said. "Smell things other people can't smell. See things other people can't see. Do things other people can't do."

"Will I be able to leap tall buildings in a single bound?" asked Berthe. Her mouth tasted sour, and her words were all coming out sour too. She could not seem to care.

She went over to the window and began to fiddle with the pull on the blind so she wouldn't have to keep looking at him.

"Medium-size buildings," he said. "Crouch first. Don't go for a skyscraper. I'd describe that as o'erarching ambition."

Berthe twisted the pull around her wrist, plastic beads digging into her flesh hard. She could not believe he was trying to make a joke.

"So you're," she said, and could not find the words in her sour dust-dry mouth. She tugged hard at the blind. "You're like me?"

The blind tumbled down with a rattle and a bang, the plastic cord suddenly slack around her waist and sudden sunlight flooding in, making her blink.

Her ears filled with the sound of the boy hissing, a cat's noise from a boy's throat. She saw him move, fast, backing away from the sudden sunlight and into a different dark corner.

There was a hand held up, protecting his face, but she could still see his bared inhuman teeth.

"No," he whispered. "I'm not like you."

This last revelation was too much, the world of strangeness expanding too far. Berthe could not bear another second in this little house.

She turned and ran, as she'd wanted to before, out into the sunlight where he could not follow her, and she told herself that it would not happen again.

She kept telling herself that. She sneaked in through her bedroom window and pretended she had got in late and slept in her own bed that night, tucked up innocent and harmless under her sheets.

She told herself that when she lied to her friends that she was all better now, she told herself that when she refused to go on the next camping trip, even though she had always signed up to go on every trip before. She told herself that lying in her safe bed, under her safe sheets, with the windows open so she could see the moon had not become bright and dangerous yet.

She could hear her parents having whispered fights all the way across the house, she could hear Natalie and Leela murmuring secrets meant to exclude her, and even though she knew she'd done the same thing with both of them, that every pair of friends had secrets between just the two of them, actually hearing it hurt.

That she could hear them hurt worse. The scar on the inside of her elbow was a silver crescent moon, shining and smooth on her skin, but the moon was long past crescent.

She could not get away from the world or herself. The night and her body lay in wait to betray her.

She stopped telling herself that it would not happen again, because she could not bear to think about it at all.

But she remembered, as well as the fear and pain, what the boy at the coffee shop had said.

You don't want to hurt anyone, do you?

She walked across town as the sun died, on the night of the next full moon, and knocked on a gray door.

The boy from the coffee shop let her in.

It happened again.

*

Berthe came downstairs in another pair of sweatpants and a T-shirt that read BEING PESSIMISTIC WOULDN'T WORK ANYWAY. She was not tempted to run out the door this time. She had spent a month running already.

The boy was standing in the same shadowed corner he had stood in the last time. Berthe noticed he had fixed the blind.

He had loomed large in her mind, the moment of hissing and teeth overwriting everything else, but he looked very much like he had in the coffee shop, dark hair swept back in a particular deliberate way, wearing fingerless gloves of all things. The room looked exactly the same as well, down to the cup of tea and the biscuit on the table.

"Thank you," said Berthe. She felt she had to, even though she didn't know how to mean it.

"You're welcome," he said quietly. He gestured toward the table. "Do you want a cup of tea?"

"Yes," Berthe said. "All right."

She walked toward the table, and sat down in the chair. "Can I—"

"I do not drink ... tea," said the boy, and smirked to himself before his face smoothed out, serious and pale. "I don't eat. It's for you."

It made her feel strange, to realize that he had gone out and bought tea and biscuits for her last month, laid them out thinking she might be hungry.

She took a sip of the tea. It was cooling, but she saw the strips of sunlight on the kitchen counter, and knew he could not have made it later. The whole room had sneaky pieces of sunlight in it.

The heavy shutters and door upstairs clearly formed his refuge from the sunlight, and she had exiled him from it.

"Thanks," she said again, and meant it a little this time. "The tea's good. Is there a cure?"

"It isn't a sickness," said the boy. "It's who you are now."

"So that would be a no."

He was silent, though his attention stayed fixed on her. Now Berthe was looking back at him, she saw why he might wear glasses: they helped hide their strange brightness and the way his eyes tracked movement, more alert than a human's would.

Or maybe he needed glasses. Could a creature like him need glasses?

"You knew what I was," Berthe said, utterly unable to talk about him smelling her. "You recognized it. So you must have met other people like me."

"I knew one. She was kind to me," said the boy. "But she can't help you. I'm sorry. She's dead now."

"What did she die of?" Berthe heard her voice shake, felt her lips tremble, and put the biscuit to her lips to hide it.

"She killed herself," said the boy, softly. He added, "I'm sorry," again.

"I'm the one who should be sorry," Berthe said, swallowing desolation and a mouthful of biscuit, so dry it scraped her throat. "She was your friend."

Killed herself, Berthe thought despairingly. Because she hurt somebody, or because she could not live being like Berthe was now a moment longer? She didn't know, and the woman could not tell her now. She could not tell Berthe anything.

"What about the—the person who bit me, in the woods?" Berthe asked desperately. "They must be like me. Couldn't we find them? Couldn't you smell them?"

The boy's eyebrows raised. "I'm not a sniffer dog," he said mildly. "Even when you were human, I'm sure you could smell a pie. I don't imagine you could wander the city streets and track a pie down by scent."

"Isn't there some way," Berthe said. She put down the biscuit and the tea, and put her face in her hands, too wretched to be embarrassed. "Isn't there any way?"

The boy cleared his throat, a soft apologetic sound, after she had sat with her head in her hands for some time. She looked up and saw him looking at the floor, at one of the strips of sunlight.

"They might still be in the woods," he said. "If they are, I don't think they'll be able to help you. But if you want, I'll go with you to look."

"Yes," Berthe said. Any relief at this point felt like overwhelming joy. "Yes, please. Thank you. Can we go now?"

"Well," the boy said. "No. I fear that if I burst into flames and died in agony it might hamper the expedition somewhat."

"Oh." Berthe felt like an idiot, and also just felt lost. She had seen him leap away from the fallen blind, seen his teeth, but with every moment spent in his company it seemed more unreal. She could run around the room pulling up blinds, and though he seemed solid and real, he would turn to ash. A shudder rang through her, all the way to her aching bones. "Can we go tonight?"

The boy said: "Of course."

"Thank you," Berthe said again. Every one of her thanks had become more real, by degrees. She turned away from her tea and the crumbs on the table, tilted her head so she was looking at him, at the strange eyes glittering behind his glasses. "I'm Berthe."

"Berthe," he said, pronouncing it correctly right off. "That's French, isn't it?"

"Yeah."

Berthe always felt a bit awkward about her name. She didn't look elegant and French, dainty and well-dressed like her mother, who she'd once heard described as everything a woman should be. Berthe was tall and blond with strong shoulders, like her dad. But they hadn't known what she would be like when she grew up.

The creepy guy from the coffee shop, the creature with the teeth who had saved her, said: "I'm Stephen."

It was such an ordinary name, it made Berthe almost smile, and then bite on her lower lip in case that offended him.

He didn't look offended.

"I can't say it's nice to meet you, under the circumstances," said Berthe at last. "But..."

He smiled, mouth closed and teeth hidden. It was, under the circumstances, quite a nice smile.

"Likewise."

The woods near her town were not full of gnarled oaks and whispered legends of a curse. The trees were all pine trees, grown for lumber, with a lot of handy campsites. Berthe had gone hiking through these woods a hundred times, and never felt the least alarm. She had been so absolutely sure that when it came right down to it, she was safe.

The woods at night, nobody but her and a relative stranger, were very quiet. It was also very bright, even considering that the moon was one night past full, a shining coin in the sky. Berthe could see the silver stir of pine needles as a tiny animal ran through them, yards and yards away. Every tree branch was a clear silver line struck against the sky.

When she looked at Stephen, he had his glasses off. She'd been right, she thought: he didn't need them for anything but concealment. His eyes looked silver too, his pupils subtly wrong, darting after every movement in the wood.

Just like her eyes were. Berthe wondered what her eyes looked like to him.

"Which of us can see better?" she asked.

"I don't know," Stephen answered. "Does it matter? We can both see very well. We are predators. But you're stronger, and faster. My kind are built for a more cunning type of hunt."

Predators. Hunt. The words danced grotesquely in Berthe's head.

Stephen blinked. "Sorry. That came out a great deal more disturbing than it sounded in my head. I'm afraid I'm out of practice with conversation."

"You don't talk to people?" Berthe asked blankly.

"Not really," said Stephen. "Not in depth. The less contact with other people, the less chance they'll notice I'm not aging. I can stay in one place longer."

"You don't," Berthe said. "You don't age. Right, obviously. Because that's how you work, with the no sunlight and the—not aging. And you talk like an old person. How old are you?"

You talk like an old person, Berthe repeated to herself. She never had known how to talk to boys.

"Sixty-two," Stephen answered.

Berthe stared.

"I know," said Stephen. "It seems glamorous and otherworldly for someone like me to be a hundred years old, or two hundred. But there is the problem of getting there."

It was a real age, an age that a person could be, the age for women with blue hair and blouses, for men with canes and tweed caps, for grandparents. That made it much harder to assign to the boy in front of her, his face smooth and his eyes faintly glowing.

"You wait until I'm a hundred years old," Stephen said, mouth quirking. "The ladies will love it."

"I'll be fifty-four by then," Berthe told him.

There was a brief awkward pause.

"I meant the ladies in general," Stephen said. "They will be lining up. I will have to carry a stick and extra dance cards, on account of how my dance card will be entirely full."

There was another silence, broken by a rustle far away that made Stephen's head turn, chin lifting, scenting the air. Berthe turned with him, trying to make out whatever he did, and caught something: wild and strange, musk and fur. She wondered if that was how she smelled to him, and then she did not have time to wonder further: Stephen was running, fleet and sure, faster than any boy who looked like he did should have been able to. Faster than anyone should have been able to.

Berthe was fast. She didn't run track or anything, but she played lacrosse and in gym she tended to win races. She wasn't fast enough to keep up with Stephen, she knew, but she tried anyway, and it was shockingly easy. Her feet found every place, tree roots and leaf drifts where she might have tripped or slipped seeming not even there. It was like running over smooth ground, and she was past Stephen, towards the wild scent, with the wild wind in her hair.

There was a dark shape at the foot of a tree, and it twisted away from her and almost ran into Stephen, who hissed at it, teeth gleaming. For a moment Berthe felt a tremor run through her, a chill of profound unfamiliarity: that Stephen was not like her, and the shape between them was.

Except Stephen was here to help her, and this was the creature that had attacked her.

"Why," Berthe said, voice tearing in the wind, "why is he still a wolf? It's not the full moon—he shouldn't be—"

"Some of you turn wild." Stephen's voice was calm because it was always calm, but there was a slight strain to the calm now. "And you don't turn back."

Berthe's heart banged in her ears like many doors slamming all at once: no answers, no hope, no help to be had, just a dumb thing with eyes shining up at her, green like her own but split with lines of yellow like lightning.

It was moving, low on the ground but with intent, toward Stephen.

The hair on the back of Berthe's neck stood up, but for once she didn't feel afraid. She felt—it was more like outrage, and she moved in her new smooth way and was standing between them, making a sound that was mangled by her human throat but not quite human.

I won't let you: challenge: mine, said the sound, and the animal backed away. It understood her.

It understood her because she was half-way to being an animal herself, because there were no answers but only this horror beyond words in the woods.

The wolf backed away on its belly, and Berthe sat down among the pine needles.

"Sometimes they still turn back," Stephen said. "I thought perhaps—I wanted there to be something here for you."

"A look into the future?"

"No," said Stephen. "They make a choice—they turn toward the wild—"

"And what other choice is there to make?" Berthe demanded. "The one your friend did?"

Berthe had to look up from the pine needle floor because she could not hear Stephen. He did not breathe and his heart did not beat; when he was still he was a creature of perfect silence and she could not tell if he was there. She was suddenly afraid that he had left: suddenly aware that things could get worse.

Stephen had not left. He was looking down at her, eyes moonlight-eerie in his thin serious face, and then he knelt down so they were on a level.

"She was very lonely," he said. "She didn't know what was happening to her at first. She hurt people. She hurt her family. You haven't done that. You're not alone."

"No," said Berthe, and thought painfully of her parents, and of Leela and Natalie. They all seemed so far away, in a world she did not know how to scramble back to. "But I could hurt them," she said. "And I can't tell them. And I'm alone with this."

"You're not," said Stephen.

"You're not like me," Berthe told him, her voice low.

She did not just mean what they were, or the feeling of being on different sides in a dark wood. He was in control as she was not: he was not tearing rooms into shreds.

"I only wanted," Berthe tried to explain. "I wanted someone who could explain this to me, from the inside out."

Stephen looked off into the trees, after the fleeing wolf, and then knelt down on the ground among the needles with her.

"I'm not telling you this to trump what you're feeling," he said, "or to try and win the argument. I was made by a man who had a whole bevy of us—teenage minions, old enough to be useful, but not old enough to survive on our own with ease. He told us what was happening to us, and what to do, how to feed, how to serve him and recruit for him. We were dependent on him, because of what we were."

Feed, Berthe thought, and whispered: "Did you kill someone?"

"I killed three people," Stephen answered, without hesitating. "The last one was the worst, though I doubt the first two would agree with me. I had a family, once. I waited for my chance to get back to them. When it came, I didn't get away clean—someone was watching me. A window broke, and I was cut, and one of the others had her teeth in my wrist to the bone. I had to tear free. They were hunting me through the streets, and I did not know what to do. I knocked on doors and a woman let me in, a teenage boy covered in blood. In return for her kindness I knocked her to the floor, ripped her throat out, and gulped down her heart's blood. I stayed in her house all that night and the next day with her body. Without her, I don't think I would have escaped.

"I wanted to get away from the man who made me and taught me. I wish I had not asked for that woman's help. Being able to depend on nobody but yourself isn't so bad."

"If you can depend on yourself," Berthe said shakily.

"You can," Stephen said, and sounded sure, calm again, the alien creature, the murderer who had saved her from hurting anyone.

"And you're *not* alone."

The night was crystal-clear and terrifying, the wolf running through the woods, and when she closed her eyes she could not hear anyone's breathing or heartbeat but her own.

But when she looked up, she wasn't alone, after all, and when she got home from the dark woods her mother made her hot chocolate. She popped in a marshmallow. Berthe looked at the tiny treat in the cup and thought about all the little sweetnesses love slipped into your daily life, almost unnoticed except that when they were added up, they meant you could bear anything.

At her next lacrosse game she was running, running across the field with her stick in hand, her parents and friends cheering as they watched. Another girl ran at her full-tilt, body-checking her.

Berthe barely paused, but she bumped the girl's shoulder— carefully, careful, she had to be so careful, you don't want to hurt anyone, do you—and the girl fell back, and Berthe ran ahead with the ball and her victory.

It was a bright sunlit moment, but the girl had a bruise on her shoulder afterward. She said in the locker room, a little admiration but mostly spite: "You're an animal, Lindstrom."

The other girl was the one who had not been playing fair. If Berthe was playing fair by playing at all, considering what she was.

Berthe went and took a hot shower, scrubbing hard at her unmarked body. She came out of it and looked in the fogged mirror set over the sink, misted glass reflecting back pieces of her grotesquely: blond hair dark, stringy with water, pale blur of flesh and eyes cut with lightning, like the eyes of the wolf in the woods. She pressed her face against the wet glass and took deep shuddering breaths, and outside the building she heard Natalie and Leela whispering secrets Berthe was not supposed to know.

When she was done taking breaths, she leaned back from the mirror, wiped it with her shaking hand, and looked at herself whole and clear.

"How do you…" Berthe said, on the third morning after a full moon, sitting with her biscuit half-eaten in her hand. "How do you feed now?"

Stephen sat in the corner away from the sunlight. He did not, as she had feared, look offended by the question.

"Not well," he answered. "There is no way to do it that's right. People who are sleeping on the street. People who are passed out drunk at parties in a garden. Stealing from a blood bank. I feed in small dark ways, but I don't kill."

It was a horrible picture, the monster preying on unsuspecting people. The savagery that ripped through Stephen's bedroom every full moon, that would rip through people, was horrible as well.

And there was something else besides horror in it, the thought of kind Stephen spending half his life desperately scavenging for sustenance.

"You must be hungry a lot," she said quietly.

He was silent.

"If you want," she began. She had brought her own clothes this time, and she fiddled with the sleeve of her warm comforting sweater, pulling it up to expose the veins on her wrist.

It could not be anything like as bad as the liquefying pain she had suffered last night, and would suffer, again and again, as long as she lived. And she would get to do something for Stephen: something that might make him happy.

"I wouldn't mind," she told him.

"My kind can't feed on your kind," Stephen said, and after a pause, very politely: "But thank you very much. I mean it. Nobody's ever offered me that before."

It hurt for a moment that her body was disqualified to do something for him. She felt monstrous for not being prey for him, and how stupid was that?

"When I'm—like I am, upstairs, can you hear me?" she asked. "Is it awful?"

"No," said Stephen.

"How can it not be?"

"How can you stand to look at me," Stephen said, "when you know what I am? Once you change things from the general to the personal, what does monstrous even mean? It's not awful. I hear you and it's Berthe, upstairs."

It didn't seem like her, and she was scared of thinking of it as her, but she gave some thought to trying to remember next time.

Berthe tucked her feet up under her. "How'd you get so smart?"

"Well, I've been around a while," Stephen said. "Gives you time to think things through, even if our minds don't mature like yours will."

"How do you know your mind isn't mature?"

"I'm speculating," said Stephen. "Of course, it's quite probable that being scared and uncertain and stupid is something you never grow out of, and I just want to think there's some way for other people to do it."

Berthe blinked at him, startled into speechlessness by the idea of Stephen being scared or uncertain.

He looked the same as ever, inhuman, bright eyes steady behind his glasses, wearing a T-shirt that seemed to be about robots, his face pale and thin and thoughtful.

"I'm glad I can't drink from you," Stephen told her. "I don't want to be a monster with you."

"You're not," said Berthe. She didn't like words as much as Stephen did, couldn't frame the right things to say the way he could, but she smiled at him and said awkwardly: "It's personal for me, too."

Stephen smiled back. She thought he might cross the room to her, but of course he could not get past the sunlight, the rays between them like iron bars.

It was three weeks more until Leela told Berthe what she had already told Natalie: that she was gay. After Berthe told Leela that she loved her, was glad to know anything about her friend that Leela had to tell because she loved her, and nothing would change that love, Leela let her know when she was planning to tell her parents, and that she wanted a sleepover at Natalie's house afterward. On the night of the full moon.

Berthe had to say no, and hurt Leela, with awkward lies. Berthe knew that in the human world, there was no excuse for what she was doing.

"You did get back to your family," she said to Stephen, as the sun was sinking behind his blinds, and her whole body wavered on the edge of the abyss. "Didn't you?"

"I did," said Stephen. "I got back to them, and I got to stay with them for two years. But after that—it was beginning to be obvious I wasn't aging, and hunting was so hard to hide. I couldn't stay with them."

Berthe could not talk to him any longer. She had to run up the stairs, lock the door behind her and feel pain twist her body into a whole new shape, casting her humanity far, far away. She lifted her face to the shut-out moon and howled because it would not stay.

The next day she did not stop for tea or Stephen, just threw on the clothes she had left outside the door and pushed her battered body, used all of her inhuman speed, for the task of getting coffee and pastries from Leela's favorite place. She ran all the way to

Natalie's house, and rang the bell with the sun still tentative and new in the sky.

Leela opened the door and looked at her, and for a moment there was a silence of hurt and hesitance, a possibility that the door would be shut in her face, but instead Leela reached out and drew her inside.

The three of them spent the day together, talking about how it had gone and what Leela was thinking and feeling and planning out things they might want to do next, discussing movies and sports and coming back around to Leela because this was her day.

They walked around town until evening came and they got to a certain coffee shop, and went in to find crowded tables and people who looked in for the long haul, student types with their laptops.

Stephen, with a book and a coffee cup he had not touched, wanting to be with people even though he didn't speak to them. Stephen who had made his house something like a home for her—somewhere he had chosen to always let her in, whenever she came—but who had been too scared to stay in his own home, had told her that he felt eternally young and scared, so scared that the only thing he could think of to do was spend all his life in hiding.

"I see a table," she said to Leela and Natalie, and marched up—the idea of it, of her marching up to a table where a boy was. "Hey," she said, as Stephen blinked inhuman-brilliant eyes behind his glasses and let his book fall onto his saucer. "Can we join you? This is Leela and Natalie. Girls, this is my friend Stephen."

Leela turned out to have read Stephen's book, and discussing it with him made them both smile. Natalie drew Leela to the register, on the blatant pretext of wanting another cookie, to discuss Stephen and Berthe with her, and Berthe stayed behind to discuss them with him.

"Won't they wonder about—where I go to school?" Stephen asked, apparently nonplussed and pleased enough to come close to Berthe's level of conversational flailing.

"Tell them you're home-schooled," said Berthe, tactfully not adding that the way Stephen talked, they might be assuming this already—though either she didn't notice how he talked was strange anymore or he was talking a bit more normally. "Or maybe a college guy taking a year out. Very glamorous."

"Do you really think I look old enough?" Stephen asked, sounding almost shy.

"Definitely," said Berthe.

"Dad," Berthe said a couple of weeks later. "Next time you have a little space between jobs, I was wondering if you could help out a friend of mine."

"Space between jobs, what are you talking about? I work my fingers to the bone keeping you in designer clothing and handbags," her dad told her, pulling on the hood of her sweatshirt. "Is it Natalie or Leela? Leela needs a bookcase set in her wall, I've been saying it for years."

"It's another friend," Berthe said. "Um. A boy. Stephen. Is his name. He has porphyria," and here she turned her face away, because she'd never lied to her dad before. "He's sensitive to sunlight. And he works at a call center, he doesn't have a whole lot of money. I thought, if we could put shutters on his windows downstairs…"

Her dad was quiet for a little while. "Is that where you've been, some nights you've been home pretty early?"

"If the boy's sick," her mother said, quick to sympathy as she was quick to anger, and her dad looked at her and then pulled Berthe into a hug.

"See what I can do," he said.

"You should bring this Stephen around for dinner," said her mother. "What does he like to eat?"

Berthe could not tell her mother that Stephen liked to eat people. She could not tell the people who loved her best in the world what she had become.

But she wasn't like Stephen. She was going to grow up, and maybe that meant becoming a little less scared. Maybe by the time she was ready to go to college, she could tell them. Maybe she could think about telling her friends.

Leela and Natalie assumed Stephen was Berthe's boyfriend: that he was a little weird but nice, that he and Berthe fit through being at opposite ends of some spectrum. Her parents clearly thought so as well. They all thought they knew what was going on.

They knew nothing about his weird staring and wonderful rescue in the coffee shop, or his silent presence in the woods. And Berthe knew nothing about romance.

He liked her, she thought. But he never did or said anything like that: he was the boy who had quietly left his home to spare his family, who did not talk to other people at all, who kept hidden.

Berthe rather self-consciously wore a T-shirt that said TOO LONG, DIDN'T READ she'd bought, because it made her think of Stephen and also said something about herself, on the night of the next full moon.

It made Stephen smile his small crooked smile as he opened the door, but he didn't comment on it. She didn't know what she was supposed to do if he didn't say anything: Stephen always knew the right thing to say.

"See you in the morning," she told him, for want of anything better, and smiled back.

She took off her shirt in his hall, folding it neatly, took off the rest of her clothes as well and realized he could probably hear her getting undressed for the first time. She went into his bedroom with her cheeks burning.

Stephen always made the bed, even though he knew she was going to wreck it. Berthe went and lay down on it, felt the cool material of his pillow against her face, and concentrated on that scrap of comfort through the pain.

When she woke up, there were more scars on the walls, but she had not ripped the mattress apart this time. It still looked as if there had been a beast inside the room, but just a little more controlled this time.

She dressed slowly, getting comfortable with being back in her own skin, went downstairs, and opened the door to find her tea on the table beside her biscuit, her Stephen in the corner shutting his book as soon as he saw her.

He had reached out when they met, she thought, taken steps with her she could not have taken alone. She could do that now, when he might be paralyzed from being in hiding, from years and years in the dark.

Berthe crossed the floor, and the sunlight was no bar to her. She approached Stephen and he rose politely to meet her approach, and she did not try to say the right thing.

She took his face in her hands, and kissed him. He moved in toward her at once, a little awkward and seeming so glad, and she was so glad too. It felt like a different kind of moonlight, moving through her and changing her.

He was a little shorter than she was now, and he hadn't been a few months ago. She was growing up, and he was not. This moment, his narrow chest against hers, could not be kept. She smiled against his mouth: a little sweetness in the cup of her life and his, having this moment and the next, and being unafraid of change.

"I was wondering," Berthe said, soft as her own breath. "What are you doing tonight?"

57 Reasons for the Slate Quarry Suicides

By Sam J. Miller

1. Because it would take the patience of a saint or Dalai Lama to smilingly turn the other cheek to those six savage boys day after day, to emerge unembittered from each new round of psychological and physical assaults; whereas I, Jared Shumsky, aged sixteen, have many things, like pimples and the bottom bunk bed in a trailer, and clothes that smell like cherry car air fresheners, but no particular strength or patience.

2. Because God, or the universe, or karma, or Charles Darwin, gave me a different strength, one that terrified me until I learned

what it was, and how to control it, and how to use it as the instrument of my brutal and magnificent and long-postponed vengeance.

3. Because I loved Anchal, with the fierceness and devotion that only a gay boy can feel for the girl who has his back, who takes the *Cosmo* sex quiz with him, who listens to his pointless yammerings about his latest crush, who puts herself between him and his bullies so often that the bullies' wrath is ultimately re-routed onto her.

4. Because after the Albany Academy swim meet, while I was basking in the bliss of a shower that actually spouts hot water—a luxury our backwoods public school lacks—I was bodily seized by my six evil teammates, and dragged outside, and deposited there in the December cold, naked, wet, spluttering, pounding on the door, screaming, imagining hypothermia, penile frostbite, until the door opened, and an utterly uninterested girl opened the door and let me in and said, "Jeez, calm down."

5. Because it's not so simple as evil bullies in need of punishment; because their bodies were too beautiful to hate and their eyes too lovely to simply gouge out; because every one of them was adorable in his own way, but they all had the musculature and arrogance of Olympic swimmers, which I lacked, being only five-six of quivery scrawn; because I loved swimming too much to quit the team—the silence of the water and how alone you were when you were in it, the caustic reek of chlorine and the

twilight bus rides to strange schools and the sight of so much male skin; and because of those moments, on the ride home from Canajoharie or Schaghticoke or Albany, in the rattling, medicine-smelling short bus normally reserved for the mentally challenged, with the coach snoring and everyone else asleep or staring out the window watching the night roll by, when I was part of the team, when I was connected to people; when I belonged somewhere.

6. Because I had spent the past six months practicing; on animals at first, and after the first time I tried it on my cat she shrieked and never came near me again, but my dog was not so smart, and even though his eyes showed raw animal panic while I was working him he kept coming back every time I took my hand away and released him, and pretty soon working the animals was easy, the field of control forming in the instant my fingertips touched them, their brains like switches I could turn off and on at will, turning their bodies into mirrors for my own, but I still couldn't figure out a way to harm them.

7. Because once, while she slept, in my basement, engorged on candy and gossip and bad television, I tried my gift on Anchal, and it was much harder on a human, because she was so much bigger and her brain so much more complex and therefore more difficult to disable, and even though I tried to only do things that would not disturb her, her eyes fluttered open and then immediately narrowed in suspicion and fear, the wiser animal part of her brain recognizing me as a threat before the

dumb easily-duped mammalian intellect intervened and said, *no, wait, this is your friend, he would never do anything to hurt you*, and she smiled a blood-hungry smile and leaned forward and said, "How the hell did you do that?"

8. Because Mrs. Burgess assigned us Edgar Allan Poe's "Hop-Frog" for English class, which helped my vengeance take shape, and because none of the boys had read it.

9. Because Anchal did read it, and came to me, after school, eyes all laughing fire at the ideas the protagonist gave her— Hop-Frog, that squat, deformed little dwarf who murdered the cruel king and his six fat ministers in a dazzling spectacle of burned flesh and screaming death, and her excitement was infectious, and we worked on my gift for hours, until turning her into a puppet was as easy as believing she was one.

10. Because *Carrie* came on television that same night.

11. Because I am an idiot who still hasn't learned how stories and movies mislead us, showing us how things ought to end up, which is never how they do; and because stories are oracles whose prophecies we can't unravel until it is too late.

12. Because Anchal worked long and hard on the revenge scenario, sketching out all the ways my gift could be used to cause maximum devastation, all the ways we could transform our enemies into an ugly spectacle that would show the whole world what monsters they truly were.

13. Because I didn't listen when she said we would have to kill them, that they were *sick sons of bitches and would never*

stop being sick sons of bitches. Because I still believed that they could be mine.

14. Because Anchal, equal parts Indian and Indian—Native American and Hindu—always smelled like wood smoke, lived with her Cherokee mom in a tiny house barely better than a cabin, and so I thought that she was invincible, heiress to noble, durable traditions far better than my own impoverished Caucasian ones, and that she could survive whatever the world might throw at her. And because she was beautiful; because she was smart and strong; because boys flocked to her; because she knew that if there was one sure thing we could depend upon, it was that teenaged boys were a lot more likely to make dumb decisions when lust was addling their brains.

15. Because Spencer, alone among my swim team mates, would smile at me for no reason, and speak to me sometimes when the others weren't around, and because some tiny actions gave me hope that he too was gay, and that we were each other's destinies.

16. Because Rex, on the other hand, an ogre of rare and excellent proportions, thick-headed but shrewd when it came to cruelty, served as the ringleader, and just as they had all obeyed him in his plan to pour Kool-Aid into Anchal's locker as punishment for stopping them from stomping my skull in, so I knew that *he* was the linchpin, the only one I would need to work, and that once I had him, the others would fall.

17. Because coach was sick that day, and our next meet wasn't for a week, so we had the day off from practice, an unheard-of

gift of free time, and I knew that this was our shot, and we couldn't waste it, so I texted Anchal *We are GO* and then after school, while Rex was alone in the weight room, I stood outside in the hallway and called her cell, and said in a maybe-a-little-bit-too-loud voice, "Hey, so, I got a couple hours to kill, wanna meet me by the slate quarries in an hour, maybe bring some of your mama's vodka?" and she said, "Yes," and I said, "Great," and whistled while I walked away.

18. Because I hid myself in a darkened classroom where I could watch the weight room through the window in the door, and I saw how Rex called them all into a huddle when they arrived from their own classes, and they rubbed their hands or licked their lips or punched each other in the arm in glee, and then they left, as one, and I knew the bait had been taken.

19. Because they had their bicycles and I had mine, and after they left I let five minutes go by, and if I had stuck to that timeline everything would have gone exactly according to plan.

20. Because as I was about to unlock my bike I heard someone holler my name, and I swooned at the sound of it in Spencer's mouth, and I stopped, and saw him standing sweaty and tank-topped at the cafeteria window, smiling, nervous, looking exactly like he always did in the dreams where we finally told each other our separate, identical secrets, and said, "Can I maybe talk to you for a minute?"

21. Because I have an easily-duped mammalian intellect of my own, and because if there's one thing you can depend upon,

it's that teenage boys are a lot more likely to make dumb decisions when lust is addling their brains.

22. Because I went to him, and said, "Hey," and he said, "Hey," and we stood there like that for a second, and his pale skin had the same faint green-blue tint as mine from soaking in chlorine four hours a day for months, and his eyes were two tiny swimming pools, and somehow there wasn't a single pimple anywhere on him. And he said, "That Edgar Allan Poe shit was pretty fucked up, wasn't it?" and I laughed and said that yes, it was, and my heart was loud in my throat and it had hijacked my brain and I could not disobey it, through several long minutes of small talk, even while I knew what it meant for Anchal.

23. Because he smiled and said, "Do you think I could, I don't know, come over some time?" and I grinned so hard it hurt, and said, "Yeah, yes, sure, that'd be great," while my mind scrolled through a zoetrope of blurry images, heavy petting on the bean bag chair in my basement, pale skin warming pale skin, us walking hand-in-hand through the hallowed horrible halls of Hudson High, me and Spencer against the world, my heinous monastic celibacy broken.

24. Because his phone buzzed, then, and he took it out and looked at it and then looked at me and said, "Yeah, uh, so, I should be going," and I saw at once that my plan had been seen through, my timeline tampered with, and I knew what even these six minutes of delay might mean for Anchal—and I left him in

midsentence, and ran for my bike and pedalled as hard as I could, heading for the slate quarries.

25. Because the long rocky road in to the quarry was littered with giant jutting slabs of slate, obscuring my view and slowing me down, so I didn't see her, or any of them, until I arrived at the top of the quarry and saw Anchal standing her ground, the five of them in a semicircle around her, but nothing between her and a drop to the jagged rocks and quarry lagoon below, and her face was bruised and bleeding but she was still on her feet and holding something in her hand, and she turned, and saw me, and saw Spencer coming close behind, and knew what I had done, how my weakness had hurt her, how only her own strength had saved her from the horrific fate I abandoned her to, and she knew, in that moment, exactly what I was, and what I was was a sick son of a bitch just like the rest of them.

26. Because Rex had taken off his jacket, and his sweater, and his shirt, even though it was mid-December twilight, and he was freezing, and goosebumps armored his torso, and he turned and smiled when he saw me ride up, and said, "Hold on for a minute, boys, let me just take care of something first."

27. Because I tossed my bike to the ground and advanced on him, unafraid for once in my life, because guilt and shame over how weak I was had overpowered the fear of physical pain that usually held me back, and one of them laughed with surprise at my aggressiveness and said, "Damn, Rex, look out," and I yelled, "Get away from her you pigs!" and Rex laughed and

said, "Or what? You'll take us all on? All six of us?"—for Spencer had taken Rex's spot in the semicircle—and I said, "I'll kill you all," and I knew, hearing myself say it, that it was true, that Anchal was right, that there was no way *not* to kill them, that being a threat was who they were, and only death would make them cease to be one.

28. Because Rex said, "Come on then!" and I reached out for him, and he evaded me, and I reached again with the other arm and he leapt back, and I wasn't throwing fists because all I had to do was touch him, bare skin to bare skin, to possess him.

29. Because the terrible thought occurred to me, when Rex had successfully dodged several of my grabs, and threw his arm out at me, not in a fist but in the same extended-finger grip as mine, *What if I'm not the only one with this gift?*

30. Because our fight looked more like a ballet than a battle, ducking and leaping and flinging our arms out, and I was gaining ground, pushing him back toward the circle and the ledge, and his friends were laughing but in a nervous kind of way, and because I knew that he was thrown off balance by trying not to make eye contact with any of his fellow thugs, but that so was I, in my efforts to avoid looking into Anchal's eyes, for fear of what I'd find there.

31. Because Anchal's arm shot out then, and sprayed the little mace canister in Rex's eyes, and he stopped like someone pushed pause, and I struck his bare shoulder with one triumphant palm.

32. Because his scream of pain was cut short in that instant, and we stood like that, frozen, touching, for a solid thirty seconds, while I battled Rex for control of his body, and I saw how ill-advised this plan had been, because only the pain and confusion caused by Anchal's mace kept him from easily turning my gift back on me, and if any of his friends had touched me my control would have been broken and I'd surely have died that day.

33. Because none of them did touch me.

34. Because once I had Rex, the rest were easy.

35. Because I reached out my left arm and Rex reached out his in a precise mirror-motion, and touched it to the right arm of the boy standing beside him, and now when I reached out with my left arm *both* boys reached out with theirs, and touched the next boy, and so on, until all six boys, including Spencer, were linked hand to hand with me, and every move I made, they made.

36. Because my gift had established a field of control that no longer depended on mere touch, and when I took my hand away the boys were my vassals, my puppets, unable to move or speak on their own, free will gone, their hearts pumping at precisely the same rate as mine, their lungs taking in and casting out air in perfect rhythm with my breath

37. Because I, on the other hand, felt nothing at all beyond the slight tension of the muscles that I always felt when I used my gift.

38. Because I raised my arms and they raised theirs; I jumped and so did they; I let loose a wolf call matched by six baying voices.

39. Because their eyes, I was surprised to learn, retained their autonomy, and the semicircle now showed me an impressive ocular display of hatred, fear, pain, anger.

40. Because Anchal stood up, and looked at me, and unlike my captive animals her eyes told me nothing, and she ran, silently, into the dark, and when I called her name those six boys said it too.

41. Because I let a long time pass, standing, listening, waiting for her to come back.

42. Because she didn't.

43. Because it is not a simple thing, to kill a man who mimics your every move.

44. Because Anchal chose the slate quarry for just that purpose.

45. Because I squatted, and they squatted, and I picked up a heavy rock, and their hands closed on nothingness, and I stood, and they stood, and I hoisted the rock over my head, and they raised their empty hands up just as high, and I threw the rock as hard as I could at Rex's head, and they made the same gesture.

46. Because Rex could neither flinch nor blink nor budge as the rock struck his face, nor even snap his head back to soften the impact by moving with the rock's inertia, and blood covered his face in seconds, and in the darkness we could smell the blood but not see the extent of the damage, and now every emotion other than terror was gone from those eyes.

47. Because I spoke, then—I shouted, and their screams formed around my words, a ghastly chorus of doomed men, echoing: *"Once I dreamed of being one of you, of having your bodies, of moving so easily and fearlessly through the world, of belonging so effortlessly to a group of friends—but now that I can taste it for myself, now that I have your bodies, now that I am you, all of you, I see it for the horrid meaningless thing that it is."*

48. Because the speech was not for them, and I'd spent a long time practicing it, and I was proud of it, but its intended audience was gone, fled, betrayed and hurt, by me.

49. Because suddenly my anger was gone, replaced by shame, and I had no more energy for our plan of a moment ago, of slowly but surely inducing them to bash each other to bits, to leave a grisly mess for forensic scientists to spend decades puzzling over.

50. Because the water at the bottom of the quarry was still an eerie blue with the light from the sky, even though the sun had already slipped past the horizon.

51. Because they were all standing so much closer than I was to the uneven lip of the quarry, and I reached out my arms and clasped my hands on air, so they were linked up in a human chain, and I ran and leapt and they went over the edge but I still had another three feet of solid ground ahead of me.

52. Because I stepped forward and looked down and there they were, far below, their backs to me, waist-deep in water and

looking down into it, still holding hands, some of them unable to stand on broken legs, and there was blood in the water.

53. Because it was more from weariness than anything else when I lay down on the ground, head pressed to the dirt, and I knew even though I couldn't see them that they were all fully underwater, and I opened my mouth and breathed in that sweet cold December night air and then breathed it out, breathed it in and breathed it out, until the tension slackened in my muscles and I knew the field was broken, because they had drowned.

54. Because I got up off the ground knowing I had lost her forever, that she had seen straight through to the cold twisted heart of who I was. And in seeing who I was, she had shown me myself.

55. Because I had been too dumb to see how this power, this privilege I didn't want but had nonetheless, far from helping me to see, had blinded me to the truth of who we were.

56. Because in the movie, Carrie's punishment for killing her foes was to die, and mine was to live.

57. Because Anchal knew what I did not: that we are what we are, and we act it out without wanting to, and only death can break us of the habit of being the bodies we're born into.

The Minotaur Girls

By Tansy Rayner Roberts

Only the hottest girls in town got picked for the Minotaur. Like everyone else when I was fourteen, I wanted it desperately. I wanted to be like willowy Amber Sanders who was taken by the Minotaur the year before. Maybe I could dye my hair from mousy brown to fire engine red, and attain the mythical, miraculous status of *glitter*.

My mates and I weren't even glitter enough to get past the velvet rope. Thin Lizzie and Fat Lizzie and Chrissy and me, we tried a few Saturday nights, but it was humiliating to stand there in our best silver bubble-skirts and white tights, frizzed-high fringes and skates hanging around our neck, hoping that the door bitch would let us past.

We never even saw the door bitch. The lads on the door wouldn't let us past the first rope to get to her. We were too young, too wide-eyed, too daft.

So unglitter.

We skated in the park instead, wobbling around the bike ramps and hoping not to ladder our tights. If we couldn't have the silver lights and pounding music of the Minotaur, at least we had this.

If we practiced and practiced, if we were hell on wheels, it wouldn't matter how we looked, right? The Minotaur would beg us to join them.

Sometimes Thin Lizzie's brother Sean and his bogan mates would join us, and sometimes they had beer. They didn't care that we were young—I think they liked trying to impress us. Eventually we paired off, for pashing and groping. This was practice too, I told myself, as I tried to keep Richie Mason's wandering hands from going too far past my bra.

A Minotaur girl had to be good at everything.

One Monday, Fat Lizzie wasn't in class. The rumours were flying around the school by lunch. She had been seen, walking into the Minotaur in broad daylight. Wearing their uniform, the crisp white mini-dress, and brand new silver skates.

Our mate had been taken, and she hadn't even said goodbye.

"Why her, though?" said Chrissy as we ate dim sims at the corner shop after school. "She's … well, you know."

"Fat," said Thin Lizzie, who wasn't especially thin.

We sat in quiet reflection of how horrible it must be to be slightly fatter than your friends.

"Must have been the boobs," Chrissy decided, and we all agreed. Fat Lizzie filled a bra like no one else.

"Listen to us," I said. "Talking like she's dead. She's on the inside, isn't she? She's still our mate. Do you think she'd let us in one night?"

There was a long silence, as we thought about that.

"She won't want to know us now," said Chrissy. "No one ever comes back."

I practiced skating even harder. The Fat Lizzie thing gave me hope. It might be my turn next. So I went to the park even when the others couldn't be bothered, and I rolled and spun and did every trick that I could.

Notice me, notice me, notice me.

One evening, I spotted a boy watching me on the bike ramps. He had a nice shirt, all silvery, and when I stopped and matched his stare with my own, I recognised him.

He used to hang out with Thin Lizzie's brother Sean last year, before the boys started noticing us. I didn't remember his name, maybe Ade or Ollie. He'd gone missing a while back and everyone thought he shot through to the big city, looking for work.

It had never occurred to us that maybe the Minotaur took boys too.

They had made him beautiful. His hair was like frosted snow, and his eyes a bright jewel-blue that didn't exist in real life. He had the perfect jeans, fitted to his hips like they were sewn on to him. Glitter all the way.

He lounged on the edge of the ramp. And oh, he was watching me.

I did a flip and skidded up the slope to land near him, breathing harder than I wanted to. "Hey."

"You're good," he said. His voice was beautiful too. It reminded me of expensive soap and Milli Vanilli.

"I practice a lot," I said, and could have kicked myself. You're not supposed to show how much effort it takes to be good. You're supposed to be floaty and gorgeous and not even try. "I mean, it's the best park for skating. I'm Tess."

Did I sound desperate or what? I flopped down next to him, not looking at those beautiful bright eyes, pretending not to care that I sounded like a dropkick.

He didn't tell me his name.

"You're one of them," I said. "A Minotaur boy."

He smiled softly. Sunlight gleamed on his hair. Glitter on a stick. "Is that what you call us?"

"What do you call the rest of us?"

A gentle shrug. "We don't think about you much at all."

Anger burned through me. "Say hello to Fat Lizzie for me. I used to be her friend." I pushed myself up, rolling down the ramp, wanting to get away from him as fast as I could.

Something flashed in the air in front of me and bounced, ringing on the ramp. I skidded and leaned down to pick it up.

A silver coin with a Minotaur printed on it, and the words Admit One stamped on the back. I'd never seen one before, but older girls giggled about them sometimes, the tokens that get you past the velvet rope. Two prefects had once had a slap fight in the quadrangle over one they'd found in the street.

The coin was warm in my hand. I looked up, shielding my eyes against the sun reflecting off the boy's frosted hair. For the first time in my life, I felt brave.

"I have two friends," I said loudly. "I go with them, or not at all."

The Minotaur boy stared at me for a moment, and then he began to laugh.

Glitter is an attitude, not just a look. I had never felt as glitter as I did that day I showed Chrissy and Thin Lizzie what I had for us. Three perfect silver coins. Minotaur tokens.

"Unbelievable," breathed Chrissy.

Thin Lizzie was frowning, turning hers over in her hand. "What did you do for this, Tess?" she asked finally.

My cheeks went hot. "I skated really well in the park, and he gave them to me."

Thin Lizzie's eyebrows went up. I hated her in that moment. If she was going to be a mole, I didn't want her to have the coin at all.

Was this why Fat Lizzie never got in touch, when the Minotaur took her? Did she think we would be bitchy about it?

"You don't have to come," I muttered.

Thin Lizzie smiled. "Of course I'm coming."

"This is so awesome," Chrissy squealed. "What are we going to wear?"

We touched our skates up with silver paint, and shared a brand new frosted lipstick. My hand was hot from holding on to the coin all the way to the club. The lads on the rope let us through, and we found ourselves stumbling through a dark corridor towards the door bitch.

Her fringe was sprayed so high it almost brushed the top of the doorway. I'd never seen anyone with a nose stud before, and tried not to stare at it.

"You're the ones Ari invited," she said, taking in our carefully assembled outfits. I waited for her to kick us out for being so unglitter.

Ari. His name was Ari.

The door bitch pulled back a dark curtain and the air was thick with music, a pounding beat that made my teeth hurt. Silver lights blazed out at us.

"Skates on, chickadees," said the door bitch, and gave Thin Lizzie a push so she ended up in front of us, sliding on the polished floor. "Ante up."

We had made it to the Minotaur, and it hadn't cost us anything.

Skates on. Ante up.

It was bigger inside than I had ever imaged. Ramps ran up the walls from room to room, and the lights dipped and spun from an impossibly high ceiling, making the shapes and the curves change every time. It was the best skating rink ever, times a million.

I lost Thin Lizzie. She was ahead of us, and plunged down a chute with some other girls, screaming and laughing. By the time Chrissy and I got there, Lizzie was nowhere in sight.

"We'll stick together, yeah, Tess?" Chrissy said, and I nodded reluctantly. The music was loud and amazing, with a beat that got inside my arms and legs. I didn't want her holding me back. I wanted to dance and skate and kiss boys and drink pink drinks and…

Chrissy seemed small.

We skated together, down a long channel into a high-ceilinged room where skaters flipped and tumbled their way up the walls, and a bright silver disco ball threw rainbow refractions against them. The ball spun, and the world shifted.

Sometimes when the light fell on them, they didn't look gorgeous at all. They looked like monsters. Their eyes glowed and their limbs undulated. Their sprayed hair became flowing lion manes, their lipsticked mouths became beaks, and there were snakes coiling everywhere, from their scalps to their pubes.

When the light shifted, they were beautiful again.

I still wanted to kiss them.

A tall monster with dreadlocked hair and kicky pink skates screeched up in front of me, grinning like a demon. I let her pull me into the maze of ramps. I did my best tricks and she laughed, clapping in delight. I spun and whirled, and if there were feathers flying from my arms now, I hardly noticed them.

I wasn't a monster or anything. Not yet.

Pink Skates tugged me into another room, and I lost Chrissy altogether. I didn't care. This one had a bright purple disco ball that cast grape-coloured shadows. The walls were soft and padded like the room was one big lounge suite. Someone gave me a drink and I gulped it gratefully before the sting hit the back of my throat and I realised that it wasn't water. It was like acid going down but then it warmed me up all over and I drank more of it.

No one was skating here, or if they were it was a long and lazy dance. Mostly they were pashing, limbs tangled together, heads tipped back against the soft parts of the walls, hands vanishing under layers of designer clothing.

I felt my face flame red with embarrassment. I don't know why. I hadn't cared at all that time Thin Lizzie and her first boyfriend started heavy petting in the park while the rest of us were right there, talking about which of the Coreys was cuter.

Some of these people were going further than heavy petting, but it was dark and the music was loud, and I didn't want to stare.

Kids were gaming in here too, with silver tokens like the ones Ari had given me. Several beautiful Minotaur Girls leaned over a green baize table, flipping coins back and forth for the customers. I didn't understand the game.

I still wanted to play.

Pink Skates turned and kissed me. My head fell back against the cushiony padded walls. I was so light, my skates were the only thing holding me down. She tasted of raspberry lipgloss.

"Bet you can't guess my name," she whispered.

Whoops and hollers awoke me from my daze. I pulled away from her, but no one was looking at us. The skaters and the gamers and the make out artists all looked up, pointing and hooting at a boy in a cage that hung from the high ceiling, gleaming like a mirrorball.

"Go on," Pink Skates said, more urgently. "Bet."

The boy was not laughing. He flinched as they threw bags of cellophane confetti at him, which burst against the cage.

He was Ari, the silver boy who had given me the coins.

"What did he do?" I breathed. Why were they punishing him?

Pink Skates gave me an odd look. "He won at the tables, and this is his prize," she said. "I'd love to be in the cage. Everyone looks at you. Guess my name, or you lose the bet."

"Rose," I said at random, the pinkest name I could think of.

"Wrong," she laughed, and kept on laughing until she could barely breathe. "I win!"

"What are you—" I started to say, and then something slammed into my chest. I gasped through the pain, falling to my knees. It hurt. My breasts were on fire from the inside out, and my stomach cramped like I was having five periods all at once.

Pink Skates did a pirouette in front of me, glowing with light and happiness. "Standard ante," she said. "A year of your life. You should be more careful who you bet with, chickadee."

"Why me?" I demanded of her. The pain began to ease, and I struggled to my feet.

"Why not? Baby dolls like you taste good. Fresh meat." She skated away, still laughing.

This was the Minotaur. Music so loud it hurt, bored kids causing pain for kicks and oh yes, being taunted in a glowing mirrorball cage was some kind of reward.

All I'd ever wanted to do was skate.

Somewhere in the dazzle and the brightness, I heard a scream. Was that Chrissy? I should never have left her alone.

I forced my way through several rooms of skaters and dancers and gaming tables and ramps, dazzling lights and dark shadows. Hands plucked at me, but I shook them off and kept going. "Chrissy!"

I found her in a ball pit below a beautiful glass ramp that looked like something Cinderella would have skated down.

"These people are skanks," Chrissy said breathlessly as I helped her climb out from under the writhing bodies. "Some of the girls were kissing other girls!"

"Yeah," I said uneasily. "Let's get out of here."

I had seen a big purple EXIT sign before, but I wasn't sure where.

"Going somewhere?" jeered a voice.

Thin Lizzie. She had come in here with us less than an hour ago, but I guess she'd made some new friends. She stood with them now, chewing gum and staring at me.

"I'm over this," I said defiantly.

Thin Lizzie glided forward, daring me to push her or prove my uncool in some other way. "They say I can stay if I stop you both leaving," she said. "I can come every night. Maybe earn my ticket into being a real Minotaur girl. Don't spoil this for me, Tess."

"I want to go home," Chrissy whined.

"You'd like it if you gave it a chance," said Lizzie. "Don't be such a chickenshit."

I faced her down. "If this place is so glitter, why are they trying to stop us leaving?"

But I knew that already. They didn't want me shouting my mouth off about how gross the Minotaur really was.

An older boy, with dark eyes and a smile I might have thought was charming about fifteen minutes ago, put his hand on Thin Lizzie's shoulder. "You can leave, babe," he said to me. "Anytime you want. But first you have to skate."

★

They took me to an arena deep in the Minotaur, with a plain round skating rink. A spotlight fell on me and I wondered for one laughable moment if this was some kind of reward, like it had been for Ari.

Teenagers leaned over balconies and sprawled across banks of velour seats.

The Minotaur girls stood at the edge of the rink, beautiful and silver and nearly identical. Never mind the spotlight, I was blinded by their pearly white eyeshadow. There were a few boys with them too, just as pretty.

My eyelashes prickled with sweat, and the audience took on other shapes before my eyes. Monsters all, teeth and claws. Laughing, sneering, glittering monsters.

I searched the crowd for one friendly face, but Chrissie stood with Thin Lizzie, their fingers entwined. She wasn't going to save me.

So I skated for the monsters. The lights grew brighter, and the music pounded in my ears only slightly louder than my heartbeat. I spun and whirled.

I could see the monsters more clearly now. Thin silver threads flowed from their wrists and ankles, spiralling upwards into the ceiling. Every time one of them moved or jerked a head, I saw a thread tug at them.

Even Chrissy had threads, though hers were paler than everyone else's.

I kept skating, pulling out every trick and flourish that I knew.

A chime rang out above the music, and the Minotaur girls joined me on the rink, wheels flashing.

While I was skating, I was one of them.

I slowed, and immediately saw the difference. The Minotaur girls turned towards me with sneers and suspicion. I sped up, did a twirl or two, and they relaxed.

No way I could do this forever. My skates felt like concrete blocks on my feet.

Thin Lizzie and Chrissy skated together. They did not look at me. Thin Lizzie's threads were almost as bright as those of the real Minotaur girls, and Chrissy's glowed as she gained confidence.

If I stayed longer, I might not want to leave either.

A silver shadow poured from the ceiling to the floor. Everyone skated around it, pretending it wasn't there. It was a rope ladder, made of those threads they all wore. A silver ladder of knotted threads. It couldn't take my weight, surely?

But it was a chance.

I spun and danced and sped around the rink, not aiming for the ladder at all. I even let a Minotaur boy or two catch my hand and twirl me around. Non-threatening. Part of the show.

Then I skated backwards until I felt the soft brush of the thread ladder against my back.

I grabbed hold and climbed, pulling it up behind me. Up and up, and I hardly needed the ladder after a while because the silver threads were a thick tangle up here, twitching in the air. I climbed and climbed, and finally grasped something solid instead of that diaphanous ladder. It was a hanging cage. The knotted ladder ended here. I could see where the web of threads had been torn around us, to make the ladder.

"You," said a whispered voice, and I saw the boy Ari staring out at me, his thin fingers grasping the bars. "Is it you?"

He was so pathetic, my stomach swelled up with anger against him. "Why did you give me that coin?" I hissed. "Why did you bring me here? This place is horrible."

Ari was still beautiful, but not nearly as glitter as he had seemed that day in the park. "I didn't have a choice," he said. "The Minotaur made me do it. But I hoped … it might be different this time. Maybe you could break this place wide open. Someone has to."

I hadn't thought of that. Could I close down the Minotaur once and for all? "Everyone would hate me," I said in awe at the very idea of it.

Ari smiled with bright teeth and yeah, I'd still let him kiss me. "They'd never forget you," he said.

I broke two fingernails getting his cage open. I had to use a skate to bash at the lock until it broke and Ari could get out. We climbed together, up the chain that held the cage, and it wasn't long before we spotted a railing at the top of the Minotaur. There was a balcony running around the inside of this upper part of the building, and we clambered across the web of threads to reach it.

If we fell, we would be caught in those threads like the net under a trapeze. So many threads, each plugged into a beautiful monster.

Ari was right. We had to blow this place wide open.

"Where are we going?" I whispered.

"Control room," Ari said back. "There's always someone pulling the threads."

"Like—a big boss?"

"I can't answer that," he said, as I climbed over the railing. Finally, solid floor under my feet. He didn't once try to help me and I wasn't sure if that was wonderful or really annoying. "A different girl pulls the threads each night."

"How does all this happen without someone in charge?"

"It's the Minotaur," said Ari. "The building is alive. It wants us to have a good time and put on a show. It loves roller skates, who knows why. If we make it happy, it rewards us. So we do."

We were outside the control room now. It had a wide glass window but I couldn't see much in the darkness.

Ari hung back.

"Aren't you coming in?" I asked.

"I don't think I can." He lifted his feet and hands. Pale threads veined away from him and down over the edge of the balcony. "They always grow back," he said sadly.

I ran inside the control room and slammed the door behind me. "So," I said aloud. "Who's pulling the threads tonight?"

"Tess?" said a small voice. "Is that you?"

As my eyes got used to the darkness, I saw her at the far end of the room. She sat on an ordinary office chair, the kind that spins around. Every inch of her body had a silver thread growing out of it. They lashed into the walls and floor and ceiling.

Fat Lizzie. I hadn't seen her in weeks, but she looked different. Gaunt and angry and so, so scared.

"What have they done to you?" I breathed.

"It's not they," she said. "There isn't a 'they'. It's the Minotaur. She hates us all."

The floor shuddered under my feet. The Minotaur didn't like us having this conversation. And since when was the Minotaur a she?

"What happens if I cut you out of those threads?" I asked Fat Lizzie.

"They grow back. Faster. And they hurt."

I turned to the control banks, all those switches and dials. I pressed a button, and a screen flicked into life slowly, in greyscale. Another screen, then another. You could see the whole Minotaur from here, every room and ramp. The girls and boys were skating, gaming, kissing and groping.

"Not much of a show," I said aloud. "What if I make it more entertaining?"

The floor stopped rumbling under my feet. The Minotaur was curious.

"You can't beat the Minotaur, Tess," said Fat Lizzie. She sounded stretched thin. "She won't let you."

That stung. Ari thought I was special. Why was she so certain I wasn't? "Why not?"

Lizzie didn't answer. Her hands moved back and forth, plucking at the silvery threads that spun out through the walls and floors.

I left the control room and went back out to the balcony, where Ari lay trapped in his own tangle of silver threads. "Why me?" I demanded. "Why did you choose ME if I'm so useless?"

He shook his head, staring up at me.

"Why am I the only one without silver threads sticking out of me?" I tried. This time, when he didn't answer, I flew at him, tearing at the threads. He yelled with pain as I pulled them out. When the last of them snaked away off the edge of the balcony, Ari sat there, breathless and rumpled but able to talk to me again.

"What are we going to do?" I demanded. I was no use on my own. I should be part of a group, with Lizzie and Lizzie and Chrissy bouncing our every word and thought off each other until everything made sense.

I missed them so badly.

"Don't ask me," Ari snapped. "This is your game, not mine. Don't you get it? You're the hero and I'm the fucking damsel in distress."

Something rang a chord in my mind, so very familiar. "What do you mean, game?"

"Ante-up, lay your bets, roll the dice," he said in a sing-song voice. "I laid my bets on you, Tess, and you're not exactly paying off."

"Who am I playing against?" I hissed at him.

He glanced past me, and shuddered. "The Minotaur."

I turned, not sure what to expect. My worst fear was that it would be one of my girls, Thin Lizzie or Chrissy, that I'd have to fight them. But it wasn't anyone I knew.

She wasn't tall. She was old like Mum, and I felt a familiar shock as I gazed at her, like meeting a long lost aunt for the first time. She was fitter than my Mum, with better hair. She had a really great suit, all purple velvet and pale pink lace, like something Prince would wear.

"You were right the first time, Tess," said the Minotaur. "There is a boss."

"I knew it," I said sourly. "No way a building is this mean all on its own."

"That's not exactly true. I am the building, and the building is me—the Minotaur and her maze. Bet you can't guess my name."

"I'm not falling for that again."

"Fair enough." She grinned at me, like she was my age. I wish I could remember where I'd seen her before. "My name is Teresa Maree Holland. Or it was, before I became the Minotaur. So long ago."

I felt small and stupid, and that made me angrier. "That's my name."

"Obviously."

"You expect me to believe that … you're me?"

"No, sweetheart," the Minotaur said, all patronising like the teachers at school. "You're *me*."

"That's not TRUE," I flung at her.

She smirked at me, and I knew that expression so well that it chilled my insides. I'd practiced it in the mirror before coming here tonight, so I'd look like the confident one instead of tagging after Thin Lizzie like I always do. "The reason you don't have threads sticking out of you is because you are all thread, my darling. That's what I made you from. Time to come home, chickadee."

The Minotaur reached out to me, and I felt something tug inside my stomach. It was true. I could feel how my whole body was made of threads, coiled tightly to make my limbs and blood and skin. If she pulled hard enough, I would dissolve into whorls of thread, spinning and dancing in the air. I wasn't real, I didn't mean anything, I was temporary...

"NO." I wrenched myself away. "I'm not you. I don't care what game you're playing..."

"Aces high," she said with a wink. "But you're more of a two of hearts, really. A three at most. Naïve enough to let one of my girls win a year of your life, which I'm rather put out about. I had plans for that year."

"I'm *me*," I said, enraged. "I'm Tess, I'm a real person."

"I was like you once. More than once. So fresh faced. I mean, look at your adorable baby doll body. Life was so glitter back then. All I wanted to do was skate, and go with cute boys, and cruise with my friends. Look at me now—I'm living the dream."

"Apart from being old," I shot at her.

She looked triumphant. "You don't think I went to all this trouble just to see a younger version of myself scampering about, do you? Look at you, my dear, all fire and outrage. Big fringe, short skirt. The power of youth. I made you, and now I'm taking you back, like I do every time. Every Minotaur does, when she grows old."

Every time. This had happened before. The knowledge fell into my head like a brick. It wasn't just her, not just this Minotaur. Kids like me, all over the world, eaten and absorbed by desperate middle-aged wannabes like her. She smiled at me, like a real mother might, and I knew it was true. I knew a lot of things I couldn't know unless it was all true, and I was the next version of her.

The Minotaur didn't want to pull my body apart into threads of nothing. She wanted to climb inside it, steal it for her own. Where would I be? Would I be her? I couldn't imagine anything worse.

"You are—so—UNGLITTER!" I howled at her.

She actually laughed, as if the word meant nothing.

I don't know what they were about, those other girls. I don't know how many of them—of me—trudged obediently to the slaughter, letting the Minotaur take them and reshape them and put herself inside their young bodies so she could do it all over again, and again, and again.

What did she do to them, to make them not want to fight for their life? I thought about my friends, and the last time I was truly happy, that day in the park when we were all together. I was ready to fight.

I was aware of every thread in this body of mine, every mote of skin and drop of blood. She had built me for one purpose, to be the next Minotaur. She wanted to rule this world of skates and dance music all over again, to control the silver threads, and so she must have built that power into me in order that it would be there when she stole my fourteen-year old body. Fifteen-year-old. That was a hard one to get used to.

I could see it all, just as I felt her reaching out to me, into me, awakening that power so that it would bring her home.

And I snapped the threads. Every time she reached for me, I severed the connection. She frowned and tried again, but I beat her back. *My body, my threads. Mine for the keeping.*

Mine to destroy.

This time, when she came at me, I yanked every thread in the place. I felt Fat Lizzy in the control room, hanging on to the threads for dear life, and I begged her to trust me, to let her burden go. They slipped from her, every thread, and snaked towards me.

The woman who thought herself the Minotaur howled, trying physically to prevent the threads from reaching me, but her power was weak and every thread made me so, so strong.

I called to them, the Minotaur girls and boys, the teens who just wanted to skate and play games, the audience, my friends, even Ari. *Come to me, give me your power, share it all with me, and I will set you free. Ante up. Bet on me.*

Offered a choice between my older self and a teenage girl who looked much like them, they chose me.

The look on the Old Minotaur face when she realised she had lost was awful. I felt kind of bad for her. But that didn't stop me setting those kids loose on her.

You thought you were free of them, grown ups with their rules and stupid lectures. But she was here all the time, telling you what to do.

They didn't like that, the Minotaur kids. They climbed to us, up the webs of silver threads, hungry and desperate and furious. The happy fun place was lost, the music had stopped, and they remembered now that they had homes and families and lives that had been stolen from them. That they had been stolen from.

They ate her alive, the horde of beautiful silver children with shiny hair and totally glitter outfits. They tore her to pieces, and I let them do it.

Afterwards they looked at me, all docile and obedient, with the blood of my older self still staining their mouths, like they wanted me to be in charge. They thought I would be better than her, because I was young like them, and they did not know how to go on from here.

Would I be the one to give them back their eternal skate party, their games and glamour and mirror balls? Would I make it all better?

"We're going to burn it down," I told them. "It's going to be so glitter. The most glitter ever. And after that, you can go home."

The Minotaur Girls | Tansy Rayner Roberts

*

The Minotaur burned, and the fire engines came, and there was nothing much left after that except charcoal and crying teenagers. I found my skates in the sparkling rubble.

"You did it," Ari said to me. "You broke the spell."

"Yay for me," I said flatly.

The parents came, one by one, to drive their kids home. Thin Lizzie's Mum cried when she saw her. Chrissy's Dad looked really fierce. Fat Lizzie's parents just looked relieved.

Ari and I waited, until they had all gone home, and it was just us.

I hadn't expected anyone to come for me. That Mum and Dad I thought I had, when we talked about our parents at school, or in the park … if they had ever existed, they belonged to the original Tess, generations ago. Gone now.

I didn't ask why no one had come for Ari. He didn't seem surprised.

"What now?" he asked.

My charred skates still had silver paint on them. "Let's go to the park," I said.

"And do what?" he said in disbelief. "Skate? After all this?"

"It's the best park for skating."

I knotted my laces together, hung my skates around my neck, and took his hand. We would skate a bit, and talk, and maybe kiss for a while. We would fall asleep on the cold grass of the park. And I would leave him there, before it got light. Where I was going next, I couldn't take him.

There were other Minotaurs in the world, in other towns. I knew that now, and I knew how to stop them. I had to locate the girls that were just like me, help them unravel the truth and the power within their own skin.

Skates on.

Ante up.

One thread at a time.

Not With You, But With You

By Miri Kim

Last night Daphne's dad became a Civil Servant. We all tried so hard not to look like we felt sorry for her, and fought over giving her our plate of cake and sitting next to her when she looked tired, which was all the time. But when the memorial was over and only a couple of us were left with her we didn't know what to say—do we tell her we're sorry or don't we?—so none of us really said anything and the room went so quiet we could hear the adults talking downstairs and then all of a sudden we could hear Daphne sniffling in her sad daisy-colored heap at the rained-over window.

From across the room Brynn gave me a look, like: *do we pretend we don't hear her?* Then Mom came up to get me and I jumped up to leave, but she made me go back and give Daphne a hug good-bye. At first she didn't even look up at me, but then, just as my hands were leaving her hair, she wiped at her face and said, "Thank you, Naomi."

I couldn't think of anything at all to say to her because what could you say to a girl with *that* for a father?

Tonight Mom and Peter leave me at home with my older sister, Jamie, who promptly goes out at eight with Dickie, who is her new Man, as she calls him. The movie Peter got for me is stupid. I turn it off and sit in silence for a while, but only as long as I can stand the dull thickness in the air, and then I play pick-the-last-digit on my phone to see who I should call. Immediately I think of the number seven, which is no good as Daphne's is the only number that ends in seven. I definitely don't want to call her even if hers is the number I picked and I almost always listen to myself; next I think of the number three, which two girls have, so I call them up in alphabetical order. Lynn picks up on the second ring but tells me she has got a thing at her church, which I know is bunk because I can hear voices in the background and they all sound like boys and they keep calling her name in a weird way. I hang up. Next is Vita but she doesn't even pick up. Then I grow tired of pick-the-last-digit and think of hanging with Brynn, but on second thought I don't want to see her.

That's when my phone rings.

It's Daphne. I hesitate instead of answering right away because I haven't seen her in school all week and in that time I started hanging with Vita, who doesn't get along with Daphne. If I like being with Vita, isn't that a way of choosing her over Daphne?

"Hey, Nomi," she says when I answer. She's calling me by the name she used to call me in elementary school. Her voice sounds thin and sad as a raincloud. "What are you up to?"

"Me? Nothing. How about you?"

"Nothing."

I stretch out on my bed and decide to use *my* old pet name for her in elementary school. If she wants to be lovey, I can be, too. After all, we are still friends, even if I haven't seen her in school all week, even if I almost chose Vita over her. "What's up, Nee?"

I can hear her sniffling. Probably she has been crying all night, maybe all week. "I've just been—thinking."

I make a thoughtful noise. Of course she has been thinking, probably about her dad. I've been thinking about her dad, too, in my own way, and I've had maybe, five conversations with him in my lifetime. More than his voice, though, I mostly remember his face. He looks a bit like a character on TV, a guy who played a cop whose name I can't remember, both the actor and character. It's just as well. Daphne's dad no longer has a name, either. Civil Servants aren't supposed to.

"I found out my dad's CSN," Daphne says suddenly.

I sit up. "How?" For some reason the word *why* bounces around in my head, but something stills me.

"It was easier than I thought it'd be. I didn't have to do anything at all. Somebody called looking for my mom, but they only had my number, and…" she trails off.

"And? Nee?"

"He sounded cool. Sort of nice. And he said—he helps put families back together. Whatever that means."

"Oh." Suddenly the room feels cold, and I'm aware of how empty the house is. Funny how big houses seem when there's only you tucked away in your little corner. I sit up and hug my knees to my chest. "So what else did he say?"

"He said my dad's Civil Servant Number is eighty-four, and he's going to be assigned downtown, instead of far away. He's supposed to be far away. That's what they promised, Nomi, but he said they almost always lie about everything."

"Oh." It comes out in a croak, and I quickly clear my throat.

There's a pause, then she says, "We didn't talk long." Her breath rattles the line. "I was going to call you, before, so I could ask you if you thought it was a bad idea, talking to somebody about my dad like that. I know how much you liked him. My dad, I mean."

I rack my brain, trying to think why Daphne would say that. I think about all the times I slept over at Daphne's, the dinners where I sat on her dad's right and stole glances at him to see how much he looked like the cop on TV whose name I can't remember. I try to remember the five conversations we had together, if we talked about something special or if it was just the same old stuff I talk about with other girls' dads: school and my family and my grades and my plans for whatever. I think everything over and I can't see why Daphne would say I liked her dad, a little or a lot. I can't think of any reason at all. "I don't think it was a bad idea," I tell her. "Anyway, that guy called *you*. You didn't do anything wrong."

"I should've hung up on him, I think. My mom—she never gets the phone anymore, did I tell you that? She has hers turned off and the landline's being rerouted to my aunt's."

"So he called you because he couldn't get to your mom?"

Daphne makes a little *mm-hmm* sound, but it's muffled like she's covering her mouth.

"When did he call you? Just now?"

"Hmm," she says. "Yeah." I think she has her hand away from her mouth now.

"Do you think he's going to call again?"

"I don't know," Daphne says. "Maybe."

I set my phone on my knees and press my ear against it so our breath on the line sounds hollow and muffled at the same time. "How come your mom doesn't answer the phone anymore?"

"People keep calling," Daphne says. "People who don't like Civil Servants."

On our way home from the market Mom and I pass Founders' Square, where people are holding a big rally, and we get stuck in a huge block of traffic. Long lines of people walk past our car holding signs that have nothing written on them, only an X. Occasionally, they thump our hood or the hoods of other cars and shout and whoop and holler. The crowd grows bigger and bigger; Mom doesn't seem to care. She lights up a cigarette and talks on her phone, but she must notice something's wrong because she locks our doors and starts drumming her fingers on the steering wheel.

"And then what'd you tell her?" she says into her phone.

Several minutes pass and the cars don't move forward. In the distance someone starts banging away on a drum and there's fresh chanting but I can't make out any real words, only a sort of mushed up shout. Suddenly there's a sharp shrill whistle, like someone's setting off fireworks, and the people in the car ahead of us get out and look up at the sky. They don't look scared, just excited, so I unlock my door and climb out, too. I don't see any fireworks.

Then there's a loud bang, and a weak little puff of smoke rises into the air. It sounds like a giant water balloon bursting, which is a funny thing to think but it's what comes to mind. A tall dark-skinned girl hanging out on the trunk of the car idling in the next lane looks over at me and says in a bored way, "Just a boob bomb," and I nod and try to look unimpressed.

But I *am* impressed. Nothing ever goes on in Founders' Square, only book fairs and farmers' markets and things like that, never a rally where people yell and throw bombs. I peek in the window at Mom, and I ask her if I can check it out.

"No, get in the car, Naomi," she says, but I tell her I can see up the street and the cars aren't moving and that I'll be right back. Before she can say no again I move away. Out of the corner of my eye I see the tall unimpressed girl and when she sees me she joins me, sort of, and together we move toward the Square.

Closer, at the edge of the crowd, the noise is deafening and there's a pressed-together high buzz in the air, but I still can't see what's happening, surrounded by all these people. The girl's still by my side and suddenly she nudges me and says, "Are you with it?"

I look over at her.

She's older than me, and she smells like cigarettes. She rolls her eyes at me like she can smell me too, and to her great disgust I don't smell like cigarettes. She turns away and slips into the crowd. I give myself one more minute of standing around looking at a wall of people until I have to go back and join Mom and the ice cream melting in the backseat.

That's when I spot him. Daphne's dad. Civil Servant Number Eighty-four. Of course, he doesn't look anything like how I remember him; only the face is familiar to me. The face they left alone, along with his broad shoulders and thick waist, but everything below his gun holster they have pulled off of him.

And then in a weird moment time seems to stand still as his gaze moves over the crowd slowly, slowly. I feel cold and tight all over, but I can't stop looking at him and finally he sees me, too. He looks right at me, as if I've called him by name.

As if he knows me, still.

I can't move. I can't feel anything but the searing sharp chill of his gaze traveling all that space to find me. Fear curls around my throat with icy fingers.

Another high, sharp sound bullets the air. This time thick black smoke mushrooms up into the sky high above us. What was an orderly wall of people starts collapsing around me as everyone tries to press forward and move back, all at once. When the smoke settles, Daphne's dad disappears from view and then I finally feel in my own skin again and I remember how to move; I want to move *away*. I turn and blindly squeeze through the sea of bodies rapidly swelling into a solid mass of claws and panicked faces, ignoring the wailing of sirens, ignoring the choked wild screams all around me, and then I'm running, running, running—

I take a taxi out to Hope Plaza to meet Daphne. Hope Plaza was her idea. My sister says you don't go to the Plaza to shop, you go there to meet boys, but since coming here tonight was Daphne's idea, I don't know how true that can be. Probably Daphne has neither boys nor shopping on her mind. And neither do I. Lately I have been seeing more and more of Daphne and less of Vita and Brynn and the others. It's not as if I want to keep seeing Daphne; it's more like I have to because every time I see her face, I can see her dad's and then I remember how it felt to be frozen with fear and I can smell the tall girl's cigarettes and hear the warble of police sirens and see the birthmark on Daphne's dad's neck that they didn't bother removing when they took away so much of him and then I remember asking Mom if I can go see the rally and it's like I'm remembering everything backward. It's kind of funny, living this way, funny and kind of exciting.

On the sixteenth floor I find Daphne sitting alone on one of those light-up mood benches that were so cool last year, but now everyone has them in all sorts of places, like bakeries and things, so they're not so neat anymore. Daphne's bench is lit-up green. I've forgotten what that's supposed to mean. Pent up, maybe, or hopeful. I can never remember.

She looks up. I give her a little wave.

"Your mood is green," I tell her.

"We can walk around now if you want."

I sit beside her and lean back. "Wait, I want to see what my mood is."

Daphne sits stiffly beside me while we wait for the bench to read my mood. Instead of her usual purse, she's holding a worn-looking book bag. It's definitely not the premium one she uses at school.

"It used to be my dad's," she says.

My ears grow hot. "Oh."

A few seconds later my side of the bench turns a pale orange.

"Do you remember what this color's supposed to mean?"

Daphne stares down at her fingers, or maybe her bag. "Cross."

"Angry?" I frown. "I'm not angry."

"White-orange means you're upset about something." Daphne shuts her eyes briefly. Her lids are heavy and pink and stretched tight over her eyes, the skin shiny like new scars, but I know it's just pink eye shadow. Daphne is easily the prettiest friend I have, though she's not really popular with the boys at school, and she doesn't even have lots and lots of friends like Brynn, who is easily the most popular friend we have between us and Brynn's not even pretty, just sort of *vibrant*.

"Well," I say, "where do you want to go?"

"I don't know." She chews on her lower lip. "Let's just walk around."

We get up and walk over to the screens, just to look because it's already half past nine and I have to go home before eleven. Daphne says she doesn't have a curfew anymore, but probably she has to get home early, too. As I watch the ads next to the marquee, I notice Daphne isn't doing the same. Instead, she's staring off into space, her big hazel eyes glassy and unfocused.

"They always play the same old stuff on these things," I say just to say something.

Daphne doesn't say anything back.

Then I catch something out of the corner of my eye: a group of boys, and they're watching us. They're older, or at least they're taller than most boys at our school. When one of the group catches me looking he gives me a wink. He's wearing his dark hair partly shaved in the sign of an X. I'm still not sure what the X means; it could mean he's anti-Civil Servants, or that he's doing it to look anti but isn't really. But definitely he's anti-Something enough to do *that* to his hair.

Suddenly I remember what the tall, older girl asked me, that day at the rally. *"Are you with it?"* I still don't understand, but the question haunts me.

Not With You, But With You | Miri Kim

I turn away from the X-haired boy and try to ignore the fluttery jagged-edged wings scratching at my insides. I don't know how my sister can catch a new Man every week; I can barely look at this one without wanting to puke and run away.

And then, he's here. The boy. Close enough to reach out and touch. He pays attention to me mostly, which is strange as most boys go for Daphne and ignore me completely. This time it's all flipped around. He looks at me and says, "I think I know your sister. You're Naomi, right?"

"Uh-huh, and she's Daphne," I say. Daphne's staring at him, hard, like she knows him, but he's acting like she doesn't even exist.

I never have anything to say to older boys, and neither does Daphne. When the silence between us grows a little too long, the boy turns to give his friends a funny little wave and that's when I see the tattoo on his palm. Probably it's been done with ballpoint or henna but it looks etched in, not smooth and vivid like a fake would be. It's a black X.

He catches me studying his palm and I quickly glance over at the ads on the walls. A new ad starts up, as if on cue: men in a row hoist guns on their shoulders and shoot into the sky. The bang isn't very loud but Daphne gives a little jump.

The boy offers us each a cigarette. He watches us and smirks to himself, like he can see right through our clothes. "Hey, let's get out of here," he says. A warmness flows through me, not quite pleasant: kind of funny and weird and ugly and nice, all at once.

Are you with it?

On impulse, I take one of his cigarettes and tap it against my palm like people do on TV.

"Are you with it?" I ask him suddenly. My heart stops beating for a moment, then pounds away fiercely.

One corner of his pierced mouth lifts into a zigzag smile. "Yeah," he says. "Sure."

Daphne frowns at me. "Nomi."

I take the boy's hand and turn it over palm-up. "Okay," I say, my ears growing hot, "prove it."

"How?"

"Don't you know?"

His expression hardens. Then, just as quickly, he's easy and careless again. "I know where they keep them," he says quietly. "The Civil Servants, when they're not out on rotation."

"What did you say?" Daphne says. Again she gives the boy a long, strange look and again I get that funny feeling that they know each other.

"I can show you," he tells her.

"You're serious?"

"Yeah. Sure."

Daphne doesn't look at me, only at him, and he only has eyes for her when just seconds before it was different. I know how stupid that is. Daphne is lit up by all these ads, and her sadness about her poor ruined father makes her even more appealing. Of course he's into her and not me.

"Show me then," she says.

I won't be the third wheel. "I have to get home," I tell the air. Later I'm on the light-up mood bench again, alone. My skirt and sweater glow with color. Not white-orange this time, but a pretty shade of lilac. I don't know what this means. I never know what anything means.

A few days later I'm with Daphne in Citizenship class. While the teacher has us type out an essay on why it's important to turn in our Body Ownership Conferral Card a year early, before our sixteenth birthdays, Daphne has her head ducked and her hand is a claw gripping her hair. She doesn't write a single thing, not even her name, and then later when we have to turn in our files, she leaves her space in Mrs. Summit's box empty and blinking. From across the room Brynn locks eyes with me and gives me a puzzled look. I shrug my shoulders.

When the bell rings Daphne slips her thin arm through mine, her face pale and her hair a messy bird's nest. "Let's ditch," she says quietly. This is the first thing she's said to me in days, because she's been a walking ghost ever since that boy with the x-ray eyes and his stupid X-hair took her away from me at the Plaza. Brynn is following us expectantly. For some reason I wave her off and she gives me a look like she doesn't know why I'm sticking with Daphne instead of her. She walks out of the room with a flip of her hair.

"Come with me?" Daphne says. There are dark shadows under her eyes and bits of red around her lips like she's been trying to chew her mouth off.

"Where?"

"Anywhere. No, wait. He's coming—he's picking me up." Daphne presses her left hand to her forehead and winces. I grab her hand and inspect it and see that her palm has gotten infected from a tattoo she's gotten. The skin around the legs of the etched black X is bright pink and swollen. She takes back her hand and presses it to her side.

"Oh, Nee," I breathe. "You didn't."

She looks at me, her face drawn and pinched. "It means I'm with it. Against them. Together we're with it. Better to be together against it than alone. That's what he says." Her voice goes soft. "Are you with it, Nomi?"

I frown. Something clicks in my head, but it's not the pieces coming together or anything like that, it's more like a latch sliding across a door.

She chews on her lip. "He wants you to come with us." She sounds like *she* doesn't want me to, but she'll ask because it's what *he* wants. Whoever *he* is—though I think I have an idea.

I feel cold all over.

"Nomi?"

I shouldn't. I'm not. But because she asked, I do.

We go around the Arts Building over to the old bike rack where there's a small hole in the chain-link fence covered by vines. Daphne goes through first and she holds the opening out for me as I crawl through.

"Where are we going?" I ask her as I straighten and brush the leaves off my sweater.

"Downtown," she says, glancing at her phone.

The word makes my stomach turn painfully. "What, *now?*"

"Come on," she says, leading the way. She has on her dad's book bag; it sits awkwardly on her thin shoulders, too high, too bulky, too big on her delicate frame.

We walk down the block and over the small hilly yard of a large brick house ringed by stinking red roses. Daphne leads the way onto the opposite street, but as soon as we're off the road, she stops me. She pulls me by the arm and forces me against a stop sign. "I changed my mind," she says. "You can't come with us."

I push her away but she's strong, stronger than she should be looking the way she does. "What's with you?"

"You can't come, Naomi," she says, her dark brows drawn together. She takes a step away, holding her tattooed hand to her chest. Her thin face twists into a mask, an old lady mask. "I changed my mind," she says. "I don't want you with me."

I start to smile, thinking she's playing at something, but her face only goes colder. "Don't follow us," she says.

She jogs away from me and down the street. I watch as she stops beside a silver car glinting in the sunlight. After she climbs in, the boy from the Plaza sticks his head out of the driver's side window. "Nomi!" he says, in a singsong voice. "Nomi, come on! Come with us!"

I lean against the stop sign. I should run out after her, no matter what Daphne said. I don't like the idea of her going off to be alone with that boy, though I know they must've been hanging together all this time that she has been away from me. But I don't. I hang back, my heart beating oddly in my chest, like I'm having some sort of attack. I know I'm not *with it*, I'm thinking, if it means going downtown. They have too many rallies there now, violent ones. They're not even real protests, just an excuse for lots of anti-people to come together to throw things at the buildings, at cars, at the police, but mostly at the Civil Servants. People have gotten hurt at Founders' Square. Lots of people. Anti- and regular old people caught in the crossfire.

After a while, I hear a car speed down the road; when I look, they're gone.

Back at school, I join the others at our usual lunch table and tell them Daphne and I aren't friends anymore and Vita looks at me with a little grin and Brynn flips her hair at all of us.

I don't think about Daphne again for the rest of the day, but as soon as I get home her face is all over the TV. Mom and Jamie are all upset and Peter rests his hand on the top of my head and the four of us stand in a V in front of the TV and I watch in a stupid daze as they replay the bomb going off over and over and over. Then Mom goes to answer the phone which must've been ringing for some time and for some reason her soft "Hello?" from the kitchen is like a balm to my right ear. Jamie wipes at her face and sits on the sofa; Peter and I don't move.

At some point the tape of the bomb going off is replaced by a recorded message from a group of masked people wearing big black X's on their bare torsos. One is a woman, and the arms of her black X are faint where they meet the curve of her breasts. They say they're responsible for today's bomb and for each subsequent bomb from now on, each one representing the ninety-three.

"Ninety-three?" Peter says thickly.

"Civil Servants," my sister murmurs, and she explains that she's been reading up about it on the underground news feeds, which talk about things that don't get talked about on TV. After a while I stop listening to Peter and Jamie talk because I'm transfixed by the carved X on one man's body, the one sitting next to the half-nude woman. His X isn't a tattoo, as I first thought, or paint like the others'. His is a scar, jagged and darkened over time. He must've mutilated himself for this cause a long, long time ago.

I move away from Peter and crumple to the floor, right in front of the TV. It's *him*. I'm sure of it. Even with the voice garbled and his face behind a mask I can tell it's him. The X-hair boy. The boy with the x-ray eyes. The boy with the silver car. The boy who took Daphne away from me.

"She died to save Eighty-four from his miserable existence," the half-nude woman with the X on her breasts says, and the video cuts to footage, more poorly shot than the one the news keeps showing but the view is closer, much closer to the fountain where Daphne died. I can make out her long black hair, the awkward bulk on her shoulders. She's running. Someone turns around, faces her. He's long and gleaming and horrible. She runs and runs and he just stands there, waiting for her, and then there's suddenly without any warning a great big gush of red, like wet goopy fireworks, then black smoke billows out into the air, flames blaze high into the sky, people run everywhere, and then the news feed goes dead. Then Mom comes into the room and tells me there's someone on the phone who wants to talk to me and *why* is my cell turned off? It's dangerous, you know, especially on a day like today.

I take my phone out of my pocket. At the sight of its dark screen something hardens between my ribs, like cold wax, and it's hard to breathe or think or see anything but suddenly I remember the way Daphne looked on the mood bench, her pale skin lit electric green—the color of sickness, not a mood at all, just sickness.

Are you with it?

I was never with it. I even turned off my phone so she wouldn't, couldn't call me, just in case. She was never with it, with me, ever.

As I walk into the kitchen I hear Mom say, "She used to be such a good girl," and I can't tell if she's talking about me or Daphne.

Mom left the receiver facing up; for some reason I don't want to pick it up. Instead I press my ear down onto it.

"Hello?"

I stare at the dull white walls of our kitchen but the only thing I can see is the big gush of red, the terrible bloom of blood where Daphne stood at the fountain for the last time with the ruined reassembled body of her dead father. So much blood, for only one-and-a-half bodies. I shut my eyes but I can still see them. It. Everything.

"Hello?" I say again into the spiral of holes. My voice sounds muffled and hollow. An echo of an echo of an echo.

Ghost Town

By Malinda Lo

1. October 31, 11:57 PM

McKenzie shows up at the Spruce Street Guest House a few minutes before midnight, dressed all in black as if she's some kind of ninja. She's even got a black stocking cap pulled over her blond hair, which is sticking out from the bottom in a luminous sheet and ruining the disguise. She's carrying a backpack, out of which she pulls a flashlight. "Ty?" she whispers.

She can't see me. I'm leaning against the back of the house, and the light of the half-moon doesn't reach that far into the covered porch. I step forward and she squeals in fright.

"Jesus! You scared the hell out of me."

"Sorry," I say. "You sure you want to do this?"

She huffs a little, as if I've offended her. "Whatever, you just startled me. I'm prepared for what's in *there*." She clicks on the flashlight and sets it on the top step while she opens her backpack to rummage through it. "I brought an audio recorder and a video recorder, although it probably won't pick up much in the dark." She pulls out a slim metallic device and hits the power button. A tiny red light glows at the tip. "Audio's on. I'm putting it in the outer pocket of my backpack so it'll be recording the whole time." She stuffs her video camera into her pocket and slings her backpack on again. "You ready?" she says, picking up the flashlight.

"I guess. I didn't bring any equipment."

McKenzie grins. "That's what I'm here for. This is your first ghost hunt; how would you know?"

"Uh … TV?"

McKenzie laughs and climbs the porch steps. "Don't believe everything you see on TV." The back door is locked, but McKenzie pulls a key out of her pocket.

"Where'd you get that?" I ask.

"Kelsey's mom's on the Pinnacle Ghost Tour staff. Kelsey swiped it and made a copy." She unlocks the door and pushes it open. The hinges whine, a thin, shrill noise as unpleasant as fingernails down a chalkboard. "You ready to see what Pinnacle's all about?" McKenzie asks.

There's a hint of a come-on in her voice, and despite everything, it gets to me. I wish I could see her face, but it's too dark. "You bet," I say, and I follow her inside.

Pinnacle, Colorado, bills itself as the Salem of the Rockies—
except there have never been any witches here, and it's not exactly
in the mountains. But people love that slogan, even if it's a marvel
of false advertising. Pinnacle is a dinky little town on the flat part
of Colorado (people always seem to forget about the flat part),
an hour and a half from the Rockies and a light year from San
Francisco, where I grew up. I moved here with my parents and little
sister in August when my dad got a job at a technology company.
They like to think of Colorado as a social experiment—a chance to
see the middle of America—but I think of it as time in purgatory. I
have one year left of high school, and then I'm heading back to Cali.

The only good part about being here, at least until tonight,
has been McKenzie.

She enters the kitchen and shines the flashlight around. It's
dirty and dilapidated and creepy: everything a haunted house
is supposed to be. A bunch of the bottom cabinets have rotted,
making the counters slope toward the floor. The upper cabinets
have mostly lost their doors, turning them into yawning black boxes
displaying a few pieces of chipped china. The ancient stove looks
like it hasn't been operational in decades, and the once-white sink
has reddish stains in the bottom. "Gross," McKenzie murmurs as
she looks down into the sink.

The Spruce Street Guest House is on Old Main, which was
the center of town during its heyday in the late 1800s. Back then,
when coal mining was Pinnacle's chief industry, this place was
the Wild West equivalent of a bustling metropolis, complete with

eight saloons, a brothel or two behind the tracks, and plenty of gunslingers who went around shooting people whenever they had a bad day. When the coal mine dried up, so did Pinnacle, and for a long time it really was a ghost town. During the tech boom of the nineties, it came back from the dead. Now there's a brand new "downtown" centered on a strip mall anchored by a Super Target. But the buildings on Old Main were abandoned, and they developed a reputation for being haunted by the ghosts of those gunslingers and their victims.

Personally, I think it's all a big gimmick, but the first thing I learned when I moved here was that the locals take their legends seriously. Every Halloween, Pinnacle dusts off Old Main to create a quote-unquote ghost town for the annual Pinnacle Spooktacular, a week of "family-friendly" activities celebrating the ghostly remains of the town's outlaw past. It culminates in the Spooktacular Spectacle, a dance in the ramshackle theatre on the eastern end of Old Main.

The guesthouse is on the western end. We can't hear the music down here, though I know the party's still going on. By now all the little kids have gone home, and the few teens who remain are being edged out by adults in sexy zombie nurse costumes. I saw some of them lurching around half-drunk on my way to the guesthouse.

McKenzie heads out of the kitchen and I follow. The only sounds are the whisper of our footsteps and the occasional groan of the floorboards. It's in pretty good shape for a building that's been abandoned, and I know it's because the Pinnacle Spooktacular has renovated it—discreetly, of course—to make sure that tourists don't accidentally fall through the floor on the ghost tour.

Still, it's definitely got a creepy vibe going on. We walk down the long hallway toward the front of the building, passing the door to the basement, a dining room with a crooked chandelier, the decrepit powder room, and finally the main parlor, where all the furniture is draped with yellowing sheets. In the foyer, a staircase that used to be grand sweeps down from the dark second floor, and McKenzie turns to face me.

"Have you heard the story about this place?" she asks.

I shrug. "Somebody died?"

Her lips curve up in a slight smile. "Yeah. Somebody died." She starts up the stairs. "This used to be a boarding house, and one of the people who stayed here was a woman named Ida Root. She was from the East Coast and came out here for a teaching job. She didn't have a lot of money so she ended up sharing her room with another girl, Elsie Bates. Ida came back from school late one night, after dark. She was feeling sick and decided to go straight to bed."

McKenzie stops at the top of the stairs and waits for me, the flashlight beam pooling on the floor. The last step creaks under my feet. "What happened then?" I ask.

"In the morning, Ida woke up. Elsie was right there in the room with her ... except she was dead."

McKenzie's a good storyteller, and a shiver runs down my spine.

"Somebody murdered her and wrote a message on the wall in her blood."

I step closer to McKenzie, so there's only a foot of space between us. She holds her ground, but the flashlight wavers in her hands. "What did it say?" I ask.

"That's the weird thing," McKenzie whispers. "There's no record of that. But there were plenty of rumors going around town about Ida and Elsie. Whether they were more than friends."

McKenzie's expression is unreadable, but warmth flushes across my own face, and it pisses me off. I've heard this story before, although it's usually set in a college dorm or at summer camp. I can hardly believe that McKenzie thinks I'm going to buy it.

"The room where Ida stayed is the third door down," McKenzie says. "Want to take a look?"

"You think her ghost is in there?"

"Maybe," she says coyly.

The door has an old-fashioned crystal handle, and McKenzie fumbles with it for a few seconds before she gets it open. She goes inside, but stops abruptly.

"Oh my God," she says, her voice quivering. "Oh my God."

I follow her in. The moonlight shines through the window, which is hung with lace curtains. The room has a rusted metal bedframe in it, the mattress long gone. A chipped pitcher and basin rest on a bureau that's missing half its drawers. A rocking chair is pushed into the corner, the woven seat eaten through in the center. McKenzie trains her flashlight on the wall over the bed. A word is scrawled there, red letters dripping down the peeling wallpaper.

DYKE.

A shock jolts through me, hot and cold all at once. I become aware of a dim buzzing in my ears as I stare at the word. The whole effect is, I have to admit, very well done. The drips look just like blood, and it ties in perfectly with the story McKenzie just told me, although I know that the word isn't about Ida and her maybe-girlfriend Elsie.

It's for me.

I've been to the Dyke March in San Francisco and seen women with the word tattooed on their shoulders or written across their chests in lipstick. I've never used it to describe myself because it sounds so old. But it doesn't bother me, either. It stopped offending me a long time ago.

Seeing it like this, though, is a lot different than seeing it tattooed on a girl's arm with a heart around it. I feel like I just got my breath knocked out of me. As if someone came over and shoved me, then spit in my face.

I hate Pinnacle.

All the frustrations I've felt since I moved here knot up inside me in a burst of hot anger. I want to punch the person who wrote that on the wall.

I know that McKenzie's watching me, trying to figure out why I didn't scream and run out of the room in terror. I'm not sure what to do. To buy time, I walk past her to the wall and reach out to touch the red letters. "What are you doing?" she cries.

The stuff that was used to write the word is still a little damp, and it rubs off on my fingers. I sniff it.

"What is it?" she asks.

It's sticky and has a chemical smell that I recognize. It's fake blood. They probably bought it at the Super Target in the Halloween aisle. "I don't know," I say impulsively. "It's kind of … warm."

"It's warm?" She sounds confused.

"Yeah," I lie. I rub the fake blood residue onto the wallpaper, leaving a streak next to the D. "I heard a different story about this house," I say as I turn to look at her.

She visibly stiffens. "You did?"

"I read it on the town blog."

"Oh?"

Her tone is skeptical, and I wonder if I'm pushing it too far, but the anger inside me is developing a reckless edge. "Yeah," I say. I cross the room toward the window so that I can peek at the backyard. There's nobody there, or at least, nobody I can see. "You want to hear it?"

McKenzie hesitates. Then she says, "Sure, why not." It's not a question. She's acting all cool, but I can tell she's trying to figure out if I know what she did, and if so, how.

It's so clear to me that the word on the wall isn't *real* to McKenzie. It's a four-letter word chosen for dramatic impact. She doesn't get that the word and her ghost story suggest that a woman was murdered in this room for being gay. She probably thinks it's funny. I almost choke on my disgust for McKenzie. But I force myself to swallow it, because now I know what I'm going to do.

"I read that back when this place was a boarding house, two

chicks died," I say. "One was probably the girl you told me about—the one who died in this room. But another girl died here a couple of days later." I pause for dramatic effect. "She hanged herself in the basement."

McKenzie's breath hitches, and I know I've got her.

I walk over to her and take the flashlight out of her startled hands. "What do you say we go downstairs and check it out?"

"The basement? Are you crazy?"

I hold the flashlight up so that it illuminates our faces from below, classic ghost-story style. I give her a sardonic smile—one of my best, if I must say—and she blushes. "I thought you wanted to go ghost hunting with me," I say. "Are you scared?"

"Of course not," she snaps. She crosses her arms defensively and adds, "It's just not safe down there. Kelsey's mom says the tours can't go into the basement."

I cock my head at her. "I thought you liked to live dangerously."

Her gaze flickers briefly to the window, then back again. "Fine. Let's go." She holds out her hand. "Give me back the flashlight."

"Not yet," I say, and lead the way out of the room.

"Ty!" she objects, but I don't stop, and since she doesn't want to be left in the dark, she has no choice but to follow.

A latch holds the basement door shut, and when I lift it, the door pops open with a sigh. A scent of dampness and rot wafts up from the darkness below. A chill runs over my skin, and I wonder if this is a good idea.

"It smells down there."

There's something prissy about the way she says it, and it completely annoys me. My anger comes back, hard as armor, and I'm not scared anymore. I want to do this, even if it's stupid, because if there's anybody who deserves to have their safe little bubble popped, it's McKenzie. "Come on," I say, and I point the flashlight down the narrow wooden stairs.

The basement is really more of a cellar. The floor and walls are hard-packed dirt, and the ceiling is the bare rafters supporting the floor above. When I reach the bottom I turn and shine the light up at McKenzie, who has paused halfway down.

"I don't think this is a good idea," she says.

I can practically feel the dark against my back, cool and slightly wet. But I see that she's on the verge of splitting, so I say, "There's nothing down here." To her credit, she descends the rest of the stairs, and when she steps onto the dirt floor, I offer her the flash-light. "You can be in charge now."

She takes it, and when our hands touch I notice that her fingers are freezing. She sweeps the light around. There isn't much to see. The room is small and bare, except for a pile of broken wooden crates next to the stairs. The light skitters over a door on the far wall, and I reach out to grab McKenzie's hand.

"Jeez!" she shrieks.

"Door," I say calmly, and guide the flashlight beam across the room. I start walking.

"Where are you going?"

"I want to see what's on the other side." Adrenaline is racing through me now, electric and insistent.

"You're crazy," McKenzie says, but she scurries after me, keeping the beam leveled at the door.

This one has an old metal knob, spotted with rust. I turn it and push, and at first the door sticks, as if there's something behind it. McKenzie's so close I can hear her breathing, quick and fast. Suddenly the door gives way, and the air that whooshes out is even more musty than the stuff we're breathing already.

"Ugh," McKenzie groans as she shines the flashlight inside the space.

There's something hanging from the rafters.

It moves in the light before darting back into the dark. McKenzie's hand clamps down onto my arm, her nails digging through the material of my jacket and into my skin. She's mumbling *oh my God* over and over again, pulling me away from the door.

Someone else is breathing down here.

It's not McKenzie's panicked hyperventilating, and it's not my own breath, which isn't exactly steady either. It's slower, raspier, as if it's coming from an ancient pair of lungs.

"Oh my God did you touch my back?" McKenzie whispers.

"You're holding my arm," I point out.

She shrieks and spins around, the flashlight beam jerking around the cellar. The thing hanging from the rafters moves again, and McKenzie screams and runs, dragging me with her, her fingers so tight around mine it feels like she might crush them.

Upstairs McKenzie sprints for the exit, but I pull away from her. "Ty! What are you doing?"

"Closing the door."

She doesn't wait for me. I'm alone in the hallway at the top of the basement stairs. I look back down, hesitating. And then I push the door shut and drop the latch in place. "Thanks," I whisper.

2. October 31, 10:49 PM

The Spruce Street Guest House's back yard is full of shadows. Spruce trees are clumped together in one area, and a dilapidated shed leans to one side near the brick wall at the back of the property. It's cold tonight, but at least it's not snowing. From what people have told me, it almost always snows on Halloween. I huddle in the dark corner between the shed and the wall, squatting in my increasingly frigid jeans so I don't have to sit on the even colder ground.

It's not long before the girls come through the broken section of the wooden fence along the right side of the yard. I hear their giggling before I see them, and I wonder if they realize how loud they are. I recognize Kelsey Fisher's voice as she says, "Watch out! Shh!"

Lauren Meier gasps a little, as if she's trying to stop herself from laughing. "Did your mom notice you taking the key?" She seems to be trying to whisper, but the question carries all the way across the yard.

"No," Kelsey answers. "She's so busy this time of year she barely pays attention."

"You guys are being too loud," says a third girl, and my stomach lurches when I recognize the voice. It's McKenzie. I'm not entirely surprised—she and Lauren and Kelsey are best friends, and they seem to do everything together—but I am disappointed. More than disappointed. A sharp pang goes through me, and I get mad at myself. I don't know why they're here yet. Maybe it's not what I think it is.

They run across the yard, crunching over the fallen leaves so loudly it doesn't matter that they manage not to say a word. I hear them climb the steps of the back porch, and then more furious whispering as Kelsey unlocks the door. It creaks as they push it open, and one of the girls—probably Lauren—squeals in fright.

"Shh!" McKenzie hushes them. "Let's go."

I wait till they're inside and then I follow as silently as I can. I'm a lot quieter than they are. They've left the door partly open, and I slide inside by pushing it just a little. It gives a barely noticeable groan.

I look around the kitchen. Luckily there's a half-moon shining through the windows tonight, because I can't turn on a flashlight and expose myself. I don't want them to see me. At first I don't know where they went, but then I hear them going up the stairs, and I pad softly into the hallway after them.

"Did you bring the camera?" McKenzie asks as she climbs the stairs.

"Yeah," Lauren says. "My brother showed me how to set the timer and everything."

"Cool," McKenzie says.

Once they reach the second floor they disappear into one of the bedrooms, and I tiptoe after them, flattening myself against the wall outside the room they've entered. Something thumps onto the floor, and a bag unzips.

"Give me that," McKenzie says.

"Jeez, I'm just trying to help," Lauren says.

"I want to make sure this goes off without a hitch," McKenzie says. She's definitely in charge, and the disappointment I felt earlier turns toward myself. I should've known better.

The first time I saw McKenzie was on my first day at Coal Creek High. I was walking down the hall outside the school office, reading my class schedule and trying to figure out where homeroom was, and I bumped right into her as she came out of the girls' bathroom.

"Sorry," I said. "I didn't see you."

She was wearing jeans and a white Oxford shirt, unbuttoned just enough to show a hint of cleavage. Her honey-blond hair hung in loose waves over her shoulder, and her makeup was flawless: not too much, not too little. She was as preppy as it got here in Pinnacle, and I bet she had a closet full of plaid skirts.

"It's okay," she said, and then looked at me more closely. "You're new."

"Yeah."

"I'm McKenzie Wells," she said, and smiled.

"Tyler White," I said, "but people call me Ty."

It took her a minute to figure out that I'm a girl. I knew when it happened, because this tremor went over her face, as if she was buzzed by static electricity. After that, she excused herself, clearly rattled by making such a basic mistake, and I was left standing there in the hallway as she practically fled toward the lockers and her friends.

It bugged me, sure. I'm not the butchest chick on the planet, and in San Francisco, enough people look like me that I'm not an anomaly. But in Pinnacle, girls don't wear boys' clothes and have short hair. I think it's my walk that confuses them the most, though. Girls usually have this swaying motion when they move, so that even from far away, it's obvious they're girls. But I've never walked like that. I walk like my dad.

I think she would have just avoided me from then on, but her last name is Wells and mine is White, so we were assigned seats next to each other in Physics and Study Hall. She was nice enough to me in class, but it wasn't like we were friends. And her friends didn't talk to me. Only she did—usually when they weren't around. She had this way of looking at me, though—kind of under her eyelashes when she thought I wouldn't notice—that made me think she thought I was cute.

I should've known better.

I hear McKenzie and Lauren arguing over where to place the camera. "We can attach it to the ledge here," Lauren says.

"It's just going to poke out if we put it there," McKenzie objects.

They decide to stick it on the top of the window. "The tape will hold it," Lauren says. "We have to point the lens down. Nobody's going to be able to see it in the dark."

Their lights bob inside the room as they rig the camera over the window. And then Kelsey says, "Look what I got to write on the wall."

Lauren and McKenzie make appreciative sounds. Kelsey wants to do it, but ultimately McKenzie prevails. "I'll use my own hands. It'll look awesome."

"Ty's gonna freak," Kelsey says gleefully.

"Do you think it's too much?" Lauren asks, sounding hesitant.

"Nah," McKenzie says dismissively. "It's a joke. Wait'll we post the video. Everybody's gonna love it. We have to do a Halloween prank—we live in Pinnacle."

A Halloween prank. I feel sick to my stomach. This is why McKenzie asked me to meet her here: to play a joke on me. I suspected something like this—that's why I got here so early—but the confirmation sinks inside me like lead weights.

I could go home right now. Stand her up. Never speak to her again. But even though the idea of running is extremely tempting, I'm also pissed. McKenzie Wells might rule the school, but she doesn't rule me.

When I hear them finishing up I slide farther down the hall, edging into the room next door. It's empty, but out of the corner of my eye I see something move. I almost jump out of my skin before I realize it's a mirror: one of those old-fashioned ones on a wooden stand. Somebody left a damn mirror behind. I let out my breath slowly, hoping the girls can't hear me.

After they leave I walk down the dark hall, back to the room they outfitted with the camera. I want to check it out, but then I realize I'll be caught on tape. Crap. Something in the house creaks, and the hairs on the back of my neck stand straight up.

I don't even have a flashlight.

I decide to head outside to wait for my date with McKenzie, and I book it down the stairs in my haste to leave.

3. October 31, 9:02 PM

The tour guide gathers us on the sidewalk outside the guesthouse. This is the second-to-last stop on the tour; after this he'll lead everybody back to the Pinnacle Theatre for the Spooktacular Spectacle. I stand on the edge of the group, the hood of my new winter jacket pulled up. The crowd is mostly adults, but there are three boys about my age nearby.

"This is the Spruce Street Guest House," the tour guide says, "which operated from 1886 to 1923, and then was briefly turned into a sanatorium before it shut down in 1929. While it was a guesthouse, it was operated by Maud Collins, a woman who married a much older man who had made it rich in the gold rush. When he died, she took her inheritance and bought this place, intending to turn it into a high-class hotel. Unfortunately for Maud, Pinnacle was never quite as sophisticated as she hoped."

The tour guide laughs dryly, but the crowd is getting restless. The boys whisper to each other behind cupped hands. I don't recognize them from school, but lots of people from the neighboring towns come to Pinnacle on Halloween night.

The guide clears his throat. "The Spruce Street Guest House is home to at least one ghost, which was documented three years ago on camera by a ghost-hunting team from the cable TV show *Ghost Seekers*." The boys shut up, and I shift a little closer to the front. "Before I tell you more about the ghost, let's go on inside and take a peek, shall we?"

An excited murmur goes through the crowd. So far we've only been inside two other buildings—both of them saloons—and this house is way bigger. The tour guide leads us up the path to the front door, which he unlocks and pushes open with a dramatic creak. I wonder if that was staged. The guide switches on an electric lantern and ushers us inside. A few of the tourists pull out their own flashlights, and we crowd into the foyer.

The guide starts up the staircase and tells us to gather around. I stand in the doorway to the front parlor, eyeing the slip-covered furniture uneasily. In the pale light of the lantern, the armchairs look like monsters. The guide begins to tell us about the history of the guesthouse and how Maud Collins was picky about the boarders she allowed to stay here, how she had rules about how late the women could stay out, and whether they could be seated next to the men during meals. The boys are clumped together a few feet away from me, talking in low voices and not paying attention.

I don't blame them. Everybody wants to hear about the ghost, but the tour guide wants to set the scene. I zone out because I already read about the history of this place last week, after McKenzie asked me if I wanted to meet her here on Halloween night. Her invitation, during Study Hall, was delivered so casually that at first I didn't get it, and she had to ask again.

"It's a Pinnacle tradition," she said with a flirty smile as she tossed her ponytail. "Every newbie has to go ghost hunting on Halloween night."

"Really?" I said, not sure if I should believe her.

"Yeah. It's really fun."

"Have you ever done it before?"

She shrugged. "It's not my first time." She gave me a conspiratorial grin and leaned across the library table toward me. "I'll bring some of my mom's secret stash of vodka and we'll make screwdrivers and stuff."

I wondered if she understood what this sounded like. Me and her, in an abandoned house on Halloween night, drinking vodka. "You aren't worried about your reputation?" I said, a slight smile on my face.

She rolled her eyes. "Oh, come on. You can tell me all about your life in California and I can introduce you to Pinnacle's finest ghosts."

I studied her face for a minute. She was all shiny-eyed confidence, and warmth spread through me as I thought about it. Yeah, I wanted to spend Halloween night with McKenzie Wells in an abandoned house drinking vodka. I definitely wanted to do that. "Okay," I said, and something like triumph flashed over her face before she gave me a dazzling smile.

"Awesome."

But that brief flash of triumph I saw stuck with me, chipping into my anticipation over spending Halloween night alone with McKenzie. The only time we'd gotten together outside of school was to work on a physics report at the library. This was totally different. As much as I wanted to believe McKenzie wasn't entirely straight, I didn't think I should count on it. So I did some research on the guesthouse, just in case. I might be new to Pinnacle, but I wasn't born yesterday.

That's why I decided to go on the ghost tour. I figured I'd get a sneak peek at the place before McKenzie showed up. I like to be prepared.

The guide finally finishes his boring recital of the guesthouse's history and says, "Let's head upstairs and I'll tell you all about the ghost, all right?" We follow him down the hallway and crowd into a room overlooking the street. There's nothing in the room but an ancient armchair that nobody moves to sit in. "I've brought you in here because we can't all fit into room number three down the hall, which is the site of one of the two deaths that this guesthouse is known for."

He tells us that in the fall of 1897, two young women boarded here, one of them a teacher, the other a seamstress. They shared a room because neither of them could afford their own, and because back then it was safer for two women to board together than alone. One night, the teacher came back from work to discover that the seamstress was dead—shot by a gunslinger who mistook her for a prostitute who had turned him down. A few days later, the teacher herself died.

"She took her own life," the tour guide says, and the whole group is silent. "We'll never know why she decided to do it. Perhaps her delicate feminine sensibilities were too upset by the untimely death of her roommate. Just before Halloween, she hanged herself in the cellar."

A noticeable shiver ripples through the crowd, and I wrap my arms around myself.

"Now, who's up for checking out the deceased's room?" the tour guide says cheerfully. Nervous laughter titters through the group. "It's pretty small, so you'll need to take it in groups of four or five."

Everybody starts moving toward the hallway, and since I'm on the edge of the group I get pushed out of the room first, bumping into one of the boys standing just outside the door. They're all wearing puffy down jackets and ski hats, and I separate them out as Tall, Medium, and Short.

"Dude, watch out," Tall says.

"Sorry."

"Hey, do you go to Westfield?" he asks. "I don't recognize you."

"I go to Coal Creek," I say, pitching my voice lower. I know he doesn't realize I'm not a guy, and I don't think I want to deal with him figuring it out. A thick rush of homesickness fills me.

I'm so sick of being new all the time. I miss my friend Jada with her blue hair, and Kendall who's obsessed with anime. I miss the warm weather and I miss—God, I miss Angie. Even if she never really liked me that way, at least she didn't think it was crazy that I liked her.

The shortest of the three guys comes back from looking over the railing at the foyer, and says, "Hey, do you remember seeing that door down there? I bet it leads to the basement. Wanna go check it out?"

"That's where the tour guide said that chick killed herself," Tall says.

"Duh," says Short. "That's why we should go down there."

"Yeah, let's go," says Medium enthusiastically. "This tour is boring."

Tall gestures at me. "Hey, dude, wanna come?"

I glance over my shoulder at the tour guide, but he's busy corralling the crowd in small groups into the bedroom. "Yeah, okay." The guys are right. This tour is boring, and I want to check out the rest of the house before McKenzie shows up.

We go back down the stairs as quietly as possible.

"What's your name?" Tall asks.

"Ty."

"Hey. I'm Brian. This is Chad and that's Jason."

"Hi," I say, nodding to them.

"What are you doing on this tour?" Brian asks.

"Just moved here. Wanted to see what it was about."

Jason's already at the door they spotted. It has a latch holding it shut, and when he lifts it, the door springs open. "Whoa," he says, and shines his flashlight down the stairs. I see dirt at the bottom; the basement's not finished.

"That's creepy, man," Brian says.

Chad is apparently the one with the most need to prove himself, because he shoves his way to the front and says, "Whatever. Don't be a chicken." He heads down the stairs, and Brian and Jason chuckle nervously before following.

I trail them down the steps into the cellar, the smell of damp dirt surrounding me. The space is pretty small, but as they shine their flashlights around the room, I spot a door on the far wall.

"Check that out," Chad says. "That is awesome."

I try to suppress the shiver that runs over me, but I can't. I'm not cold, exactly, but there's definitely something eerie about the air down here. It feels thick against my face, as if I'm walking through fog.

Even Jason seems a little freaked out. "Dude, do you really—"

But by then Chad has already crossed the basement and opened the door in the wall, and the scent that spills out is foul.

"Something must've died in there," Brian says.

We all go stiff with silence, until Chad says, "Yeah, dude, like a rat."

Jason gives a nervous laugh and joins Chad at the threshold. They sweep their lights through the space. I'm standing behind them, beside Brian, but I can see a little. It's a big room; I think it goes underneath the whole house. There are several piles of furniture in it, chairs and tables and an old tufted armchair that must have once been pretty nice, but is now clearly a nest for whatever died.

Something flutters at the edge of the flashlight and Chad curses out loud, bumping into Jason. "Dude, get away from me," Jason growls.

"Shut up—check that out." Chad shines the light up and for one terrifying second I think there's a body hanging from the rafters. "It's a sheet," Chad says triumphantly. "Somebody tied a freaking sheet to the ceiling."

The boys start laughing, and I join in—I can't help it—it's just a sheet nailed to the rafters. It's not a ghost at all; it just looks like one.

Something touches my back, and I glance over at Brian, who's closest to me, but he's at least three or four feet away.

I freeze.

There's something behind me. I want to turn around but I'm paralyzed. The boys are joking about how someone got that sheet up there in the first place. They don't notice that I've stopped laughing. The impression of five fingers on my skin—even though I'm wearing my own puffy jacket—is unmistakable. And then I feel someone lean over my shoulder, an unseen weight bending toward my head. I feel breath against my ear. Even though I want to scream, I don't, because of that *hand* pressing against me as if to say, *don't say a word.*

Suddenly the door slams shut, and Chad and Jason and Brian shriek and leap back. One of them trips on something and falls onto his butt, his hands scrabbling in the dirt, and *still* I'm unable to move. I'm stuck in place as if roots have grown out of my feet and dug into the ground.

"Move, move, move!" Brian shouts as they race toward the stairs.

Their feet pound up the steps, and I'm alone in the dark with this thing.

The breath on my ear is like a kiss: cold lips against my warm skin. I know I should be scared. I should be pissing my pants with terror. But the feeling that sweeps through me isn't fear; it's awe. There's something *real* down here in the cellar. Something that upends everything I've ever believed about life and what comes after.

As if this entity, whatever or whoever it is, can sense my wonder, the fingertips slide over the small of my back in a cool caress. It's almost inviting. And for some reason I remember that day in the library with McKenzie and our physics homework. It was just the two of us, with nobody there to see the way she looked at me. Her flirty grin, her body angled toward me, leaning into the possibility.

I don't want to leave.

Something on the other side of the door in the wall thumps, like someone's knocking. *Get. Out.*

Cold ripples across my skin as I realize there isn't only one entity in this cellar. There are two. And one of them does not want me here.

The hand on my back shoves me toward the stairs, unsticking me from the ground.

I run.

December

By Neil Gaiman

S ummer on the streets is hard, but you can sleep in a park in the summer without dying from the cold. Winter is different. Winter can be lethal. And even if it isn't, the cold still takes you as its special homeless friend, and it insinuates itself into every part of your life.

Donna had learned from the old hands. The trick, they told her, is to sleep wherever you can during the day—the Circle line is good, buy a ticket and ride all day, snoozing in the carriage, and so are the kinds of cheap cafes where they don't mind an eighteen year old girl spending fifty pence on a cup of tea and then dozing off in a corner for an hour or three, as long as she looks more or less respectable—but to keep moving at night, when the temperatures plummet, and the warm places close their doors, and lock them, and turn off the lights.

It was nine at night and Donna was walking. She kept to well-lit areas, and she wasn't ashamed to ask for money. Not any more. People could always say no, and mostly they did.

There was nothing familiar about the woman on the street corner. If there had been, Donna wouldn't have approached her. It was her nightmare, someone from Biddenden seeing her like this: the shame, and the fear that they'd tell her mum (who never said much, who only said "good riddance" when she heard gran had died) and then her mum would tell her dad, and he might just come down here and look for her, and try to bring her home. And that would break her. She didn't ever want to see him again.

The woman on the corner had stopped, puzzled, and was looking around as if she was lost. Lost people were sometimes good for change, if you could tell them the way to where they wanted to go.

Donna stepped closer, and said, "Spare any change?"

The woman looked down at her. And then the expression on her face changed and she looked like... Donna understood the cliché then, understood why people would say *She looked like she had seen a ghost*. She did. The woman said, "*You?*"

"Me?" said Donna. If she had recognised the woman she might have backed away, she might even have run off, but she didn't know her. The woman looked a little like Donna's mum, but kinder, softer, plump where Donna's mum was pinched. It was hard to see what she really looked like because she was wearing thick black winter clothes, and a thick woollen bobble cap, but her hair beneath the cap was as orange as Donna's own.

The woman said, "Donna." Donna would have run then, but she didn't, she stayed where she was because it was just too crazy, too unlikely, too ridiculous for words.

The woman said, "Oh god. Donna. You are you, aren't you? I remember." Then she stopped. She seemed to be blinking back tears.

Donna looked at the woman, as an unlikely, ridiculous idea filled her head, and she said, "Are you who I think you are?"

The woman nodded. "I'm you," she said. "Or I will be. One day. I was walking this way remembering what it was like back when I … when you…" Again she stopped. "Listen. It won't be like this for you for ever. Or even for very long. Just don't do anything stupid. And don't do anything permanent. I promise it will be all right. Like the YouTube videos, you know? *It Gets Better*."

"What's a you tube?" asked Donna.

"Oh, lovey," said the woman. And she put her arms around Donna and pulled her close and held her tight.

"Will you take me home with you?" asked Donna.

"I can't," said the woman. "Home isn't there for you yet. You haven't met any of the people who are going to help you get off the street, or help you get a job. You haven't met the person who's going to turn out to be your partner. And you'll both make a place that's safe, for each other and for your children. Somewhere warm."

Donna felt the anger rising inside her. "Why are you telling me this?" she asked.

"So you know it gets better. To give you hope."

Donna stepped back. "I don't want hope," she said. "I want somewhere warm. I want a home. I want it now. Not in twenty years."

A hurt expression on the placid face. "It's sooner than twen—"

"I don't *care!* It's not tonight. I don't have anywhere to go. And I'm *cold*. Have you got any change?"

The woman nodded. "Here," she said. She opened her purse and took out a twenty pound note. Donna took it, but the money didn't look like any currency she was familiar with. She looked back at the woman to ask her something, but she was gone, and when Donna looked back at her hand, so was the money.

She stood there shivering. The money was gone, if it had ever been there. But she had kept one thing: she knew it would all work out someday. In the end. And she knew that she didn't need to do anything stupid. She didn't have to buy one last Underground ticket just to be able to jump down onto the tracks when she saw a train coming, too close to stop.

The winter wind was bitter, and it bit her and it cut her to the bone, but still, she spotted something blown up against a shop doorway, and she reached down and picked it up: a five pound note. Perhaps tomorrow would be easier. She didn't have to do any of the things she had imagined herself doing.

December could be lethal, when you were out on the streets. But not this year. Not tonight.

An Echo in the Shell

By Beth Cato

Despite the bitter autumn chill, Jonah's kiss warmed Allison's lips and sent unaccustomed heat swirling through her belly. Gravity didn't weigh her steps as she hopped up to the front porch. He had kissed her. He had held her hand and kissed her. Allison squealed and spun in a dizzying circle.

Feet away, the walls of her house shuddered. Something heavy smacked against the inner window, unseen behind the thick cover of nailed plywood. In that instant, the heat from the kiss evaporated and reality grounded her like an anvil.

Grandma.

Allison flung open the screen and fumbled with the key to unlock the doorknob and both deadbolts. She jumped inside.

Glass squealed and crunched beneath her flats.

"Shut the door!" screamed Mom.

Allison kicked the door shut and slammed the locks in place. Grandma's solid weight impacted against Allison's back, sending a gush of air from her lungs. The doorknob gouged her gut. Grandma's knobby fingers inched up her arms towards her neck. The buzzing sound grew louder; the earthy, indefinable odor more potent.

Then Mom was there. With a sharp squeal, Grandma released her hold. Allison slipped around just in time to catch Grandma as she slumped to the ground. Mom stood there, panting, her hair electrocution-wild. A syringe gleamed in her hand.

"She took an extra long nap and was too quiet when she woke up and then I couldn't catch her." Mom blew stray hair from her lips, tears filling her eyes. "Her first Kafka rage."

"So how long were you chasing her—oh." As Allison heaved Grandma onto the couch, she finally had a good look at the room. Broken glass littered the floor. Two side-tables lay broken, one leg embedded in the wall like a spear. Through the arched doorway to the dining room, she saw more overturned chairs and the light of the gaping refrigerator door. Grandma had broken things before or tried to bust out, run towards lights outside, but nothing like this.

The rage. The next symptoms ... no

"Oh, Grandma." Allison stroked Grandma's shorn scalp.

"Looks like she has some cuts and bruises. I need to take pictures of her and the room and then I can sweep up this glass."

"You should have called me," Allison said.

"Like I had a chance," Mom snapped. "But no, you had to go on your little date. I hope you enjoyed it, because you aren't having another one for a long time. She always seems to respond best to you." Mom gnawed at her inner cheek as she stared at Grandma.

"Mom! That's not fair!"

"Life's not fair. You're sixteen, Allison. You'll have plenty of time for boys and all that nonsense later on. Go grab the digital camera for me."

Glass crunched underfoot as Allison stalked towards the hall. Like Mom had any place talking to her about boys, seeing how Dad left, seeing how Mom hadn't even attempted a date since Y2K.

But maybe Mom was right, too. Maybe Grandma had missed Allison. Maybe that was why she flipped out. Maybe this wasn't "the rage" doctors talked about. Maybe it was something ... weird. A tantrum. That's all.

She made a slight detour to shut the fridge and reset the child-proof latch. The office door was open, which meant Mom must have been working when Grandma's rampage started. No surprise there. Mom tried to squeeze in freelancing whenever she could. The monitor was darkened in screensaver mode, the green light beneath blinking like a heartbeat. Allison grabbed the camera from its dock.

She took pictures as she walked through the house. A new hole in the wall. She stopped in the doorway to the living room and took in an empty spot on a high bookshelf. That broken glass used to be her great-great grandmother's vase. The one that used to be Grandma's favorite.

It was just a vase.

There were no curtains over the board-covered windows. A Plexiglas shield covered the TV, and that was frosted and scratched. Any shelves were bolted to the walls, cupboards secured with childproofing snaps and locks. Mom leaned against an open cabinet beside the TV, set something inside, and shut the door. A shot of whiskey, probably. As if Allison didn't know. Mom would probably finish off the bottle when Allison was in bed and bury the evidence at the bottom of the recycling bin, as usual.

Grandma sat up on the couch. Her eyelids blinked as she stared dully into space. Her crudely-shorn hair lay flat against her skull, dull metal grey against pasty skin. Her shadow cast against the front door revealed the truth. Long antennae curved from her head and arced a foot in height. Two mandibles protruded from her face and worked at the air. From her shoulders, diaphanous wings clung to her back and stretched the length of her body and through the couch itself. None of that was visible to the human eye, of course. Not yet. Light revealed the strengthening curse, that Grandma's body had become the husk of a soul-stealing bug.

That was the proof that Grandma suffered from Kafka Syndrome.

★

Grandma used to be Loretta Christiansen. Retired letter carrier for the United States Postal Service. Sunday school teacher for thirty-five years. Widow of Johann Christiansen. Mother of one. Grandmother of one. Game show junkie.

Really, when Allison thought of her grandma and who she truly was, her game shows were the first thing that came to mind.

"Come on, you banana brain," Grandma would yell at the TV. "The answer's the Mississippi River! The Amazon isn't even on this continent." Grandma had declared that Alex Trebek was dead to her after he shaved off his mustache.

Funny and old game shows were the best of all. Checkered bell bottom pants and big hair were standard issue, along with cheesy orange studio sets. Allison was crestfallen at age ten when she realized no other kids knew about *Match Game 75* and Charles Nelson Reilly or the hilarity of the Whammies on *Press Your Luck*.

Oh, how Grandma would laugh as she watched, light and feminine and free, and descend into giggles and wheezes.

One day as Grandma and Allison walked the two blocks from school, Allison saw Grandma's shadow. The horns were mere nubs then, the wings like little fists from her shoulders.

Allison wasn't scared. She reached for Grandma's hand and squeezed, and stood close enough so that the shadow couldn't be seen.

The curse had been on Grandma and others for decades and the victims never even knew. Back in the early '70s, some group of animal rights radicals laid a sleeper curse on laboratory workers in five states. Their goal: make the workers become their own test subjects. By the time the illness manifested in shadows decades later, there was nothing magic or medical science could do.

Grandma had delivered mail to all the labs within the complex. For some reason, the Asian cockroach room's curse was the one that clung to her soul. Ate it away.

But Allison swore that sometimes a flash of clarity returned to Grandma's eyes. Sure, she might not be able to talk anymore, or laugh. She ate with her fingers gathered like pincers. Sometimes she hissed when surprised. And at dusk, she fixated on the lights outside, especially the ones reflecting on the lake behind the house—so they boarded up the windows. That attraction made the Asian cockroach different from other kinds. They hungered for light.

They were also supposed to be really strong flyers.

Allison refused to think about that final stage. It was a long way off. But there were only some five thousand people under the curse, a few hundred with the Kafka variant. No one knew the exact timeline. Doctors said that most would die during that final physical transition, anyway.

Until then, Allison had Grandma to love and care for, and that was all that mattered.

The next morning, the house looked normal again. Spartan. The sharp stink of fresh paint made Allison's nose run.

With the phone to her ear, Mom paced along the bay window in the dining room. "I know you're still building the Kafka wing, but this was her first big incident of the rage. Yes, I read the report—no, we aren't sending her to that lab. The whole point of that curse was to force her to be some lab animal, damn it!" She took in a deep breath. "Sorry. Sorry. She signed a living will before—uh huh. I'm sorry. Last night was just really rough and…"

Oh. Mom was talking with the people at that special home for National Lab curse patients. It was down near the University of Washington. A really nice place. They were building it for compatibility with a dozen different curses-in-progress.

Mom's voice slurred. Maybe the person on the phone wouldn't notice. Allison's stomach clenched in a knot. She hated mornings now.

Mom trailed a hand down her face. "Yes. Yes. Thank you." She pressed a button on her phone and set it down on the table, staring at it between her fingers.

"No progress?" Allison asked.

Mom's lips worked for a second and she shook her head. "They can't build it any faster. Other than that, they said we can sedate her more if necessary. I just…" She looked away, blinking, her head bobbing slightly. "Hey, don't you have that biology test today?"

"That was last week. But all of my homework is done. I had everything taken care of before my date, remember?"

"Oh yes. Your date. That's right, it's Monday morning." Mom stared at where the calendar used to hang. Now only a few gouges from tacks marked the spot. "I'm losing my mind."

"You could drink less." Allison tried to keep her voice light.

"That's none of your business." Mom made no such attempt at levity.

"It is if I hear you slurring like this first thing in the morning."

Mom sucked in a sharp breath, the sound so like Grandma's cockroach hiss that it sent a rush of cold along Allison's spine. "How dare you. I'm an adult. I'm in complete control of how much I drink. It helps me sleep. Last night I needed all the help I could get, after that."

Allison grabbed an apple from the fridge and made a quick retreat towards the front door. She couldn't bear to even look at Mom.

Grandma was still asleep on the couch, her jaw gaped open. Asleep, she looked so normal.

"Hey Grandma," Allison whispered, her throat hot with tension. "I've gotta go to school. I'll miss you. Maybe this afternoon we can hang out?" Without waiting for an answer, she planted a kiss on Grandma's forehead. It was a shame the game show channel had changed their whole line-up a few months before. All their old shows were shuffled around.

"Allison. She's gone. This is just a shell—"

"Don't say it. I'm sick of you saying that."

"Reality's going to crash down hard on you when it comes, Allison. You can't be in denial forever."

"Denial? I know Grandma's sick—"

"She's not sick, damn it, she's gone! Dead! That's not her on the couch, get it?"

It was the whiskey, it was that stupid whiskey that made Mom all awful every morning. Allison backed up to the front door, her nails digging into flesh of the apple in her palm. She swung her backpack onto one shoulder and fled. She hit the sidewalk running fast enough that the tears tipped from her eyes and flew away without touching her cheeks.

"Come on, Grandma. It's time to get ready for bed."

With her hand curled beneath Grandma's armpit, Allison walked her down the hall. They staggered together, Grandma's steps small and shuffling. She fitted Grandma in fresh disposable underwear and a pink paisley nightgown that snapped up the sides. Then she guided Grandma to her room. Mattresses sat on a bare concrete floor. Scratches gouged the walls. Allison tried not to see it, tried not to compare the room to how it used to be with its dense '70s wood furniture and Currier & Ives prints on the walls.

She tucked in the old woman, taking care to layer the blankets and cover her wrinkled feet.

Allison laid a hand against Grandma's cheek. By Mom's account, it had been an okay day. Nothing good, nothing bad. Allison's day—well.

"Jonah asked me to go out with him on Friday," Allison whispered. "I didn't say no, not straight out. I mean… I know how he'd react. He's a cool guy, really. But…" She could only say "no" so many times. Most of her old friends had moved on for that very reason, or were content with just hanging out at school, never mentioning the possibility of anything after.

"It's hard sometimes, you know? But I know Mom won't let me go."

Grandma's teeth bared in a grimace. If her shadow had been visible, no doubt those pincers would be working as if they could bite. But there was no shadow. Just Grandma.

"Good night, Grandma. I love you." She planted a kiss on her forehead.

Allison shut the door and bolted it on the outside.

Mom was holed up in her office, working frantically on her work backlog. Probably would be until late. Allison disgorged her backpack's contents onto the couch and turned on the TV. She had already gotten a decent start on her homework by staying late after school—not like she was in a rush to get home for more quality time with Mom—but the terrors of algebra awaited.

Out of habit, she picked up the remote and flicked it to the game show channel.

"—*Match Game* Marathon!" boomed an overly-pleasant announcer.

Allison's head jerked up.

A *Match Game* Marathon this Friday. Twenty-four solid hours of bell-bottoms and orange shag goodness. Grandma would love this!

From the office, the chatter of computer keys continued, punctuated by dark, indecipherable mutters.

Mom wouldn't agree. Mom would say it was pointless, that

Grandma wasn't in there, that it was all just a waste of time. She would yell and rant and do everything she could to make sure the TV stayed off. Allison's hand clenched the remote as if she could strangle the plastic. Grandma would love this marathon. If anything could coax her out of her shell, this would be it. Mom had even said Grandma responded best to her.

Mom needed to be out of the house that night.

Grinning, she reached for the phone and dialed up Mom's best friend, a friend who'd already pestered Mom for months to cut loose and relax for sanity's sake. "Hey, Shayna?" she said. "Allison here. Mom's really needing a break. You think we can tag team her?"

A few minutes later, she hung up. A devious plot was already underway. Shayna knew how to score tickets for some overnight bed and breakfast deal over in Leavenworth this Friday night. If Shayna had already shelled out the money, Mom would be more likely to cave in and go. It'd still take a few days to wear her down, but Allison knew it would work. On some level, Mom knew she needed a break, too. This was the excuse.

Allison finished up her homework as the TV droned in the background. For the first time in ages, she hummed aloud, a smile on her lips. This Friday was going to be the awesomest night ever, for all of them.

When Allison crawled into bed, she was still smiling. An incessant buzzing sound shivered through the wall. Grandma slept one room over, her breathing like a mob of a thousand mosquitoes.

Down the hallway, the door clicked open. From the living room came the soft thud of the opening liquor cabinet and the clink of glass. Mom was getting ready for bed, then.

Allison stared at the blackness of the ceiling. Her happiness dwindled away as a sick knot resumed its normal place in her stomach. Mom was the one who was really gone, not Grandma.

The terrible susurrus continued from next door, from Grandma. "It's just buzzing," Allison whispered, as if saying it aloud made it true.

She drifted to sleep, and the buzzing droned on.

"I shouldn't go." Mom clutched her suitcase handle and paced the living room. "You know what happened on Sunday—"

"She's been fine all week. If it gets to be too much, I'll call 9-1-1," Allison said. "Now go. If Shayna has to shut off her car to come get you, the neighbors might call 9-1-1 before you even leave."

Mom laughed, the sound abrupt and nervous. "Yeah. Riding tied up in the trunk might look suspicious."

"Go." Allison held open the door and pointed to the sidewalk.

Mom ducked her head like a chastised child, casting glances over her shoulder as she walked halfway along the path. "If you need me—"

"I'll call. Go!"

Allison bolted the door and stood there, shivering. It was going to be awful cold tonight. Through the peephole, she watched the car drive away. Mom was probably crying now, apologizing to Shayna, saying she shouldn't go. Shayna would keep driving.

"Well, Grandma, this is our big night," said Allison.Grandma sat on the couch with a slack jaw. Her dead eyes stared ahead at the television.

"That's right, it's TV time! We've already missed some twelve hours of the marathon. We're slacking." She powered on the television and squealed as she sat down beside Grandma. "Look at Charles Nelson Reilly in that snazzy red suit! Geez, I think I saw Brett Somer's dress on sale at the mall last week. And you said the '70s would never come back in fashion."

Grandma buzzed softly. Allison leaned against her knees and giggled as she watched. "Oh, gosh. I'm surprised that comment made it past the censors then. That was awfully double-edged, even for now." Rain drummed a soft rhythm above their heads. Another episode came on, then another.

"That was a cop-out answer. That could have been smarter or funnier." Allison shot a furtive glance at Grandma, in search of agreement.

"Charles Nelson Reilly! Best player ever! Remember when I showed you the song Weird Al made all about him? Wasn't it awesome?

"That hair. Crazy. Did she stick her finger in a light socket or what?"

Buzzing answered. Only buzzing.

Two hours passed; three.

Grandma's laughter wasn't there. Grandma wasn't there.

Allison turned off the television. She stared at the black screen. Through the marred protective glass, she could see their reflections. Grandma's expression never changed.

Grandma was really gone.

The realization was quiet. Cold. Back when the diagnosis first came, Allison had tried to joke that the curse wasn't real until Grandma had wings. Now she understood. It wasn't about how Grandma looked, or even her shadow. It was about ... Grandma.

She stood. In the blank screen, she saw Grandma stand as well. Grandma pivoted, hunch-backed, and dove at the taped-together lamp on the end table. It crashed to the carpet, and in a blink, the room was cast into darkness.

"Grandma?" No. This wasn't Grandma, not really. It wore her skin, but soon, it wouldn't even wear that. Mom had injected Grandma before she left—her regular dose with a little extra.

It wasn't enough to quell the rage.

There was a long, cockroach hiss and the shuffling of feet and Grandma was there, those hands scratching at Allison's neck.

She sidestepped. Grandma grunted, swinging towards her. Allison retreated towards the TV. Lamp shards skittered and crunched underfoot. Pain pierced the sole of her right foot, followed by the intense warmth of blood.

In scant grey light, Grandma advanced, her feet wide like a sumo wrestler. Her mouth gaped, glare reflecting from her teeth. Her gaze—empty. No hatred. No malice. Allison was just ... a thing. A target. Prey?

Grandma was gone. Dead. She was dead. She wasn't in that body anymore.

Anger rippled through Allison and clogged her throat. Anger at the hippies and their curse, anger at Mom and her alcohol and her work, anger at doctors for doing nothing. Anger at Grandma.

"You were supposed to fight this!" Allison yelled. "You're supposed to still be in … there!"

Grandma launched herself forward. Allison slipped aside, her bloodied foot tacky on the carpet, and Grandma plowed into the liquor cabinet. It rattled, glass tinkling and liquid jostling.

Allison hated that cabinet. Hated it. She turned, throwing her shoulder into the cabinet. It rocked against the wall, unable to fall because of the straps securing it in place. She hugged it with both arms and yanked with all of her body weight. The cabinet pulled from the wall. Then Grandma was there, tackling her. Allison met the next wall with a grunt. The cabinet crashed into the carpet at Grandma's heels.

Mom could buy more alcohol. She undoubtedly would. But there was something amazing about hearing those bottles shatter. There was just enough light to see a gush of dark fluid seep through to the floor, as if the cabinet itself bled.

"You should have laughed during *Match Game*," Allison whispered. "You would have laughed."

How long would the curse drag on? How many months, years? How long would this thing wear Grandma's skin? How long until—that Asian cockroach emerged? The wings. The antennae.

The shadow come to life. And Mom—how would Mom change? What facade would she wear?

Nausea punched her in the stomach. Suddenly it was all real. All too real. Grandma hissed, and Allison stepped back. Her bare feet kicked through more pieces of the lamp. Pain zinged all the way up her leg and caused her to gasp. If she made it across the room to the switch, Grandma would go for the light instead. That would distract her until...

Light. Outside, the light would be on down at the dock. A light that attracted clouds of bugs.

The awfulness of the thought froze her for a moment. Then the fumes of weeping liquor stung at her nostrils, and she knew what she would do.

She glanced at the door to the back patio. The story poured into her head: she would say she heard that old tom cat on the porch, that she opened her door to check. That Grandma attacked her. It was close to the truth. That they had fought throughout the room and then ended up back at the door. The door that lead to the stairs and the lake and the light and the cold, rainy night.

Allison staggered across the room and towards the door. Grandma's nails gouged at her neck. An earring ripped free from Allison's lobe. She worked the locks as Grandma's body dragged from her arm. The door swung free, iciness a wave over her skin.

Grandma hissed, grabbing Allison's neck with both hands, and shoved. Allison's head met the hardness of the doorjamb. Stars danced in the middle of the room as she fell to her knees. The loosened snaps of Grandma's gown clacked at Allison's head level.

"You're free," Allison whispered. "Go."

Then, the old woman was out the door, her bare feet smacking on wet cement. Allison forced her head to turn.

Rain fell in wavering sheets. Out on the nearby lake dock, a single yellow light stood as a sentinel. Grandma, hunched, was like a gray shadow in the blackness as she scurried away. The unsnapped gown trailed behind her like wings. Then she met the stairs. She tumbled, feet over head. Allison listened to the rasps of her own breaths. Grandma's head was visible again, barely. She still worked towards that brightness below, just like the Asian cockroach she was.

Allison could have screamed for help. She would have, if Grandma had been somewhere within that frail shell.

A slow ooze of blood coursed Allison's cheek. She lowered herself to the frigid linoleum before the door. The gallop of her heart was louder than the buzzing had ever been. She quivered as she heard a distant splash, and clenched her eyes shut. The light from the dock still burned through the blackness, and as the minutes passed and the chill sank in, the relentless rhythm of the rain soothed her like a lullaby.

Dan's Dreams

By Eliza Victoria

Dan used a cheat sheet for the first time for his last set of exams before graduation. He was slogging through senior year as a scholar in a science high school where grades meant everything, and he needed near-perfect scores to maintain the top spot. Pressure was high for him to be valedictorian and get a scholarship for college. His mother said so in not so many words when the acceptance letter from UP arrived in the mail. UP was the cheapest among the big universities, but a thousand pesos a unit would be a big blow to his family's finances. If he graduated valedictorian he'd get an excellent shot at getting a scholarship. That was how Dan thought about his life those days. His thinking pattern resembled overlapping circles, a stray dog that couldn't get rid of its leash. Scores, valedictorian, scholarship, college. Round and round it went. In the end he did more worrying than studying, so he got up at dawn and scribbled a cheat sheet for the Physics exam.

He was not caught. He put the cheat sheet in his clear plastic envelope, and put the envelope under Samantha's chair right in front of him. If the proctor glanced at him, she'd only see him staring hard at the floor, thinking, thinking, because he was Dan, number one, the whiz who brought home gold at the Science Camp. All of the Physics formulae were crammed in his head. Ah, but pressure was high. The proctor would look at Dan, and Dan would look as if he were trying hard to find the formulae on the classroom floor. Poor kid.

The punishment for cheating was immediate expulsion. Groveling wouldn't work, crying wouldn't work, your mother crying wouldn't work. Nothing would work. For Dan, expulsion meant death.

After the Physics exam, Dan's legs felt like jelly. Desperation hung heavy over his shoulders. He wanted to talk to someone. He wanted to weep. But there was no one to weep to. That was the price of being number one. The students at the school thought he was strange. He mumbled under his breath during lunch, stared off into space for hours at a time. Dan didn't have any friends.

The closest thing to a friend he had was his roommate. Dan knew nothing about him, not even his name. Dan hadn't even seen his whole face. He tried telling this to his parents but they didn't comment on it. They just gave him more food and told him again how proud they were, how proud they all were.

The roommate arrived with a small bag a month ago. When he came in he was wearing a black cap with the brim pulled down low. In his head, Dan called him Bob. *Hey, Bob*, he'd say under his breath.

Bob had a very predictable routine. Wake up at five, out by six. Dan would wake up and see Bob fixing his hair or buttoning his shirt uniform in front of the mirror, in the dark. *Why are you up so early?* Dan would ask Bob's back, and Bob would say, *I just like starting the day early.* When Bob got home at four in the afternoon he would sit on the edge of his bed, his back to Dan, and apply a generous amount of Kiwi on his pair of black leather shoes that never lost their shine anyway. He would hum whenever he polished, a happy tune that Dan didn't recognize. Other times Bob would sit at his desk and read or write in a notebook. Dan would invite him to grab dinner at six, but Bob always declined. By seven Bob would be in bed, wrapped in a blanket and facing the wall.

Dan once checked the room assignments at Admin, and saw that his room was listed as having only one occupant. Dan wasn't bothered. Admin took a long time updating things.

The night after the Physics exam and on the eve of the Chemistry test, Dan dreamed that he was driving through a very bad storm.

On the backseat was a single pile of clothes, a flashlight, batteries, two bottles of water, a pair of boots, and a grocery bag filled with canned goods, bread, and chips. Dan drove through a flooded street and water splashed on either side of the car. He heard the batteries fall to the floor. Rain came down in a steady, frightening stream. The wipers, overwhelmed, stopped functioning. Everything looked gray and distorted through the windshield. *I need to get to safety*, Dan thought. *I need to get to safety*.

Dan glanced at the rear-view mirror and saw Bob on the backseat.

Dan woke up with a start, upsetting the pile of notebooks he'd left sitting on his chest. He sat up and swallowed a scream. Bob was sitting on a chair beside his bed. Dan's gooseneck lamp was bent in a way that the light coming from it illuminated Bob's torso but kept his face in shadow.

"Are you all right?" Bob asked.

It was disorienting to not see Bob's face at all, not even an outline of his head. "Yeah," Dan said, and it was like talking to darkness, to empty air.

"You were groaning in your sleep."

"Oh? Sorry."

"That's all right." Bob stood up and went back to bed.

Dan tried to go back to studying, but he couldn't focus. His heart wouldn't stop hammering in his chest. He took out his notes and made another cheat sheet.

He tried sketching the face he saw in his dream but he was too scared.

The Chemistry exam went well. That night, while studying for Math, he dreamed he was bundled in furs and knee-deep in snow. He was with a group of men who were trying to reach the South Pole. They had marched for thirty days, spending Christmas and greeting the New Year in snow and in the cold, away from their families. And for what? Glory, of course. To be the first expedition to reach the South Pole.

But someone else had reached the South Pole first. When Dan saw who it was, he turned around and walked away as fast as he could, as fast as anyone could in the cold of Antarctic winter. His companions caught up with him. *A month's journey, and for what?* they shouted. They were right. History doesn't remember second placers. He fell and couldn't get up. The men were hungry. They had consumed almost two-thirds of their supply on the polar march. They didn't have enough for the way back. *Yes, you do,* Bob said inside his tent on the South Pole, and Dan screamed as the men hacked him to pieces.

"Ma, I'm tired," Dan said. "And I'm scared."

His mother's voice sounded so small coming through the phone. "Why would you be scared?" she said. "You're doing so well. Just a few more exams and you can come home and rest."

"What if I fail?" Dan scrunched up his eyes and started to cry. He hadn't studied for Math.

"You don't fail, Dan," his mother said.

Dan was caught looking at a cheat sheet during the Math exam. The proctor was a new teacher and eager to prove his worth, and as he was walking around the room he caught Dan looking at something on the floor and saw the plastic envelope. "What is that?" the proctor said, all pomp and theatrics. Dan and the plastic envelope were hauled out of the room and sent to the principal's office, where Dan was read his death sentence.

Dan felt numb the whole time, but when they sent him back to the dorms with a pair of teachers to guard him as he packed his things and waited for his parents, he burst into tears. All those years of studying, and for what? Glory? They would be marching him out of the school in a few hours. He wouldn't be going to UP. He wouldn't graduate. From one to none. He began to shake. He didn't want to face his parents.

Surely it would have been better to just fail than to end like this? Round and round it went.

He fell asleep while folding his shirts. He began to dream. He was walking down a school hallway. At the end of the hall he entered a classroom, but instead of finding rows of chairs and a desk on a raised platform he found two beds, two study tables, two closets, a mirror. His dorm room. Bob was on his bed, polishing his shoes, humming that happy tune.

When Dan walked up to him, Bob stopped humming. *You need to get to safety*, Bob said, and Dan nodded. Bob got up and went out and closed the door, leaving Dan alone with his shoes.

When Dan woke up he was sitting on the edge of Bob's bed, holding a Kiwi-streaked rag, the smell of shoe polish clogging his nose. His parents were talking to a boy on the other side of the room. His mother was crying. Eventually they all straightened up and got ready to leave.

Dan looked at them as they walked to the door. None of them glanced at him. He could finally see Bob's face now, but Bob was wearing his face.

"How could you do this, Dan," Dan's father said to Bob with the Dan-face, whispering furiously under his breath. "Look at your mother. Look how she's crying. How could you embarrass us like this." Dan's father gripped Bob's upper arm, the Dan-flesh turning white from the pressure. Dan saw Bob trying to contain his laughter, as though amused by an inside joke.

The door slammed. Dan picked up a shoe and, humming, began polishing it with the rag.

As Large as Alone

By Alena McNamara

As the boat slowed, Julia watched the girl on the public raft. She wasn't pretty, in the normal way, but her whole body inclined toward a secret hinted at in the curve of her fingers toward her knee and the way she raised her head, half self-conscious.

When the girl met her stare, Julia glanced away. Their father gave her a grateful smile from the helm for watching her sister for the day.

Julia balanced a moment on the edge of the boat, and then jumped. Clutching a kickboard white-knuckled against her lifevest, Mandy eased into the lake after her.

Mandy reached the raft first. The water from her splashing kicks rang hollow on the metal raft. "I'm Mandy," she said, climbing up. "Who are you?"

The girl gazed at her, and then at Julia. "I don't have a name."

Treading water, Julia held her breath while the boat's wake rolled past. It lapped against the bridge of her nose and her ears.

"Why not?"

"I'm a mermaid," the girl said. Her purple swimsuit was worn down to lavender in places, like Julia's after her junior high season on the swim team. "We don't need names."

Mandy grinned. "Yeah, right."

"Mandy," Julia said automatically.

Ignoring her—as usual—Mandy crossed her arms. "Prove it."

The girl looked surprised. Not quite graceful, she unfolded to slip off the raft. Her sidelong glance walked pricks of raised hairs up Julia's arms.

The water swallowed her. Mandy settled in to wait.

Julia told her, "We're talking later," and dove into the lake.

Just cloudy water, for a while, featureless. Little air bubbles stole out of the corner of her mouth, rushing for the surface. She let herself keep sinking. Fish flicked against her ankles, slick with scales.

At the bottom the girl lay in a bed of weeds, leaves and stems tangled olive-green around her. Deep rough wrinkles ridged her pale skin under the purple swimsuit, and her arms and legs lay swollen, angles not quite right. White foam clung to her nostrils, tiny drops of red to her ear where her hair drifted away. The skin on her leg peeled back so far that the bare white bone showed through.

Lack of oxygen tightened Julia's chest. She touched bottom with one foot, pushing off against a rock slimy with algae, and shot upward. Her breath raced her to the surface.

"Well?" Mandy called.

Julia swallowed the tang of silt and lakeweed. She swam over slowly and hung on to the raft, not quite up to treading water. Not a mermaid. Vulnerable, lonely. Dead. "She's down there."

"Bet you she'll be up soon," Mandy said, smug in her certainty.

Swimming laps, slow steady strokes that curved her around the raft and back again, Julia tried not to count the minutes. She was at the furthest point of her circle when Mandy shouted, out where the weeds met the area cleared for swimming.

The girl pulled herself up onto the raft, water running off her body. She looked just like any other girl, now, settling down next to Mandy, but Julia couldn't keep herself from glancing at her with every stroke.

The tone of their conversation drifted across the water: Mandy excited, exclaiming, counterpoint to the girl's voice, low and amused. When Julia's path took her back around to the raft, Mandy was saying, "Just icky weeds? Don't you eat fish?"

"Would you eat humans?" The girl caught Julia's eye.

She knew the secret gleaming in that smile now.

"You don't look like a fish. You don't have scales," Mandy said.

Out of the corner of her eye Julia could tell the girl still looked at her. Barely loud enough for Julia to hear, the girl said, "You just can't see them."

Tucking the memory deep away, Julia dove underwater again and kept swimming.

"We met a mermaid today," Mandy said during dinner.

Their mother smiled. "Did she have a fish tail?"

"No. Not that I could see, anyway." Mandy fiddled with her fork and the pile of thawed peas before her.

At her mother's glance, Julia said, "Some new girl was out on the raft. Her family must've just moved in."

Their father looked thoughtful. "There's that couple over on the west side, they were up last weekend supervising the guys building them a dock," he said, "but I didn't think they had kids."

"No, they did," her mother said, and their father let it go.

Julia thought of lake-washed bones disturbed by new construction, and laid the peas out into rows across her plate.

"You saw her," Mandy said later in their shared bedroom. "You did!"

"I know," Julia said, sitting down on her bed. "I saw her. But you know them—they think you're too old to be making things up." They'd started telling her that even earlier, seven to Mandy's eight.

"But it's not just stories." Mandy plopped down on her own bed, slapping at a mosquito that had found a way into their cabin. "I know made-up things aren't real. But she's not imaginary."

"I know," Julia said again. The back of her neck itched with the grit of dried lakewater.

"If it's real then they should know about it. But they won't even listen."

Leaning forward, Julia said, "Let's promise to keep it a secret between us. To keep *her* a secret between us."

Mandy pinky-swore with her solemnly. Julia padded over to turn off the lights. Just before she flicked the switch she looked back at her sister, now just a huddled lump of sheets that shifted to snatch again at the mosquito's thready whine.

"Got it!" Mandy said.

In the darkness Julia felt her way back to bed and lay there, staring up at the ceiling.

Pinky-swear or no, she didn't believe that Mandy would keep their promise.

Julia sat backwards in the boat the next morning, watching the last lingering mist swirl over the water in their wake, and only looked around when the motor cut out and the boat drifted to a stop.

The raft floated light under the weight of morning sun. The girl had never promised to be there again when she'd slipped into the lake the day before, but Julia had thought—

Maybe she'd never come back. Julia hoped she wouldn't. Mandy didn't need any more confusion over what was true.

Mandy leaped off the boat, splashing her. Julia followed her in.

The water wrapped over her like a second skin, and she wondered if this was what it felt like to be a mermaid.

Not, she reminded herself, that mermaids were real.

Mandy took up her perch on the raft, dangling her feet in the lake. Julia wanted to sit and wait with her, but her shoulders ached to swim laps. She'd made her circuit seven times, strokes pulling her muscles loose and easy, when she caught a glimpse of something underneath her.

Holding her breath, Julia plunged her head beneath the surface and opened her eyes, gliding. The girl swam ten feet beneath her, arms moving languidly through the water, as whole and pristine as she was on the surface with Mandy.

Julia surfaced and took a few more strokes. Her chest felt empty, buoyant. Without quite a conscious decision, she drew in a deep breath and looked down again.

The girl met her gaze and pushed off the bottom with one foot. She drifted up through the water. No air in her lungs to buoy her up to the surface, she just floated there, much closer now. Close enough to touch.

Her eyes were as dark as the bottom of the sea.

Julia reached out, half-afraid her skin would slough off at a touch, or feel rubbery and loose over rotting muscles. But it was just cool and slippery, like fish scales, and her fingers slid along it easily.

It was easier to think of her as a mermaid when they were touching like this.

Gently, the girl drifted closer. Their lips touched. Julia let her eyes close, savoring the contact. The girl's mouth slipped open over hers, and Julia's lips parted without a thought.

Water rushed into her mouth. She pulled away, escaped air whirling in bubbles around her, and kicked for the surface. Breathless, floating belly-up, she rubbed the water from her eyes.

By the time she'd recovered, the girl sat on the raft with Mandy, answering her questions about mermaid life.

Julia swam laps the rest of the day. Even when her fingers had wrinkles like raisins, she stayed in the water, sneaking glances toward the raft.

The girl ignored her completely.

It stormed the next day, hard enough that the window-screens still held water a day later. They caught Mandy trying to start the boat, wearing only her swimsuit and shivering so hard she couldn't shift the clutch. Before the end of the evening she had a cough and a slight fever, and their mother tucked her up in bed early. She was still sick the day after, when the rain had stopped but the clouds not yet cleared, wrapped in blankets all but her scowling face.

"Julia," she said.

"What is it?" She crouched by Mandy's bed.

"Tell her I'm sorry I couldn't come today."

Julia swallowed. "I will," she said, and, when Mandy's scowl deepened, "I promise."

"I thought I might take the canoe out today," Julia said at breakfast. Only one motorboat's growl had broken the quiet of the overcast lake since dawn.

Her father glanced at her mother.

"Take a lifejacket," her mother said with a sigh.

Outside, the air still smelled like rain, and the water gave back the matte grey of clouds. The weeds near their dock tangled around the paddle. The green stems against pale wood made her think of the girl. Julia shook them off.

Coming up alongside the empty raft, she leaned over to tie the canoe up and then eased herself onto the platform. The metal slats pressed cold against her legs. Huddled there, hugging her knees for warmth, she waited.

The girl's head broke the water first, shattering the tiny ripples any calm lake had. They just looked at each other for a moment, Julia keeping in her head what she needed to say. Slowly, the girl swam to the raft and pulled herself up. Their arms brushed.

Julia leaned away. She said, "You have to stay away from Mandy."

It wasn't, she thought with grim amusement, what the girl had expected her to say.

"She tried to go out and see you yesterday. Even after she couldn't start the boat. She said that she'd be fine below the water, that down there it didn't matter whether it was raining." Julia pressed her thumbs together, squeezing until the nailbeds turned white. She couldn't, didn't want to imagine Mandy's body dredged up from the bottom of the lake looking like the girl's. "Now she's in bed with a fever. What do you think would've happened if we hadn't caught her in time?"

"I'm sorry—"

"She would have *drowned*."

The girl had fallen silent. She picked at the abandoned spiderwebs wadded on the side of the raft, not meeting Julia's gaze.

"Because of all your stories about mermaids." Julia stared out at the lake, determined to say nothing more.

"They're true," the girl ventured.

Julia whirled around, the wet bottom of her swimsuit skidding on the raft. "I don't care if they're true," she said. "I care about my sister believing that she's a mermaid too, that she can breathe water and live in a lake."

"No," the girl said, considering, and Julia stared at her. "You do care if they're true. You care more than she does."

Julia swallowed.

"But you don't believe." She leaned closer. "Do you believe this?"

This time when they kissed the lake stayed where it should. The girl's teeth were cool and slick, and they tasted of weeds and deep water.

Both Julia and Mandy stayed in the day after that, though the weather was fine. The girl was waiting for them on the raft when they came the next day, though, legs curled under her like a tail. Mandy scrambled up next to her, and Julia turned to wave her father off. It had taken Mandy fifteen minutes to convince their mother to let her out on the lake; Julia had had to promise that she'd make sure Mandy didn't stay in the water too long.

The boat's engine muttered over the water as her father pulled away from the raft. The wake spread out across calm waters.

"Where do all the other mermaids live?" Mandy asked right away. "Is there a mermaid kingdom?"

The girl darted a guilty look at Julia. Pushing off from the raft, Julia started to swim laps, splashing loudly until she was far enough from them that she wouldn't hear the answer.

Later, the girl coaxed Mandy off the raft. More comfortable in the water than Julia had ever seen her, Mandy paddled around with her kickboard, pretending to be a mermaid. Julia slid up to the raft again and hooked an arm around the rail to watch. The girl swam alongside Mandy, laughing and beckoning her on, never quite there when Mandy reached for her.

Kicking harder, Mandy splashed the water high, and the girl swam back around to show her how to move more smoothly. Ten minutes later, she was raising much less water and noise.

Joining Julia at the raft, the girl glanced after Mandy. Something twisted in Julia's chest. Over the years, she had made three attempts to teach Mandy that kick, but Mandy had never even tried.

"She's getting better."

Julia nodded, curling her fingers. She wanted to touch the hollow of the girl's elbow. She wanted her to go away, to stop filling Mandy's head with tales of mermaids and teaching her to kick right. She wanted Mandy back in the cabin, and the girl's fingertips against hers with all the weight of solitude behind them.

"I didn't tell her," the girl said. "That we have a kingdom."

Pulled back to the water, Julia asked, "What—"

"I told her mermaids live in lakes like this. Alone."

Their gazes met for a long moment. "And what's the truth?"

The girl just turned back to watch Mandy, smiling a little.

Near midnight, Julia woke with a start at a scratch on their window. A tree branch, she thought, and turned over to go back to sleep.

The girl's face rose pale against the glass, and Julia was half standing before she knew it, fumbling her slippers onto her feet.

When she came out of their cabin, easing the screen door shut behind her, the girl stood on the end of their dock, watching the lake and waiting. Brushing through a cloud of gnats and leaving a trail of footprints across the dewy grass, Julia went to her.

The girl turned as Julia stepped onto the dock, one hand chafing her elbow as if she were cold. "Is everyone asleep?"

"Worried about Mandy?" Julia smiled, sleepy. "Never let her know you can go off the lake."

"I hardly knew, either," the girl said. "I just kept going. But that wasn't what I meant."

Looking up at her, she said, "I don't want to be lonely. Not tonight."

When Julia didn't back away, she threaded her hands through Julia's hair, one finger at a time. "I like your hair down."

She kissed Julia, and for a moment Julia lost herself in it. Then she pulled away, stepping back. "You're—" None of the ways to finish that sentence ended well. Julia took a deep breath. "I can't. I'm sorry."

"What?"

Julia could still taste the lakewater on the girl's teeth. "I don't even know your name," she said, helplessly. "You said mermaids don't have them, mermaids don't need them, but you're a dead girl lying on the bottom of the lake and I don't even know who you were."

All the girl needed to say was, *You know who I am now. Isn't that what matters?* But she just stared.

Around the dock, the lily pad blossoms were moons against the dark circles of their leaves.

"A—dead girl?"

Forced into her suspicions, Julia said, "You don't even know who you were." She shivered against the night chill. "I can't."

"I'm not dead." She touched her face, her arms, hugged her body. "Am I dead?"

Julia had been as stupid as Mandy.

"How could I be dead? I can walk, I can talk, I can—breathe." Her fingers flew to her throat. "Oh my God," she said, her eyes wide. "I can't breathe."

"It's okay," Julia said. She reached out. "It'll be okay."

The girl pushed her hands away. "I'm dead! It won't be okay. It isn't okay." She spun and ran, diving off the dock before Julia could open her mouth. Weeds danced wildly around the spot where she'd vanished, lily pads bobbing in the ripples.

Julia stood alone on the dock.

Tucking her slippers far under the bed to hide the damp marks of dew, Julia slid into her bed. The quiet sounds of their parents' sleeping breath came through the wall.

"She's my mermaid," Mandy said, conversationally.

Julia—startled—sat up. "How long have you been awake?"

"Long enough. I guess I'll share her, though," she said.

She flopped back down. "Good night, Mandy." Maybe if she pulled her sheets over her head Mandy would leave her alone.

"I figure," Mandy said, yawning, "you probably won't get another chance."

Julia stared through her sheets at the ceiling, listening to the high-pitched whine of that one mosquito that had managed to get in again. After a time she sat up again and groped under her bed for her slippers.

Mandy, if she was awake, had the good sense not to comment.

Dawn found her on the raft, buckled into a lifejacket and huddled underneath a heavy blanket, canoe tied up and nudging the raft with every swell of water slopping hollow against the shell. She yawned, rubbing at the gritty corners of her eyes.

The girl surfaced a few feet away, water running off her dark hair. She swam to the raft, as easy in the lake as ever, and pulled herself up to sit next to Julia. After a moment, Julia offered her a fold of the blanket. They edged together, not quite touching.

"Your hands are cold," Julia said.

She reached out and, carefully, tucked one of them between hers.

"They aren't going to warm up," said the girl.

With great concentration, Julia laced her fingers through the girl's. She thought before she spoke, of mermaids and death and loneliness.

Finally, she said, "I know."

Random Play All and the League of Awesome

By Shane Halbach

yrus sat on the couch and crunched on a bowl of frosted wheat. Normally he would have sat at the table, but the table was currently covered with papers, folders and charts. His mom was finalizing her budget with her new business partner, Herman. There wasn't much room in the one bedroom condo, so Cyrus was bumped to the couch.

He was sick to death of business plans and marketing and how much will it cost, so he put in his ear buds and switched his MP3 player on. He hit next to get a random song.

Can't trust me but it's not about trust

I make no sense, I am the walrus

Cyrus sprayed milk all over the coffee table.

He had been looking directly at Herman when that line played. He always thought Herman looked like a walrus, with his droopy mustache and big belly.

"Cyrus, what is wrong with you?" asked his mother, irritated. "Hey, aren't you supposed to be going to school?"

Cyrus was still chuckling as he mopped up the droplets of milk.

"Yeah Mom, I was just leaving."

"And take those headphones off. Your ears are going to grow around those things."

"Sure mom," mumbled Cyrus, but he made no move to take them out.

Between his mom's work and night school, he was pretty used to taking care of himself. She used to say it would be better when she graduated, but as soon as she had her business degree, she started spending all her free time developing her plans for "From Chi-town, With Love", a specialty bakery. Cyrus knew she had been working towards this moment for years. Say what you want about Sarah Durham, but when she had her sights set on something, she didn't quit. He was proud of her, and proud that, with her investment partner Herman Miller putting up half of the money, her dream was only two days away from becoming a reality.

Cyrus threw his bag over his shoulder, grabbed an old, baggy sweatshirt to protect against the fall chill, and checked himself in the mirror by the door. His tight, black hair was maybe a little frizzier than normal, but other than that, he looked about the same as he always did.

He skipped ahead to the next song on his player and smiled.

I'm sick of this, the time has come
for me to move along
And you can all just miss me when I'm gone.

Perfect exit music, as usual.

Cyrus ran his ear buds up through the sleeve of his sweatshirt. With the volume low, he could listen to music while pretending he was idly resting his head in his hand.

He was killing time until class ended, doodling in his notebook and writing down snatches of lyrics that struck him as interesting. He had just finished writing:

You weren't looking for something new,
You don't find destiny, it finds you

…when the bell rang. He ripped the page from his notebook, crumpled it, and tossed it in the trashcan on the way out the door.

He tossed his books in his locker and grabbed his bag. He wondered if his mom would be home for dinner, or if he would be on his own again. He slammed his locker door, revealing Milo Baumstein, who had apparently crept up while he was rummaging in his locker. Milo was skinny and white, with a perpetual smirk. He looked like he would be annoying, and he was.

"Cyrus, Cyrus, bo-byrus, just the man I wanted to see."

"What's up Milo?"

"Is this your handwriting?"

Milo smoothed out a wrinkled piece of paper and held it up for Cyrus' inspection.

"You're taking my papers out of the trash? That's creepy, Milo."

"What can I say, I have a crush on you." Milo laughed once, too loudly, like a donkey's bray. "So it is yours then? I thought so."

Cyrus snatched the paper out of Milo's hand.

"Yeah, it's mine. So what?"

Milo snatched it back.

"Dude, we've got to talk. How did you do it?"

"Do what? It's just trash."

"No, it's not. It's the future, man. You wrote the future!"

"Milo, what are you talking about?"

"Look, on Monday you balled this up and threw it at the trash can. It bounced off the rim and rolled to my feet."

"And you kept it?"

"Yes, and I'll explain why in a minute. But just listen! You wrote this on Monday, and everything you wrote came true on Tuesday!"

I Ic had Cyrus' attention now.

"Look, here's an example. You wrote:

The fire and the rain,

All my life is pain,

...and the League of Awesome | Shane Halbach

I'm sick of this

and then someone pulled that fire alarm in 3rd period, and we all had to stand outside in the rain. And then here you wrote:

Jammed up,

Slammed up,

Hard to even move when I'm so dammed up.

and that was the day Neveh Jimson hit Tonya Bradley in the parking lot and nobody could move their cars for forty-five minutes. It's like a magic iPod or something!"

"Milo, what are you talking about? I just wrote some song lyrics down. That's a song by Breaking Cashflow. It doesn't mean anything about an accident. I don't even drive."

Cyrus tried to push past Milo, but Milo stepped in front of him. The halls were clearing quickly as everyone left to go home.

"It's alright, man. Don't be ashamed! I have a superpower too. It's how I got this in the first place."

Milo waved the crumpled paper.

"Your superpower is getting things out of the trash? Or just being really annoying?"

Milo was unfazed.

"No, my superpower is getting information." He leaned in close. "They call me The Ferret. Get it? Because I ferret out information."

"By digging in the trash."

"I didn't get it out of the trash. That's what I'm trying to tell you. It rolled over to me, remember?"

"Milo, I gotta go home now."

"This is *serious*, Cyrus! I really mean it! I can't help it, information just finds me. I pick up the phone and overhear the name of the boy my sister likes. I go to the store to get milk for my mom, and I see Jamarcus Fisher coming out of the movies with Carrie Smith, not Wanda Pierce, who he's dating. Notes fall out of notebooks into my lap!"

"It sounds like you're trying to justify a lot of snooping."

Cyrus pushed past Milo and headed for the door. Milo trailed after him.

"Fine, you don't believe me? How about a demonstration?"

He ran past Cyrus and yanked open a classroom door at random. Inside, Mr. Blythe, the chemistry teacher was pawing passionately at Ms. Pastor, the librarian.

Cyrus' mouth dropped open, and hung there.

"Way to go, Mr. Blythe!" shouted Milo into the stunned silence.

"Milo…" warned Mr. Blythe, but before he could say anything more, Cyrus turned and ran. He wasn't sure if he were running to avoid getting in trouble, or just fleeing from the embarrassment of it all.

He ran to the end of the hall and skidded around the corner, not stopping until he passed through the glass doors into the stairwell before the exit. When he got there, he bent over, catching his breath. When he had it, he began to laugh. Hysterical laughter that kept him doubled over, holding his stomach. He was still laughing when Milo burst through the doors a couple of seconds later. Cyrus wiped the tears from his eyes.

"How did you know they were in there?"

"I didn't, that's my point. It's my superpower."

"You just, what, stumble upon things?"

"I ferret out information. That's why they call me The Ferret. How do you think I keep from getting beat up every day?"

They sat in silence for a while before Milo continued.

"I have a superhero group. It's called the League of Awesome. We need you. There's crime out there that needs stopping. You could help stop it."

Cyrus stood up.

"Milo, you're crazy. I've got to go."

He turned and pushed open the door without looking back.

"Think about it!" Milo called after him.

Cyrus was sitting on the front porch, listening to his MP3 player and enjoying one of the last few nice evenings before fall reminded everyone just how much winter was going to suck. He skipped from track to track, trying to find something he wanted to listen to. It was no use; he needed some new music.

His mom and Herman must have finished their strategy meeting because Herman came out the front door.

"Hey, you coming to the closing tomorrow?" he asked.

"I don't know, maybe."

Cyrus really didn't care about some dumb paper getting signed, but he knew it was a big day for his mom. Once they owned the spot, the bakery stepped out of the realm of a dream, and became a reality. Cyrus kind of wanted to be there when it happened.

"Alright, maybe I'll see you then, kiddo."

Herman left down the front walk and took a left, fishing in his pocket for his keys. He must have been distracted, because he didn't see a boy walking in the other direction, and the two collided hard. Herman's hand shot out for balance, and the contents of his pocket, including his keys and wallet, went flying everywhere.

The other boy was Milo.

Milo had been knocked to the ground, and he reached over and picked up Herman's license from where it had fallen next to him.

Herman snatched it out of his hand.

"Watch where you're going, kid!"

"Hey, same to you, pal!" replied Milo.

Herman hurried off, and Cyrus sighed as Milo turned in towards where he was sitting on the porch.

"Was that your dad?"

"Milo, he's white."

Milo just blinked up at him, so Cyrus continued.

"That's Herman. He's just my mom's business partner."

Milo got a strange look on his face, confused and suddenly intense.

"Did you say Herman? Why did his license say his name was Jack?"

Now it was Cyrus' turn to be confused.

"What are you talking about? Why would Herman have someone else's driver's license?"

"It had his picture on it, and the name was Jack Covington. I never heard of Jack being short for Herman."

Cyrus shrugged.

"I don't know, Milo. There's probably a million explanations."

Milo had a gleam in his eye, and it was getting brighter by the minute.

"This looks like a job for the League of Awesome!"

"No! Uh-uh. No way. He's a nice guy who's helping my mom buy her bakery tomorrow. Leave him alone, okay?"

"Not a chance! There's something going on here, and I'm going to get to the bottom of it. That's why they call me The Ferret!"

"Nobody calls you The Ferret, do they?"

Milo was already heading for the sidewalk. He shouted back over his shoulder, "I've got to assemble the League! We'll pick you up in an hour!"

Cyrus shouted back, "You're not doing this, Milo! I'm not going to let you!"

"You can come with us or not, but I'm going either way."

That left Cyrus without much of a choice.

A ratty gray sedan rolled up in front of Cyrus' house. Its bulk gave it a somewhat stately appearance, despite the occasional rust spot.

Milo poked his head out of the driver's window.

Cyrus said, "Hey Milo, nice boat! I thought you were bringing a car?"

Milo grinned.

"This is the Ferretmobile. Official League transportation. Hop in."

Cyrus opened the door and slid in the backseat. Next to Milo in the front seat, was a big black kid that Cyrus didn't know. He filled up most of the front seat, but he looked solid, chubby more than fat. He was just that big. His head was shaved smooth, and he had big wrinkles in the back of his neck. He was about the polar opposite of Milo. The boy had a rubber superball, and every few seconds he would bounce it off the dashboard, up into the windshield, and back into his hand.

Milo turned to face Cyrus, still grinning.

"Welcome to the League!"

"I'm not joining the League."

"This is Rudy."

Rudy stopped bouncing his ball long enough to turn and shake Cyrus' hand.

"And what's your power?" Cyrus asked wryly.

"I entertain myself," said Rudy, and he punctuated it by bouncing the ball in its two-bounce pattern.

"He never gets bored. Rudy's perfect for a job like this. We call him Stakeout Boy."

"Stakeout Man," corrected Rudy.

The car pulled away from the curb.

"So who else are we picking up?"

"Nobody else, you're it."

"So the League of Awesome is you and Rudy?"

"And you."

"I'm not part of the League."

They rode in silence for a while, with only the boc-tic-whap, boc-tic-whap of Rudy's ball. Cyrus found it more annoying than soothing.

"Isn't that hard to do while he's driving?"

"That's what makes it a challenge."

Milo spoke up again.

"Now that you're a part of the League, you're going to need a superhero name. We can't just call you Cyrus."

"Why not?"

"How about Shuffle Man?"

"How about Cyrus?"

"The Shuffler."

"That will inspire fear into the hearts of my enemies. It makes me sound like an old man!"

"Shuffle Master. The iPoder."

"Come on, Milo. Besides, my MP3 player isn't even an iPod."

"Well, what do you have instead of shuffle?"

"Random play all."

"Random Play All ... I like it. Nice ring to it. Random Play All."

"You're not really going to start calling me that, are you?"

"No, of course not. Only at League functions."

Mercifully, they were just pulling to the curb at their destination. It was an old brick warehouse at the end of a run-down, industrial looking dead end street. The shadows were dark in the gathering twilight, except for a lone light over a nondescript, windowless door.

"Where are we?" asked Cyrus.

"Jack Covington's place of business," replied Milo.

"Who's Jack Covington?"

"Who indeed? That was the name on the license that your mom's business partner dropped. The only Jack Covington I could find around here apparently owns a company named Triple A Imports. But it's weird, it's like the company doesn't really exist. All I could find was a phone number. No address, no company website, nada. So I called up Tony's Big Slice and gave them the number for Triple A, and they repeated this address back to me, to confirm. In fact..."

A beat up hatch back with a glowing "Tony's Big Slice" car topper was just pulling up across the street. Milo shut off the car and went to go get the pizza.

"So what do we do now?" asked Cyrus.

"Now, we wait," replied Rudy.

He put his superball in his pocket and glanced around the car. He grabbed a nickel out of the center console.

"Heads or tails?"

★

After an hour or so, Cyrus couldn't take any more.

"This is ridiculous. Nobody's come in or out of that building all night. You don't even know for sure that this place belongs to Jack Covington, and even if it does, you don't know why Herman had his driver's license. And if I wanted to play heads or tails all night, I could do it in the comfort of my own home!"

Milo thought for a minute, and then came to a decision.

"You're right. We need to get in there."

"That's not exactly what I meant."

Rudy tossed the nickel back in the console and Milo opened the door.

"Hey, wait a minute guys! That's breaking and entering. You could go to jail!"

"Since when has that ever stopped a superhero?"

"Guys! I'm not going to let you do this!"

Cyrus' complaints fell on deaf ears. Milo and Rudy were already out of the car and crossing the street. Cyrus opened his door and hurried after them.

On the side of the building, there was a row of high, small windows. Milo picked one at random, and Rudy boosted him up. The mechanism was broken, and Milo was able to pull it open easily.

"You've got to be kidding me," Cyrus muttered to himself. "What are the odds of that?"

There was no way Rudy was fitting through the window, even if he could have reached, so Milo had to wriggle through and then open the front door for them. As Cyrus waited for the door to open, he felt like every eye in the neighborhood was on him. It seemed to take forever, and when the door finally opened, Cyrus jumped inside as fast as he could.

Milo flipped on a bank of lights. The harsh fluorescents illuminated a mostly empty industrial space. In the far corner, chain link formed the walls of a small office, with a desk and filing cabinets. It was the only part of the big room that really looked used. The rest was mostly empty, with a few filing cabinets, a stack of wooden crates, and a worktable with a few papers on it.

"I guess we start with the office," said Rudy.

"You guys take the office … I want to check out those filing cabinets," said Milo with a far-off look in his eyes.

The office wasn't much. There was a desk in the center of the chain link "room" with a desk lamp and stacks of papers on it. A metal filing cabinet was in one corner with a few magnets stuck to the side, including one for Tony's Big Slice, a sprinkle covered doughnut, and a rainbow colored rectangle that said, "Don't worry, be happy!" A fan was sitting on the floor next to a well-worn boom box, both plugged into the same power strip as the desk lamp.

Rudy headed for the filing cabinets, so Cyrus took a look at the desk. There were receipts for what looked like a construction project of some sort. Gingerly, Cyrus pinched the corner of the top sheet and peeked beneath it. He wished he'd brought gloves or something.

"Hey guys, over here!" called Milo. He was holding up a manila envelope he had found in one of the drawers.

Cyrus and Rudy jogged over to him. Inside the packet was a series of false IDs and documents. Cyrus scanned through them quickly. He saw at least six driver's licenses from various states, each one bearing Herman's smiling face next to names like Ted Brinkman and Alex Miller.

"Looks like Herman has a lot of irons in the fire," smirked Milo.

"Indeed I do," spoke a low voice behind them.

Herman stood pointing a small, black, snub-nosed gun at the three of them. His eyes were cold and his face was expressionless.

"Drop the envelope."

Milo dropped it. Herman motion with the gun.

"Into the office."

Cyrus didn't think he looked like a walrus anymore. More like a tiger.

Herman closed the chain link door and snapped a lock through the clasp.

"It's nothing personal, Cyrus. It's just business. I've been working on your mom too long to have it ruined now."

He set the key down on the worktable, well out of the reach of someone trapped in the office. Next to it, he placed the telephone handset he had removed from the office, as well as the cell phones he had confiscated from Milo and Rudy, and Cyrus' MP3 player.

"The key is right here. I'll make sure somebody stops by here tomorrow, after I'm long gone."

He picked up the packet of identities and a few other papers. He glanced around the room to make sure he hadn't forgotten anything.

"Be good, kiddo. It's not personal, I mean it. I like you. If I didn't, I'd kill you."

Herman smiled affectionately at Cyrus, but Cyrus felt less than warmed by it.

"You're stealing our life's savings, Herman. You lied to us from day one. I'd say it's personal."

Herman shrugged.

"Suit yourself. Doesn't make a difference to me."

He turned and walked toward the front door.

"I'll call the cops! I'll track you down myself!" shouted Cyrus.

Herman didn't even look back as he left the building.

Cyrus wrapped his fingers in the chain links and yelled as loud as he could, screaming out all of the impotence, frustration and rage.

When he was through, Milo said, "We have to get out of here. We have to stop him before he gets the money from your mom."

Cyrus rounded on him.

"Yeah? And how are we going to do that? Anybody in "The League" have super strength? Laser vision? Huh? Or are we just a bunch of dumb kids stuck in a cage until some adult comes and lets us out?"

Cyrus was in Milo's face, but Milo didn't back down.

"We're not dumb kids. We're superheroes, whether you believe it or not. I believe it. I *know* it. And as far as predicaments go, this one's nothing. Any superhero worth his salt should be able to crack this one."

Milo started pacing in a circle around the desk.

"We've got to rely on our powers. It's our one advantage. I can't see how my power can be of any use, or Rudy's. Cyrus, it's got to be you."

"We don't have any powers, Milo! Besides, even if I did, my magic MP3 player is out there. I'm helpless."

"Maybe not," said Milo.

He reached down and picked up the old boom box, placing it on the desk.

"What if the power is in you, not the MP3 player?"

He flicked a button, and music suddenly filled the room. Oldies.

Cyrus reached out, his hand hovering over the tuner dial.

Please. For Mom, he thought, and gave the knob a vicious spin.

The radio hissed and popped as it spun past stations, and when Cyrus' hand stopped, it settled in on a station.

"...nobody does doughnuts like Devil's Doughnuts. Sinfully good!"

Cyrus stared at the radio for a second, and then turned it off.

"Sorry Milo." Cyrus said coldly. "I guess I don't have any super-powers after all."

Cyrus, embarrassed that he had even given it a try, couldn't look Milo in the eyes. Just for a second, he had almost believed Milo's delusion...

His eyes fell on the filing cabinet in the corner, and in particular on a magnet. It was round with a hole through the center and colored sprinkles around the edge, advertising a doughnut shop. Devil's Doughnuts.

Cyrus walked over and snatched it off the side of the cabinet for a closer look. Surely it was a coincidence. Could it just be a coincidence?

"Uh, guys?" said Cyrus, turning the magnet over in his hands.

Suddenly, he had an idea. Quickly he rummaged through the desk and looked on the floor.

"Do you guys see any string or rope or anything?"

Rudy and Milo started looking around, but quickly covered the small office, turning up nothing. Finally, Cyrus took the beaten up radio and unplugged it from the wall.

"If this works, I owe you," he murmured to the radio, wrapping the cord double around his hand. He set it on the floor, put a foot on it, and yanked as hard as he could. The cord came loose from the back.

He peeled apart the end of the cord and wrapped it around the doughnut magnet, twisting the exposed wires together to secure it. He walked over to the chain link wall closest to where the key lay on the table.

He couldn't push his hand through the chain link, but the magnet fit through. He held on to the plug end of the cord and stuck what he could of his fingers through the fence. Awkwardly, he tried to throw the magnet towards the key.

The cord was long enough, but Cyrus' throw wasn't even close. He reeled in the magnet and tried again, this time at least smacking the table before the magnet dropped to the floor. The next three tries were about the same.

"Mind if I try?" asked Rudy.

Cyrus reluctantly handed him the magnet and the cord, and stepped aside. Rudy bounced it in his palms a few times, weighing it. Rather than mashing his fingers through the fence, Rudy placed the magnet flat on his palm and held it up to the fence. He squinted one eye and lined up his shot carefully. With the index finger of his other hand, he flicked the magnet hard.

The magnet arced through the air and landed with a click on top of the key. Cyrus' mouth fell open, and he turned to look at Rudy.

"How did you do that?"

Rudy shrugged and allowed himself a little smile.

"Do you know how many times I've practiced flicking something at a target? It's a great way to kill time."

Rudy reeled in the magnet and retrieved the key.

"Way to go, Stakeout Boy!" crowed Milo.

"Stakeout Man," corrected Rudy mildly.

Cyrus took the key and opened the door.

"Rudy, you're definitely the man! Let's go warn my mom."

When they pulled up out front, Cyrus could see the light was on in the living room. They went inside.

Cyrus burst through the door.

"Mom? Mom! I have to tell you…"

Cyrus froze, and so did Milo and Rudy behind him. Herman was sitting on the couch across from his mom. He was smiling, but his eyes turned cold when they looked at Cyrus.

"Cyrus, I didn't expect to see you tonight."

Cyrus kept his voice level.

"Mom, what is he doing here?"

"Herman was in the neighborhood, so he stopped by to get the check a little early, so we'd be all set for tomorrow…"

Her voice trailed off as she noticed how Cyrus and Herman were looking at each other.

"Just needed the check a little early, huh Herman? Why's that?"

Herman stood up and took a step towards Cyrus. His voice was jovial, even if his expression wasn't.

"I was just driving by and I thought I'd stop in and get it."

"Cyrus, what is going on here?" demanded his mom.

"Mom, Herman isn't who he says he is. He's a con man, and he's trying to take our money."

Her face flushed red.

"Young man, I don't know what you think you're doing, but you will not talk to Mr. Miller that way! You should be ashamed of yourself!"

Herman kept his eyes on Cyrus, but he laughed. "I've been called a lot of things, but never a con man."

"Yeah, right," mumbled Milo.

It was quiet for a moment, before Herman broke the silence.

"Alright, well hey, no problem." Herman took another step towards Cyrus, and towards the door. "It's no big deal, Sarah, I'll just get it when I see you tomorrow."

Cyrus prepared to dodge or fight, but Herman just stepped around him and walked toward the door. As Herman walked between Milo and Rudy, Milo's hand darted out and slipped into the pocket of Herman's sport coat. It came back out holding the manila envelope of Herman's fake IDs. Milo's face lit up triumphantly.

Herman backhanded him across the cheek, knocking him to the floor.

"Should have gone for the other pocket," he sneered, pulling the gun out with his left hand and pointing it at Milo.

"Hand over the envelope."

Mom drew a deep breath, but didn't scream. Milo looked defiant.

"Don't be an idiot, Milo, give it to him!" said Cyrus.

Herman cocked the hammer back.

Time slowed to a crawl for Cyrus. He tried to move, to react, but there was nothing he could do. Milo wouldn't give Herman the envelope, he was sure of it. Herman was going to shoot Milo. There was no movement, no sound. Nothing but the gun pointing at Milo's chest.

A tiny "thonk!" brought Cyrus back to reality. Rudy's superball ricocheted off the kitchen cabinet and struck Herman directly in the eye.

Herman hissed and raised both hands to his face in surprise. Cyrus crashed into him a moment later, grappling for the gun. It went spinning across the floor, under the kitchen table. Rudy piled on a second later, using his bulk to pin down Herman's legs. Shortly, Milo jumped into the fray.

"Mom, get some rope!" shouted Cyrus.

Herman didn't say anything, but he fought and kicked like a cornered animal. With Rudy on his legs, Cyrus on one arm and Milo on the other, his struggles soon lessened.

Mom came back into the kitchen carrying the yellow rope they had used to tie a Christmas tree on top of Uncle James' SUV two years ago. The tree hadn't been worth the hassle, but at least they found another use for the rope.

She tossed it to Cyrus, and Herman was quickly tied as securely as Cyrus and his mom could make him. Milo gagged him with a dish towel. Herman's eyes smoldered.

Mom put her face next to his.

"Herman, I don't know what this is about. But if you think you can pull a gun on a kid in my kitchen, then you've got another thing coming."

"Thanks, Mom," said Cyrus.

Mom rounded on him. "Start explaining," she growled.

Milo produced the packet and spilled its contents onto the table.

"Herman isn't exactly who he says he is."

Cyrus quickly explained about the fake IDs and being trapped at Triple A Imports. Mom looked skeptical at first, but Herman's face smiling up from half a dozen plastic rectangles spread across the kitchen table was hard to dispute.

"So, what do we do with him?" asked Rudy when Cyrus finished.

"We deliver him to the police," said Mom, scooping the IDs back into the envelope.

Milo produced something white from his pocket and tossed it at Herman. It spun through the air, bouncing off Herman's chest and into his lap. It was a business card with a "TLA" logo in bold green and purple letters. The League of Awesome.

"Our first collar," said Milo

Cyrus closed his locker with a bang and jumped when he realized someone had been standing behind the door.

"Come on, Milo, don't do that to me!"

"I have something for you."

He held up a brand new MP3 player.

"It's already full of songs. Thousands of them. I figure the more songs you have, the easier it is for your power to talk to you. This thing's like a power boost times ten."

"If I take it, do I have to be in the League?" asked Cyrus.

"You're already in the League," replied Milo.

Cyrus took the MP3 player and skimmed through it. It really

did have everything on it: rap, country, alternative rock. He started to walk to his next class, and Milo trailed after him.

"You know, I think there's something shady going on at the dry cleaners by my house. I just got a funny feeling when I went in there the other day. I was standing in line and the door opened, blowing a receipt off the counter onto my shoe..."

Mah Song

By Joanne Anderton

A rain of stars heralds the descent of the Nine Lords, and the rest of my family celebrate. Mother burns fragrant handfuls of carefully preserved flowers, Father fills tiny cups of recycled tin with cheap rice wine. Later there will be sticky cakes of preserved red beans, and the entire crop of my mother's window-grown spinach served wilted, and heavily salted.

I do not join the celebrations. Instead, I go in search of Aroon. It's important to see him before the Mah Song takes him again.

He sits in his room, as he always does, plugged into a world we cannot see. Cables run like mangrove roots from dozens of sockets in his shaved scalp. They continue beneath the floorboards to intersect with the ancient optical and copper streams that twist through the ruined city.

"Aroon," I whisper, and crouch beside him. "Little brother."

I touch his shoulder to get his attention. "How long before they land?"

He is sitting as if in meditation, legs crossed, hands on his knees, palms up. Beneath his shirt the fan in his chest whirs gently, like calm breathing. He turns toward me and his eyes are glowing: flicking green and red numbers in his right eye, a complex array of charts in his left.

"Hello big sister," he replies. He closes one eye and concentrates for a moment. "Two days." His voice is unsteady, but it's not nerves. Long gone are my little brother's childhood days, when he clung to my leg and wept each time the Lords descended. It's hard to believe he is only ten years old. He carries himself with such dignity now.

His voice is unsteady because the last sacrifice hasn't had time to settle into his body. A complex design of pins on either side of his neck, each lit by a tiny bulb of a different colour. I don't know what they do, and he has not offered to tell me yet.

My heart drops. Two days is so soon. "Shall we walk by the river, then? I have credits enough for khanom jark. A whole one each."

A faint smile, nothing like the grins and sticky fingers I remember so clearly. "The taste of coconut is nothing but data," he says. "Chemical reactions translated by the brain." He traces the plugs in his head. "There's too much inside me now to leave any space for taste. Do not waste your credits on me." He blinks unevenly, one eye after the other. "But that's not the point, is it? I forget sometimes. Yes, we must walk. It's time."

I give him the space to get ready. As he goes through the complicated process of disconnecting himself, my preparations are far more mundane. I tie back my dark hair without brushing it and change into slightly cleaner clothes. The night is humid, but the sleeves of my blouse are long, to hide the scars—old and new—across the underside of my forearms.

The result of my failed Mah Song tests.

"What shall we pray to the Lords for?"

I turn. Mother stands in the doorway, arms crossed, all her good humour gone.

"Good health," I answer, head down. That's what the Lords are for. "And a Mah Song to carry our prayers."

"Or a husband?" Her tone is bitter. "One less mouth to feed."

I am the third of three daughters. I should have been born Mah Song—according to my mother, at least. That burden does not rightly belong to the miracle son she should have been too old to carry to term. She had me tested, over and over. My scars are ropey, like the wires the monks shoved beneath my skin when, really, I was too old and had failed too many times to try.

Aroon tells me memory is only data. The stink of the temple, the razor in a monk's wrinkled fingers are just like the taste of coconut. If I want, I can erase them.

The inoperative nodes sewn into my arms convince me otherwise.

It's no cooler outside, but the air feels lighter. Aroon has gathered all his cables into a scarf, wound cloth around his forearms and dressed plainly. He can't do anything about his eyes, so he still draws attention. His gait is awkward thanks to a sacrifice in his hip, but at least he can walk, and enjoy the night.

Every time the Lords descend, and I take him to the riverbank for sweets, I wonder if this is the last time.

I buy substandard khanom jark and we sit beneath the bare tree branches in our usual spot to eat it—where the fence has rusted clean away, and we can dangle our feet over the river's grey water. The palm leaf it's wrapped in is dry and cracked, the coconut tastes like dust, and the sweetness isn't from sugar. Two bites, and I toss it to the monitor lizards lurking below.

"It's an energy converter," Aroon says, pointing to the sacrifice in his neck. "The first step towards making me self-sufficient. I've felt no hunger since it was installed, so I believe it's working."

"It won't be long, will it?" I lean against him, and he tips his head so our temples meet. He vibrates, ever so softly. His fan. Not fear. "Until the last sacrifice. The one where the Lords take you away."

"Two more descents," he answers, eventually. "Maybe three."

I close my eyes to the lights from the Ayutthaya slum behind us, the foaming river, and the toxic, empty lands running off to the horizon on the other side. "But we're not ready."

Mah Song do not live long, and they grow less human with every descent. I can't stop this any more than I can take my brother's place, but I'll be damned if I'm going to sit back and watch him disappear before my eyes. We've worked together since he was just a very little boy to come up with a way to save him. And now, when we are so close, when we've finally found something that might actually work, the Lords are back.

He threads his fingers with mine, and I'm not sure who is comforting who. "The data key will work, sister. It just needs repairing. Fix it up, and it will have the space to hold several small boys like me." A deeper smile this time, almost genuine. "Remember, we are all just data. The Lords want this body, but this body is not all I am."

"And then what?" I whisper. "Once we upload you to the key, what will you do? A key can't talk, or walk. A key can't hold my hand. How can you think I'd doom you to a life like—"

"We don't have any other options," he interrupts, so calmly. "I've been scanning, every minute of every day, tapping deep into the ruins, as far as I can access. The key is all we have. It's insane, and rotting away, but you can fix that. You know how. You know where to get the parts."

I say nothing. No one argues with a Mah Song.

"Promise me you will, big sister. When I'm gone, look after me?"

Nodding, I resist the urge to rub at the nodes in my wrists, and the freshly cut skin, taut and sore against them. Yes, I know how. I can fix all kinds of things.

Two days go by so quickly, and too soon Aroon is gone. Oh, he still sits in his room in his meditative pose, and his eyes flash so many signals in green, but he isn't with us. Not really. The Mah Song trance has taken him.

So it's time for the procession to begin.

We dress him in simple white pants. I pry away the cap that covers the fan in his chest, and loosen the thin wires that crawl across his stomach and shoulders, freeing them from the fine layer of skin that had started to grow over them. They look like tattoos—a complex pattern of colour and line.

Then Father seats him on his steel-pipe and plastic-mesh Woh, the four strongest men from the street lift him one at each corner, and he is carried from the house.

I refuse to chant and stamp and wail like everyone else. Instead, I return to his room, wait until I'm sure no one has followed me, and pick up one of his toys; a metallic lizard standing on its hind legs, spines down its back, mouth open in a ferocious expression. We dug it out of the ruins together, when Aroon had enough space in his brain for play.

I pull off the head, tip the body upside down, and the data key lands in my palm.

The data key is shiny, wiggling, and resembles an insect. A head of flicking bulbs and connectors, a golden body riddled with tiny tubes and resistors, a tail of copper and plastic-coated wire, and wings of tissue and blood.

The data key is old world tech—a complex mixture of electronic and organic circuitry, similar to the Nine Lords themselves. At least, that's what Aroon tells me. He located it after the last descent, buried deep, its signal shielded. It attacked me when I dug it out, but it rather likes Aroon. He's not too different, after all.

I pinch its body between forefinger and thumb, and it stabs wildly at me with the sharp tip of its tail. Eons trapped, all alone beneath the earth, have driven it insane. Aroon tells me not to personify it like that. The key doesn't have a mind, not really. Its organic processors have rotted away, fragmenting its protocols and ruining whatever information it once stored. That's all. It's perfectly repairable. In fact, for the past two days we have discussed, over and over, how I will do just that. Fix the key, plug it into my little brother, and he will do the rest.

Even so, I can't help but feel sorry for it.

"Phailin!" Mother calls from the street. The procession is about to begin. I wrap the key in cloth, and shove it into my pocket.

When I emerge, the Lords have filled the sky.

The Nine Lords remind me of the ruined city beneath us, except polished, clean and alive. Aroon calls them satellites and orbital stations, but these words don't mean much to me. As they hover above us they look to me like upside-down buildings and empty streets. Arches of pale steel. Engines burning like close suns. Smooth, reflective glass. Rippling liquid crystal in more colours than I have names for. Their searchlights scan over us, the beams hot and intense. Green lasers flicker across our rusting streets. They are accompanied by an ever-present hum, a taste of metal in the air, and the incense of burning plastic.

"Phailin."

My mother waits beside Aroon's Woh. She has acquired a small huddle of tourists—an older couple, and their son. They stand out. Tall and thin where my mother is short and round, black suits with clean shoes instead of loose sarongs and slippers. They have a look I know well by now: wide-eyed, slightly terrified, definitely in awe. It's the look of a wealthy tourist, caught in my mother's web.

"My daughter," Mother tells them. "Sister of Aroon. And almost a Mah Song herself."

I curl my lip at *almost*. My mother does more than pray for a son-in-law, she actively hunts them. Tourists are her speciality. My two elder sisters have both left Ayutthaya in their company.

The procession begins, and the tourists' son falls into step beside me. The crowd grows as we proceed. All around us is chanting, singing, and everywhere red. Red cloth, red face paint, red candles and fireworks.

Behind me, Mother is shouting over the din. "She came so close. Mah Song blood in her, don't you doubt it. Sadly, she's still alone. Spends all her time caring for her brother when she should be caring for a husband and child of her own."

The tourist smiles at me. "Philip." He shouts to be heard, and holds out his hand. I take it only because I know Mother will be watching. He has fine, pale hair, his skin is uncomfortably pink, and his clothes are already heavy with sweat.

The procession ends at the top of the temple steps, and Aroon is set down. The monks emerge, carrying a giant pile of tech scavenged from the ruins and an array of knives. Head tipped back, not watching what he is doing, Aroon stands. Calmly, he selects what he needs to make his sacrifice. A bundle of clear cables, parts of broken circuit boards. A small, very fine knife.

Behind me, the drums start playing. Above me, the Lords start rattling. Aroon opens his mouth, grips his tongue with one hand and the knife with the other—

And I can't watch.

I look at my feet, swallowing nausea, and anger, and an overwhelming hatred for the people around me.

"Oh my God," Philip gasps, beside me, and I shift my attention to him. I'd forgotten he was there. "How can he do that? Doesn't it hurt?"

"When the Mah Song takes him," I say. "He knows no fear. No pain. No weakness."

A moment, a pause, in which Philip presses his hand to his chest. "Amazing." The word escapes on a reverent rush of air.

Sprinklers open in the skies all across Ayutthaya, and the Lords' healing, life-giving waters gush forth. It's a downpour, cold compared to the humid air, at once painful and refreshing.

The tourist lifts his arms to shield his head. I grab his wrists and force them down. He's surprisingly weak.

"Let it fall on you!" I hiss into his shocked face. "This is why you're here, isn't it? The Mah Song sacrifice to the Nine Lords, and they bless us in return. This rain is their blessing!" I release him, and draw a wet, shuddering breath.

He stares at me, blinking too much, not accustomed to the rain's sting. "This? Yes, yes of course. I don't know what I was thinking."

Around us, the sea of red bodies revel in the rain—singing, whirling, drinking, eating, kissing and even fucking, hidden in the tight alleyways. It is happening all along the river; nine temples for Nine Lords, a Mah Song sacrificing in front of each of them, and the people celebrating. Red electric lanterns are strung up between buildings, piles of gunpowder go up in sparks, and there is food everywhere—left out in the rain until it is sodden, disgusting, and so precious.

"It's just not what I expected," Philip says. "The Lords are far away. I've read all about them, I was so excited to finally see them. But now I'm here, I can hardly see anything at all." He shrugs and looks up.

I glance at the temple. "From here, sure. But if you are willing to make an offering you can see them closer—well, a part of them. In the shrine itself." A plan is forming, even as I say the words. This is perfect. The shrine is just where I need to be.

Philip goes through a complicated dance to remove his shoes before I can lead him up the temple steps. He blithely makes what seems to me to be a sizeable donation of credit, and the monks are more than happy to let us in.

Inside the temple is dark, and the moment we step out of the rain and away from the noise, I begin to regret it.

I never wanted to come here again.

Numbers flicker, needles tremble, and patterns of light flash across the switches set into the walls. A bloodied table in one corner—*don't look at it*—and tech piled everywhere, all scavenged from the ruins and brought in tithes. We keep going. In my previous trips to the temple, the shrine has been empty. A great round room with an open roof, walls painted a too-perfect blue and decorated with pale masks—the sightless and impassive faces of countless children. The floor is tiled in crimson and steel, and dried flowers burn in large golden bowls.

This time, the shrine is full. The Lord above us is so massive it fills the sky, and this is its smallest part, slotted in through the hole in the roof when it came in to land. A tumble of wiring and bone, veins and rivets, skin and transistors, with several faces all merging into each other. Dials for eyes, plugs in place of open mouths. Imploring hands spread wide, palms up, holding keyboards or screens.

It could be a statue to worship, except that it is hideous. And it breathes.

"Amazing," Philip whispers. "It's just the way my research described it. A true bio-mechanical computer from the old world."

"And parts of dead Mah Song," I whisper, in reply.

This is my brother's future. Does anything of these people remain behind their empty faces and rigid hands? Can they remember the taste of khanom jark by the riverbank?

I leave Philip peering at an outstretched keyboard, and circle around the Lord until he's out of sight. The key is having a fit when I take it out of my pocket. I keep half of it wrapped, and run a practiced finger down its shivering body to open the casing. A smell like rot and the Lords' own electric haze wafts out on tendrils of smoke.

The parts I need come from the Lord itself. This is the only place to find them whole and living, not ancient and decaying. I use the key's tail to slice into the blue flesh around eyes and mouth then dig into the shallow cuts. They don't bleed. From within the Lord I pull a fine thread of pink and wiggling wire. Carefully, I slide it into the key. It squirms inside, and I repeat the process.

I'm not accustomed to this kind of circuitry. The wires I use tend not to be alive. I'm a little disturbed when all the pink wiggling things bind together, winding themselves into ever more complicated knots before pushing out the old, decomposed wiring until I can pinch and remove it entirely.

"What are you doing?"

I spin, heart in my mouth, but it's only Philip, peering down at me in his innocent-tourist curiosity. I close the key and pocket it as I stand. "Nothing." I smile, but I'm shaking, and it doesn't work very well. "Have you had a good look?"

"Oh yes. It's incredible." He still seems far too distracted by my pocket.

"Good. Let's return to the party then, shall we?"

The key feels heavy as we leave the temple, heavier than it ever was before. It's hope. Hope that my repairs have worked, hope that Aroon's right and the key is big enough to carry all of his memories and personality, so when the Lord takes his body, the rest of him can stay here with me.

But as soon as I see him, all that hope falls away.

Because Aroon will never speak again.

He has split his tongue for the sacrifice and embroidered the inside of his mouth with optical fibre. Blood has dyed his once-white pants red. It colours the puddles on the temple floor around him. It will take days more to get the sacrifice just right. Days of tweaking, of bleeding, and with every adjustment, the Lords bless us.

How will I know if the data key works, if he can't tell me?

Mother is a frenzy of activity, as wild as the full river. The house is as clean as a house built of metal sheets and ancient stones can be. She is using the Lords' bounty to its full, cooking kanom-tom to snack on, cool khao chae, and half a dozen different curries. Philip and his parents accepted her invitation to dinner. I can't imagine why they would want to eat here, when they're staying in the raised tourist annex, further back from the river and accessible only by cable car, but apparently we will make a delightful part of the tourist experience.

I don't have it in me to sit, wait, and pretend to care. Instead, I wander down the alleyways between tin-shed houses baking in the afternoon heat. Life is springing up in the wake of the rains. Skeletal trees are green again, a thick blanket of moss softens every hard surface. Bright yellow orchids burst out of grates in the road. The land of the other side of the river has changed completely. For a few short weeks, it will be clean, and every kind of crop will flourish there. Bridges of rope and iron have been strung up across the rapidly flowing water, ready to harvest the rice, already sprouting.

This is the power of the Lords' blessing. Only yesterday, Ayutthaya was a dark slum, rusted and dead. Now, it is a forest.

This is what my brother, and the other Mah Songs, buy us with their blood.

My brother. All I can think about is the data key, still safe in my pocket. I can't imagine engaging these tourists in conversation. I can't even imagine eating. Another thing Aroon won't do ever again. No space in his head for taste, and now none in his mouth for chewing. He probably doesn't even need to. That's what those power-converters in his neck are for.

"Phailin?"

I'm so distracted, I almost walk right into him. Philip, coming the other way. He checks himself, visibly surprised, then relaxes into a smile. "Oh—I'm so glad I saw you!" He turns and falls into step beside me.

I frown at him. "What are you doing walking around on your own?"

"I just wanted to see the temple some more." It's raining again, and Philip plucks at the front of his shirt as we walk. It's plastered to his chest, wet and heavy. "I must have got lost."

"You must have."

"How do you stand being wet like this all the time?" Philip shakes himself as we negotiate the puddles pooling in the rusty holes and uneven dips in the pockmarked iron road. His feet squelch in those ridiculous shoes. "I've never been so uncomfortable. And trust me, Phailin, I know about being uncomfortable."

I turn, ready to tell him I very much doubt that, when I notice something on his chest. The rain has made his shirt transparent, and his skin is a criss-cross of scars. That stops me in my tracks. Dark, ropey lines and large, circular plugs in shiny chrome.

"Don't let anyone else see those."

He lifts questioning eyebrows, and I nod at his chest.

"Only the Mah Song should augment themselves," I explain, as he reddens further and does up the buttons of his sodden jacket. "At least, that's what the monks teach us."

"It's not exactly augmentation." He crouches to brush away vines tangling around his ankle. "As much as necessity."

And that's when I realise what he is, and why he is really here. "I've heard of people like you. But I didn't believe you existed. So sick your own doctors can't cure you. The blessing of the Nine Lords is your last resort."

He nods. "My nervous system is breaking down. Slowly." He doesn't sound too sad about it. Just resigned. "It's degenerative. Do you know what that means? It's getting worse, gradually. Inexorably. Soon, I won't be able to walk, and then stand, and then, finally, breathe."

I swallow hard.

"It might be uncomfortable," he continues, suddenly bright, "but this rain is amazing stuff. Since the first shower, my hands are steady. No tremors, not even one." He runs his fingers through the wet knots in his pale hair. "Nano-enhanced bacterium, repro-grammed viral matter, and whole strings of hyperactive progenitor cells. No one really knows why the Lords come here to release it. I've read theories that it's a misfiring repair function designed to literally rebuild organic matter from a sub-cellular level."

"You seem to know a lot about the Lords. For a tourist." I can't share his enthusiasm.

"Research!" He beams at me. "I read all about it before I came. The Nine Lords aren't the only relics, you know. There are other satellite and subterranean beings still in existence. But they're the only ones who interact with us. Don't you wonder why? What's going on, behind those faces you showed me? What could they teach us, if only we could get them to speak?"

"Actually, I couldn't care less. Your research means nothing to me. I only care that they need Aroon to cut himself, over and over, until it finally kills him. Slowly." I take a deep breath, try to stay calm. "Think of it as... *Degenerative*. That way you'll know how he feels."

Silence. When I glance up, Philip is staring at me, red-faced and horrified. "He's just a boy, isn't he? To you, I mean. Just a boy, not a sacrifice, not a saviour. Not a wonder of bio-mechanical engineering."

"He's Aroon." I'm having trouble meeting his eyes. I've made him feel guilty, I can see that clearly. Part of me is sorry, because of the plugs in his chest and the death that's stalking him, but part of me is so very glad. I'm not sure which part I want him to see.

"I think we should be honest, don't you?" he says, after we push our way through a crowd that's gathered to catch fish suddenly hatching in a large pothole. "This was not my idea any more than it was yours. But we both know what's going on. Your mother wants a son-in-law. My mother wants a Mah Song grandchild."

I gape at him. "She *what*?"

He sighs. "I know. My doctors have sent me here because they can't help anymore. But it's hardly a permanent solution, is it? No one knows when the Lords will descend, and the boats are few and far between. We waited here for three months before the rain of stars came, and who knows how long before we can go home again? So she's decided if we had a Mah Song of our own, if we could make them come to us—"

I'm shaking my head. "It doesn't work that way. It's not inherited; just because Aroon is a Mah Song doesn't mean anyone else in the family will be."

"That's not the way your mother tells it."

"That sounds like her." I snort a bitter laugh. "Who's to say the Lords would come to you anyway? Have you ever seen one, before coming here? Ever danced in rain that can heal your wounds, grow forests out of nothing, and cleanse ancient poisons from the earth?"

He shakes his head.

"That's because they're our Lords, not yours. This land, this people. Our sacrifice."

He nods. "But I am my mother's son. She is willing to try."

"And what about you?" I squeeze my hands into fists, digging nails into my palm. It doesn't matter, by the time we get home the rain will have healed them. "Would you really wish that on your child? A slow death just to save yourself? One life for another?"

He just looks so damned torn.

"Could you really?" I whisper. "If you had the choice?"

Dinner is awkward.

Late that night, when all the house is sleeping, I take a small blade and sit on the floor in Aroon's room. Light from the Lords filters in through the plastic-sheet windows in steady yellows and greens. It rained again while we were eating, and a cache of tiny geckos exploded out of the ceiling into Philip's mother's hair. I think their affection for us is waning, and I am grateful.

One life, to save another? I know what choice I would make. I've already started.

I work a node in my upper forearm free, catching the blood in an old, soiled towel. The pain is nothing, I tell myself the whole time. Just data. Even as my arm shakes. Just data.

Aroon has taught me many things. In between descents he scours the ancient networks, always plugged in, always searching. Technology and toys are his favourite things, but as his sacrifices increased and his mobility waned, I learned to do the digging and the fixing for him. I can weld the tiny limbs of tin soldiers back in place. I can paint the eyes on dolls. From soldering motherboards to healing organic filament, my skills are growing.

And I have been practising on myself.

Aroon doesn't know this. He would never agree to it.

I pull out a gory plastic and copper mess from my skin. My nodes are inert; they never responded to the Lords in the temple, no light in their bulbs or signals from my brain. But I have repaired computers centuries old. The key is older than history, and I have given it new life—all by following Aroon's instructions. Why can't I do the same for myself? So I've replaced my parts and rethreaded the wires, and sent little shocks of electricity through my palm and dripped rain into the open wounds, in the hope that something, anything, will establish the connections between node and nervous system that the monks were unable to stabilise.

But the key doesn't react to me. I shove its tail of wires in as deep into my nodes as they will go. "Come on," I hiss. Nothing. I don't even know what to expect. Voices from the ancient world, stored on the key, transferred to whisper fragmented and damaged in my brain? A twitch, a flicker of bulbs, anything to indicate we've established a connection?

Still nothing. Either I didn't fix the key properly, or I'm just too broken.

I pull the key free and tie the towel around the wound. Either way, it's not enough. Even if I can transfer his mind to the key, I refuse to leave Aroon alone to rot in madness in an ancient memory device. If I can get these ridiculous nodes working, then I won't have to. I will save him. No matter the cost.

I replace the towel with bandages made from torn sheets and head out into the never-dark night. Back to the temple, in search of more parts.

There's a single family making offerings before the temple, arranging junk in a small pile and burning bowls of flowers. It's odd that the monks aren't there to accept them. The family chant softly, eyes closed and bodies rocking, and take no notice of me as I kick off my slippers and climb the steps.

Aroon, of course, doesn't notice me either. He jerks as I walk past him, lifts an arm, and digs his fingers into his cheeks, wiring away the face I know and love. Right on cue, the sprinklers open.

I duck into the temple just as the rain starts—and pause. It's unusually dark inside. The switches in the walls have been dimmed and even the lights from the Lord in the shrine have gone out.

I drop to all fours and crawl forward into the darkness. Until my hand touches something soft. Warm. I feel around. An arm, a limp hand, fistfuls of cloth. I bend forward, my eyesight gradually adjusting. It's one of the monks, lying prone beneath me. There is blood from a blow to his forehead. I can't tell if he's alive.

I sit back, uncertain. I should leave, now. Raise the alarm, now. But if I do that, I won't have the chance to get back inside here, unsupervised. The throbbing pain in my arm is insistent. I must do what I came here to do, and fix myself, so I can help my brother. Worry about the monks later.

But as I reach the shrine, I begin to hear noises. The scratching of metal and muttered curses. I creep closer.

It's Philip. Philip, naked from the waist up, examining the body of the Lord. Illuminated in the faint light from a single lamp, the plugs in his chest are ugly, ungainly things, and have none of the smooth beauty of Aroon's sacrifices. They poke out, the skin around them red and irritated, criss-crossed with stitches and staples.

I'm so shocked I just stand there, and he sees me.

"Phailin?" He looks tired. Great shadows haunt the skin beneath his eyes, his cheekbones are stark, ribs clear to see. I had not realised how thin he was before. "Why do I keep running into you?"

"What are you doing to the Lord?" I hiss, and take a shaky step forward.

He lifts a gun and points it at me. "Don't move."

We had never found guns. Maybe Aroon didn't look for them, or maybe they'd all been found and removed long before we were born. Even so, I know what one is. And what it can do. "Philip, don't—"

"Just stay where you are. Don't interfere."

I glance back over my shoulder. "The monks?" I whisper. "Was that you? Did you—?" I can't believe it. I can't even say it. Philip, who smiled so readily at me, who was so eager to see the temple, who read so much about the Lords he was desperate to see—

Suddenly, something doesn't feel right. "Wait." I hold his gaze and he narrows his eyes at me. "So eager to get into the temple, all that research? You said the Lords have the technology to cure you." I gesture at the Lord. "Is that why you're really here?"

"You were right, of course," he says, mouth a firm line and expression unreadable. "About the unlikelihood of a Mah Song child. It was the desperate plan of a desperate mother, and the only way I could think to convince her to bring me here. She would never have agreed to the truth." He runs his free hand across the Lord's closest face, and I realise it's the one I cut. "I have, indeed, done my research. And when I saw that little brother of yours, bloodied and pain-free on the top of the steps, I knew I was right. Only the Lords can save me. And not with their fickle rain but their technology. Their very selves."

Knives taken from the monks' testing table lie on the ground at his feet. I think I know what he has in mind. The same thing as me.

"But now that I'm here," he continues, and begins to sound uncertain, "it's nothing like the diagrams." His fingers still on the tiny incision I'd made. He turns to me. "Actually, come here."

My hand is over my pocket, where the key and knife are hiding, but he's watching me so closely I don't dare try to grab them. Not yet.

"You fix me," he says. "I saw you do it, here before. To the data key."

I must look as shocked as I feel, because he smiles, grimly.

"Did you think I wouldn't see? That I was too awestruck to notice you fix it, or that I was just a foolish tourist and wouldn't know what it was? I told you, I've done the research. I know a data key when I see one. Old world tech. Just like your Lords. So you can do the same for me. Take what you need out of the Lord, and fix me."

"Fix—?"

He shakes the gun at me. "I suggest you work faster than that. "

As I approach the Lord, I gesture at Philip's chest. "I'm not even sure what those things are supposed to do. How can I fix them?"

He places a faintly quivering hand over his plugs. "They feed immune suppressants and stabilising neural charges straight into my spine. They don't fix the problem, just maintain it. They also hurt like hell and are constantly getting infected. Unlike your little Mah Song out here, I don't have a Lord to dull the pain."

I look down at the ugly blades scattered across the floor. "I don't think I can help you."

"What?"

I pull back my sleeve and unwind my bloody bandages. "It won't work."

"What are you doing?" Desperation in his voice now. A dangerous sound.

"I've been trying to do it too." I hold out my ruined arm. "My mother wanted me to be a Mah Song, but I failed her. Over and over, I failed her. But I've been trying to fix it. With everything Aroon's taught me, with all the parts he's found and now, tonight,

I was coming here to do the same thing you are. Wire myself with living technology." I let my arm fall, and blood dots the floor. "But I don't know how. You say we've lost the knowledge and only the Lords' have it now. Well, they haven't chosen to share it with us. They chose my brother in his pain-free trance instead. And we just have to accept that."

Philip stares at me, unable, unwilling to comprehend. "But—"

I understand, oh how I understand.

"Well then." He spins, stares back out of the temple. "Maybe he can help me instead." He rubs at his chest and shakes his head. "Just have to wake him up, right?" He stoops, collects a knife, and heads out of the shrine. "Let's see just how pain-free this trance really is!"

"No!" I run after him, but my feet tangle in the tech on the floor and I trip. Even as I fall I grab at his legs but cannot get hold.

He staggers. It's easy to forget how weak he is. He slips to his knees, twists, points the gun at me and fires. But he's unsteady, and he misses. Instead, the bullet goes straight into one of the Lord's stolen faces.

For a moment, there's nothing but the ringing of the shot, then silence.

Until the Lord begins to move. A great shuddering fills the temple. The remaining eyes open, the hands flex, those plug-filled mouths twitch and begin to scream. I grip my ears. It's piercing, so loud, too loud, not only coming from the faces in the shrine but above us, around us. The Lord is screaming. It is full of anger, and of pain, and a desperate confusion. And why wouldn't it be? How much of the Lord is made up of Mah Song, and how much of the Mah Song remains within it? Children, all of them, frightened, modified children.

Philip scrambles to his feet and I follow. Tears pour down my cheeks, the Lord all rage and fear around me. I don't care about the gun anymore. Let him shoot me, it can't feel worse than this. So I leap onto his back and knock him down. I straddle him, grab his arm and beat the gun out of his grip. He's too weak to fight me without his weapon.

I grab a large piece from a scavenged engine and lift it above my head. But even as I look up, there's a figure in the doorway. Small, thin, silhouetted against the light from outside—flashing red now, a sky full of furious Lords—and instantly recognisable. Aroon.

Maybe the Lord is too busy screaming to keep Aroon in his Mah Song trance? Maybe the bullet damaged some vital piece necessary to create the trance to begin with? Either way, the boy that stands in the doorway is free. I can tell, instantly, just from the way he holds himself. He's human again.

I drop the engine and stagger over to him. He wraps his arms around me and I hold him close. He's shaking and bleeding all over me, but he doesn't hold me for long. He pulls back, takes my hand, and leads me to Philip.

Aroon can't speak, so he gestures instead. Philip's trying to stand, I push him down again. "Please?" he gurgles. "Hurts." I roll him onto his back. His plugs did not survive the struggle well—they've been pulled out of alignment, the red skin around them torn, leaking blood and clear, infected pus.

More hand waving from Aroon—desperate, hurried, fearful—and I run outside, to the pile of wires and blades and needles he's been using to sew himself with. I gather them all, barely noticing the chaos below. The Lords are sitting lower in the sky, their vents closed, sirens and lasers and lights beat down instead of rain. The streets are full of people, all heading for the temples, but no one is dancing. We don't have much time. Whatever Aroon is doing, he has to do it quickly.

I pass him his tools. His mouth moves but the noises that come out aren't words. The fibres sewn into his cheeks stretch in what I hope is a smile.

I help him, alternating between holding Philip down, finding Aroon what he needs, and completing the delicate tasks his fingers struggle with. With fibres, wires, nodes, circuit boards and organic matter taken from the screaming Lord itself, we open up the poorly made plugs in Philip's chest. It looks like a terrible mess to me, but Aroon seems to know what he's doing. He did something similar to himself once, to install that fan.

As we rewire Philip, I whisper to him. "Shh there, you're okay. Just a little more." I try to be soothing. "It's what you wanted, isn't it? The technology of the Lords to fix you?" After a while I'm not sure he can hear me anymore. Blood pools around us; my arms are slick up to my elbows. "We're all just data, after all."

When Aroon and I have finished, Philip's plugs are completely different. They lie flush against his chest, and they're wired into his heart, lungs and spine with the Lord's organic filament.

Aroon sits back, and holds out his hand. But I shake my head. "I don't know if I did it properly," I whisper. "I don't know if I fixed the key right. What if it doesn't work?"

He doesn't move. Is that trust in his ruined face?

Voices outside, the temple shuddering, and I know we don't have any time left. So I prod at the skin around the edge of his fan, to the hidden plug there. The one he made himself, not under the influence of the Mah Song. It's different from the rest of his sacrifices. Rusty copper tipped with green.

I slot the key in. For a moment, nothing seems to happen. Then Aroon closes his eyes, tips back his head, and the key flutters, flashing. Alive.

It pops back out on its own. It's warm, and solid, and still.

No time for doubt. People in the doorway, voices shouting, shadows and fitful light. I spin and slam the key into one of the plugs in Philip's chest, as Aroon stands, and walks calmly into the shrine.

He never comes out again.

I lost track of Philip in the chaos—the monks from other temples, the sirens and the screaming and Aroon, choosing to destroy himself to repair the Lord. Someone dragged me away, so at least

I didn't see him in the very end. It hasn't rained since, and barely enough food has grown to feed us. Already, there have been fights, and an entire neighbourhood poisoned by freshly dried rice.

The wounded Lord called a new Mah Song before it ascended. A tiny girl—she looked as young as three—who cried as they carried her in a terrible and solemn procession to have her first incisions made.

The tourist ships have left, following the river back out to sea. My mother disowned me. And now, I scavenge a poor living on the tech I can dig out of the city below. I still remember the places Aroon sent me, and I will forever keep the skills he gave me. But there isn't much of a market for toys, and some weeks, I am forced to beg for what food I can. On the riverbank, where we used to walk, where we planned a way to help him escape. Aroon, my little brother and Mah Song. Gone.

Empty and alone, I sit at our usual spot, my legs dangling over the river. The lizards watch like they are waiting for me to fall in.

Then a man sits beside me. At first glance, I don't recognise him. He has a heavy cloth wrapped around his head, and bare feet. Then he hands me khanom jark. "I know it's only data," he says, smiling. "But I've missed the taste of coconut."

What We Ourselves Are Not

By Leah Cypess

T he second Zach's mother walked into his room, he knew it was time for the Talk. She was biting the side of her lip, the way she did when she was really nervous, and she gave his picture of Amy an extra long look before she sat down on his bed.

Not that he was surprised. It was his seventeenth birthday, and the copy of *Dealing with the Teen Years* she kept on her nightstand recommended seventeen as the ideal age for chip implantation. Which made sense: it only became legal at sixteen, and was usually impossible by the age of twenty, due to decreased brain plasticity.

Secretly reading that book had been one of the best moves he'd ever made. Now he always knew what to expect when his mother got nervous.

"Zach," his mother said. Despite all the signs of nervousness, her voice was casual and even. *Dealing with the Teen Years* also recommended "practicing important conversations" and "preparing responses for expected arguments." Though Zach was pretty sure his mother had no response prepared for what he was going to say.

Since she had done all that preparation, though, it seemed polite to at least let her get through her speech. He minimized his v-screen and said, "Hey."

"So." His mother smoothed the blanket over his mattress. "I know a couple of your friends have chips now, and I was wondering if you were thinking about it."

Zach grunted. Suddenly, despite the fact that he had prepared for this, he wanted to put off the inevitable.

"I also know that some of your friends have opted not to be chipped, and your father and I will respect your decision if that's what you want. But we really think getting a chip will be the best thing for you."

Amy's parents had thought the same thing. They had even paid big bucks for the custom add-ons she had asked for.

His mother's brow furrowed, and Zach realized that she was waiting for a response. He tried to think of one. "Uh—why?"

"Because it can be difficult, in today's world, to hold on to who you are and what makes you unique." She launched into the speech with evident relief. "It's so easy to be swallowed up by the majority, and that might even seem like an attractive option to you. But a world without diversity is a poorer world…"

He tuned her out while pasting an attentive look on his face. The school had been organizing discussion groups about chips for months now; he knew all the arguments and all the counterarguments. They merged in his head into one vast swirl of confusion. It didn't matter. He had made his decision, so he didn't have to think about it anymore.

His mother drew in her breath, and he blinked at her. She was looking at him with concern; maybe his attentive look had slipped. She winced, then said, "If you … want … we can get the version without the Holocaust."

Wow. They really wanted him to get the chip.

But the wince helped. It seemed to stake out some part of the decision as his own instead of his parents'. There was something about his mother's pride in his accomplishments that could bring out the worst in Zach—as if her happiness wrapped itself around him and stifled him, leaving him no space to breathe. It was easier to be rational around her when she wasn't completely thrilled with him.

"All right," he said with a shrug. "I'll check out both versions and decide which one I want."

His mother peered at him. This was not the response she had been prepared for. "You're sure? You mean … you've already … you're going to get a chip?"

"I am," Zach said. And then, since she seemed to have nothing to say, he pulled up his v-screen again. Hopefully, that would signify that the conversation was over.

The v-screen's audio pickup was obviously working well, since the first thing that popped up was an article called, "Are Chips Making Society More Fragmented?" The answer seemed obvious, so Zach ignored the article and switched back over to the game he had been playing.

But his mother wasn't done. "Zach. I'm very happy to hear that, but I want you to be sure."

"I am," he said. And then, for no reason, "Amy already got one."

"Oh." He could see her struggling with herself. She took a deep breath. "This should be your own decision, Zach. Not something you're doing to be more like your girlfriend."

A harsh laugh slipped out of him. "More *like* her? Not really."

"Zach. I know how you feel about Amy, but the two of you are still in high school. I know it's hard to see now, but someday…"

"Stop it," Zach said, already regretting the slip. There was a reason he usually kept his love life off limits in conversations with his parents. "Not someday. Today."

"What?"

"Amy and I broke up."

"Oh." She shot another startled glance at the picture on his desk. "I'm sorry."

"No, you're not."

"Zach—"

"It's fine." He restarted the game and scowled with concentration at the new challenge he had just opened. "I just don't want to talk about it. It has nothing to do with the chip."

Which was a lie. But his mother didn't question it, since it was what she wanted to hear.

He saw Amy in school the next day, and for the first time in a week he didn't turn and head the other way. He didn't head toward her, either, though that had been his plan. He just stood and looked at her, standing like an idiot in the middle of the hall, feeling as if his heart had frozen and was blocking his ability to breathe.

He had never believed she would break up with him. Even after she got her chip, even after the school's discussion group on how chips could change relationships, even after days of subtle but definite distance between them. He hadn't believed it until she had told him, and then...

Well, then he hadn't handled it very well.

"I don't want to hurt you," she had said, after about ten minutes of him making a fool of himself. "And I'm sorry, Zach, I'm so so sorry. It's just that I'm part of something, something that is big and important and that shouldn't disappear from the world. I don't want to be a part of making it disappear. I have an identity and a purpose, and I want my children to have that too."

"We can make our own identity." Even as he'd said it, he had been grateful none of his friends were around to hear him begging.

"We don't have to be tied down to the past. Cultures change all the time."

"Changing isn't the same as disappearing."

"You were Korean before! Do you think Koreans who haven't been chipped aren't real Koreans?"

She had flinched at that, making him shamefully glad. "No. But it's ... it's more of me, now. It's the base of what I am, not just a part of who I am. I can't imagine who I would be if I wasn't Korean."

"I can."

She had stepped back then, giving him a look that made it clear that not only was he not getting it, he had just said exactly the wrong thing. He had seen her drawing away and known there was no way to stop her.

"It doesn't have to be like this!" He couldn't help sounding desperate. "Don't blame it on the chip. You and I, we were talking about *forever*." He had almost been crying. Okay, not *almost*. "I love you, Amy. We were planning to go to the same college. We were happy. How can something be good if it ruins that? What's more important than people being happy?"

"I know you don't understand." If only she had been crying too. But her face, though pale, had been calm. "I don't expect you to, Zach."

He hadn't expected to either.

But today, he was full of hope for the first time in days. He took a deep breath, then another, then another, until it was almost easy. And then he walked right up to her, as if he had a right to, and said, "Hey."

Her friends exchanged looks, then scattered. They didn't even bother making excuses.

"Hey," Amy said warily. Her dark eyes were red-rimmed, but Zach knew better than to assume she had been crying over their breakup. The first couple of weeks after implantation were said to be tough.

"I'm getting my chip this afternoon," he said. "My parents talked me into it."

Amy peered at him from under her red-streaked bangs. She knew him better than anyone. She knew his parents hadn't talked him into it.

"Good," she said finally. "I think you should get a chip."

"I'm aware of that."

"I think everyone should know where they come from."

"Spare me the pep talk."

She narrowed her eyes. "I also think you should be doing it for the right reasons."

Zach swallowed hard, suddenly very aware of the overlap between grand romantic gestures and pathetically desperate wussiness. "I'm doing it for you."

"Oh, Zach."

"Once I have a chip too, I'll understand you again, and we'll—"

She shook her head so sharply that the ends of her black hair whipped into his face. He hadn't realized he was standing so close to her. But she didn't step back, so neither did he.

"Don't you want that?" He had definitely crossed over the wussiness border now, but he couldn't make himself stop. "You said I couldn't understand you anymore…"

"You won't be getting the same chip as me, Zach!"

Zach tried to imagine telling his parents that instead of the Jewish chip, he wanted the Korean one. Even in his mind, he couldn't pull it off. "I read this article last week. It said the gap between the chipped and the non-chipped is far greater than the gap between those whose chips are from different cultural backgrounds."

"That makes sense." Amy stepped back, squashing Zach's impulse to lean in and kiss her. Which was probably a good thing. "Now that I have the chip, I feel a connection to everyone who's proud of their differences, even if they're not different in the same way I am."

"So once I have a chip—"

"Zach." She bit her upper lip, a habit she had developed back when she was trying to cure her overbite. He had always found that habit oddly sexy, but now all he felt was a roil of misery and confusion. "Don't. Even if you get a chip, we're not getting back together."

This time, he was the one who stepped back. "Fabulous idea, then, isn't it? After all this time we've spent learning to respect our common humanity, to know that we're all the same deep down, let's divide people up into distinct little groups again. Like we don't have enough ways of making people more distant from each other."

"Zach." She stepped forward, and he held up both hands as if to ward her off. "You already are distant from almost everyone who exists. The chips make you closer to the people you *can* be closer to." She bit her upper lip again. "But that's not the point. If that's how you feel, you shouldn't get a chip."

She was so calm, so reasonable. He couldn't even make her mad anymore. It was like they had broken up a year ago instead of last week.

She hadn't cried at all. Not over him. He had; he had sobbed in his room the night they broke up, with his music cranked up loud so no one could hear. But he was sure she had not cried over him, not one single tear. And he knew it was horrible, but he wished that she would.

The silence stretched between them. She kept her beautiful dark eyes on him, careful and considering. It wasn't just that they were red and puffy. They were … old. Older than seventeen. Burdened with knowledge and experience.

I don't want eyes like that, Zach thought suddenly. He drew in a ragged breath, and heard himself say, "I hate you for this."

Amy blinked. Then she reached out and touched his cheek. "No, Zach. You don't."

He'd had a response all ready, but her touch froze him. "How can you—"

She smiled, a smile as old as her eyes. "Because I know what it's like to really be hated."

And soon, he guessed, so would he.

He didn't cancel the implantation. He didn't have the energy to face that fight, not after how excited his parents had been all day. At least someone was happy.

"So," his father said, in the gray-walled waiting room. "About the Holocaust…"

The woman in the seat next to them, a black woman with a bored-looking teenage boy, glanced at them and then looked away. Zach wished his father would lower his voice.

"You know," his father said, not lowering his voice, "the whole reason the original chips were developed was because of the Holocaust. Because the last survivors were dying, and people were saying it never happened. They wanted to make sure the next generation would never forget."

Zach knew the history. But his father always took a long time to get to a point, so he just nodded. He hadn't thought he was opposed to getting the Holocaust memories, until his father started going on about them. Now he was starting to wonder what he was even doing here.

If that's how you feel, you shouldn't get a chip. But he didn't know how he felt. He wished he *did* know, the way Amy did.

On the end table next to their faded brown chairs was a pamphlet with red block letters across the front: *Will your culture still exist a century from now?*

He couldn't possibly tell his parents he was rethinking the whole chip idea, so he stuck to the subject he was allowed to argue about. "It's not like I plan on trying to forget about the Holocaust," he said. "But I'm not sure I want it hardwired into me. Shouldn't I have a choice?"

"A choice about what?" his mother said. "About whether these things happened? About whether they happened to people related to you? About whether you choose to forget everything they did and suffered and lived for and died for?"

His father took a deep breath. But before he could start circling around the point again, the receptionist sang out, in a bored voice, "Levinsons, please make your way to Room 173."

They had to wait for the tech, so his father got to review the history all over again, reading most of it straight from one of the glossy brochures, while his mother sat watching them anxiously.

There were three Jewish chips. The first — "more for historical interest, really" —was Holocaust-only; the impending deaths of the last Holocaust survivors twenty years ago had been the impetus for the first chip.

The second was the broader cultural chip, a collection of memories put together by a coalition of Jewish organizations: Holocaust survivors, soldiers in Israel's War of Independence,

American Jews rallying for Soviet Jews, an Egyptian Jew being forced to sign the Pledge to Never Return, an Ethiopian Jew stepping off a plane onto Israeli soil. His father didn't mention the fact that there was still daily squabbling in the Jewish papers about why one person's memories had been chosen over another's. Not that Zach read the Jewish papers, but he'd had to do a term paper about it last year. Every ethnic group had the same kinds of arguments about their chips. Some had refused to try to put together a chip at all, finding the whole idea impossible or even offensive. One of Zach's bandmates was Han Chinese, and wanted a chip but couldn't get one; his parents didn't have the multi-millions necessary to create a personalized chip from scratch.

Along with the history, there were the non-specific memories: complete knowledge of Hebrew, Ladino, and Yiddish (either the full language, or just the jokes and curses), a repertoire of ethnic recipes, a song repository, and the basic traditions of all the Jewish holidays.

And then, of course, there was the third choice. All the knowledge and all the memories—except the Holocaust. His father was just getting started on that when the tech entered the room. She was a short, older woman—young enough to be hot, though—with light brown skin and severely-cut hair. Zach watched her face as she described the chips in a detached tone.

"None of the memories will make you feel like you're reliving them," she said. She had a pleasant, reassuring voice. Zach wondered if her voice was the reason she had been hired to do this. "They'll feel like exactly that, memories. Some you might never even 'remember' unless a circumstance calls them up. If you choose to add personal memories from your own parents and grandparents, those are usually more vivid…"

She lifted an eyebrow, and smiled faintly when Zach's parents shook their heads. "I didn't think so. Some ethnicities tend to be more interested in the family memory option than others."

Amy's family add-ons had cost almost as much as her original chip. Zach's parents had never even mentioned them.

"However, there are those who feel that the Holocaust memories are so traumatic as to be debilitating. You probably know that in San Francisco, implanting chips containing Holocaust memories is illegal without a prior psychiatric evaluation."

"What is your opinion?" Zach's father said.

The tech half-smiled, half-grimaced. "Even though the input is the same, everyone filters it through their own personalities and experiences, so outputs vary widely—for all aspects of the cultural memories, but especially for the Holocaust. Most of my patients who take the full implant adjust quite well. There are those who have a lot of difficulty, especially those who didn't understand the full extent of the Holocaust before they got their chip. The more you've read up on it in advance, the easier the transition will be. I see you go to Hebrew school once a week. That will help a lot." She rubbed her forehead. "You do have to understand that the chips can't be un-implanted. The procedure is not reversible."

"Do you have a chip?" Zach asked.

"Zach!" his mother said.

The tech chuckled. "That's all right. A lot of people ask. The answer, Zach, is that I don't. I'm half Hispanic, one-quarter Native American, and one-quarter Irish. I wouldn't even know where to begin."

"Then how can you participate in this?" He didn't have to turn around to know that both his parents were glaring at him. "Your parents and … and ancestors … if they hadn't bridged the differences between them, you wouldn't even exist. Do you think differences between people are a *good* thing?"

She tilted her head to the side. "Say there were no differences between people. Who should we all be like?"

"Like—like people who can choose their own way. Who don't want to be trapped by history. Who care about everyone equally. Who are free. People like…" His voice died before he could finish. *Like me.*

She smiled. "Everyone does choose their own way, Zach. And for some people, the way is a chip. This might surprise you, but after everything I've seen working here, seeing how much meaning people can find in their culture and history, I'm considering getting a chip myself. Probably the Irish one, because it's my Irish grandmother who…" She stopped and gave a little laugh. "We don't need to get into that."

"Aren't you too old?"

"Zach!" His father, this time. His parents tended to take turns like that.

The tech just shrugged. "There are new chips being developed that will work even on people whose brain growth is minimal. Twenty isn't the limit anymore."

Zach's father blinked, then leaned forward eagerly. "I hadn't heard about those."

"They're not publicly available yet."

"When will they be?"

The tech hesitated. Zach wondered if she wasn't supposed to tell people about this. "There will be a limited run in December. If you want to sign up as a possible participant—"

"I do," Zach's father said instantly.

His mother sat silent.

Zach turned and stared at her. She was biting the side of her lip. "Mom?"

She looked away from him.

Zach stood up. "Are you kidding me? *You* don't want a chip?"

"I'm not eligible for one."

"I'll give you a moment," the tech said hastily, all but scrambling to her feet.

"That won't be necessary," Zach's mother said. "This isn't a secret. It just … never came up."

"*What* never came up?" Zach asked.

His mother took a deep breath. "That I'm not Jewish."

★

Necessary or not, the tech seemed pretty eager to leave once the yelling reached a certain level. The door swung shut behind her.

"We weren't hiding it from you," Zach's mother said, for the dozenth time. "And I did convert, though not, technically, in a way we could prove."

"We agreed to raise you Jewish," his father said, "so we thought—"

"*Why?*" Zach kept his focus on his mother. "*Why* would you agree to raise me Jewish? With all this talk about the past defining me and not forgetting who I am. What about who *you* were? Why was it okay for that to get lost?"

"I had nothing to *lose*." His mother lifted her head. The more Zach shouted, the calmer and more in control she became. "My parents lost it for me. I had no idea who I was, where I came from, and they thought it didn't matter. They thought there should be no differences between people. That I should be exactly the same as every other person in the world, no matter where they came from, no matter what their history or culture."

"Sounds good to me," Zach said bitterly.

"It wasn't coincidence that I married your father. We met at a class about Judaism. You can't imagine how much it appealed to me, the idea of being part of a people who had endured through centuries against unimaginable odds, who never let go of who they were. I wanted to be part of that and I wanted my children to be part of it. And I understood that you can't have it both ways. If you want to be part of something bigger than yourself, Zach, then there are choices that have to be made. It's what I tried to explain to you about Amy—"

"I'm seventeen, Mom! I wasn't going to marry Amy!"

"But whoever you marry. If she's not someone who shares your culture, then you have to make a choice, when it comes to your children."

"What if we don't? What if we're not so damn dramatic about it, and just wait to see what happens, instead of deciding that one culture has to lose?"

"Then the minority culture loses," his mother snapped, her control finally breaking. "Then after all those generations of holding fast, you let go of your identity just because you couldn't be bothered to care."

"I don't see why I *should* care about a bunch of people who lived and died before I was ever born, just because I happen to share their DNA." His mother flinched, and his anger broke, a bit. He didn't mean that, not really. Or at least, he wasn't sure he did. "Besides, it's not quite as simple as that. In case you haven't noticed, neither Amy nor I are exactly part of the majority culture."

"Don't be ridiculous," his mother said. "You both were."

Were. Until last week, when Amy got her chip.

Someone rapped on the door, and the tech peeked her head through. "I'm sorry to interrupt. But we don't have much time, if you're planning to go ahead with the procedure."

The silence was absolute.

"Also, Ms. Levinson? I want to point out that there are no eligibility requirements for any of the chips. You don't have to prove anything. If, er, if that's what you want."

"Thank you," Zach's mother said, her eyes on Zach. "That's what I want."

Zach looked back at her, then at his father, who was watching his mother. Then he looked at the tech.

"I'm ready," he said. "I know what I want, too."

Amy came over to him once he was back in school. Her eyes were clear again, though still oddly old, and she was wearing the short pleated skirt she had worn on their first date. Zach met her eyes, then turned and walked down the hall and out the front doors of the school.

He wasn't sure she would follow him. But she did, all the way down the block and around the corner, into a small deserted park they used to sneak out to whenever they got a chance. Just being there with her made his blood heat up.

But other memories overlaid that now. That first sight of Amy had been a shock, calling up a memory of a girl who looked a lot like her, singing and laughing in Pagoda Park, her face full of hope, a line of Japanese policemen advancing slowly behind her.

When Zach turned to face her, that faded. It was just Amy, beautiful and brilliant and brave, who, despite what he'd told his parents, he had fully believed he would marry someday. He couldn't imagine ever meeting anyone better, or loving anyone more.

"How are you adjusting to the chip?" Amy twirled a slack strand of hair tightly around her finger, a habit she had been trying to break for a year. She had asked Zach to mention it when he saw her doing it, but this didn't seem like the time.

"They're okay," he said. "It takes some getting used to. I have nightmares."

Her finger stopped in mid-twirl. "They?"

"Especially about the 6.25 War," Zach said. "The one where I'm watching my village burn to the ground. I can't shake that one."

She dropped her hand. Her hair sprang free.

He laughed at the expression on her face. "I got both. Jewish and Korean."

She stood there, frozen, staring at him. The silence stretched so long that he heard himself saying, awkwardly, "I can give making kimchi a shot now—I've got a bunch of different recipes in my head, and a lot of good memories associated with the taste. Though I still can't promise I'll like your mother's soup."

Amy drew in a sharp breath. "They let you do that?"

"Not just let me. Once I explained my idea, they were all excited about it—they even paid for it, when my parents wouldn't. There's going to be an article about me and everything." He couldn't stop smiling, even though she wasn't smiling back. "I was thinking that once I adjust to these, I can get all the chips. Understand everyone's culture. And once people know it can be done, maybe I won't be the only one who makes that choice."

"God, Zach." She was staring at him, but not in the wonder he had anticipated. There was horror written across her face. "You had no right!"

"The tech said it was an amazing idea. Said it could change the world. Can you imagine—" He stopped. He was babbling, which was *his* nervous habit. "But I didn't do it for the world. You know why I did it."

She turned abruptly, leaving him staring at her hair and her back and her trembling hands. "I did it for you. Because now we can go back to being what we were."

"I didn't want to be what we were!"

That hurt, more than anything else she had said or done to him. It was a moment before he could speak. "That's not what you said. Not at the dance, or that time on the bridge. Remember?" He stepped forward and raised his hand, but let it drop before it touched her hair. "You said we were different. And we *were*. We are. We have a future together, Amy."

"I know!" She whirled back, and he saw that her eyes were bright with unshed tears. "I know we did, Zach. Don't you see? That's why I did this. Because of you."

"Because of—"

"I *do* love you! The chip doesn't change that."

Do. Not *did*. His heart suddenly felt lighter than it had in weeks. "Then what does it change?"

"It changes what I want my life to be. Or how badly I want it. Being Korean is important to me as a way of life, and I want to pass it along to my children *as a way of life*. Not as a colorful addition to being just like everyone else."

"But being just like everyone else could be a *good* thing. Especially if the reporter is right, if what I did catches on." He lifted a hand toward her face, and she didn't turn away. His fingers touched her cheek. "Don't you see? It's not about erasing differences. It's about erasing divisions. I identify with everyone, now."

"No." She slapped his hand away. Her eyes were bright, dark and shining. "You skipped the part where you learn how to do that. How can you identify with everyone when you can't even identify with your own people?"

His hand was shaking as he lowered it to his side. This wasn't how this was supposed to go. "That's exactly the sort of narrow-minded thinking I don't want to be forced into. Do you *want* to divide people from each other? To divide me from you? What if it doesn't have to be this way? You said I could never understand, but I do now. I *do*."

"You don't! I'm trying to make you understand, and you won't. No matter how much I love you, Zach, I can't have the life I want if I'm with you."

"But I—"

"Grafted it on like it was an interesting extra-curricular? My culture, along with *everyone's* culture? No, Zach. That just proves how little you understand." She began to cry then—finally, after all this time—and it didn't make him feel better at all. He felt cold and empty. Tears dripped off her chin as she spoke. "You've done exactly what the chips were created to prevent. You want to erase all our differences. You want to make us all the same."

He wanted to brush away her tears. He wanted to hold her close. Instead, he held himself very still. "Yes. Because it will be a better world that way. I did this because *every* culture is important to me."

"No." She stuttered, but kept going. "What you're setting out to do is destroy my culture. Mine, and yours—"

"Don't pretend you care about mine!"

"I *do* care! I care about everyone's. I'm not afraid to be different, so I'm not afraid of other people being different. But you are."

"Maybe you should be," Zach said. "Differences between people aren't so simple. They can be dangerous. Read some history."

"Read some *more* history. People will find things to fight about no matter what. And fighting is better than persecution, Zach, which is what you get when you try to force everyone to be the same."

"I'm not trying to force anyone to do anything! That's what you and your precious chips are about. I'm just trying to help people move past worrying about persecution, past being stuck in history, past being obsessed with their own narrow ways of life—"

"So we should all be the same? Is that really what you want?"

"I want—" He stopped. He took a deep breath. "You know what, Amy? Yesterday, all I wanted was to understand *you*. But today I want more than that." He forced himself to look straight at her. "Now I'm part of something more important. Something bigger than I would have been a part of if I'd only implanted one chip."

"I don't think so," she said.

He managed a trembling smile. "I know."

She brushed away her own tears, and they stood in silence, facing each other.

He was the first to step back. They stood looking at each other for a few moments more, and then they turned and went back to school, walking side by side but with a significant distance between them.

The City of Chrysanthemum

By Ken Liu

Bobby is the first off the school bus. He always sits in the front seat on the right; first, because the driver can offer some protection, and second, because he can get out quickly.

He does not look behind him. He can feel their gazes.

It's still fifteen minutes until homeroom, and this is among the most dangerous times during the day. He makes his way to the east wing, and dodges through the crowd of eighth-graders like a minnow among bigger fish.

The art room is empty. He shucks off his backpack and pushes it under the sink, then crawls into the cubby himself.

The dim space and the silence reassure him. He lets out a held breath, a mixture of shame and relief.

He thinks about what he'll draw, later, when he's free from this prison called school: a ball gown, sleeveless, with a beaded bodice and a full skirt. He imagines patterning the swirling, smoky silk like a sun-dried rainbow so that when spun it will look like a blossoming chrysanthemum…

"There you are!" says Tom.

"Think you can hide here all day?" says Gene.

They drag him out by his hair. He slaps at their arms ineffectually.

"That's for running away," says Tom. The punch to the small of his back makes him arch over and drop his backpack.

Gene pinches Bobby's arm through his shirt and twists as he applies pressure. "Cry, sissy, cry."

Bobby doesn't make any sound. Tom and Gene are very smart. They never touch his face, which might raise questions.

They open his backpack and dump everything on the ground.

"Where are the girlie pictures you like to draw?"

He bites his lips and closes his eyes.

At sunset, the concentric layers of carp scale shingles on top of the Palace reflect the golden light so brilliantly that visitors to Chrysanthemum know right away how the city got its name.

The Prince spins in secret in his room.

The City of Chrysanthemum | Ken Liu

He gathers the gossamer roving on his distaff by sneaking into the empty garden before sunrise, when spiders spin webs between the giant flowers to capture the dewy dawn.

Once, when the King found his drop spindle, he had lied and said it was a top.

As he spins, the threads capture the light coming through the stained glass window, and the yarn winding around the shaft glitters like a lazy rainbow.

"Don't feel well?" Mom asks at dinner.

He shakes his head.

"Were those boys bullying you?" asks Dad. "You seemed afraid of them when I picked you up."

He immediately denies it.

"I can talk to the teachers," Mom says.

Fear threatens to overwhelm him. That parents can be such fools still astonishes him.

Dad comes to his rescue, sort of. "Elaine, he has to learn to stick up for himself." He turns to his son. "How about we practice throwing some punches?"

He wishes he could tell his father the truth. But this is the real world.

Reluctantly, he nods.

*

The Prince weaves the yarn into cloth. The fabric is full of light, playful, warm to the touch. He thinks wearing it will be like wearing a summer's worth of afternoons. He's so absorbed in the task that he doesn't hear the King entering the room.

"What is this?" asks the King. "You're a boy. You should be learning to fight, to be strong and brave."

"I don't like to fight," says the Prince.

And because this is Chrysanthemum, the explanation actually works. The Prince shows the King the dress he has in mind and the King admires it, smiling.

Bullies back down when you stand up to them, Bobby repeats to himself. He makes fists the way Dad showed him.

But Tom and Gene don't back down. His punch is easily deflected, and Gene laughs as his kick connects with Bobby's stomach.

Blinded by the pain, Bobby waves his hands wildly and manages to grab onto Tom's hands by the thumbs.

"Sissy wants to dance!"

Powered by rage and desperation, Bobby puts all his strength into his hands as he bends Tom's thumbs backwards. He sees fear and pain in Tom's eyes.

But Bobby is not a fighter. He lets go.

They hurt him. A lot.

He will not cry.

The City of Chrysanthemum | Ken Liu

In Chrysanthemum, the girls do not have to spin and weave and the boys do not have to learn to use a sword.

"There are other ways to be strong and brave," says the Prince. "Sometimes, it just means doing what you love."

Megumi's Quest

By Joyce Chng

Megumi heaved herself up the cliff, her fingers raw and tender from gripping the sharp-edged nooks and crevices. Her thighs felt as if they were on fire. Beside her, her wolf Tetsu tackled the ledges with surefootedness, his tongue lolling out of his mouth as he panted.

Once over this cliff, we would be done with the challenge, she told herself.

She pushed up, up, up, and finally reached the top, panting. At least, her spiritual body was far healthier and agile than her physical body connected via a tenuous silver cord. Megumi glanced at Tetsu who joined her, his tail wagging slowly. His ears flicked upright, twitching at the slightest of sounds.

We find the eggs now, the white-blue wolf said in her mind.

Yes, the eggs that bred the monster. Megumi placed her hand on the plush soft fur. *Let's go. Time is running out.*

Already the lumps on her body were spreading. She looked at them with disgust and focused wholly on her journey.

Patient is now in REM sleep. Monitoring, monitoring. The situation appears stable.

Megumi and Tetsu trotted across thorns that cut their legs, trailing blood all over like cobwebs of crimson treacle. They leapt across rivers of crystals and creeks that oozed clear water with the smell of antiseptic, like Dettol used by her mom when she mopped the floor. The sky above them was a gentle sea-shell pink and the mountain ridge reached up like jagged fingers chewed off by an angry animal. She stared at the mountain, feeling a spike of fear. It loomed, about to claw at her. She had experienced that same fear when the doctor told her about her illness. *Cancer*, the doctor said so matter-of-factly. *End of Stage 3*. She was only sixteen, too young to die. In school, she was a top swimmer with gold medals that made her parents proud. She was top of her class for Math and English. The next thing she knew, she was in the hospital, going through a battery of tests, attached to machines and gadgets. She missed her friends. She missed life outside the hospital. She wanted her body back. She wanted life to be back to normal.

She just wanted to be a normal teenager.

"I'm dying," she told her best friend over the phone. She missed her cell phone too. Pink with Hello Kitty on it, embedded with gems and sequins. She had bought it with her allowance. The next week she was brought to the hospital, having collapsed suddenly in school. She felt like a cyborg attached to so many appliances. A machine helped her breathe. Another machine fed her liquid food.

The monster resided there in the mountain. So did the eggs.

Hurry, hurry, Tetsu warned her with a curl of his lip. He always looked as if he was smiling. He had always urged her on, given her strength. He was the combination of all the good and nice things in her life.

I am! Megumi said, catching her breath. *Wait, wait, wait for me. Tetsu?*

The quest was not going as smoothly as she originally thought. They had encountered so many challenges that she had lost count. She just pushed on. The cliff was the hardest, so hard, so hard. She felt weary, despondent and on the verge of giving up. She had to push forward. She was a competitive swimmer, an athlete. She recognized the wall when she saw it.

Tetsu was the animal who came to her in a dream. He was her guardian, her protector. In this quest, Tetsu accompanied her.

More thorns blocked their ways. Interlocking brambles with fiendishly pointed spikes bristled at them. Tetsu growled softly.

Megumi bit her lower lip. They moved forward and the bramble rattled ominously.

Patient is displaying signs of elevated heartbeat and breathing. Monitoring.

The thorns were alive, lashing at them like nightmare whips. Tetsu was caught and flung across the earth, his chest bleeding, his muzzle disfigured with bright red wounds. Megumi screamed and when she screamed, the lumps on her body flared up like poisoned tattoos dotting her limbs. She screamed even louder, out of sheer shock. Pain awoke in her, sharp knives drilling right into her bones. Was it even possible to feel such horrific pain in her spiritual form?

TETSU!

All she heard was a whimper, a puppy's distress call for its mother. She knew how it sounded because she had a puppy once who cried the whole night. Her parents bought the puppy as her birthday gift. She named him...

TETSU!

She flung out her hands and paper origami cranes shot out from her fingers. They attacked the thorns and the thorns retaliated back. Shreds of paper filled the air like New Year's confetti, like mid-winter snow. She loved snow. But this snow was a hateful and loathsome one. Megumi screamed and the cranes flew on, stronger and determined, weaving around the thorns and squeezing the life of them.

TETSU!

She had to save the wolf.

She had to.

A tendril gripped her ankle and she fell.

Patient is now showing signs of distress. Abort mission? Query. Query. Urgent. Urgent.

Megumi swung in the air, dizzy as blood rushed to her head. She saw the thorns had a mouth, that the thorns were actually part of a creature with a moist, sharp-toothed mouth in the middle. It drooled blood, sap and something else she didn't like the sight and smell of. It smelled like a clogged sewage drain outside her family house. It smelled vile, evil, filled with dead and decaying things.

Remember the tools! Tetsu's voice was weak and growing weaker by the minute, but Megumi heard him clearly. *Remember what you have!*

Megumi reached deep inside her and reached out her katana which she used to slice at the flailing thorny tendrils. The katana resembled her oji-san's. She had loved the ancient blade ever since she saw it displayed reverentially at her grandparents' home. She sobbed aloud as she cut and cut and cut. She couldn't—and shouldn't—stop cutting. The tendrils seemed to go on forward. Blood flew everywhere, the creature's blood-sap. She got it on her face, in her mouth. It tasted mucus-gross like natto. She must be one of the rare few who hated the gooey and stringy fermented soy beans. She always refused to eat it, even at family gatherings. "Try it. You might like it with hot rice," her mother often cajoled her. No. She wouldn't touch it.

She chopped even harder and this time, the creature dropped her, evidently hurt and weakened. She collapsed, katana falling off her hands. She hit the ground hard.

Remember who you are! Tetsu's voice was weaker now. He was rapidly fading away.

Megumi got up on shaky legs and retrieved the katana. Evading the flailing tendrils, she made for the heart of the creature. She plunged it into the soft center; the creature screamed and screamed its defiance. She forced her thoughts into it, thought hard about the sakura viewing festivals and her obasan's beloved samisen as she sang traditional songs under the cherry blossom trees. Hanami. Happier times then when Megumi wore brightly-coloured kimonos. She even missed wearing her cotton yakatas for hot summer festivals. She had grown too thin and too self-conscious. She had even lost her hair. Perhaps when she was better, she would go and indulge in her favorite food, grilled tako.

Sakura, sakura, SAKURA!

The thorny tendril trembled and shook, as if to resist the sudden transformation. Gradually, cherry blossom buds emerged and opened, pink, white—and soon the entire creature was covered with cherry blossoms. The creature rustled violently as if it was in pain.

Backing away now was a good idea. She found Tetsu lying on his side, his flank heaving. His breathing sounded extremely labored. Like her puppy who became a dog who then grew ill. She had to put him down because he was beyond help, too weak and too old to cope with the illness. She had cried for days. On the table in her room stood a small blue urn containing his ashes. She had never forgiven herself.

She was not going to do the same to Tetsu. She couldn't let him die.

Blood welled up from Tetsu's open wounds, bright and red and warm.

Let me heal you, Megumi cried, tears streaming down her face.

Too late, too late.

No, no, no. Don't die, Tetsu. Please, please, please.

Megumi went through her bag of tools and found none. She was only left with her katana, paper cranes and cherry blossoms.

Mission not aborted. Monitoring, monitoring. Advise introduction of tranquiliser. Query?

Defeated, Megumi cried even more and the crystal tears washed the blood away. Tetsu began to shine, a miniature sun lit in the middle of his chest. He glowed brighter and brighter, until he looked like a wolf consumed by fire. Okami. Okami. Okami. Like Amaterasu, the goddess of the sun.

Thank you, Megumi! Tetsu was on his paws and was growing larger until he was the size of a horse. Megumi gasped and clapped joyously, knowing that she had accomplished yet another task. She smiled. Things would look up now and victory was at hand. She would kill this monster.

She sat on the giant fire wolf, unhurt by the flames. She was a warrior of the sun.

Now, to the eggs, she whispered to Tetsu and they bounded off to the mountain.

Riding Tetsu felt like flying. Megumi laughed as the wind hissed straight into her face. She had not laughed since she had fallen ill. Tetsu ran, swift as the wind, powerful as the sun. When they reached the bottom of the mountain, Megumi held her katana aloft and the blade caught the sun's light.

Let's destroy the eggs, Megumi said determinedly. They moved up the mountain's slope. She would hear the monster, hissing, rasping, a mother viper protecting its brood. She had seen snakes do that when threatened. She hated snakes. She found a nest once, in a little forest creek near her school. The eggs gleamed. She hated them with an awful bitter taste in the mouth.

The mountain was the color of flesh, of the insides of blood vessels. There the monster resided, a gigantic snake of emerald green, curled around several transparent quivering orbs. It was a beautiful monster.

Monsters could be beautiful too. Like cancer cells under microscopic scrutiny. She read up about her type of cancer on the internet. They looked like intricate patterns, interweaving with each other. They were the bringers of death. They were her body rebelling against something. Was she a monster?

But monsters had to die.

Megumi and Tetsu attacked the monster without warning. It was the only way. She had to get rid of the eggs and the monster snake beast. The eggs bred the monster and the monster bred the eggs. Both were dangerous. Both had to be destroyed.

The snake woke with a thunderous rattle and a hiss shaking everything about Megumi. The eyes were of the brightest gold and they gazed at her like the wrath of a god.

Patient is experiencing respiratory distress. Alert doctor. Alert doctor.

She angled the katana so that it was aimed right between the snake's eyes. It thrashed its body. More eggs appeared, dropped off from an orifice in its agonized throes.

Die, Megumi shouted. *Die, beast, die!*

Tetsu aimed his fire at the eggs and they caught fire, burning. The snake screamed its horror. The cavern shook like summer thunder.

Danger. Danger. Abort. Abort. Abort.

The katana pierced through the snake and kept going in. Megumi was engulfed in the creature's lifeblood. Indeed this snake had been growing big, fat and healthy by eating her inside out.

Fury drove her on and she dug the katana in, making sure she was causing maximum pain to the creature. *Push through it*, shouted a strident voice very much like her coach. *Push through it, ignore the pain, use the pain as fuel*. Her coach would pace beside the pool while she sliced through the water, shouting, encouraging, yelling. He would be more anxious than her before competition time, pacing the pool up and down.

Tetsu's sunburst seared the eggs with gouts of flame. The sweet smell of burning skin and flesh filled the air. The eggs burst and membranous fluid flowed out, turning the flesh-colored earth into rivulets of red.

Megumi's chest constricted, a phantom hand squeezing her heart in a vise-like grip.

Yet she pushed on.

Cardiac arrest. Cardiac arrest. Alert response team A. Immediate. Immediate. Danger!

The snake tumbled, a huge tree falling backwards. Megumi was pulled along by the force of its falling, trapped in its traction. She screamed. Tetsu howled. The roaring was the roaring of gigantic waves crashing into them.

I want to live, she spat furiously at the heavens. *After coming all this way! I want to live! Let me live!*

The snake crashed and the entire fleshy cavern shook in an earthquake. Megumi grabbed Tetsu as the seismic waves made standing difficult. They weren't even standing. They were been borne aloft on the tidal waves of rock, dead snake and membrane. *That's it*, Megumi thought in sorrow. *We are going to die. I am going to die. I have failed.*

Then, there was a bright flare of light. She held onto Tetsu, burying her face into his fur. The smell of his fur comforted her. The light caught them, consumed them whole. She felt the light going into her body like the thick barium solution she had to drink for the CAT scans. Blistering fire streamed through her blood vessels. She was on fire. She would emerge from the battle a fire bird, a Ho Ho. She would scream her song to the heavens.

I want to live.

I want to live.

I want to live.

★

"She's ok," Team A leader, Dr Han, said, wiping his brows with a clean tissue. "Made us panic a bit. But she pulled through. Let us run more tests on her later. But the danger has passed." He smiled warmly. The night was indeed frightful, one which he wouldn't forget for a long time. As senior consultant, he wanted the teenager to live. She had a future ahead of her. He had a daughter of his own and this was the kind of horror any parent wouldn't want their child to go through.

"Thank heavens," Mr and Mrs Tetsuya held onto each other and cried happy tears. The ordeal was over. The pain was finally over. Outside the hospital window the cherry blossom tree was beginning to flower and the snow had started to melt.

Meanwhile, Megumi slept on, her arms wrapped tightly around a white-blue wolf plush. Her emaciated limbs were still connected to tubes and wires. They trembled as she fought another battle.

Persimmon, Teeth, and Boys

By Steve Berman

The fight happened on the second floor of C-wing, the science wing. Cecil was climbing the stairs to get to Physics when other kids started to rush past him, pushing his slight sophomore frame back and forth between painted cinderblock wall and metal banister as they called out that there was a fight upstairs. *The promise of violence at high school spreads faster than any rumor or video message*, Cecil thought. He knew, of course, who was involved: Bergen Gold versus Robbie Delaski. An image of a mime being stomped by a Tyrannosaurus, the school mascot, came to mind. Then a second image: the dinosaur belching out a bloody, black beret.

A clot of eager, clamoring students choked the far end of the hallway. Cecil was thankful for all their yells; he didn't want to hear Bergen being beaten to a pulp. Still, guilty that he was in some way responsible, or perhaps negligent might be more apt. He tried to press his way through the mob even as teachers came running.

He emerged at the mob's center to see Bergen, his thick nose bent and bloody, lying on the linoleum and staring up at Robbie, whose face looked far worse: dripping red from rutted forehead to chin. Cecil stood amazed that Bergen could have inflicted such a wound—okay, maybe he came to school all sociopath and brought a knife. According to those forensic cable television shows, scalp cuts were supposed to bleed a lot. Then Cecil saw the paint can on the ground near where Bergen lay. A puddle leaked from the open lid. Persimmon. Poor Bergen. Even when he chose a color as a weapon, he still picked one with a gay name.

Just as the teachers penetrated the inner circle, Robbie's foot slammed into Bergen's jaw. The surrounding kids went silent. Or maybe Cecil stopped hearing their roars. Spittle and blood and teeth erupted, but the only sound was the awful thud of the strike. Bergen didn't whimper, not even as he tried to crawl away as the adults grabbed Robbie.

Cecil watched as they helped Bergen to his feet and off to the nurse's office. The vacuum where the boys fought, where the paint and blood spilt, was disturbed as the class bell rang. He spotted a tooth on the dirty tiles. Off-white, broken, tipped crimson. Before someone kicked it away, he snagged it. A sharp end bit into the soft pad of his thumb. Bergen's blood mixed with his own. And Cecil found himself late to class because he began thinking of that hokey notion of blood brothers, the stuff of tree forts, frosted cereal, and 1950s television. Eventually, he put the tooth in his pocket, next to his iPod and went to hear all about Bell's inequality.

On the bus ride back home, Cecil found himself scribbling on the front of his Physics notebook. But he didn't realize he was doodling until after he'd sketched out a lune, a penny, and a molar. He looked down at the ballpoint drawings as if they were hieroglyphics not rough sketches. No, worse than hieroglyphics. Alien script. Because Cecil knew he didn't doodle. Not when bored, not whenever. He didn't like art, which seemed to work against math—despite what creaky Mrs Felisky promised when she handed him a paintbrush.

After today, he really hated art, but it had started the fight forty-eight hours earlier: as part of the School Beautification Drive of '13, all the upstairs halls were to feature student artwork. Mrs Felisky envisioned Lemane High's C-wing painted with the faces of famous scientists. Mr Sedgewick, infamous for torturing every student, favored or hated, by opening the classroom windows during any Physics test so that a kid either shivered or sweated, was against such décor. But Mrs Felisky was more liked than any other teacher at school—little surprise as no one ever secured less and a B- in her courses—so art was going up on the walls.

After class, Mr Sedgewick questioned why Cecil volunteered to help—with his grades, Cecil didn't need the extra credit that was the only way to entice the many hands needed to finish the work in two weekends. Cecil shrugged and muttered something about keeping busy to fend off boredom. There were some curiosities he couldn't, he wouldn't, express to a science teacher.

Such as his curiosity with Bergen.

Besides being the most talented freshman at Lemane, Bergen was known for being the sole out boy. Ever since freshmen year, he had accentuated a slender build with tight jeans normally worn by girls. He dyed his sneakers while the other cool kids worried over how to keep them bleach white. He moussed his hair into a new shape every week. Even wore a wig or two on occasion. Most of the students either were baffled by him or laughed at him. Since September, Cecil had considered himself in the former. Robbie Delaski was the leader of the other camp.

It was Bergen who devised the clever idea to paint the scientists as they had looked in their younger days—"I'm tired of seeing Mark Twain Einstein," he said with a dismissive wave of his hand. "I want Albie when he was a hot boychik on the prowl for some E equals MC laid."

Tamara Washington tittered. Cecil had trouble deciding where to look: at Bergen, who was pale and wispy, or Tamara's chest which was the opposite but just as bouncy.

Mr Sedgewick, who had stayed late grading papers, stepped out into the hall. "These murals are about respect, Mr Gold. The students' choices will be vetted by the science teachers before they grace our walls. I don't want Timothy Leary smiling down at me."

So they agreed to poll the various science classes. The results were the usual boring bunch. Cecil vetoed George Washington Carver—why were the other black kids always stuck on him?—and picked St. Elmo Brady because he had the most awesome name, was really good-looking, and had a Ph.D. Cecil admired all of those attributes.

Bergen insisted on choosing a scientist also. Or else he wouldn't help. Leonardo da Vinci.

"The painter?" asked Tamara. "As in the Mona girl?"

Bergen sighed. "He invented all sorts of things. And he liked men."

"Then why didn't he paint the Mona Larry?" Tamara lifted her hand to Cecil for a high five. He looked at her like she had prions on the brain. Her hand drifted down. "So what, you have a photograph of young da Vinci?"

Bergen bit his lip. Cecil noticed Bergen wore lipgloss. He wondered what flavor. Did boys who wore lipgloss choose different flavors than girls? Maybe there weren't masculine flavors—Bergen would probably roll his eyes at ever being called masculine—but Cecil was curious. Very curious.

"No. I've only seen his self-portraits when he was an old man."

"Guess you'll have to imagine him young." Molly smirked.

"Guess you'll be needin' to go to the men's room for that."

"Oh, where's my diamond ring?" Bergen cupped his mouth a moment and then raised his middle finger to Molly. "Here it is."

"Pisshap. Like some boy is ever going to give you carats," she muttered.

Cecil should never have gone searching the 'net for a younger da Vinci. He couldn't explain why he did it. There was some urge to impress Bergen. To make him grateful. But the consequences of that muddled in the stricter corners of Cecil's imagination. He could not want to know what flavor lipgloss Bergen wore to make his mouth reflect fluorescent lights so well.

After school, he had found Bergen alone in C-wing sketching faces on the wall.

"What's this?" Bergen asked when Cecil handed him the color print out.

"I think it's called a palimpsest. Da Vinci must have erased an earlier self-portrait from the page—vellum, that's sheepskin—and written over it. I mean, over the blank. So now, using tech they've reconstructed what he looked like. I mean, what he drew. Of himself."

Bergen smiled. Yes, his lips did shine pink as a peach, pink as a conch shell. "For me?"

Cecil felt his face grow warm. "Uhh, for the wall."

"Of course." Bergen leaned close. "Since there's the tiniest chance someone might come along, I won't hug you," he whispered.

But then the entire school discovered in the morning that Robbie

Persimmon, Teeth, and Boys | Steve Berman

Delaski, a bully who lacked senior status due to being held back once, and had more hair than a junior should on his face, had spray-painted F A G over Bergen's finished youthful da Vinci. He refused to brag about it, or even take the credit, even after he was escorted to the principal's office, but the way he laughed made it clear to everyone that he wasn't the least bit sorry.

And later that day, Cecil found himself shocked by Bergen's revenge with the paint and the resulting brawl. Robbie was given detention for a week. Bergen was suspended from school for three days—but then, Bergen was also in the hospital for observation.

Cecil was in his room, ready to do his homework at his desk, when he found Bergen's lost tooth in his shirt pocket. He went to the bathroom and washed it clean. The cut on his thumb throbbed and bled fresh. He added antibiotic ointment and an oversized bandage.

Again, he found himself acting weird, his thoughts drifting off to nothing in the midst of an Algebra II problem. When he looked down at the page, the Xs and Ys and Zs had been erased—he could see faint impressions of where they had been written—and poor renditions of mouths with broken smiles covered the page. A plop heralded a red dot on one set of lips. Blood had oozed through the gauze around his thumb and dropped onto the notebook. Cecil rushed the thumb into his mouth, and then remembered when he was a kid, his mother had to put some nasty-tasting medicine onto both thumbs to keep him from sucking them while he slept.

The combination of blood, cotton, and ointment sickened him.

He went into the bathroom, not sure if he was going to throw up or not. He had to be sick. That explained everything. He looked at himself in the mirror. Other than wide eyes behind his glasses, he looked the same. He tried smiling to earn a comforting reflection. The grin, toothy, looked fake, like the expression in every school picture taken since elementary school. Then he vomited in the sink.

His mother insisted he drink chicken broth and eat some crackers. He tried for chocolate ice cream, but received a glare from both his parents: No. In bed early—at eight PM, he felt ten not sixteen—troubled by homework not even half-done, he tossed and turned, unable to get comfortable. His hand went underneath the pillow and grazed something sharp. He sat up in bed, lifted the pillow and saw Bergen's tooth lying on the mattress. He had no memory of putting it there.

The nightlight clicked on, transforming the bland ceiling into a canopy of pale, yellow stars surrounding a fat crescent moon. Cecil rose, gawking at the display. He'd forgotten how his mother would turn the nightlight on before bedtime; he'd been so little then and afraid of the dark. Then he remembered that after he turned twelve he'd asked his mother to throw away the nightlight. He was too old for such things. She had given it to one of her co-workers who had a newborn.

"Very nice, very nice," said a silken voice.

Cecil fell off the bed. When he stood up he saw a man sitting on top of his desk. His skin was darker than cousin Chuck's, and he wore a dove gray tuxedo but lacked shoes and socks.

"Twas a horny night for Mister Moon
when he saw a youth with a balloon.
The boy gave a cry,
his toy reached the sky.
What a shame they both popped way too soon."

Cecil should have been shocked. Scared. Something. But all he felt was an odd calmness, so he just said, "Hello."

The man raised a hand to his temple in salute. Then he slipped off the desk. "I'm afraid that with the recession all I can offer is a dollar." He reached into his cummerbund and pulled out one of those golden Sacajawea coins. He flipped it up in the air where it glittered and drifted down onto his palm rather than falling. "She had terrible teeth, by the way. Clark and Lewis wagered a dollar—" the coin turned to tarnished silver "—as to whether she'd lose her top incisors or bottom first." The man chuckled. "When haven't men argued over tops and bottoms?"

Cecil nodded though he didn't understand.

"Of course, of more value than a dollar—and let's face it, what would this really buy you anyway?—is wisdom." The man tapped his chin a moment and began walking around Cecil.

"I'm a straight-A student," Cecil said.

"Perhaps you should be giving me advice? Listen to the wise but speak to the fool, I always say." The man's teeth gleamed like washed pearls.

Cecil looked back at the bed. He saw himself lying there, twisted in the covers, mouth open. For a moment, he thought, *I'm dead.* Then Cecil-in-bed turned. "I'm dreaming," Cecil said and Cecil-in-bed echoed the words with his lips and sleepy breath.

"Of course," the man said. "No one awake ever sees me. That would be dreadful. Just dreadful."

"You're the—"

The man produced a business card from his cummerbund. It featured a black mouse with gray, old-fashioned nightcap atop his head and a pair of pliers in his paws. No words.

"You have to—" the man gestured, rolling his fingers " —you have to turn the card over."

Cecil found the other side read *Not this side!*

"Over, over."

He flipped once more. The drawing of the mouse had been replaced. Mr Bistre S. Ouris. Tooth Sprite.

Mr Ouris tsked tsked. "I know, I know. Not that Cecil is anymore … contemporary than Bistre." The way he said it, the name rhymed with mystery.

"Tooth sprite." Cecil snapped his fingers. "So that's why you offered money."

Mr Ouris nodded. "Which you so graciously refused. My retirement thanks you." He slapped his hands together and rubbed them, which made a whispering sound. "So, what are you going to teach me tonight?"

"Tonight?"

"I am here, aren't I?" Mr Ouris folded his arms, but only for a moment. It seemed impossible for the sprite to remain still.

"Me? Teach you?"

"Well you offered. Boasted even about your studies."

"I guess—"

"Ah, ah, ah, first things first." And Mr Ouris stepped over to the Cecil-in-bed. He reached into his tuxedo jacket and pulled out a wicked pair of needle-nose pliers with mother-of-pearl handles. He snapped the jaws once, twice. "Must get what I came for."

Cecil called out, telling himself to wakeup as Mr Ouris leaned down with the pliers, but Cecil-in-bed just muttered and snored like the last dodo must have before the dogs tore it apart. The pliers hesitated above Cecil-in-bed's parted lips and then, the hand behind them moved fast, slipping the pliers beneath the pillow and out again. The silvery jaws clutched Bergen's tooth.

"Ahh, this one's a fighter. Either biters or fighters." He lifted a loupe from the cummerbund and started examining the tooth. "Hold on, hold on." He glanced down at Cecil. Back at the tooth. Then back at Cecil. He frowned. "This isn't yours…" By the circling starlight it looked like Mr Ouris had grown a foot taller.

Cecil's eyes widened. "I can explain—" he lifted up his hands, pointing to the tooth.

Mr Ouris gasped. "I knew it. Knew it. You're a thief. Cunning little hugger-mugger. Well, you won't get a dime off me. I'm broke. Utterly broke."

Cecil backed up against the wall against his poster of the Periodic Table of Accidents between Bi (Blue ice falling from plane passing overhead) and St (Cooking s'mores in toaster).

Mr Ouris laughed. "Relax, my friend. I'm only licensed for milk teeth. Permanent ones are taboo. Oh, so tempting but taboo, true black-market trade." He said the last in a mock whisper as he slipped the tooth into his cummerbund. "Well, I must be off. I could say it's been a pleasure, but that will probably be what you dream of after I'm gone." He winked.

"Wait. You don't owe me anything—"

"Damn right," Mr Ouris said.

"—but you should at least leave something under Bergen's pillow. I mean, the boy whose tooth that is."

Mr Ouris sighed and bent his head. "Fine." He practically spit the word out of his mouth like it was poison. He then went to the window. He paused, looking back at Cecil. "You know we'll have to break this."

"Why?"

"I must have words with the Superintendent of All Schools. What are they teaching you?"

Mr Ouris tapped the glass with his pliers. "The quickest way to get inside any hospital is by breaking something. Tibula. Fibula. Nibula." He struck the glass pane, which shattered outwards.

Cecil could see that what lay beyond the jagged edges wasn't ten or so feet off the ground but a white-walled, white-floored, hallway. "Hospital?"

"That's where you told me the boy can be found."

The hospital seemed deserted. They passed an empty nurses' station. All the doors in the hall were closed. All but one. Bergen's room.

He looked so small under the white covers. His face looked both less and more striking thanks to bruises. Flowers and cards were on a bedside table along with a pastel water glass, which Mr Ouris opened, sniffed, then put down with a frown.

"Water." The word came out with disgust. "When did the world turn against high fructose corn syrup. Oh, sorry day." He sat down in the chair across from the bed, placed his elbows on the edge of the mattress and his long chin on said elbows. "So you like this boy."

"A little. I think."

Bergen snored then, which brought a smile to both their lips.

Mr Ouris whistled a jaunty tune. "Ahh, young gay love. It's a thing of beauty. Like caries."

"Don't call me gay."

"Ahh, young gay love in denial—"

Cecil shook his head. "I'm not gay."

The sprite rolled his eyes. "And I'm no fairy."

"Label chatter, that's all that is. I hate being labeled. I don't call myself Cecil the Black Kid. Or Cecil the Nerd. I'm an individual. Don't classify me like I'm something found on a museum shelf."

Mr Ouris tugged at his lapels. "What's wrong with some class?"

"No. Not funny." Cecil looked down at Bergen. "It's not fair."

"Fair? Why should anything be fair?" Mr Ouris took off his hat and twirled it around one finger. "What do you want, Cecil? Or am I not allowed to ask that because it would be too … labeling?"

"I want…" Too many answers, too many fantasies choked him. Bergen up and whole and smiling, hopefully at him. For the fight never to have taken place. For the fight to have happened and Bergen to have beaten Robbie. For some measure of fairness. Or justice. But that sounded like a bad movie. What slipped out of his mouth was a single word that pushed its way past the other idle thoughts, much like he had the crowd surrounded the fallen Bergen: "Punishment."

The syllables left a sick taste in his mouth. Coppery. As if he had lost a tooth. He realized he hadn't helped in the fight, just picked up a scrap. His thumb ached and he saw it dripped blood on the clean, sterile-looking bedsheets.

"An eye for an eye, a tooth for a tooth?"

Cecil nodded.

Mr Ouris slipped a very tarnished penny out of the slot of his cummerbund and tucked it under Bergen's pillow without even disturbing his sleep. "Some would call those evil thoughts."

"Maybe there's no good or evil, either. Why aren't they as much labels as gay and straight. There's no absolutes in the world."

"So I'm not a good fairy?"

"You're no angel. They don't exist. You should have free will to do what you want, and the consequences … well, that's what makes someone good." *And I did nothing good*, Cecil thought. *Nothing to help Bergen.*

"But doing something wrong wouldn't make me evil, since that's just as much another label, another easy way to classify me, make me easier to understand. There are no tooth spites, eh?"

"Everyone does something wrong in a day. Sometimes more than once in a day…"

"Hmm. Thanks, my friend, I think you did teach me something after all."

Then Cecil woke. He felt warm, stifled by all the covers. He had an embarrassing erection that distracted him for several moments before he searched for Bergen's tooth. He did not find it under his pillow. Or on his desk. He would never find it again.

Bergen never returned to Lemane High. For several days after the fight, students gossiped: his strict parents sent him upstate to therapy and to "cure" him; he ran off to San Francisco and was a street artist; he was afraid. All of them said he was too afraid to return.

Robbie prowled the halls with a fresh-kill smile. His ranking in the cruel hierarchy of high school had improved.

Cecil had stopped doodling. Now and then he would pause in front of where Bergen's portrait of Leonardo da Vinci had been; now the same dun-colored paint used on most of C-wing's walls covered up the space between St. Elmo Brady and Albert

Einstein. Every time he dawdled and stared at the gap, he felt ugly, like looking into the mirror, smiling and seeing one of his front teeth missing.

In study hall the next day, Robbie Delaski screamed as he lifted his head from the table. He'd been napping, his leg a-twitch like a dreaming mastiff, and now he was clutching his mouth and shrieking. Blood poured everywhere. Spilling through his fingers to stain the front of his football letter jacket. Spotting the table, the linoleum.

The janitor never found any of Robbie's teeth. They closed the cafeteria for the rest of the day.

That night, Cecil received a Facebook message from Bergen: *When I was in the hospital I dreamt that you came to visit. You brought me a black mouse. I hope that doesn't sound … I don't know, all racist.*

Cecil read the message again and again—he took comfort that Bergen hadn't disappeared entirely, but truthfully he had forgotten his dream of Mr Ouris until Bergen reminded him.

He typed several possible replies. None were great. They rambled, asked too many questions. He didn't even know if Bergen expected or wanted a reply.

What Cecil settled on was the least pathetic, the least revealing, but he was tired and frustrated and just wanted to click Reply. *School seems more intolerable without you. Perhaps I could visit you for real later this week?*

The night passed like water dripping from a faucet—cold and

slow and impossible to ignore or sleep away. He would get out of bed every so often and check for another message. Nothing.

A substitute teacher manned Mr Sedgewick's Physics class. He didn't seem to know why the teacher who rarely ever was absent, had called in sick. The DVD player and television were rolled out to the front of the classroom and an episode of *Nova* played. In the dark, many students whispered, goofed off, and one worried. Cecil was sure that he had seen a bloody molar on the whiteboard pen tray as he had walked into class. But when he left, there was nothing there other than red stains that could have been left by a leaking marker. Maybe.

Cecil's mood lightened when he saw the reply from Bergen in his message box. *That would be cool with a cap Q.* Seven digits followed. Why did the act of entering this boy's number into his iPhone seem more momentous than when Cecil asked Jackie Mosley for a kiss in seventh grade on his first date or getting punched in the stomach the next year for staring at Rigoberto Vasquez's uncircumcised penis in the locker room or watching a *Dr Who* marathon while having influenza and delirium made Cecil convinced these were some lucky guy's home movies?

Most of the students who went to Lemane High had smart-phones, shopped at the mall and not a Wal-Mart, didn't lack for braces. Not that the surrounding suburbs were rich, and Cecil's parents didn't drive anything with leather interior, but when one of Lemane's teams visited another school district, especially the ones many miles away, the difference in clothes and mannerisms was sobering.

Bergen's home was even more deluxe. Cobblestoned driveway. Awnings of beaten copper.

"Hey," Bergen said when he answered the doorbell's pleasant chime. He wore a prep school blazer over a white dress shirt—slightly unbuttoned—and khaki slacks. "Just to warn you, my mother is an ovo-flexitarian, so there's a fifty-percent chance of meatball tonight."

"Okay."

"So, what do you think?" Bergen twirled around once in the foyer.

"Nice house."

"No." Bergen pouted and gestured at his clothes. "The uniform?"

"Oh. Preppy."

Bergen groaned. "Not dashing? I know. Navy blue? Can't they make the blazers in a color you don't dare wear to a funeral?"

"How are you feeling?"

Cecil quickly learned through a non-stop ramble on Bergen's part over dinner that the boy's parents were divorced, his father was in Dubai, his mother was an attorney and liked to use her utensils to accentuate whatever point she was making during dinner—which was meatballs, thankfully. His mother seemed unfazed by her only son's disclosures. As first the salad fork, then the entree fork, stabbed the air as she asked Cecil about himself.

"Mother put me in a prep school."

"It's safer," she said. "No offense, Cecil, but the sort of children who attend public schools have the social skills of Neanderthals."

Cecil wasn't sure if the "No offense" was because he still went to Lemane, was black, or didn't know which fork to use first.

"Do you regret throwing the paint?" Cecil asked. As soon as he said it, he saw by her expression, that Bergen's mother did not approve of the question.

"Nope. It was the only time Robbie looked pretty."

She took a sip from her wineglass. "The entire situation should never have happened. And we're not allowed to discuss the matter while there's a lawsuit pending."

After dinner, Bergen took Cecil into the den, which could have swallowed a classroom. The flat-screen television would give the whiteboards a run for their money.

"So." Bergen slouched on one of the comfy white sofas.

"Yeah."

"Mom's intense."

"I think it's part of the rules," Cecil said.

How would his own parents react if he brought home a boy? A boy like Bergen? Shocked that Cecil was into guys? Thrilled that if it was a guy, he came from money? His parents' mindset was an utter blank to him; they never pressured him to date, never asked him anything embarrassing around Valentine's Day or about school dances. He had learned about pregnancy and adolescence's rollercoaster of hormones from a book they had left for him on his bookshelf when he had been a naïve twelve-year-old and opened wide the flap in the front of his pajama bottoms to his father and asked him about the black wiry hairs around his penis.

His dad had never given him a condom. He had bought him a membership to *Smithsonian Magazine*.

"But I think she'd let me date a Neanderthal if I could, you know, *My Fair Lady* him."

"Huh. What?"

"It's a movie." Bergen laughed. "Oh my gawd, your eyes went so wide."

"Sorry."

"Listen, it's the twenty-first century, so I feel there's this pressing need to just stop all the hints and whiffs."

"Right." Cecil had no idea what Bergen was talking about. He realized that, outside of the hospital, this was the only time he had seen Bergen without lipgloss. The uniform diminished much of his … flamboyance.

"So," Bergen put a hand on Cecil's shoulder. His fingertips pressed, rubbed, stroked a little. "I'm just going to ask you out."

Cecil nodded, even as words tumbled out of his mouth. "So you think I'm gay?"

Bergen rolled his eyes. "I practically have my arm cuddling you and you haven't moved away."

"Yeah." Cecil breathed in deep. "Remember how that word 'faggot' bothered you—"

Bergen slipped his hand off Cecil. "Bothered is a little mild … try offended. And he ruined my—"

"True. All true. I just … I just don't know if I want to be called gay. By anyone."

"It's not as bad as faggot—"

"No. I know. But, I wouldn't want you to be introducing me around as your black boyfriend anymore than your gay boyfriend."

"Everyone would know you're my gay boyfriend since you'd be me with. Or are you bothered because I'm too flaming for you."

Bergen rose and paced the room a moment, then turned on the television with the remote and began exploring all that Netflix had to offer that day. He didn't look at Cecil when he said, "It's not easy to step out of the closet. I mean, I've known forever. Everyone has to come out there own way. And some of us like to burn bright."

"I love how you express yourself." Cecil stood up and forced himself to walk over to where Bergen stood staring at the listing for Musicals. "I think it's amazing you doused Robbie in Persimmon. And you're wittier than anyone I've ever met."

"There's a 'but' coming…"

"I think—I think I was arguing this with someone else. Trying to make him understand. Words like 'gay' and 'faggot' are like nametags we stick on our shirt. Or like when our moms wrote our names in our clothes when we were in kindergarten. You don't have to wear them."

"You're afraid." Bergen turned around. They were close enough to kiss but Cecil knew by Bergen's furrowed brow that was not going to happen. "You're afraid of being called a faggot, too."

"No. I'm scared that I'm going to have to abandon the things I do care about just because I'd date another guy. That I'd only be accepted if I like fashion." He took the remote from Bergen. "Or musicals instead of science fiction movies. I don't want to change myself to fit a label. I didn't know what Persimmon looked like before I met you. I don't want to have to know all the other colors just so you would feel comfortable with me."

"I—I don't understand. It's not like saying you're gay suddenly turns you into a drag queen."

Cecil hung his head. The sight of their so different shoes in the thick carpet made him think back to the last time he had gone to a quiz bowl at a poorer school. His sneakers were worn around the edges. Dingy. Bergen had shiny loafers. They looked like they had not only been bought at two totally different stores but two different cities. Or even countries.

"Can I—do you have any aspirin. I kinda have a headache…"

"Sure." Bergen looked deflated. Insulted. "I'll go—"

"Just tell me where the bathroom is. I have some, uhh, other business I need to do, too."

Cecil opened the medicine counter. As he anticipated, the nearest prescription bottle was for Bergen. Vicodin. Under the masking sound of the running tap, he shook out two pills and pocketed them.

When he came out, he took hold of Bergen's arm. "I did want to spend time with you. Can we still watch a movie?"

Bergen gave a weak smile and nodded.

That night, Cecil took both Vicodin. He waited until he felt dopey, almost waited too long as he began to stumble and had to sit down at his desk and his arms slipped now and then. He had to be precise as he lifted the pair of needle-nose pliers he had found in an old toolbox in the garage. But he didn't want to feel the pain as he clenched the metal pincers around one of his back teeth.

He didn't even remember pulling; it must have been hard work because both the pliers and the tooth flew across the room. He felt warm fill his mouth and run down his numb lips. He brought up an old shirt to soak up the blood.

The tooth, still gory, was slipped beneath his pillow. He lay half-under the covers, brought one arm over his eyes, and counted for as long as he could remember which was not very long.

Whispering in his ear woke him. "Bribery? Oh, my boy, you know me too well."

Cecil opened his eyes. He sat at his desk. Stretched out on his bed, hat tipped to cover his eyes, was Mr Ouris. He wore animal slippers, fuzzy mice.

Cecil didn't feel the drowsiness of the drugs or the pain of the lost tooth. He tongued the empty spot in his mouth but it didn't set his nerves on fire.

"You must be desperate," Mr Ouris said. "Or worse, have a conscience. You asked for revenge, and I've been obliging you. Just tonight I removed some rather nicotine-stained teeth from a very loud-mouthed girl you dislike. I'm inundated with incisors, bristling with bicuspids—"

"Stop."

Mr Ouris raised his hat and frowned. "What? Now? But I've been having so much fun since you taught me I don't need silly trademarks or denominations."

"No. Stop. Talking."

"Someone is snappy." Mr Ouris chattered his teeth a few seconds then covered his mouth with one hand, the other gesturing for Cecil to speak.

"I don't even know what I was thinking summoning you. But you're different, you're in this world, you're not, you're the only one that ever seemed to have listened to me—though I'm kinda scared at what has happened from that.

"I just want things to be simple. But they can't be because simple means classifying everything. This is gay. This is not. This is a kiss, this is not. There aren't any in betweens. People don't want there to be. They need to have everything defined and I feel like if I do that, instead of finding myself, I'm losing myself altogether."

"My turn?" Mr Ouris mumbled through his fingers.

Cecil nodded.

"Je suis une souris. Je suis aussi une fée."

"What—"

"My turn, remember. Merci. What I just said are facts. And what I just said are meaningless because you do not understand French. Life and love can be both true and meaningless, alas."

He held up Cecil's pulled molar. "Call this a tooth, a snag, a chopper, a clicker ... whatever you like, but it will do what it is meant to. Everyone knows that but we like words like we enjoy play. Referring to this as a bit of ivory might get you a bad grade in English class but it won't make it any less a tooth.

"So you like boys. And you've liked girls in the past, too. You can howl at the moon all you like, but you will be called gay or queer or tapette as much as you will be called black, African American, maybe even nig-nog. Again, I say words can be both true and meaningless."

"So, then Bergen was right. I am just scared of being called a faggot."

Mr Ouris tossed Cecil the tooth. "Perhaps. That's what happened to him, so he thinks it's true and he thinks your fears are meaningless. But perhaps, you're right. You're simply a Cecil Gibson. Fact. And all that people will call you in this life is meaningless as long as you stay true to who Cecil Gibson is."

"I don't even know who I am half the time. I asked that girl out years ago. Now I want to be with Bergen—who probably never wants to see me again—and tomorrow, who will I be then?"

"Put the tooth back in."

"Hmm?"

"Stop playing with it and put your tooth back in."

It fit perfectly in the empty socket. Didn't even wiggle loose.

Mr Ouris appeared over Cecil's shoulder. "I don't think mortals were ever meant to live past fifty. Otherwise you'd have milk teeth and beer teeth and then prune juice teeth. But your kind does live long these days. Gone are the old rules. I'm not even following them now. I don't know what will happen tomorrow. Maybe I'll be tired of all the grisly effort and stop haunting your school. Maybe I'll go back to plucking the teeth of babes. Or I could try collecting from sharks. I hear they never stop growing teeth. Imagine that. Though they don't sleep do they?"

"Mr Ouris—"

He waved. "No thank you needed. But as you once said, actions are what define you. If you're willing to tear out one of your own teeth, you're pretty damn brave. And foolish. So, act on your feelings and whatever others call you, whether it's true or not, treat it as meaningless."

Mr Ouris slapped Cecil on the back, which knocked the tooth out of his mouth. "I never really planned on giving this up…"

And when Cecil woke, he wished he had saved one of those Vicodin because the pain was terrible. But not enough to stop him from texting Bergen an apology. Or doodling a plan.

Google found the image he wanted. Software added a sepia tone. Staples turned it into a poster that would stick to any wall. And so, before going to lunch, Cecil went to C-wing and the blank patch among the scientists' portraits. He slipped the cardboard tube out of his backpack and stretched high on his toes to ensure that a young da Vinci returned to where he belonged.

And before anyone could take it down or stain it, he took a photo with his phone and sent it to Bergen, who, moments later replied with a toothy grin emoticon.

Flight

By Angela Slatter

The feathers were tiny and Emer hoped they would stay so.
Indeed, she prayed they would fall out altogether. They were
not downy little pins. Small, but determined, their black shafts
hardened as soon as they poked through her skin, calcifying under
her touch as she stroked them in dreadful fascination.

All day she'd felt something happening beneath the gloves hastily
donned after her morning's escapade. The sight of those ladylike
coverings had brought approving nods from both her mother and
governess, as if they were a sign she was *finally* listening to their
exhortations. *A princess does not run. A princess does not shout
or curse. A princess keeps the sun in her voice, but off her fair
skin. A princess sits quietly, back straight. A princess smiles at a*

gentleman's tasteful jest, but never laughs too loudly. A princess never furrows her brow with thought. A princess does not chew her nails.

Emer had been determined that nothing untoward was occurring; that the healing salve she'd sneaked from her mother's workroom would put everything to rights.

But that night, when Emer closed her bedchamber door and finally peeled away the doeskin gloves, she found that the wound in her palm was sprouting dark fronds around its ragged edge. They looked like the collar of her mother's favorite cloak—except those feathers with their vibrant eyes were from the palace peacocks. A great ball of fear threatened to stopper her throat.

It had been the madness of a moment, to sneak away and run through the gardens with the sky so blue, the clouds so white, the grass such a vibrant green. Trembling in the breeze, the flowers shone like delicate gems: wine-dark amethysts, sun-bright topazes, heavenly sapphires, rubies red as blood, beryl the color of a storm-tossed sea and, stranger still, the roses.

She'd danced and run, bounded and rolled like a child of five not a young lady of thirteen. Not like a princess on the eve of her fealty ceremony, someone who shouldn't frolic until her gown, once a triumph of pink embroidered with daffodils, had its hem torn and trailing, one sleeve held in place by four tenuous threads, and grass and dirt staining the pattern. Tradition decreed the heir—even if, to the regret of many, she was female—be left unattended this day, not so she could *play*, but so that she might stand vigil, alone, unsupervised and mature, meditating on her future life of state. Preparing to pledge herself to the land, to be its sovereign and its succor, now and always.

Leaving the manicured lawns upon which she was usually permitted a chaperoned stroll, Emer had wandered into unkempt areas where the demarcation between garden and myrkwood was little more than a rough boundary of aged briars. Smooth malachite stems spiked with roses' thorns—roses black as ebony!—entwined seamlessly with the gray and brittle barbs of the brambles.

A burning glow from the heart of each bloom had compelled her closer; an opalescent flash of green and red and gold, orange and azure and magenta had drawn her. She'd reached out to touch the nearest one, careful to avoid its prickles. The petals were like velvet. As she pulled away, she felt a stabbing pain in her upturned hand.

One moment the air in front of her was empty and the next, a raven, which had sat so still that it'd been invisible in the chest-high hedge, occupied the space with regal mien, its claws fixed tightly around the briar barrier. The crimson wound in the center of Emer's palm showed where it had made its mark.

Emer stared at the bird; its feathers glistened tenebrous-dark, yet radiant as if moonlight had been woven into their undersides. The raven gave a harsh cry— if she hadn't known better, she'd have said it sounded apologetic—and Emer noticed its eyes burned with the same fire as the blossoms, colors flickering and dying, only to be replaced by the next brilliant hue. The creature took off, flying higher and growing smaller until finally it dove, plummeting straight at the girl, veering at the last second and shooting into the shadowy depths of the forest.

That was when Emer's nerve had broken. Hitching her skirts, she'd fled to her rooms, changed her dress and hid the destroyed one. She'd smoothed her hair and washed her face, slipped on the snug gloves, and spent the afternoon, heart aflutter, sitting in the solar, feigning contemplation of the book on her lap whenever her mother or governess swept past, and hoping ever so hard that nothing would come of her misadventure.

Now, Emer removed her frock slowly, fearfully, wondering why she did not feel the cold. She stood in front of the mirror and turned. An inverted feathery triangle lay across her back and shoulders. At the nape of her neck were knots and twists where her tresses had begun to tangle into a kind of plumage. Her nails had toughened, lengthened and grown points. Her thumbs and little fingers were shorter.

Yet she did not call for help.

Emer knew the price of magic—something outlawed since the beginning of her father's reign. Herbcraft was acceptable; although leechwork was a gray area, its benefits were acknowledged; but witchcraft? Enchantments had enabled the Black Bride to bring calamity, to blind the King to the one he loved, to almost ruin a prosperous land, and to leave the Queen permanently scarred. Emer, transforming as she was, must be committing sorcery, even if it wasn't her choice.

No, she would not call for help. Surely it would go away. Surely all she needed was to apply more of her mother's lavender nostrum. Surely in the morning, she thought, upending the bottle of ointment and slopping it up her arms, surely by then this would all be gone.

At dawn, as the final act of her vigil the princess dressed all by herself for the first and last time.

A cream silk wimple, a veil of amaranthine gossamer, and a circlet of engraved gold hid the tight calamus cap her hair had become. Only Emer's un-feathered face remained visible. Her high-necked ruby robe had sleeves long and loose enough to conceal her glossy black body and her arms, which were rapidly knitting into wings. Stubbornly, she fumbled with gloves, but didn't bother with shoes—her legs had wizened, toughened with dusky gray skin, finished with pronged feet. Now three clawed toes *click-click-clicked* as she walked.

And so it was that the kingdom's firstborn, pride and joy (and occasional frustration) of her royal parents, entered the great hall with a strange new gait. Her eyes, once blue, were black, and her head moved this way and that, taking everything in with a darting gaze. She promenaded along the ermine carpet to where her parents sat, enthroned and enthralled by her terrible progress.

When she stood before them, dropping into the queerest curtsey ever seen, the Queen and King began to weep and wail respectively.

Emer's hands convulsed and the delicate gloves, which had been shoved onto the tips of her transmuting fingers, fell away as the flesh melded. The gown, too, was rent, and soon the princess was jiggling about on one leg then the other, kicking away the rags. Her head grew rounder, tinier, and her ears disappeared; the coronet slid down to sit around her neck like a collar. Wimple and veil hung loose until she shook them off. Emer's nose and mouth speared into a scintillating beak.

Ladies-in-waiting screamed and lords bellowed. The noise was astonishing; it swelled until the crescendo broke over the raven-girl and she tottered about, looking for escape. One of the high-reaching windows was open to allow the cool breeze in, and she half-ran, half-skipped towards it, shrinking, until the golden circlet slipped away and she leapt through the opening as if performing a circus trick. She hopped onto the sill, gave her parents one last look, and *caw-cawed*, a sound that echoed the whole sad length and breadth of the chamber.

With one swift beat of her new wings she caught an updraft. Her parents, released from their paralysis, ran to the window and watched as their daughter joined a waiting unkindness of ravens that greeted her with croaks. The sun kissed her wings and she and the birds were gone, faster than thought, faster than possibility.

They flew toward the horizon. Emer-that-was wondered how far they'd come—and when they'd stop—as they floated over fields and rivers, mountains and valleys, towers and turrets of rulers petty and great. But Emer-of-feathers did not ponder, merely obeyed instinct and followed her fellows. They flew for so long that Emer-that-was despaired of ever finding her way back.

When finally they began to descend, it was toward a huge granite edifice positioned astride a river, nothing like Emer's hilltop home of polished marble and clear glass. This was a castle fit for battle, with windows so slender they were suitable only for shooting arrows through, or sending out the occasional pigeon bearing a message to an attacking general, saying he may as well piss into the wind, for this bastion would never fall to the likes of him.

The flock aimed itself at the closed portcullis, winging precisely through the grille, Emer as lithe and light as the rest. They traversed a deserted courtyard, thence towards a great set of doors hewn from oak and banded with silver. The doors, as if sensing their approach, opened at the very last moment, but the winged host did not slow, did not hesitate, as if cooperation was to be expected.

They flew along hallways lined with threadbare tapestries and paintings of people who'd been obscured not by time but by the tearing and shredding of canvas. They flew through rooms lined with rows of weapon racks filled with rusting swords and battleaxes, unstrung bows, decaying spears and toothless morning stars. They flew through bedchambers so thick with dust they had to rely purely on intuition to navigate. They flew until at last they came to a hall as lofty and lengthy as a cathedral's nave, as cool and dim as one too, for most of the tall pointed windows were shuttered. At the farthest end sat a woman.

Bustling around the chamber was an army of servants. Here and there, valets and footmen, butlers and a majordomo, maids and ladies-in-waiting, some of them in the costume of courtiers and some of them in rustic attire, but Emer had no doubt they were all, without exception, slaves. No matter their garb, none wore human form. Each was canine, walking upright and wearing a motley mix of livery, using fans, carrying trays, bearing tea pots and saucers, one the lord of a samovar, another king of the canapés.

Emer glided onwards, unaware that her companions had dropped behind. She slowed, and descended, carefully avoiding the shifting mass of what appeared to be large rabbits—no, hares kicking at each in occasional ill-temper. She alighted on the shabby red carpet leading to the dais upon which a cushioned throne was set. Three short steps separated her from black-booted toes.

Lifting her gaze, Emer took in the woman's face, gypsy-hued, marred with long-healed scars; her hair and eyes like jet, lips like a damson plum. And the features somehow familiar, yet Emer could not place them. The woman in a long charcoal dress, with carmined nails, smiled down at the raven who was a girl. Emer shuddered deep inside her hollow-boned body. She wished to fly, to flee, but her limbs would not obey.

The dark one limped down the stairs to gather up the bird. She tucked Emer under her arm as one might a chicken, and stroked her with a hand almost entirely curled in upon itself. Emer recoiled, willing her talons to lash out and tear, her beak to stab and shred, but her body was contrary. All she could do was shiver. Clicking her fingers, the woman produced a chain as fine as thread from thin air. The thing shone and shimmered as she twisted it twice around the raven's right foot. Emer watched as the metal fused. The other end was looped through the intricately carved rose-and-briar pattern adorning the top of the throne.

The woman's voice, when she spoke, was strange, a mix of the sweet and the discordant—only later would the girl realize it came of the scars at the base of her throat.

"Now. Now you are secure, my little one, the game has begun."

Emer, finding her own voice unaffected by whatever paralyzed her body, gave an answering cry.

"Come, come—you want to help me, don't you? And if I take my fun at the same time, then what harm?" She laughed. "Would you like a story, my dear one? My sweet sister's darling child? Shall we begin thus? Once upon a time…"

And Emer listened as her unsuspected aunt told of two sisters, one swan-white, the other raven-dark. All the while the girl wondered how long she would be in this shape. How long before all she began to think of were bugs and beetles, worms and carrion. How long it would take for someone to find her. And Emer despaired because she knew her parents believed the Black Bride defeated and dead. They would never find their raven-daughter because they would never think to hunt for a ghost.

★

The girl spent many months feathered and tethered.

Each night she heard the Black Bride's version of the tale Emer's governess had told in hushed tones. Her mother had tenderly sworn it was no more than a story, and even though Emer pretended to believe her, she had seen the evidence on the Queen's very flesh: the blemishes around her neck where the gold band clutched too tightly, the left hand missing its smallest finger where her wings had been clipped so she would not flee the palace pond. By the end of her first month in captivity, Emer was acquainted with every cadence of the new account as surely as she was her own heartbeat.

How the Black Bride's mother had two perfectly serviceable husbands, one after the other, and produced one lovely daughter with each. How both girls were raised with equal affection, and how, when an exceedingly fine suitor—a king-to-be—came a-courting those very girls, this very same mother refused to choose between her daughters, so the dark girl had no choice but to make her own fate. How the prince had made his preference for the snowy girl known—and the girl of shadows had determined *her* will would prevail.

It wasn't as if she'd harmed her sister so terribly, said the Black Bride with a shrug. Turned her into a swan, certainly, but as she was sure Emer could attest, a few feathers never hurt anyone. And hadn't the swan sister's revenge been a terrible over-reaction?

When she came to this point in the tale, the Black Bride always fingered the scars on her cheeks, neck, breasts, where spikes hammered into the barrel had pierced her as she was rolled up hill and down dale until that barrel had finally hit a tree and burst asunder, leaving her bleeding and dying, the tiny child within her withering as surely as an ice-lily on a summer's day.

How, when she'd thought her last breath was spent, she was found by a woman, a witch—not kindly—who mended her and taught her greater things than she'd ever imagined. Marvelous magics, legends of objects that might grant every wish, but none of this imparted fast enough for her wanting or wishing. There was still much to learn when the Black Bride held a pillow over the old woman's face and stifled *her* last breath, but the girl was simply tired of waiting for her to step aside and let a new order begin.

How, after years of plotting and planning, everything she'd worked for threatened to slip from the Black Bride's grasp. Though she'd schemed and marshaled her resources so she might yet play on, she had failed to get what her heart most desired: healing. It was tricky, balancing the time she had left between revenge and recovery, but she refused to relinquish one for the chance of the other. No matter how it taxed her, she could be—*would* be—whole once more, and all scores settled with her sister and the King.

Emer listened and watched, watched and listened, although no one spoke to her but the Black Bride. She paid attention to the comings and goings of the shadowed woman's pilfered court, noting the frequency and severity of the woman's wet cough, the sweet-sour dying scent of her breath. There were suitors—for her wealth, though stolen, though dusty, was not insubstantial, and the strength of her sorcery was of great value. Aside from these charms, in certain lights, the ravages of her punishment were not so obvious. So, the willing grooms came, though none of them ever left.

In the cold hours, after the woman had talked herself out, after she'd muttered at the windows *when will she come, when will she come?*, then gone to bed, Emer would work with her sharp beak at the deceptively fragile-looking chain, more out of habit than hope, but inexorably, insistently.

Peck-peck-peck.

Peck-peck-peck.

Peck-peck-peck.

"About time."

Emer, perched on the padded armrest of the throne, was enduring the Black Bride's caress, staring out the only unshuttered window. Normally, she divided her time between eyeing the roiling mass of canine domestics, the fluttering carpet of ravens who came and went at the Bride's bidding, and the hopping, kicking sea of fur that had once been the courting princes—all now transformed to fine, fat hares. This day, though, the sky had her undivided attention. She ignored the dark woman, assuming the remark was addressed to someone else. But the Black Bride's next words—and her tone, so soft and sad—dragged the raven-girl's gaze back to the room.

"Did you think yourself forgotten?"

Emer was startled—it was precisely what she was beginning

to think. She had lost track of the days, weeks, months, but the turning of the season outside told her winter was arriving for what seemed the second time. She wasn't sure—speculations about bugs and beetles had occupied her mind of late. A tentative movement at the entrance of the chamber made her head tilt in curiosity.

The figure was willowy, dressed in white furs, a hood of silver fox framing her pale face. She moved with all the grace of a bird on the surface of a lake, effortless. She hesitated as if, unable to find whom she sought, she was unwilling to commit deeper to the room.

"You should know," continued the Black Bride, her touch stilled, "that she raised an army to find you. Your father failed and wept, wasted away—trust me, my girl, I have my spies. But she, oh *she* mobilized their vassals, rode at their head, slept in the saddle, scoured all the lands that could be covered by foot and sea. I'll warrant she'd have given her very soul to take to the skies if it meant she might find you that way."

Her hand slid to the black chain. She toyed with the liquid length, unconsciously worrying at the dent Emer's beak had made. She stared at the woman hovering in the doorway and seemed to realize that there would be no further progress without some kind of carrot.

"In the end, though, I sent for her. Reports of her mourning, her burning anguish, warmed my very soul. I could *imagine* it for I know her as well as I know myself. But there is no true joy in suffering that one cannot witness, child," the Black Bride said, then she snapped scarlet-tipped fingers, and the ankle chain evaporated. Before Emer could take advantage of this freedom and make it to the open window, the Black Bride wrapped both hands around the raven's trembling form. She held the bird as if intent upon stilling her heart, then kissed the top of her head. Whispering *flux*, she threw the girl—not upward, but forward.

The raven-girl's shape became fluid, like water tossed from a bucket. Her feathers disintegrated, her beak receded to a pert little nose, legs lengthened and grew feet with soft pink toes, the tips of her wings split into fingers. Emer plummeted like a surprised stone, landing half on, half off the fusty carpet, scattering canine courtiers and confused coneys as she went. Naked and suddenly cold, she sat up slowly, feeling sick, stunned. Her mother, as if released from a cannon, sped toward her, hands reaching, lips curving, focusing entirely on her child, drawn by that agonizing relief which makes caution flee.

The Queen's hands were not as Emer remembered; once soft as silk and pale as moonlight, they were now red, the skin split and dry, callused, coarsened from gripping sword and reins. But the eyes, silvery blue, the gaze wide and wise as an owl's—those were her mother's without doubt. Emer nestled into the embrace, feeling as much as hearing a *thrum* as the White Bride crooned her love.

"Oh, sister, how sweet!" The Black Bride teetered on the edge of the dais, shuddering with the effort of her magic. "What was lost is found. You didn't look for me like that, not even to make sure I was dead."

"A mistake I will not repeat, sister," said the White Bride as she rose.

"Now, now, sister, don't be too hasty. Didn't I give her back? Isn't she safe? Isn't she lovely and whole, unlike we who still wear our battle scars? Didn't I give you hope?"

"Only as one doles out breadcrumbs, sister, for without hope, suffering tastes flat," said the White Bride, which set the Black Bride off into peals of laughter.

When she calmed, wiping spittle from her lips, she looked fondly at Emer and the White Bride. "Didn't I say so, little one? That we know each other as well as we know ourselves? You should find *this* no surprise at all then, sister dear."

And the Black Bride clapped with a noise like a lightning strike and shouted something Emer couldn't quite comprehend, a word that slipped over her ears like oil across skin, and left nothing in its wake but a slight ringing. Where her mother had stood, half-buried under the fox fur hood, was a sleek alabaster she-hare with eyes of silvery blue. Emer could do nothing but stare through hot tears as the Black Bride hobbled down the steps and scooped up the animal that made no move to run.

"No feathers for you on this occasion—I do like variety. I would we had more time for thrust and parry—I could play this game forever—but you've taken so long to find us that my time is running short. Your child must be swift if she wishes to save you."

An iron cage, which had not been there moments before, appeared at the foot of her throne. The Black Bride urged the animal in and latched the door. "Best keep her here, though I'm sure she'd be terribly popular with the boys," she cackled, then shuddered into a fit of coughing that resulted in something nasty spattering on the stone floor. A spaniel footman hurried forward to lap it up. Emer shuddered to think of her mother at the mercy of the legions of bucks, whose noses twitched at the smell of a female.

Unsteadily, the girl picked herself up and wrapped her mother's cloak around her, clinging to the warmth left within. She worried at the hood between her fingers as she tried her voice, found only a raucous sound, tried again and managed, "Why? Why all this?"

The Black Bride gave her an astonished look. "For the sport, of course. The vengeance."

Emer looked at the hare, the Queen-that-was, and quivered. "If I was the bait, then she's taken it. You win… What use have you for me now?"

"I thought I'd have more time," the Black Bride murmured, not to Emer, but to the ghosts, the nobodies with whom she regularly conversed. Blinking, she looked down at the girl, as if calculating fitness for purpose. "You'll have to do."

"Do what?"

"You want your freedom, don't you?"

Emer nodded. The Black Bride mirrored the movement and went on.

"Retrieve something for me, and we'll see what we shall see about *that*."

"That's hardly a bargain," Emer said, surprised at her boldness. The Black Bride ignored her.

"I've sent that lot many times." She shrugged dismissively towards the milling crowd of ravens. "And all they've brought back are excuses and complaints about the loss of this cousin or that brother. What I need can be obtained only by someone with pure intent—and we both know that's not me—once it's taken, of course, it can be handed over to whomever the acquirer pleases. It seems a fair price to me, for your liberty."

"And my mother—her life, freedom, her true form," Emer said. She had listened for so long to the Black Bride's tricksy tongue, to conditions that seemed carelessly worded but were not, to deals she'd made with all those princes who now wore fluffy tails and pointed ears.

"Very well, clever little miss." The woman frowned, curious. "What did you think about? When you were bird-brained?"

"Worms. Sky. Flight." *Home. Mother. Father.* Emer's short life had been determined by the whims and demands of others; therefore, she chose to keep some truths for herself this time.

"Ah." The Black Bride seemed disappointed, and sat back on the moth-eaten damask cushions of her throne. "So. There is a castle atop a mountain of glass, almost a day's distance. Inside is a very special crown, which you will retrieve."

"And how do I climb slopes of glass? Will you give me wings again?"

"No, I can't trust you not to fly away. You said yourself, in that form all your thoughts were those of birds—you'll lose focus, grow forgetful." She shook her head. "In the stables, there's a horse—actually there are many, but you can't miss this one. A suitable beast, but with a foul temper." The Black Bride sighed. "You're a clever girl, Emer, so listen carefully: there are no second chances for you. If you do not return here before the turning of a day and a night with the crown, I will kill your mother. Understand? I'm sick with waiting."

"Is there a map?" Emer inquired stiffly.

"Follow the river—that'll be map enough."

"What's so special about this crown?" demanded the girl, her spirit growing the longer she stood on her own two fleshy feet.

The Black Bride's eyes slid to the animal in the cage at her feet. "Enough questions. Go, and be quick about it."

The bird had spent all the time since they'd left the castle pattering across the horse's broad shoulders, up and down its neck, and making occasional forays onto saddle's pommel. In turn, the roan had not stopped whickering in irritation and shaking itself hard enough that both bird and rider were almost dislodged. The raven—Bertók by name—also kept up an unrelenting monologue.

"And *that*," he said with a meaningful look at the gingham bundle tied behind Emer, "if I'm not mistaken, is a loaf of bread and a flask of wine that will never run out. Purely magical, very valuable. The dog, I'm sure, was not meant to give you *that*."

A tired-looking Alsatian with sad eyes, green waistcoat, fawn breeches, and mauve frockcoat, had been instructed to find Emer clothes and food and send her on her way. He'd led her to a room decorated with colorful arras, furniture of pale honey wood, and brightly bleached linens. An alcove housed a tub; ancient copper plumbing rattled as the valet drew a bath. In all the past months, Emer had never suspected a room like this existed here.

She was provided with trousers and shirt, highly polished leather boots, and a worsted wool cloak, all in varying shades of black. Emer ignored the cloak, keeping instead her mother's fur and hood. When she was washed and dressed, her guide took her to the stables and pointed out her steed.

The Black Bride had been right—so many princes had left many, many horses—but this one stood out. At least twenty hands high and with a burnished hide, he wore no shoes for his hooves were of spiked bronze. When Emer knelt before him, his golden gaze was measured. She held out the apple she'd kept back from her own quick meal and he deigned to sink his sharp teeth in its firm flesh. The dog, noting the beastie's compliance, swiftly—and with palpable relief—saddled him, while Emer explored some of the stalls, patted the more biddable animals.

"Ahem. Excuse me, miss?" came a voice from the shadows.

At first, Emer couldn't find the source, but when her eyes adjusted to the gloomy corners she saw a withy cage hanging from one of the rafters. Inside was a defeated-looking raven. His eyes were dull until Emer approached. Then, a flare of recognition and something else: a fire within, a swirling conflagration of green and red and gold, orange and azure and magenta.

"You!" she'd screamed, rage rushing through her, and strode forward, intent upon throttling the bird. The raven flapped wildly, shouting, "Now, don't be hasty, I can explain!"

"This is all *your* fault, with your lying in wait and your pecking. Give me one good reason why I shouldn't wring your scrawny neck."

"Well, strictly speaking, you need to shoulder some of the blame—you were alone, wandering about outside. Well-behaved princesses—" he broke off as Emer began to shake the cage. "I'm sorry! Don't hurt me, I can help you."

The bird's terror broke through her fury and Emer suspected that the anger she felt was the sort of ire her aunt gave in to every day. She stepped back, shuddering with shame.

"No, I'm sorry I scared you." She reached for the latch and lifted it. "How is that I can understand you?"

"You were one of us for an age, it's bound to stick," he said, tentatively climbing out onto her proffered forearm. "If you're going where I think you're going, I really can help. Please let me come along."

It had seemed like a good idea at the time, but now Emer's head was fit to burst.

"When the old bat finds out what he's done he'll be a pair of slippers in the blink of an eye. Mind you, might come in handy," wittered Bertók.

"Why were you in that cage again?"

"Injustice! As always. "Bertók, you talk too much. Bertók, you ate all the wild cherries. Bertók, you didn't bring me back that crown. Bertók, you're snoring too loudly." It's getting so a bird can't fart let alone express an opinion without getting locked up."

In the brief respite while he took a breath and Emer used the chance to change track. "You mentioned a giant?"

"Giantess. Always hungry—I don't know if they're all like that. I wonder—"

"So, this giantess lives atop the glass mountain and has the mysterious crown and eats everyone who comes to visit?"

"Well, except us—except the ravens—not enough meat. But it doesn't stop her using us for target practice."

"And the crown can only be gained by someone with pure intent? I don't imagine that would include you." The bird didn't answer. "Raven?"

He gave a shrug of sorts. "Well, that's what we told her—the part about pure intent."

"You lied?" Emer was less scandalized than delighted by this breathtaking bit of avian bravery. "You lied to *her*?"

"She doesn't know everything, you know," the raven squawked. "She's just so... We couldn't bear the idea of losing more of our number every time she sent us off on one of those quests. She's crippled but she's got everything and it's never enough. Imagine her with that crown, whatever it does, still demanding more, more, more! We—I—thought if we put her off long enough, maybe she'd run out of time, so we haven't been trying too hard to do what she's asked."

"Why are you helping me? After all, you were the one who started this whole thing." She waved at him so he could see the scar still marring her palm. The bird had the good grace to look embarrassed.

"It's not easy, you know. Disobeying her takes effort and it hurts. And I had no idea of what she was planning. I'm sorry for what I did. You deserve no more torment, nor does your mother. You saved me from that cage and I owe you a boon. I'll help you retrieve what you need; what you do with it after is something you must consider carefully."

The journey had been interrupted only by the raven's chatter. They had covered leagues and leagues, the line of the river easy to follow, the roan tireless and intent. Yellow eyes gleamed from shadows and thickets, hands gnarled against tree trunks as their owners peeked out. Emer heard snuffles and snorts, snarls and grumbles, but nothing came near them. Wolves and trolls, ogres, and things with no name watched as they passed, but left them unmolested. She wondered if the Black Bride's power stretched this far, or if these brutes simply sensed her touch on Emer. Or worse, she thought, sensed that they shared blood.

Their destination was less a castle than a single stout tower of ochre-colored stone. Inside, the main chamber was topped by a stained glass dome that, on sunny days, showered the room with shafts of color. The air was icy, however; it leeched the hope from Emer's bones and she wondered if she'd ever see the sun again. She could feel the raven trembling on her shoulder. He'd been silent ever since they set foot in the bastion.

The giantess, all big bones, protruding eyes and corkscrew auburn hair, was ensconced in wingback chair, knitting, and giving Emer the same look one might bestow on a beef roast. Emer was glad she'd left the horse—who had taken the glass mountain at a canter and danced a kind of jig to show how pleased he was with himself—outside. Along the wall behind the enormous woman was a series of hooks, almost all hung with ill-made scarves. The scarf-free one held a huge bow of elm wood and a leather quiver filled with arrows longer than Emer's arm.

"How accommodating of you to arrive at lunch time," rumbled the giantess, who began to roll up her knitting. The door behind Emer shut with a *clang* and she rubbed sweaty palms against her trousers. She lifted her chin defiantly and wished she could fly away.

"My lady," she quavered and the giantess seemed taken aback to be so politely addressed. "I've come to ask—to beg with pure intent—for the crown."

They both looked to the crystal plinth in the center of the room; it was topped by a primrose cushion that held a circlet of white and black feathers.

"Ask as purely as you like, my girl, you're still going to be eaten.' The amazon nodded, rose, and reached for her weapon.

"Wait!" yelled Emer, and something in her tone stayed the woman.

"And why should I? I don't like to wait and I'm starving—always starving."

"I imagine it's hard to get enough food when you're stuck up here, madam," said Emer.

The giantess loomed and Emer quaked. She hurried on. "I do not ask your bounty for free. I offer you something most valuable in return."

"What could you possibly have to interest me, you little thing?"

"What if I were able to provide a loaf of bread that is never depleted and a flask of wine that never runs dry? Would that not sate your hunger, mistress?"

The giantess crossed her arms over her mammoth chest, contemplating. "And where would you find such a treasure, little scrap?"

"Outside, on my horse," answered Emer, hoping the stallion hadn't taken it into his head to go for a run elsewhere.

"Then bring it hither. I demand proof before I agree to consider this bargain. And I am not saying I will…"

Fifteen minutes later, when the giantess had attempted and failed to entirely consume the loaf and the wine three times, Emer thought her troubles were over.

"And so, my dame? Do we have an accord?"

"Let's not be hasty, little speck," said the woman slyly. "What's the point of eternal food and drink without companionship? It's been decades since I've had a chat—what with my tendency to eat my guests. Stay awhile."

"My lady—" began Emer, aware of the night's hours bleeding away.

"My lady, this young one is no fit companion for you—she has not lived long enough. What stories could she possibly tell? How she once wet her bed nightly, what frocks she has worn?" The raven began to wax lyrical. "I, on the other hand, am no mere bird."

Looking into the creature's swirling, sparking eyes the giantess admitted this fact. She seemed to nod more than was necessary. It was no wonder the woman normally shot birds out of hand; it was dangerous to listen to them. Bertók's voice swooped low, its ragged edges barely discernible as he promised hours, days, weeks, months, and years of conversations. The woman, Emer thought with a tinge of sympathy, had no idea what she was getting herself into.

By the time the raven had finished, the giantess leapt to her feet, removed the delicate crown from its cushion, and held it toward Emer.

"Thank you," Emer said, as she reached out. "Thank you."

"You're welcome," growled the giantess and snatched the crown away, while wrapping one meaty paw around both of Emer's wrists. "Did you think me a fool to fall for sweet words? Anyway, what's a sandwich without meat?"

Emer's heart hammered, and her mind emptied of all thoughts but these: feathers and air, lightness and flight. Just as her memory retained the language of birds, so too her flesh kept recollection of their form. This time the shape was *her* choice—no one else's to give or take or impose. She gladly shifted, shrank, sprouted plumes. Within seconds, the giantess clutched only emptiness, for the girl had slipped the fleshy bonds and snatched the crown of feathers with her beak.

The door to the chamber remained shut. Emer flew around the room, faster and faster, higher and higher, knowing the giantess was reaching for her bow. She heard the nocking of an arrow, curses thundering from the woman, the twang of a bowstring. She braced herself, heard a thud, but felt no pain. Risking a glance, she saw another black body hurtling downwards. Resolute and determined not to waste Bertók's gift, she raised her head and aimed towards the stained glass.

The raven-girl pierced the dome, raining colored shards on the giantess. She shot upwards, a shadow against a pallid sky. With the dainty adornment gripped tightly in her beak, she flew on, tracing the snake of the river back to whence she came.

If the Black Bride had been surprised to see Emer feathered once more, she did not show it. The girl landed and transformed, steadfastly meeting her captor's gaze.

"Give it to me, girl," said the Black Bride, her tone limned by longing, and not a little desperation.

Emer shook her head. "My mother first. Restore her."

A brief, tense standoff took place while the Black Bride insisted her niece hand over the artifact before anything else occurred. Emer remained adamant. In the end, a rage-induced coughing fit tipped the balance in Emer's favor. The Black Bride was forced to concede that she did not have enough time left to indulge in a battle of wills.

When her mother at last stood beside her—shaking, dazed—Emer held out the crown. The Black Bride snatched at it greedily, turned it this way and that, held it up to the light, her eyes shining. Then she faltered, looked at her sister and niece and asked plaintively, "How does it work?"

And Emer recalled the story from her aunt's own lips, how she had done away with her mentor before full knowledge could be passed on; for all her power, the Black Bride was a half-written book—she might well know what an object did, but not *how*.

"Put it on, I'd imagine," Emer said, then asked quietly, "What does it do?"

In an equally hushed voice, the Black Bride replied, "It mends broken things," and, reverently slid the delicate diadem onto her blackavised brow. She waited, breath rattling, eyes wide and avid, a covetous child expecting a treat. Seconds stretched to minutes as she attended, with increasing impatience, for any sign of change, of *amendment*.

When it became apparent that no healing was forthcoming, the Black Bride's face seemed to split with rage.

"What have you done? Did you think to defy me?" She turned on Emer, stalking towards her, spitting out every horrible name she could muster. "I told you there would be no second chances! Both of your lives are forfeit."

Emer and her mother stumbled backwards, transfixed by the sight of the Black Bride summoning her power, watching as it coursed around her body, and sparked at the fingertips. Wanting, but not daring, to turn tail and run—for that would be certain death.

The dark woman drew back her unmaimed hand, and just as it seemed she would strike Emer down, the White Bride, in a flash of ash and silver, threw herself at her sister. The attack, so brutal and brave, so unexpected, threw the Black Bride off balance and she retreated under each enraged blow her sister rained down. The firebolt-bright magical charge around her stuttered and snuffed, but she struck back, her nails tearing furrows along her sister's smooth cheeks. The White Bride snarled and leapt, not noticing how close they had come to the windows, and the force of her bound sent them crashing into one of the shutters. The wood, brittle and ancient, splintered like twigs and both women were oh-so-briefly silhouetted against the winter sky … then gone.

Emer rushed to the sill and peered down, too terrified to catch enough breath to scream as she watched them fall. She clung to the hope that her mother's flesh would remember the shape of wings, that she might fly; but it did not.

Flames erupted when the Brides hit the cobbled courtyard. Emer waited. The fire burned down quickly, leaving a cloud of dust and cinders that swirled and circled and, finally, found form.

Where two women had fallen, only one remained, unfurling like a lily, her hair a mix of light and dark, skin a creamy melding of the two extremes, limbs intact, unharmed. A single woman, lovely and whole. The mother-aunt raised her head, looked at Emer and beamed.

"Come home," she called. Emer stared, an uncertain smile on her lips, and she heard the echo of the Black Bride's voice: *She raised an army to find you.* She thought of her mother as she had always known her, the docile White Bride, so kind and loving; wise, but so bound by convention; always passive, meek and accepting—until the loss of her daughter. It had taken tragedy to give her the strength, determination, courage the Black Bride always had but used selfishly.

And Emer reflected on her entire life, on how it was moved by the ebb and flow of others' desires. She thought of her mother and aunt remade, all their chances given to them anew. She contemplated updrafts and thermals, swooping and diving. She looked at the sky, at the horizon.

"Come home," called her mother-aunt again.

Emer shook her head, only vaguely aware of the ruckus in the chamber behind her, of hares returned to the shape of men, and dogs released from servitude.

"I shall find my way there ... some day."

Emer-that-was thought herself weightless. She thought herself plumed, skipped onto the sill and pitched out to spiral down and hover in front of the woman. The raven-girl memorized the new face, the familiar features, so she might recognize them later, then with a powerful flap of her wings, Emer-of-feathers rose towards the dawning firmament.

We Have Always Lived on Mars

1.

I have never seen the sky. Or the sun. Or the stars. Or the moons.

My great-great-great-great-grandparents along with the others on their crew came here on an exploratory colony mission, but they were left here long ago when Earth went silent. We will never get home. This is where we live. We have always lived on Mars.

I have never taken a breath of fresh air. There has been a storm raging for decades. There is a cloud cover that never goes away.

There are rules for living here. Recycle the water. Tend to the hydroponic plants. Breed the farm animals. Manage the air. Fix all parts of the habitats. Everyone follows the rules. Everyone works at living. Or else we all die.

We are few. We never number more than twenty-four. We cannot ever grow the colony to more than what we can fit into the habitats. Sometimes if there are too many of us, one of the older members of our community walks outside unsuited to make room. I have never seen them do it. They go at night, not long after a new babe is born and when almost everyone is asleep. We wake up and one of our members is missing and we know. I know that one day when I am old I might do it myself.

"We are the last humans, Nina," my mother reminds me every time I put on the suit to go outside. The suit was not made for me, but it fits me perfectly. I must be built a lot like my great-great-great-great-grandmother, Lt. Commander Yu. According to our history, she was the tenth person to step on Mars.

"What's the point?" I always ask. My mother just shakes her head. Everyone is all about survival of the species even though we cannot grow past what the colonists started with. But I feel differently. I hate this cramped life. This small space. This constant living on top of one another. I long to run. To be alone. To be away from these others clinging to the end of humanity. To not have to check my gear one million times before I step outside.

We Have Always Lived on Mars | Cecil Castellucci

It would have been easier if more colonists had come. But
they never did. I have learned about how my great-great-great-
great-grandparents waited for the second wave of colonists and
supply ships to come. But they never arrived. The storm came and
everything about our world went dark. The radios only spout static
now, although we are always listening. The sky is always covered
with a never-ending haze.

"All systems go?" my mother asks.

"Yes," I say, checking all the valves and the oxygen levels. I am
good to go. My mother taps my helmet, giving me the all-clear
signal. I step forward into the air lock along with Devon, my
walking partner, and we wait for the depressurization and the
sudden feeling of lightness. The suit never seems heavy when I
step outside on my daily errands to check for any growth between
the red rocks. We have been trying to infect the planet with life so
that we can make it ours. But it is slow going. Sometimes there
is moss.

I like to walk outside. I always keep my eyes out for scrap.
Something that might be uncovered by the storm. Something that
we missed that we can use. It was said that fifty years ago a rover
rolled in. It had probably circled the whole planet. It wasn't much,
but it had samples and it had parts. The colony made good use of
it. Once when we were young, a satellite fell near the habitat and
there was something useful in it. If we find enough materials we
might be able to build a new habitat and add six more people to
our colony. We would finally be able to grow.

A few decades ago we expanded the habitat when we dismantled the tiny observatory that housed the telescope. I'm sure it was not an easy thing to do: we'd waited for so long for the sky to clear. But since the storm came, no one has seen the stars, and survival now is more important than looking up at some unknown future date. Now the telescope lays open to the elements.

I have seen pictures of the sky. I know that there are two moons that orbit our planet. I know that Earth would look like a little blue star in the sky. But I have never seen it. I never will.

We only go out during the day. At night it is too cold. This planet hates us.

"A planet cannot hate," my father says. "It can only be."

I disagree with him. Mars never wanted life. That's why it never had it. Not even a single-celled organism. We try to live and thrive. But we are always near to failing.

At first, we tried to keep a sterile environment protocol, in order to not mess with any potential bacteria. But after Earth fell silent, my great-great-great-great-grandparents began to experiment, first inside the habitat. Now outside. We come from scientists after all. And even though most of the science is forgotten, we are survivors.

2.

Devon and I shuffle along the ridge looking for any hint of green. The walking is also part of our necessary exercise to keep our bones strong. He heads toward a cluster of rocks. I head toward the telescope. I stroke it with my gloved hand as if it is one of the goats we keep. The telescope is useless and discarded. Already picked clean for parts. I wonder what it would be like to look through it.

I turn my head up toward the covered sky. I wish I could see what lies above those dirty clouds.

I head down the hill. The gravity is not the same as inside the habitat, or maybe it's the suit that always makes me so clumsy and so I fall. As I do I seem to fly in the air. I love the feeling when I trip, like I can fly, but then I hear the sound. A rip. It's my suit.

It was the rock I landed on that did it. I feel a rush and know that I am losing air. I am going to die. I look toward my walking partner, Devon. Devon drops his bucket and springs toward me. I can't see his face due to the solar visor that he has pulled down. I can only see a reflection of me. I seem calm when I see myself lying on the ground. I know that he's probably distressed at the situation. We train for rips. We train for emergencies. The suits we wear are so old and threadbare that it is bound to happen. It has happened before and no one has survived for longer than four minutes. I place my hand on the rip as I was taught, trying in vain to hold it closed. Hoping that somehow my oxygen won't run out. I feel weak. My knees buckle. I watch as my tank hits zero. I start to pass out as I feel Devon's arms hook under mine and drag me toward safety.

3.

When I wake up inside the habitat there are five faces leaning over me. They are smiling. And then, when I cough, they begin to clap. I do not understand why I am not dead.

"It's a miracle," my mother says, pressing her hand on my forehead.

"It's finally happened," my father says. "A child has adapted to Mars. Our founders' work on breeding is paying off."

"We must do some tests," Boaz, the oldest of our colony, says. He knows more about the science that has been passed down than anyone. He will never step outside to sacrifice himself.

All my physicals show nothing different than anyone else. My heart is good. My lungs are good. My bones are good. My DNA shows small mutations but nothing that has never been seen before.

"We must send her outside," Boaz says.

It frightens me to try to step outside the habitat without a suit. But my father will go with me. And there will be precautions.

"What if I can't breathe?" I ask.

"We'll know in the first second," he says. "And we'll close the air lock and come back in."

My father suits up and puts on his helmet. We sit in the air lock, waiting for the light to turn green and the outer door to open.

The light turns and the door opens.

I am struck by wind. My eyes close from the particles that fly about me. I take a big gulp of air. First, I smell things I've never smelled before. It makes me gag. I start to cough. I clutch at my throat. My father takes this to mean that I am dying so he slams on the button to shut the air lock.

The air we can breathe fills the room. When the alarm sounds he takes off his helmet and then grabs my face, looking at me to see if I'm okay. I am still coughing.

"Are you okay? Are you okay? We've made a mistake! She can't breathe out there."

The inner door swings open and the others rush in. I cough and cough but put my hand up.

"I'm fine," I say. "I could breathe. It was the dust that startled me."

Everyone heaves a collective sigh of relief.

"We'll try again tomorrow, Nina," Boaz says.

I must admit that I can't wait.

4.

The next day everyone gathers at the air lock to watch me go outside. I have covered my face with a cloth and my eyes with goggles.

The light turns green and I go outside.

I breathe in. I breathe out. There is no problem. The air is sweet. My lungs fill in a way that they have never been filled before. I feel clearheaded, as though my body is getting something essential into it, something that has been missing from the habitat. I turn back to my father, who is standing by the door, and give him the thumbs up. I begin to walk.

I have been told that, without the heavy boots or the artificial gravity that we have inside the habitat, walking will be strange. That I will be lighter and less grounded. But everything feels the same. I walk the circle of our habitat. I walk the yard I know so well. And then, light-headed from the crispness of the air, I make my way back inside.

That night there is a feast. There is excitement and joy.

I notice a change in everyone toward me. They stare at me. The little ones think I am magical. The adults look at me with envy.

I will be able to leave the crowded habitat and be alone with my thoughts. I will be able to walk farther than the two hours the oxygen tank allows for. I might be the beginning of the much dreamed-about expansion. They look at me like I am the future.

Boaz comes to visit me after dinner. He shoos my family out of our room and shuts the door so we can be alone.

We both sit on the corners of the bed. He has his hands folded in front of him.

"Being the eldest has its responsibilities and its secrets," he says. "And being the first that can breathe without a suit has them as well. I have decided that you will be the next elder."

"I am too young," I say. "An elder should be old."

"Yes, perhaps," he says. "But you can answer questions that no one else can."

I understand that to him, I am no longer a child. I nod.

"One question that has been asked by us all since we landed here is why did Earth go dark? It is the eternal question. Are we alone? The last gasp of a once-proud species? Have we been abandoned? Does life still exist on Earth?"

"It is hard to be alone," I say. "I often do not know why we try so hard to survive."

He puts his hand up to quiet me from saying things that I know nothing about.

"I have always had a question, and now it looks as though you will be able to answer it," Boaz says. "Why did our founders lie about the amount of oxygen that a tank can hold? Why did they not want us to walk farther than two hours from here?"

"The tanks can hold more air?"

I am stunned.

"Yes," he says. "That is one of the secrets that I keep."

I shudder at the thought of what other things he might be holding back from us all. I am suddenly uncomfortable with the idea of becoming an elder.

"I cannot answer that question, Boaz."

"But you can breathe outside without a suit. You can walk for more than two hours."

I nod. I knew that I was free now, but in this moment it strikes me how free I am. The whole planet is mine to explore. Perhaps there are satellites that fell elsewhere. Perhaps the supply ships crashed on another part of the planet.

"I want you to go out and walk south for half of the day, and then I want you to return and tell me what you find."

"I will find nothing," I say.

"Most likely," Boaz says.

5.

We do not tell anyone of the plan. Boaz and I give each other knowing looks before I go out of the air lock. I have packed a bag filled with food. He has given me a compass. I will walk farther than anyone has ever walked. I must turn back in precisely five hours or I will surely be killed by the cold Martian night.

I walk. Two hours leads to the base of the large rocks. There is no change in the scenery. But I realize that we are situated in a valley. Tall rocks and small mountains surround us.

We are so wired to return before two hours and to never venture this far that I begin to worry about myself and feel as though my lungs will stop breathing. As though I will collapse. But the dust swirls. The clouds hang. The rocks are orange as they have always been. And I am tired, but fine.

I begin to climb. It is slow going. Perhaps I should have walked the other way? Perhaps I should have gone east, or west, or north. It takes me two more hours to get to the top. I head down the other side and that is when I see something strange cutting the orange landscape. It is a ribbon of black. I check my clock. I still have an hour before I must turn back. I head for the ribbon as my destination.

When I get there, it is different from anything I've ever seen before. It is almost unnatural. It cuts in a perfect line. Not behaving like the rocks I am so used to. I struggle to remember the ancient word for what it looks like.

Road.

There are cracks and buckles everywhere in it, but it goes along a path. I notice something farther down and hike toward it.

It is a piece of metal on a metal pole laying on the ground. That is lucky. I wonder how heavy it is and I lift it up to see if it's possible to salvage for the habitat. When I lift it, I see them. The words. And in a sickening instant it hits me. And I know the truth. I know the answer to Boaz's question.

Highway 24
Earth Planetary Society / Mars Research Habitat / UTAH
Off road site →
Grand Junction 160 Miles

We are on Earth. We have always lived on Earth.

About the authors

Joanne Anderton

Joanne Anderton lives in Sydney, with her husband and too many pets. She enjoys blurring the lines between science fiction, fantasy, and horror. She is the author of the multiple award winning short story collection, *The Bone Chime Song and Other Stories,* and The Veiled Worlds Trilogy: *Debris, Suited,* and *Guardian.* Visit her online at joanneanderton.com

Steve Berman

Steve Berman sold his first short story at age seventeen. Since then, he has published almost 100 articles, essays, and works of short fiction. His novel *Vintage: A Ghost Story* was a finalist for the Andre Norton Award. He resides in southern New Jersey, the only place in the entire United States that has an official devil.

Sarah Rees Brennan

Sarah Rees Brennan was born and raised in Ireland by the sea, where her teachers valiantly tried to make her fluent in Irish (she wants you to know it's not called Gaelic) but she chose to read books under her desk in class instead.

Sarah recently completed her second series, the Lynburn Legacy, a Gothic mystery series about a school reporter who discovers her imaginary friend is a real boy, one of the strange family who have returned to the sinister manor on the hill that looms over her town. Her last short story, about a harpy boy, was published in Kelly Link and Gavin Grant's *Monstrous Affections* anthology.

Cecil Castellucci

Cecil Castellucci is the author of books and graphic novels for young adults including *Boy Proof, The Plain Janes, First Day on Earth, The Year of the Beasts, Tin Star* and *Odd Duck*. Her picture book, *Grandma's Gloves*, won the California Book Award Gold Medal.

Her short stories have been published in *Strange Horizons, YARN, Tor.com,* and various anthologies including, *Teeth, After* and *Interfictions 2*. She is the founding YA editor of the *Los Angeles Review of Books*, Children's Correspondence Coordinator for *The Rumpus* and a two time Macdowell Fellow. She lives in Los Angeles.

Beth Cato

Beth Cato is the author of *The Clockwork Dagger*, a steampunk fantasy novel from Harper Voyager. Her short fiction is in *Inter-*

About the authors

Galactic Medicine Show, Beneath Ceaseless Skies, and *Daily Science Fiction.* She's a Hanford, California native transplanted to the Arizona desert, where she lives with her husband, son, and requisite cat. Follow her at www.BethCato.com and on Twitter at @BethCato.

Joyce Chng

Born in Singapore but a global citizen, Joyce Chng writes mainly science fiction (SFF) and YA fiction. She likes steampunk and tales of transformation/transfiguration. Her fiction has appeared in *Crossed Genres,* the *Book of World SF Vol II* and *We See A Different Frontier.* Her YA science fiction trilogy is published by Singapore publisher Math Paper Press. She can be found at *A Wolf's Tale* (awolfstale.wordpress.com).

Leah Cypress

Leah Cypess (www.leahcypess.com) is the author of several young adult fantasy novels and numerous short stories. Her most recent book, *Death Sworn,* is about a reluctant tutor of assassins-in-training, and will be followed by a sequel in March 2015. She lives near Washington, D.C. with her family. Her story reprinted here owes its inspiration to Michael A. Burstein's "Kaddish for the Last Survivor," and its title to Vaclav Havel's "The Need for Transcendence in the Postmodern World."

Neil Gaiman

Neil Gaiman is the bestselling author of books for adults and children. The recipient of numerous awards, his works have been adapted for film, television, stage and radio.

Some of his most notable titles include the novels *The Graveyard Book* (the first book to ever win both the Newbery and Carnegie medals), *American Gods* and the UK's National Book Award 2013 Book of the Year, *The Ocean at the End of the Lane*.

Born in England, he now lives in the US with his wife, the musician and writer, Amanda Palmer.

Shane Halbach

Shane Halbach lives in Chicago with his wife and two kids, where he writes software by day and avoids writing stories by night. His fiction has appeared in *Escape Pod*, *Redstone SF*, *Daily Science Fiction*, and elsewhere. He blogs regularly at shanehalbach.com, or can be found on Twitter @shanehalbach.

Miri Kim

Miri Kim was born in South Korea, a nation with four normal seasons, but grew up in Los Angeles, where the weather gods have preset it to perfect. She writes science fiction and horror but considers all of her stories misunderstood romances. Send her a message at noircissus.tumblr.com.

About the authors

Ken Liu

Ken Liu (kenliu.name) is an author and translator of speculative fiction, as well as a lawyer and programmer. A winner of the Nebula, Hugo, and World Fantasy Awards, he has been published in *The Magazine of Fantasy & Science Fiction, Asimov's, Analog, Clarkesworld, Lightspeed,* and *Strange Horizons*, among other places. He lives with his family near Boston, Massachusetts.

Ken's debut novel, *The Grace of Kings*, the first in a silkpunk epic fantasy series, will be published by Saga Press, Simon & Schuster's new genre fiction imprint, in April 2015. Saga will also publish a collection of his short stories later in the year.

Malinda Lo

Malinda Lo is the critically acclaimed author of several young adult novels, most recently the duology *Adaptation,* a Bank Street College Best Children's Book of 2013, and *Inheritance,* winner of the 2014 Bisexual Book Award. She is the co-founder of *Diversity in YA*, a project that celebrates diversity in young adult books. She lives in San Francisco with her partner and their dog, and her website is www.malindalo.com.

Juliet Marillier

Juliet Marillier was born and brought up in Dunedin, New Zealand, and now lives in Western Australia. Her historical fantasy novels and short stories for adults and young adults have been published internationally and have won a number of awards including the

413

Aurealis, the American Library Association's Alex Award and the Sir Julius Vogel Award.

Her lifelong love of folklore, fairy tales and mythology is a major influence on her writing. Juliet is currently working on the Blackthorn & Grim historical fantasy/mystery series for adult readers. The first novel in the series, *Dreamer's Pool,* was published in October 2014. When not busy writing, Juliet is active in the animal rescue field, and she has her own small pack of waifs and strays. Her website is at www.julietmarillier.com

Alena McNamara

Alena McNamara (alenamcnamara.com) is a graduate of the 2008 Odyssey Writing Workshop and Viable Paradise XV. Her stories have appeared in *Kaleidoscope, Crossed Genres Magazine,* and *Lightning Cake.*

Sam J. Miller

Sam J. Miller is a writer and a community organizer. His work has appeared in *Lightspeed, Nightmare, Shimmer, Beneath Ceaseless Skies, Electric Velocipede, Strange Horizons, Daily Science Fiction, The Minnesota Review,* and *The Rumpus*, among others. He is a winner of the Shirley Jackson Award and a graduate of the Clarion Writer's Workshop, as well as the co-editor of *Horror After 9/11,* a critical anthology published by the University of Texas Press. Visit him at www.samjmiller.com.

About the authors

Nnedi Okorafor

Nnedi Okorafor is a novelist of African-based science fiction, fantasy and magical realism for both children and adults. Her novels include *Who Fears Death* (winner of the World Fantasy Award for Best Novel), *Akata Witch* (an Amazon.com Best Book of the Year), *Zahrah the Windseeker* (winner of the Wole Soyinka Prize for African Literature), and *The Shadow Speaker* (winner of the CBS Parallax Award). Her short story collection *Kabu Kabu* and her science fiction novel *Lagoon* were released in 2014. Her young adult novel *Akata Witch 2: Breaking Kola* is scheduled for release in 2016. Nnedi is an associate professor at the University at Buffalo, New York.

Tansy Rayner Roberts

Tansy Rayner Roberts (tansyrr.com) is an Australian fantasy author, blogger and podcaster. She won the 2013 Hugo for Best Fan Writer. Tansy has a PhD in Classics, which she drew upon for her short story collection *Love and Romanpunk*. Her latest fiction project is *Musketeer Space*, a gender-swapped space opera retelling of *The Three Musketeers*, published weekly as a web serial.

Sofia Samatar

Sofia Samatar is the author of the novel *A Stranger in Olondria*, the Hugo and Nebula nominated short story "Selkie Stories Are for Losers," and other works. She is the winner of the John W. Campbell Award, the Crawford Award, the British Fantasy Award, and the World Fantasy Award for Best Novel. She is a co-editor for *Interfictions: A Journal of Interstitial Arts*, and teaches literature and writing at California State University Channel Islands.

Angela Slatter

Specialising in dark fantasy and horror, Angela Slatter is the author of the Aurealis Award-winning *The Girl with No Hands and Other Tales*, the World Fantasy Award finalist *Sourdough and Other Stories*, and the Aurealis finalist *Midnight and Moonshine* (with Lisa L. Hannett).

Angela's fiction has appeared in *The Mammoth Book of New Horror #22 & #25*, *Fantasy*, *Nightmare* and *Lightspeed* magazines, *Lady Churchill's Rosebud Wristlet*, *Fearie Tales*, *A Book of Horrors*, *Steampunk II: Steampunk Reloaded*, and Australian and US *Best Of* anthologies. In 2014 three new collections were published: *The Female Factory* (with Lisa L. Hannett), *Black-Winged Angels* (Ticonderoga Publications) and *The Bitterwood Bible and Other Recountings* (Tartarus Press).

She is the first Australian to win a British Fantasy Award (for "The Coffin-Maker's Daughter"). In 2013 she was awarded one of the inaugural Queensland Writers Fellowships. She has an MA and a PhD in Creative Writing, and is a graduate of Clarion South 2009 and the Tin House Summer Writers Workshop 2006. She blogs at www.angelaslatter.com about shiny things that catch her eye.

About the authors

Lavie Tidhar

Lavie Tidhar's latest novel, *A Man Lies Dreaming* ("A twisted masterpiece" – *The Guardian)* is out now in the UK, and *The Violent Century* is out 2015 in the US. Lavie's previous novel, *Osama,* won the World Fantasy Award in 2012, and he is the author of several novels, novellas and collections, as well as numerous short stories. His comics mini-series *Adler* is currently in development with Titan Comics.

Eliza Victoria

Eliza Victoria is a Filipino author. Her books include *Dwellers* (2014), *Project 17* (2013), and *A Bottle of Storm Clouds* (2012). Her fiction and poetry have appeared in several online and print publications in the Philippines and elsewhere, including *Daily Science Fiction, Stone Telling, Room Magazine, Story Quarterly, The Pedestal Magazine, Neon, Southern Pacific Review* and the *Philippine Speculative Fiction* anthologies. Her work has won prizes and nominations in the Philippines' Carlos Palanca Memorial Awards for Literature, the Free Press Literary Awards, the National Children's Book Awards and the National Book Awards. Visit her at elizavictoria.com.

Honourable Mentions for 2013

The following is a list of stories we found worthy, but didn't include in our final selection.

Some of them were discounted due to being more middle grade or adult than YA according to our definition of YA.

Others were very good but didn't end up in our final list for various reasons including having chosen a similar story already to wanting to select stories from a wide variety of fiction venues.

The honourable mentions list is in alphabetical order according to author's last name.

Ahmed, Saladin, "Without Faith, Without Law, Without Joy", *Rags and Bones*

Alering, Alisa, "Everything You Have Seen", *Writers of the Future Volume 29*

Alexa, Camille, "Over It", *Futuredaze*

Amundsen, Erik, "Live Arcade", *Strange Horizons*

Bell, Helena, "In Light of Recent Events I Have Reconsidered the Wisdom of Your Space Elevator", *Shimmer*

Black, Holly, "Millcara", *Rags and Bones*

Burgis, Ben, "Contains Multitudes", *Tor.com*

Caine, Rachel, "The Cold Girl", *Carniepunk*

Fleming, Sam, "What the Water Gave Her", *Fish*

Gaiman, Neil, "The Sleeper and the Spindle", *Rags and Bones*

Gonzales, E. K., "Frozen Delight", *Horror: Filipino Fiction For Young Adults*

Goss, Theodora, "Estella Saves the Village", *Queen Victoria's Book of Spells*

Howey, Hugh, "Deep Blood Kettle", *Lightspeed*

Jeffers, Alex, "You Deserve", *Bad Seeds, Evil Progeny*

Jones, Stephen Graham, "Thirteen", *Halloween*

Kanakia, Rahul, "Another Prison", *Futuredaze*

Kornher-Stace, Nicole, "On the Leitmotif of the Trickster Constellation in Northern Hemispheric Star Charts, Post Apocalypse", *Clockwork Phoenix 4*

Kress, Nancy, "... And Other Stories", *Shadows of the New Sun: Stories for Gene Wolfe*

Large, Chris, "Girl Finds Key", *Next*

Lay, Anaea, "Hiding on the Red Sands of Mars", *Strange Horizons*

Lee, Yoon Ha, "The Coin of Heart's Desire", *Once Upon A Time*

Lien, Henry, "Pearl Rehabilitative Colony for Ungrateful Daughters", *Asimov's Science Fiction*

Lingen, Marissa, "Things We Have in the House for No Reason", *Analog Science Fiction and Fact*

Liu, Ken, "Ghost Days", *Lightspeed*

Liu, Ken, "The MSG Golem", *UFO 2*

Loenen-Ruiz, Rochita, "Of Alternate Adventures and Memory", *Clarkesworld*

Marino, Andy, "The Oregon Trail Diary of Willa Porter", *Tor.com*

Mastura, Kelly, "The Banshee's Initiation", *Visibility Fiction*

Mok, D. K., "Morning Star", *One Small Step, an anthology of discoveries*

Moraine, Sunny, "Event Horizon", *Strange Horizons*

Ogawa, Yukimi, "Icicle", *Clockwork Phoenix 4*

Okorafor, Nnedi, "House of Deformities", *Kabu Kabu*

Okorafor, Nnedi, "How Inyang Got Her Wings", *Kabu Kabu*

Olley, Kirstie, "Short Circuit", *Oomph!*

Olley, Kirstie, "Stolen Hearts", *Redlitzer Anthology*

Pike, Aprilynne, "Nature", *Defy the Dark*

Punsalan, Elyss G., "The Running Girl", *Horror: Filipino Fiction For Young Adults*

Ratnayake, N.A., "The Parched Lands", *Crossed Genres Magazine*

Revis, Beth, "Night Swimming", *Defy the Dark*

DIVERSE YA SCIENCE FICTION AND FANTASY STORIES
EDITED BY ALISA KRASNOSTEIN & JULIA RIOS

kaleidosco pe

Garth Nix   Sofia Samatar
Sean Williams   William Alexander
Karen Healey   Tansy Rayner Roberts
E. C. Myers   Vylar Kaftan

What do a disabled superhero, a time-traveling Chinese-American figure skater, and a transgender animal shifter have in common? They're all stars of **Kaleidoscope** stories!

Kaleidoscope collects fun, edgy, meditative, and hopeful YA science fiction and fantasy with diverse leads. These twenty original stories tell of scary futures, magical adventures, and the joys and heartbreaks of teenage.

Featuring New York Times bestselling and award-winning authors along with newer voices:

> Garth Nix, Sofia Samatar, William Alexander, Karen Healey, E.C. Myers, Tansy Rayner Roberts, Ken Liu, Vylar Kaftan, Sean Williams, Amal El-Mohtar, Jim C. Hines, Faith Mudge, John Chu, Alena McNamara, Tim Susman, Gabriela Lee, Dirk Flinthart, Holly Kench, Sean Eads, and Shveta Thakrar

"**Kaleidoscope** is one of the best anthologies I have read for a very long time.... engaging and beautiful and thoughtful and brilliant..." – *Tehani Wessely*

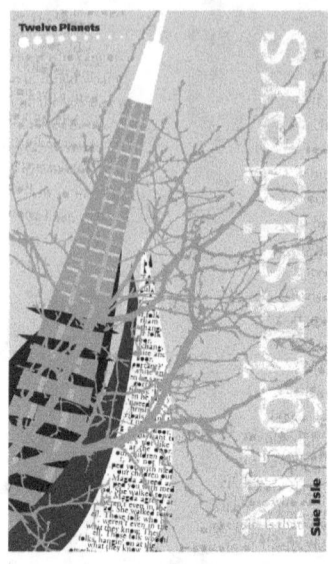

Nightsiders

Sue Isle

In a future world of extreme climate change, the western coast of Australia has been abandoned. A few thousand obstinate, independent souls cling to the southern towns and cities, living mostly by night to endure the fierce temperatures and creating a new culture in defiance of official expectations.

A teenage girl stolen from her family as a child, a troupe of street actors who affects the new with memories of the old, a boy born into the wrong body, and a teacher pushed into the role of guide, all tell the story of The Nightside.

'... [Isle's] writing is uniquely hers, direct and honest and crowned by a deft ear for dialogue.' – *Marianne de Pierres*

2012 Tiptree Long List Finalist
2012 Norma Hemming shortlist

Twelve Planets

Locus
Recommended
Reading List for
Best Collection
in 2011

aurealis
awards
FINALIST

Love and Romanpunk

Tansy Rayner Roberts

Thousands of years ago, Julia Agrippina wrote the true history of her family, the Caesars. The document was lost, or destroyed, almost immediately.

(It included more monsters than you might think.)

Hundreds of years ago, Fanny and Mary ran away from London with a debauched poet and his sister.

(If it was the poet you are thinking of, the story would have ended far more happily, and fewer people having their throats bitten out.)

Sometime in the near future, a community will live in a replica Roman city built in the Australian bush. It's a sight to behold.

(Shame about the manticores.)

Further in the future, the last man who guards the secret history of the world will discover that the past has a way of coming around to bite you.

(He didn't even know she had a thing for pointy teeth.)

History is not what you think it is.